Three Corner Rustlers

— Second Edition —

Happy Trails
K. Hamilt

A Novel by

K. Hamilton

THREE CORNER RUSTLERS
Copyright © 2015, 2020 by K. Hamilton Hutchison

ISBN: 9781657836280
LCCN: 2015954149

Front cover photo by K. Vogee
Back cover photo by William Wyckoff

This book is dedicated to my mother, Anne Kidd Hutchison. She nurtured my creativity from the day I was born. She inspired me to write this story, loved it in its infancy, encouraged it at every turn, and cheered me on constantly.

Mom, I miss you more than I can ever say.

ACKNOWLEDGMENTS

There are so many who have helped me finish my first novel, and I am so grateful to everyone who put up with me as I wrote it! Thank you.

To my editor, Cris Wanzer, my first professional choice and my best one! Thank you for being so amazing. I am so fortunate to have found you.

To Robin Leach Bosche, from the moment I shared this with you, you steadfastly believed in me. Your support is a huge reason it made it this far. Thank you.

To Bruce Johnson, extra credit! You didn't even know me and yet you shared your amazing photography of this beautiful country, your vast knowledge from hiking the three corner region, gave me answers to my questions, mapped out a route the thieves could conceivably take, inspired me to add a certain character, and made anything I needed instantly available. You have been so generous and your help made a huge impact. Thank you.

To Robert Mattos, Lyle Smith, Roger Preston, Will Wyckoff, Jim McDermott, and Joseph Pacini thank you for letting me pick your brains and for tolerating me when I did so! And to Greg Yates, Keli Hendricks, and Monte Kruger.

To Lacy Bulterman, Shar and Toby Tobin, and Cherie Cross, Thank you my dear friends.

To my husband John, thank you for listening all those hours in the car as I read to you between California and Oregon!

To RHF Rhabyn, Symba's Doc Vayder, Doc's Lyttle Lea, NV Santiago, and Gold's Tuffie Floyd, thank you for everything, I am so blessed to have had you in my life.

Have you rode the Three Corner country,
in the bunch grass where the free cattle graze?

Have you searched for something you lost,
and learned the high desert's ways?

Trails of the world be countless
and most of the trails be tried.

You tread on the hoof beats of many,
till you come where the hoof prints divide.

K.H.V.
Bend, Oregon 7/2015

PROLOGUE

The steering wheel jerked violently in his hands. "God damn it, move!" the range detective swore through clenched teeth.

The truck crossed up, slid sideways on the narrow track, and bumped the last of the cows out of his way. His hands spun the wheel to straighten the rig as it skidded over the slippery ground. He was impressed by how sure-footed their horses were. The fleeing riders were in sight one second, then obscured by swirling snowflakes the next. It was difficult to see the rough two-track road, and he used the hoofprints in the fresh snow to keep up with them. Slick conditions made the truck lose traction again, but he managed to keep them in sight. The chase was on.

Above, bumped about in the turbulent weather, the pilot made one last pass over the pursuit below. He angled the high-winged Cessna for a better look. Earlier, he'd radioed the range detective about the two buckaroos he'd spotted with a small herd. They had the looks of the men they were after. He'd kept them in sight from the air while the detective closed in on their position from the ground.

There had been sporadic sightings of the wranglers who might be the cattle thieves. To the casual observer, they appeared to be a couple of buckaroos out for a short ride—no bedrolls or halters, just a couple of guys moving a herd. But these rare sightings seemed to occur only in extreme weather, which didn't make sense. When the pilot first saw them and passed low to check them out, neither of the buckaroos looked up, and this affirmed his suspicions. The cattle spooked, but they didn't. It had to be

ix

them.

A narrow beam of sunlight pierced the thick clouds, briefly illuminating the cockpit with light and warmth. Frozen slush pelted the plane's canopy and slithered in flattened rivulets along its surface. The pilot checked his digital weather radar again, which confirmed that he had to return to the airfield.

Beneath the wings of the Cessna Skyhawk the high desert stretched for miles in Oregon's remote southeastern corner—vast country rarely, if ever, visited. Spanning more territory than Connecticut and Rhode Island combined, fewer than six hundred hardy souls lived there, where cattle outnumbered people a thousand to one and free-grazed the bunch grass on open rangeland. The pilot had a contract with the Oregon Cattlemen's Association, which helped pay for his passion for the latest in aviation technology, and he used it to look for cattle rustlers. A big fan of old-style Westerns, the irony amused him.

He turned eastward toward Idaho and home. "I'm heading back. Good luck," he said into his headset to the detective in the truck below.

There was no reply. The detective was preoccupied, navigating a series of vicious ruts that nearly concussed him into the roof of the cab. Bits of notes, a map, and business cards fell from the visor. He let them fall and concentrated. He hated to slow down. Bluffs that bordered either side of the track gave way to a ridgeline, and he felt the land disappear from both sides of his truck. For a second it crossed his mind that the buckaroos might lead him into a wreck, and in the middle of that thought, he realized that he couldn't see a road or track of any kind. He cranked the wheel to avoid a group of boulders and skidded to a halt. He set the brake and launched out of the truck at a full run.

The spit of ridgeline offered few options for escape, and to double back, they'd have to come through him. He had his heavy Maglite flashlight, and he unsnapped his holster on the fly. With each stride, his hand swung past it. Just yards ahead he heard scrambling as hooves met harder ground, then scattered loose earth. The late-season snow wasn't the real thick stuff yet, though it promised, and he was grateful it had held off. He wiped away the sweat that began to bead on his temples.

One of the wranglers stole a backwards glance to see how close their pursuer was. Like a camera, the detective's mind clicked a description: older man; thin white guy; angular, even features; mustache; late forties, maybe early fifties; and about one hundred fifty pounds soaking wet. The detective was close enough to hear the horse's breath and see it in the cold air.

Having spent the best part of his wind to get this close, the detective tripped over a rock and swung his arm wildly to catch his balance. The Maglite slipped from his numb fingers and bounced off a flat rock. He scooped it up without missing a beat, then stopped.

He was alone.

He swung around to look behind him. Snow swirled in every direction, and he felt the rush of air as it blew up the cliff face. He inched closer to the edge, saw nothing, then scanned around the narrow plateau with the powerful flashlight.

On the ground, hoofprints showed only forward motion, no sliding stops or sharp turns. The horses had gone where their riders had bid them.

"What the hell?" he muttered, then held his breath as he strained to hear them.

There was no sound. Nothing except the wind. They had vanished like smoke.

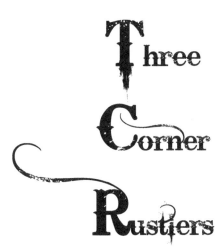

Three Corner Rustlers

ONE

The bus swung a wide turn. Its wheels crunched on the ground as it came to a stop by a set of high, reinforced gates. A series of these gates had to be negotiated to get into the secure parking lot of Colby State Prison. The buildings inside the perimeter were barren, concrete, bland in structure and color; typical of minimum-bid government contracting.

A group of men walked between armed guards toward the bus. C.J. Burk blended into the wall as he waited at the back of the line. His brown hair needed a trim, and his brown, gold-flecked eyes watched the guards. Tall and strong, his face was attractive, but reflected no joy in life. That was long gone. One of the guards handed him a black cowboy hat. When C.J. returned later that day, the same guard would take it back.

C.J.'s life choices had led him there, to another wait for another bus with bars on the windows. But this bus would take the men to a place far from other places they'd known; a place where they would be working with animals more wild than those they knew in prison. For C.J., it was a ride he'd been taking for about a year, and something he looked forward to each time.

William Wyker, an experienced horseman working with the Colorado Correctional Department, waited for the bus to arrive, his border collie, Tammy, at his feet. It was hard to know exactly how old he was. Probably somewhere in the middle-aged column; dark-haired, with tan, weathered features and a smile that revealed very white teeth. His temperament was calm, even-handed. He was a considerate man who laughed easily and often.

The Rockies gleamed with early sunlight off in the distance. He removed his hat and smiled at the beauty. The ranch area behind him was a ramshackle mix of odd structures, typically made of weathered wood, and repaired more often with whatever was at hand rather than new material.

Wyker was in charge of a program where prison inmates got a chance to come to this remote Colorado ranch and work with wild mustangs. There were dozens of horses in training in pipe-paneled paddocks, which were adjacent to a long row of larger fenced areas that held the rest. Many of them spent time in long-term holding facilities, their fates unknown, but hopefully to be trained and adopted. The unique training program helped both the horse and the inmate; Wyker had seen it.

An estimated thirty thousand horses remained free on government-managed land. The wild herds had few predators, and their overpopulation on the rangelands had a negative impact on cattle ranchers. Wildfires and encroaching developmental issues had created a situation where the Wild Horse and Burro Program, operated by the U.S. Department of the Interior Bureau of Land Management (known simply as the BLM) was forced to round up thousands of wild horses and burros. They were held in facilities located mostly in the Midwest, with a large population in Nevada, where wild horse advocates struggled to save them. They worked hard to get the horses adopted to good homes. It was the best hope for a very small percentage of them. Many more tracked a dead-end path to auction yards, kill buyers, and slaughterhouses.

Wyker leaned on the fence of a round pen, watching a black colt pace back and forth with separation anxiety. He turned to look at the men who had arrived on the bus. The colt watched too. At the orientation at Colby, he'd met the inmates chosen, knew their names, and why they were there. It was a diverse mix; a couple of homeboys, a Chicano, and a few white guys who'd earned the privilege of working with the BLM mustangs. After their initial orientation, the prisoners had attended a meeting to outline the traditional principles of the Vaquero Style, or natural horsemanship. Now these men were here to meet the horses and begin the program. These early encounters were always interesting to Wyker, because most of these men had never seen a real horse. They had no concept that horses simply responded to truth and gave it right back. But they would learn.

TWO

On the Three Bit Ranch, two Mexican cowboys were on foot, working a herd of cattle through chutes. The large bodies were pressed tightly together, and their big eyes peered between the metal slats. They bumped into each other, maneuvering for a way through and out the other side. They had been checked and counted, and the men were now moving them forward to a corral. The older man slapped his leg with a reata—a coiled rope made of four strands of braided rawhide about sixty feet long. He preferred the reata because the length allowed the "dallies," or loops, to slip and stop an animal more smoothly and farther away when lassoed.

The older man blew an ear-piercing whistle from pursed lips, and hollered, "Hey cow, hey cow, *vamanos!*"

Their horses were saddled and tied to the rail. Nearby, two herding dogs crouched, focused, or "hooked on," to the cattle and ready for work. The older man, Luis, hopped the fence, checked the girth on his horse, and mounted up. He turned and watched his son, Jorge, secure the gate behind the last cow.

Jorge said something to his dogs. He ran a hand over his upturned face, checked his cinch, then put foot to stirrup. Once settled into his well-worn Mexican saddle, he moved his horse off toward the far gate of the corral with the dogs in his wake. It was midmorning and mist still clung to the low hollows as they began to work the cattle from the pen.

The cattle called to each other as the dogs watched patiently. A signal came, barely discernible from Jorge, and the dogs jogged into position on either side of the herd. Cloven hooves left patterned prints on the ground. It was cold, like a winter without snow. There were about seventy-five head, their breaths billowing steam from round, pink nostrils, and their presence filled the air with a language that was their own.

The riders and the dogs moved the herd slowly toward a crease in the hills that led to open land north of the ranch. The cattle split off as they meandered along a path between the low brush and the dry grass that grew belly high in the summer. The winter's grayish-brown hues were deceptively barren; they would soon transform with spring and become a palette of colors that defined that part of the high desert.

Nearby, a bird called as Three Bit's owner, Kitzie Collins, stood outside the big barn and watched them go. The cattle looked like living ships cruising through a sea of vegetation. She returned to her office, and shut down the laptop that she had entered counts and breeding status data into a few minutes earlier. The wind caught a strand of gray hair that hung loose from her baseball cap. She brushed it back, then reached for her coat and woolen scarf. Kitzie was slim, late middle-aged and attractive, but not overly so. She possessed a useful beauty—the durable, timeless kind. She had brown flecks that streaked out from the pupils in hazel eyes, and she lit up the room when she smiled. She wore boot-cut jeans, a plaid flannel work shirt, and a bandana at her neck. "Dressing up" would be her best boots, a Stetson hat, a hand-tooled leather belt with her enormous championship buckle, maybe a clean shirt, and the same jeans she'd spent the day in.

Less than a week later, the Three Bit was quiet, and inside the barn, the horses chewed their hay contentedly. Kitzie looked up into the high, open trusses to the windowed spire where natural light poured in. A cathedral of rough-hewn beams, it was architecturally beautiful. A wide expanse covered what could have been a small arena, and stalls lined the sides. Her daughter Carson used to imagine that dust fairies played in the shafts of light that filtered across the floor, and that if she watched long enough, she'd see them flying in the air. For both of them, it was the horses—the smell of leather, grain, and hay—that made the world perfect.

Beyond the tack room was Kitzie's office, with two back-to-back desks, filing cabinets, shelves, and lots of pictures on the walls. These rooms were attached to the barn, a couple of small windows casting the only natural light. Kitzie flipped a switch and the overhead lights hummed to life. Down at the other end of the office was a narrower passage, a bathroom, and a smaller, rectangular room. It had tack lined neatly along its walls, bridle and saddle racks, more shelves, and a cleaning station with a sink.

Lined along the top of the walls of Kitzie's office was a "ribbon record"—a timeline of years of being on the road at horseshows. Some were long, trailing ribbons with complicated rosettes at the top and rippled folds fanning out from the center like an Elizabethan collar. Each had a metal center, some with either a symbol of the show or a venue name. Some ribbons were double or triple rosettes with highlighted bands of accentuating color. Time had faded them to the point that one had to look closely to see what color they originally had been.

Kitzie's husband, "Tuff" Collins, was passionate about cutting horses. The Three Bit Ranch, located near the small town of Martin, needed lots of work when he got it from his mother. She didn't want it after his dad had passed, so it became a rental, and maintenance had been deferred for years. Tuff was obsessed with making it perfect, and parts of what he created were considered out of character for the region. They built a huge, covered arena at one end of the barn, and he put in a covered round pen. There were corrals on the property constructed nearly a hundred years ago, one of which was a huge, circular corral made with rough-hewn, pole-shaped pieces of wood still held fast with rawhide strips instead of wire. It was badly worn in places by weather and neglect, so Tuff repaired and upgraded it while respecting the heritage of those who came before him. His ranch was an anomaly— really stuck out as odd and in the wrong place—but Tuff wanted what he wanted. The folks in town thought the whole venture crazy. They'd gossip about them, saying, "Folks here don't put their horses in stalls. That's not the 'cowboy' way."

So what if the townsfolk thought they were crazy? They could have their opinions. But it was amusing that those opinionated ranchers changed their minds when Collins Cutting Horses became successful. Nothing changes critics to fans faster than success. It astounded the locals that people would pay five and six figures for yearlings, futurity horses, and foals purchased before they were born. Kitzie smiled to herself as she remembered.

Tuff never cared what people thought; he just loved his horses. He was devoted to their breeding program, and to the thoughtful training of their horses to maximize their natural talent to cut cattle from a herd. Though he'd made his money in a suit and tie, he had a keen eye for talented horses and people, and he surrounded himself with both.

It was on the circuit that they'd met. Kitzie's given name was Kathryn, but her friends called her Kitzie, and she was at the Worlds showing her horses. It was a big class. She and Tuff competed against each other that day and she won. They were formally introduced at the show awards dinner that night. Though he was much older than she was, they talked for hours, and before the night was through, both felt they'd never be as comfortable with another human being as they were with each other. Besides their attraction, Kitzie and Tuff shared a vision to breed and train a line of smart, athletic, fine-looking cutting horses.

And so, their life began at the Three Bit. Tuff bought their foundation stallion before their daughter, Carson, was born, and they covered a lot of miles doing the show circuit. Kitzie showed some, but mostly she ran the business end; sales, embryo transfers, developing the breeding program, and marketing. They earned a reputation in the industry as good horsemen and excellent competitors. Tuff personally saw to it that the young horses were brought along to the level they were prepared for, not "rode down into the ground and lamed to get results." He understood that some owners were more interested in winning than the long-term health of the horse, and Tuff wasn't one of them. He believed in the horses he bred, believed in their talented training staff, and he avoided the training techniques that gave some in the industry a poor reputation. He was courted regularly to join the Cutting Horse Association's board of directors, but he loathed the petty politics. Their success was dependent on constant training, preparation to compete, packing and unpacking, and lots of hauling. Lots and lots of miles.

That same piece of hair slipped out again as Kitzie stared at a show photo of seven-year-old Carson on a solid gelding. The horse was a veteran of countless shows, and he had carried this little button of a girl to many junior show championships. Carson had an exuberant expression on her face as she posed with her trophy. And beside her was another new saddle she'd won. Her trainer, her barn friends, and family all posed supportively for the picture. She was a "show baby," part of a generation of kids that grew up around horses, training, and horse shows.

"She was better at it than all of us; a natural," Kitzie murmured to Tuff's picture. She looked out the window at the trailer, once their "home"—a six-horse hauler with living quarters, now long parked and neglected.

Unbidden, the memory came and she shut her eyes. After Tuff was gone, she'd felt as long as she had their foundation stud to care for, part of him was still there with her. She looked at the picture of the stunning sorrel stallion with the white blaze, his wonderful face, his expressive eyes. She recalled Tuff's words when he talked about buying him. She had balked at the cost, but he was convinced. He said, "He's the one, Kitzie, the one that takes us all the way. You'll see."

And the stud had been that and more. Nothing ever bothered him. The stallion wasn't a hard keeper, he always ate and drank well on the road, and if he was a bit sore, you never knew it. He always brought his best to the show ring, and then into the breeding barn. All his babies had a lot of try in them, like him. But the day finally came when she had to do right by him. The vet barely spoke a word as she held the halter rope and he administered the first of the two shots that would end his suffering from a ruptured intestine they could not cure. And when it was done, Kitzie started up the backhoe and drove up to the hill where she and Tuff used to picnic—"their" spot where they'd watch the yearlings run and play. She dug the hole, brought the body up there with as much dignity as she could, and buried him. The men wanted to help, but she'd have none of it. This was her responsibility and she needed to take care of him...alone. When she finally scattered Tuff's ashes in the same place, she spent a long time up on the hill with both of them.

Her vision swam as she wiped some dust from the bottom edge of the picture frame. Her gold wedding ring reflected in the glass. With a sigh, she turned off the light and left the room.

Kitzie scanned the surrounding horizon and landscape as she closed up the barn and headed to the house. It was habit to take in the view. She was not just taking in the waning day, she was looking for someone; actually, two someones. Luis and Jorge had been gone for a few days. The weather was building from the west, and they were due back. She stopped walking, thinking maybe she'd seen something off in the distance. More hair came loose and blew across her face. She brushed it out of her eyes, squinting to see if anything was there. Wyatt and Lulu, Kitzie's miniature Schnauzers, were barking, wrestling, and running toward the warmth of home. Wyatt was in the lead, as he was more sensitive to the cold and wanted to get inside faster. Lulu's thicker hair made her immune to the chilly air. They got along fine on the ranch even though they were not working dogs. Those would be Jorge's two cattle dogs; and they were still out there with Luis and Jorge looking for the herd.

The herd, Kitzie thought grimly, and her smile faded. Her heart was heavy again as each footfall dislodged bits of hay and manure onto the frosty ground.

A significant part of the Three Bit herd was missing— about forty-five pregnant cows—and she was really worried. She hoped this wasn't a result of rustling, like other ranchers in Malheur County had experienced. She wondered if it would be any different if her mountain of a husband were here running things instead of a widowed ranch wife. As many as twenty ranches had been hit by cattle rustlers, with a dozen taking the brunt of the losses. Kitzie had hoped her range was too far north to be of interest to the mysterious thieves. They were stealthy, and there was little information to go on. It was surmised that they drove their plundered stock on horseback, carefully skirting around ranches and people, remaining invisible.

Not that there are all that many people out there, she thought.

The way the cattle were disappearing, the rustlers had to be pretty solid buckaroos, good with horses and cattle, and very tough. She hoped that Luis and Jorge would return with good news, but in her heart, she felt the cows were gone. The cattle produced excellent calves yearly. This was a chunk of valuable animals, and their unborn calves too. The rustlers knew what they were doing, getting two for one.

Tuff had been dead for ten years. His was such a presence that Kitzie hardly went a full day without alternately missing him, and hating him for not being there to manage this dilemma with her. Working the ranch without her husband had been hard before the economic collapse. She managed now, but just barely.

Back in the house, she opened the fridge, looked at the contents with a blank stare, and quickly concluded that she was uninspired. She'd rather make a meal for a crowd than something for herself. She missed the sound of laughter, of people talking to each other about the details and funny stories of their day. It was like a river that flowed and carried her along. Now she was just a leaf on the stream. She felt jostled and pushed about. This Kitzie was not the Kitzie from before. Not the strong, confident woman who made things happen; the woman who felt certain she had a good bead on things. Now life seemed to be happening *to* her and she felt lost. She'd begun to feel that it was the losses that measured her out, and not the gains. She'd been pretty lucky for a lot of years, and while she appreciated those good times, she was emotionally unprepared for the big changes that came along.

"Too much junk rolling around in my head," she muttered, and refocused on the thought that she should eat something.

She leaned over the kitchen sink and looked out the window again. The light had faded and it was hard to see.

She wished they'd get back soon, even with bad news. She gave up on food, put her coat back on, and got her boots at the door. She grabbed a flashlight and headed out to close up Luis's barn. Critters would get in if she didn't.

Wyatt and Lulu bounded out the door ahead of her, then Wyatt stopped with a frozen stare into the darkness. He barked. She heard it too; horses trotting in. The cattle dogs, Tucker and Dusty, ran up and got a warm welcome from Wyatt and Lulu.

Kitzie opened the big barn door sliders and hit the lights. Heads came up from inside the stalls. Curious eyes peered out, blinked, and adjusted to the sudden brightness.

Father and son were tired and cold. The dogs trotted to the water dish and drank noisily, splashing water out of the bowl and onto the dirt. Luis smiled. He always smiled, but his eyes told the truth.

THREE

Silicon Valley had been Carson Anne Collins's goal— a personal milestone and a definitive measure of how far she'd gone. She looked down at her black Jimmy Choo pumps, and the thought of spending that much money on footwear now appalled her. They'd worn well and she appreciated that they still looked good. Her leather Bradley briefcase held the latest version of her resume, and true to her nature, she'd arrived early for her interview.

She studied her reflection in the glass of the big, polished doors and looked better than she felt. Her long, auburn hair was swept into an old-fashioned French twist, not too harsh. A few tendrils were gently pulled loose, softening the effect around her face. Her gold-flecked green eyes complemented her minimal make-up, and she was grateful that stress had not made dark circles under her eyes. She got her wire-rimmed glasses out, put them on, and wondered whether they made her look bright and capable, or just blind. Not totally sold, she pulled them off and returned them to her bag with a sigh. She was annoyed at how it seemed awkward to look both professional and feminine, or businesslike without being a total hard-assed bitch. Hell, she could ride, rope, brand, and vet cattle, but no one here cared what she could do in the high desert. They wanted to know how she could improve their bottom line in the current market, and whether she could find profit margins where others had failed. When she first got there, she felt like she could do it all, have it all, and deserved it all. Where had it gone? It had all changed and few of the rules still applied. Carson took a deep breath, flashed her best version of a winning and confident smile, and pushed her way into the chrome-trimmed marble entry.

Hours later, her coat still on, the handle of her briefcase slipped from her fingers. The briefcase landed perfectly upright before it teetered and tipped over with a *whap* on her kitchen floor. Carson looked at a stack of mail, then took a corkscrew out and set it on the counter. She stood at the cupboard, fingered a crystal glass, and rejected it, then chose something that would carry half the bottle, filled it, and proclaimed it, "Dinner!" She stood at the kitchen table and looked at the pile of bad news. She took a swig from the goblet and held up one of the envelopes. "Yup, from the mortgage company. Oh, and here's one from the county servicer. What a surprise."

The morning paper lay open to the legal notices section where Carson's name and address had been in print for the past few days. She'd circled herself with a pink highlighter, then added flames beneath that in red pen. The auction date was close, very close. Eyes welled with tears, the last bits of uncried frustration, and she sank into a chair. Leaning on the arm, chin in her hand, she looked out the window at the garden, once so lovingly tended and a source of immense pride, now desiccated evidence of her failure. It all used to be so perfect.

The silence of the house was deafening. She sat up straight, wiped away the single tear that rolled down her cheek, and spoke out loud to no one, "Location, location,

location." Carson hummed the words as she stared out the window. She looked at the last of the furniture—beautiful things bought at the height of her financial strength—and recalled how cavalierly she had purchased it when cost wasn't a consideration. And the lovely parties— entertainment for high-end clients in her *designer* home, expensive social functions she remembered as she swirled the inexpensive red table wine, took another long drag on the goblet, and then reread the Trader Joe's brand label on the half-empty bottle.

Her phone was silent. He had not called for weeks. "Busy. Busy with your beautiful wife, your life, and your happy family," she murmured.

The real truth of things had settled over her and there was no longer a way to justify what she'd been doing. The part-time affair could not fix the emptiness that enveloped her. The roller coaster of attention and distance had never been good for her, and she finally realized she didn't have the resilience to tolerate it anymore. In fact, it had begun to amplify her anxiety and depression when what she really needed was stability. He would not, and could not ever offer that.

She had an epiphany; a slow realization that crept into her consciousness as the sand ran out of the hourglass. She was out of choices. It was time to go, and there was only one place left to go to.

Carson ran her finger rhythmically around the rim of the glass, then topped it off, rose to her feet, and gazed down at all the stupid mail. She didn't have to open any of it; she already knew what was there. Sliding her hand along the cool surface of the table, her graceful, outstretched fingers began to brush the pile onto the floor one or two unopened envelopes at a time. They scattered like a broken mosaic. Everything was so quiet. The once ubiquitous drone of cable television was gone, and without it, the house felt lonelier and even more empty. Even if she wanted to have a good cry, she couldn't. The tears were all used up, like her. She picked up the bottle and went into what was once the luxuriously decorated living room. She stepped out of her shoes as though stepping out of herself, and crossed the big room in her stocking feet. Completing a faux pirouette, Carson slid down the far wall, feet out before her. God, she was so tired. Her eyes went to the cold fireplace across the room.

She didn't realize she'd lapsed into a state of mindless staring. Her weary pupils dilated into space. When she refocused, Carson settled her gaze on the enormous painting that hung over the fireplace. Recessed lighting illuminated it perfectly. Painted from a precious photograph her father had taken of her many years ago, she could almost see the breeze rustle the high-desert grasses, hear the birds, and feel the warm sun on her back. There was a slender young girl, bareback on a sorrel Quarter Horse, leaning back with one arm resting on the horse's rump.

"I hope I can fit it in the truck. I can't afford to ship it."

Carson drove the first part of the journey in silence. She enjoyed the sound of the truck's V8 motor. The weather was clear, not a cloud in the sky, and dawn appeared on the horizon to her right. Carson couldn't shake the feeling that she was still attached to all that stuff; to the house, the car, the urban stress-filled life, and the piles of unpaid bills. She wanted to think she'd outrun the guilt. She'd said no goodbyes to friendships she'd made. She'd bailed on everyone, which led to a strange realization—the farther from there she drove, the more she felt like she could breathe, like a weight was lifting. Carson thought of him and how that undiscovered betrayal had worn her down. She felt like she'd been suffocated by a lie. It was her final conclusion, her resignation about that relationship, and the certainty it had cut both ways. She could not make right where she'd done wrong. Best to say nothing and just leave.

FOUR

C.J. rode past the round pen where Wyker worked with some of the inmates. Sometimes he felt like he was back in his native Australia, back when things were simpler, and today was one of those days. C.J. had put a successful ride on a gelding that would be going to adoption very soon. He had an even, kind temperament, and C.J. had a good feeling about his future—an easily adoptable candidate. He took him to the shed and untacked him, brushed him down, and checked his feet. The gelding's head hung slack, relaxed. C.J. led the gelding down the breezeway to a paddock and turned him out. The horse walked a few steps, promptly circled a soft spot, and rolled. C.J. watched as he did the knot on the rope halter and coiled the lead. "Thanks, mate. So much for making you all nice and pretty." He shook his head and laughed as he walked back toward the round pen. He was curious to see how things were going.

There were two round pens at the ranch; a ten-foot-high, wood-walled pen, and this one, forty-five feet in diameter, made of pipe panels that had plywood set horizontally in each panel with a smaller plywood piece that fit the gate. Thicker boards ringed the bottom so that when a green horse scrambled around inside, it wouldn't get a leg caught. There was an open section across the top of each panel, and it was easy to see inside and watch what was going on. There were a couple of blocks set around the outside of the round pen so shorter people could get a view.

As C.J. approached, the horse inside the pen made hard contact against one of the panels, which startled the observers, and they jumped back away from the wall. C.J. moved in and leaned against the fence to watch one of the rookies, an inmate named Lester.

Lester, a former gang member with a do-rag on his head, was completely terrified. He held two sturdy plastic sticks that had rounded leather tips on the ends and handles like the ones found on golf clubs. Wyker had instructed him to plant the tip of one stick in the center of the pen and hold the other one, tip to the ground, and face the colt. The black colt was as frightened as Lester.

"Face him?" Lester whined, rotating his body like a top to face a mustang that had experienced only minimal human contact, and most of that unpleasant. He almost tripped over the sticks, which Wyker reminded him were aids; one to keep Lester in his space at the center of the pen, and the other to act as an extension of his arm to keep him at a safe distance from the business end of the horse.

His erratic movements threatened to unseat the ratty straw cowboy hat perched on his head. The colt bolted across the pen and came close to running him over. Lester dropped the sticks, ran toward the rail with a squeal, and left his hat in the sand.

During orientation, Lester had bragged, "Gonna ride me a horse like John Wayne."

At the time, Wyker had an answer for him. "Before you become 'the dude,' you have to know how to be around a horse from the ground, and you've no business being on top of one till you master that. We begin in the round pen with free work, then progress to ground work, where your connection to the horse is more physical. And then maybe—and I do mean *maybe*—you get to learn to ride. It is a process. This is a process for you and for the horse. You are going to learn how to help each other, and it is my job to help you both."

The colt held his ground on the far side of the pen. Lester tiptoed toward his hat, ignoring the stick aids.

Wyker said, "Forget the hat," and told him to get back to the center, then added, "Lester, you need to establish your space and help him stay in his space. If you give ground, he will fill it."

Lester swung his stick wildly about like a sword. The colt shied and threw out his right rear leg, almost catching Lester. Lester howled and scrambled again to the wall of the round pen. The colt cut across the pen to the opposite side and looked like he wanted to jump out.

Wyker spoke in a relaxed voice, "Get off the rail and back to the center."

One of the inmates joked, "That's what they call whispering to the horse, right?"

The group chuckled.

Lester looked every bit like he'd cry, but caught himself and realized he had to do what Wyker said as a matter of pride. He'd never live it down if he didn't. He returned to the center of the pen and positioned his aids.

Wyker encouraged him. "Make your moves easy. Go slow and ask him to respect your space." He watched Lester's movements for a moment. "Okay, he's not quite respecting that, so elevate that 'ask' to a suggestion. Yes, there, you see? The colt felt the pressure and moved back along the rail. Don't keep that stick out there after you get a change. After you get what you have asked for, release the pressure." Then Wyker added to the whole group, "The tools are only good if you don't overuse them. If you throw one-hundred-percent energy at him, and you don't get a change, then what? Try a measured amount of pressure and then release."

Wyker tried an analogy Lester might be more familiar with. "Horses are a herd, like a crew, okay? The lead horse communicates with pressure and releases that pressure when he gets what he wants. With a look, he can send one of his crew somewhere. That herd member goes because he knows the leader means it. The first try is persuasion."

The colt had taken a position by the wall and stopped. It was a moment where they both could take a breath.

Lester said, "Like, ya know yo ass is kicked if he says it twice?"

The colt's sides heaved.

Wyker was good with the break and told Lester, "We give these animals a bit more leeway, and they need our help to understand what is being asked of them. We need to do less to make a change. Allow the colt to make a mistake, then correct it, release the pressure, and try again. The mistake, the same mistake, may happen over again, but you will see a change if you are consistent." And then he added a truth from a horseman he admired greatly: "To quote someone who has forgotten more than I'll ever know: 'Make the right thing easy and the wrong thing hard.'"

C.J. felt himself breathe. When he was around the

horses, it was as though he hadn't taken a full breath in a long time. When the pressure was released on the horse, C.J. felt it too.

Lester began to manage his communication aids. He seemed more aware of his own body language and how it affected the horse. The colt stayed along the rail, then surged back into a run, but slowed. Sweat glimmered on his neck and chest, speckled his back, and lathered between his legs. When Lester got too far ahead of the colt, out of the "driveline," the colt spun and changed direction.

Wyker told Lester to stay in the center, and Lester shifted back into position. "You got ahead of him. You did that; you made him turn. You made that change without meaning to. Can't fault him for doing what you asked. Remember your body position to his. You get lined up slightly ahead of him, he turns." Wyker's calm voice carried across the round pen. "Get him going back in the direction you had him. Get a little ahead of him again. You won't need your stick, use your body. There, that's it."

Lester's small, pivoting steps in the center of the round pen matched the horse's. He got a little ahead of the colt's withers. Lester focused on the colt's eye and that put his own body position more ahead of the colt's shoulder. The colt was sensitive and responded to the pressure by rolling back in a turn on the hindquarters away from Lester and going the other way.

Lester was startled and stepped back, which opened space, and the colt filled it. He came in close, broke down from the lope, and took up a fast trot in the desired direction. Lester was startled, but stayed put. Laughter erupted from outside the pen.

Lester swore at them. "Gonna laugh my ass off when you're in here!"

The colt moved at a slower trot in the direction Lester wanted. Lester looked relieved and tried to resume the correct position to his horse, and kept his aid down as the colt stayed on the rail.

Wyker spoke to him. "It's like you have a bubble around you and that is your space. The horse has one also. You are learning to use your energy, your space, your bubble, to influence his."

Lester was more relaxed and seemed to understand. He moved with the horse, but moved a step away, changed his bubble, and the horse moved slightly off the rail. Lester moved back to the correct position, the colt slowed to a trot, and moved back to the rail. Wyker encouraged him. It was the first "glimmer of feel," he said.

Wyker spoke to the whole group, repeating what he'd told them before. "Remember the three parts of the horse that our movements influence: the head and shoulders, the midbody, and the back end. We drive the horse from the back section. We push the body to the rail by positioning to influence that section; and we stop, turn, and push the front from the shoulder to the eye. As you get better with the concept of 'feel', we'll lose the sticks. You will know how to be around horses when this knowledge becomes habit."

Wyker spoke directly to Lester. "Slow your steps, but stay with him. Now breathe deeply and relax, Lester. Think 'walk' and see what happens."

The colt moved around the pen, his eye on Lester and

his inside ear cocked in his direction. For a few laps there was no obvious change. The colt respected Lester's space and didn't come off the rail, which helped Lester's confidence.

"Stay with it and wait for the change. It's coming. Move your feet more slowly, but stay with him, stay in position. That's good."

Then the trot became a walk, the colt's head and neck relaxed to be more in line with his back, and his tail lost its elevation. Every rookie around the pen was silent. They could see the change.

C.J. smiled. It was his favorite part—that moment when you realize there is a connection.

Wyker smiled. "Let that be, just keep doing what you're doing."

Lester relaxed his shoulders and visibly released his tension, his fear almost forgotten.

"Let him walk on the rail for a bit. I'd like him to catch his breath, let him relax a little. You too, but stay with him. Walk in your bubble and stay in the driveline. I want you to wait till he looks at you. He'll be checking in with that inside eye and ear. When you see that, when you feel he's 'hooked on,' I want you to stop, take two steps backwards, and breathe. That will create space for him to come into the center."

Lester tensed for a second and Wyker added, "It will be a place of rest. The 'release' is with you, and you will be communicating that he has done the right thing."

The colt turned an eye to Lester and his inside ear tipped to the center toward him.

"Now, take two steps back and stop. That's it. Watch

what happens," Wyker said.

Lester exhaled, his shoulders relaxed, and the new horseman took another step back. The colt slowed, turned his head, then turned his body to face Lester. For a second, Lester was afraid, and he stepped back another foot. The timing was good; the colt dropped his head and stepped in slowly to fill the space Lester had given. The tip of Lester's stick rested in the sand, almost forgotten, and in a low voice Lester asked, "Um, how close is he going to get?"

"Do exactly what I say. Raise the tip of your stick only five inches off the ground and hold it there till the colt's feet stop," Wyker said.

The colt's feet stopped the second the stick rose.

"Now, put it back down on the ground."

The horse stood square, all feet evenly on the ground, his breathing audible but more normal, his eyes softening.

"That's it, he's with you."

Everyone was amazed by what had just happened. A huge smile lit up Lester's face. There was a realization that had come over him, a shift in attitude, and C.J. appreciated the feeling he must be experiencing at that moment.

Wyker said, "That'll do. Lester, place the sticks on the ground and walk easy to the gate. You both did well."

Lester did so, and when he closed the gate behind him, he was surprised to see that the colt had quietly followed him. Lester's face softened and it was obvious he was pleased to see him there.

To the group, Wyker asked, "Can anyone tell me what just happened? That colt moved, followed him. Why?" He glanced around at the faces and stopped at C.J.

C.J. looked at the others before he spoke. "That was real hooked on, seems to me."

Several nodded in agreement.

"So it was. Who's next?"

FIVE

Outside, the temperature was in the teens, and Kitzie was up before first light as usual. The air over the valley had held a layer of fog and low clouds for several days. She thought about the conversation from the previous night. They all agreed that the cows were probably gone. Kitzie's heart was heavy as she made a cup of coffee and stood in the semi-dark kitchen, looking at the patterned glow on the frosty ground outside cast by the kitchen light through the window.

Some fifty-odd miles away, the rustled Three Bit cows were tucked away in a little box canyon with a spring, far from where they should be. They were mixed with a smaller herd, stolen weeks before from the Bitteroot, that the rustlers had driven all night from a nearby "stash canyon." From there, they planned to skirt the Steens Mountain Wilderness and make the rendezvous.

As dawn began to break, it revealed a fairyland. The fog had frozen to every surface, in some parts known as a "hoar frost"—hauntingly beautiful, a delicate perfection grasping hold of every surface with infinite glittering forms. The grasses, branches, and rocks wore prismatic, crystalline cloaks that completely transformed them. This panorama existed only briefly, the sun illuminating the fleeting moments between frozen and gone. It was nature's art revealed in long streaks of light and sparkle, the frost vanishing in the bright, and clinging in the shadows.

Two riders, heads tucked under hats and scarves wrapped close across their faces, spoke little, if at all. When they had something to say, it sounded more like muffled grunts. Their gloved hands held coiled ropes and they slapped their chaps with them to keep the herd moving. Clouds of steam rose from the many nostrils and the collective body heat of the group. They crossed an open valley of low scrub dotted with rocky bits that looked like enormous diamonds. The winter wonderland the frozen fog had made became more apparent as the light grew, and even these hard men looked around in appreciation of the fragile beauty the night had made.

No one would be about; no one would see them. They moved steadily toward their destination, which was still some days in the distance. But this morning, in spite of the white, frozen beauty, they were glad it was not snow, or snowing. As cold as it was—and it was bitterly cold—it was better than the driving snowstorm they'd been caught in the previous year, when they had been forced to stop and make shelter for themselves in a long-abandoned homestead. Might have been a half-collapsed chicken house, the wood taking decades to fully decay, the high-desert elements fading wood to colors of slate and sand dappled with yellowish lichen. Weather had blown dirt and weeds, wind-packed them into the cracks, and over the years the accumulation had crept higher up the windward side of the tumbledown. It was uncomfortable, but better than open ground. The cattle had bunched together nearby. Even they didn't want to move much; they just grouped together, their backs to the wind and snow in the lee side of the burned-out shell of what was once the main house. Most of its roof was still there and a few walls, though the flooring was long gone. There was a small barn built next to it at a right angle, its tin roof also still intact, and the cattle had instinctively grouped out of the weather in the crook of the manmade shelter. They had been stuck for a couple of miserable days.

But today they knew they'd make good time. These cows were good-sized, healthy, and they blended together easily. They'd picked out the twenty-five best of the Bitteroot herd, added the Junction Ranch Angus, and now they were in position to meet up with the truck within the window of time allowed.

Both men were range hardened and experienced. The taller of the two—face weather-carved, in his early fifties—was in charge, and up to this point, there were no complaints. He possessed the connections and was the only link between where to find the cattle and who would get them. The rest of the chain of people needed to carry out such a big operation weren't his concern, nor did he want it to be. He was paid handsomely, and though he was careful not to trust his boss, he did trust the money. Besides, he figured his neck was way out there too. Each link in the chain relied on the other to rustle cattle on such a large scale.

The rustled cattle were moved into an established operation, one whose reputation was above reproach, and big enough to absorb what they rustled and moved through the Three Corners. Sometimes the routes they rode took them east into Idaho, and they'd meet up there; sometimes they'd go south into Nevada, then turn east and meet in another location in Idaho. And they'd often cross the reservation and pass over Indian land. Whichever way they chose, the result was the same; load the cattle and truck them to the next stop in their journey. By rustling the bred female cows in the mid-to-late winter, it'd be late spring before some would realize what their losses were.

The rustling had gained so much momentum that they'd begun to check the cattle for GPS tracking devices. In the vast Great Basin, proud ranchers had been reluctant to speak of the cattle they couldn't find, until the losses became impossible to ignore. Things were changing, and they talked about it now. He'd heard about a sixty-thousand-dollar reward offered for information leading to their arrest and conviction. That might get tempting to certain people if the pressure became too much. There had been increasing motivation from several quarters to put a stop to it. The tradition of neighbor helping neighbor had been part of the cowboy way of life since the settling of the West. The mystery of who might be behind it was vexing—what if it was someone they knew, that they rode with at brandings, or sat next to at barbecues? And if the right person got a good look at him (his name was Stiles), they'd say he looked familiar. And they'd be right, because he was that person they rode with, saw at church, and trusted. It was a very long time ago, but he had been one of them. There was no honor among thieves.

Times are hard everywhere, he thought. *Must be careful.*

He decided to check with his contact in town to make sure she hadn't gotten careless.

SIX

Even when C.J. was in a good mood he was tight-lipped, humorless, and remote. Yet Wyker enjoyed watching him with this red-roan colt, and in the days and weeks that followed, this unlikely pair had formed a bond.

At the ranch, he was called Rio Rojo, a red roan much bigger than the others, with a good eye and thick, strong neck. His size and scope reminded Wyker of the Spanish-bred horses that had mixed with the wild mustangs many generations ago. Rio's reddish-brown mane was thick, very long, and always tangled, as was his tail. His forelock went halfway down his face, and there was a bit of white between his eyes only visible when the wind blew. His body coloring was a spattered red mixed with white, and he had a darker, brownish-red stripe that ran from his withers to the top of his tail. He was built; his back wasn't too long or too short, the line of his shoulder was angled correctly, he had a good broad chest and long, solid legs. His feet were solid too, well-shaped and balanced, not broken down from years in the backcountry.

The horse was technically too old to be considered a colt, as he'd been a stallion when he was forcibly rounded up and split from his band. It was a good guess that he was maybe four or five years old and probably had had maybe one or two mares. He'd been separated from his herd, knocked out by a dart, and gelded late. "Proud cut" some call it, which meant he knew what it was to be a stallion, and he was really pissed off. He had lots of scrapes, healed scars, and he didn't suffer fools at all.

If there was a hard way to do something, this horse would find it. Nothing about him was easy. Every grain of trust, every tiny measure of respect, was earned. It became clear that teaching and learning with this one was just all around harder. He required an extraordinary level of patience and consistency.

When Wyker first saw this big gelding moving around the pen with fifty other wild mustangs, his eye was drawn to this horse. Just couldn't help it; there was something special about how he moved, easy and graceful for a horse of his size. He was a leader, and his was a tempered leadership. He was the real thing to Wyker, all the elements he looked for in a horse, and he saw great potential in this unlikely prospect. He was a totally wild package, and yet, if you could find a way in, this would be a horse you might never see the likes of again.

The weeks went by as Wyker watched the progress— or many times the lack of it—in the relationship between C.J. and Rio. The other inmates made progress too, each at their own pace, and some did better than he expected. Sure, some got a little beaten up; not real hurt, just some bumps and bruises that briefly checked their growing enthusiasm. Wyker watched their fear change to confidence. They lived in the present, in the moment. They had begun to understand what they were doing, and very little would diminish this most important aspect of their lives, and the horses' lives.

They were all prisoners. The horses were prisoners, too. The BLM ordered them to be captured and held.

They had to learn to work in this alien system, and they needed guidance to find their way in this unnatural life that had been thrust upon them. And they had spirit. They fought back—not in a hostile way, but in an honest way. Horses never lie, and the inmates learned that this was a trait to be respected, and perhaps to be attained. They saw something of themselves in the spirit of the horses, that truth and survival were one and the same to a horse. They began to see that the horse had something to offer them, showing them a way, a path, in life.

On this particular morning they were in the round pen, and Rio responded well to C.J. as he moved the gelding around. Wyker knew that C.J. was in the correct position. With people, C.J.'s cold defenses created discomfort. When he communicated with the horses, this changed to, "I'll lead you, follow me."

Earlier that morning when the prison bus arrived, C.J. was last out and Wyker had watched him walk down the alleyway between the paddocks straight to Rio. Rio shifted his gaze and watched C.J. approach. At the gate, C.J. stood, one arm resting on the top rail, thumb tucked into the front pocket of his jeans close to where leather gloves stuck out from his waistband. Wyker came up alongside him, and for a long while neither man spoke. They observed the herd, appreciating the silent communication and the body language of the leader and the followers. It was the language of a look; the tip of an ear, the dropped head, ears laid flat, and a silent, stern message was sent. All of these signals created the social fabric of a herd of horses, a language that served them and saved them from predators. The two men watched as sensitive muzzles searched the ground for the tiniest remnants of breakfast.

Wyker was first to break the reflection. "What you thinking of working on today?"

C.J.'s facial expression revealed nothing, and there was a long pause before he answered. "His feet are getting too long."

"Yup. How do you want to approach that?" Wyker asked.

C.J. said, "Very fucking carefully."

Wyker laughed as C.J. continued.

"The other day I asked him for one of his front feet. For the first time, he didn't bite the shit outta my back. Start there, and if that's fine, I'll ask him easy, and make my way toward that back end."

Wyker pushed off the fence and started down the breezeway. "Sounds like a plan. First you gotta catch him."

C.J. was patient and consistent with Rio. Wyker was pleased as he watched each session, and with how C.J. was good at helping the other inmates with their skills. Refinement was his forte, and his help made things easier. The horses improved and the inmates improved. They all became handy around the horses to varying degrees. With the better-trained horses, the inmates did cattle work, moving cows and separating them, along with some branding and vetting. A few would find a way to use these skills beyond their incarceration. Wyker suspected there would be some success stories coming out of this group.

The time came when C.J.'s sentence was served and he got parole. He still hadn't ridden Rio, and he wanted to before he left. Wyker arranged it on C.J.'s last day.

Rio moved around the pen smoothly in both directions, saddle on, fenders and stirrups moving against his sides with each stride. Wyker said nothing, and C.J. didn't need him to tell him when to make the try. Using his body language, C.J. slowed Rio to a trot, then a walk. He then moved Rio at the walk for several revolutions, C.J.'s boots shuffling in a matching rotation in the soft ground. The horse's breaths slowed to match the more relaxed gait as C.J. prepared to hook him on. Rio's ear flicked in C.J.'s direction and C.J. picked that moment to take a step back. It was perfect timing and Rio hooked on effortlessly.

C.J. stood at the center with rope halter in hand and waited for the horse. Rio moved into the center at a walk and stopped close to him. C.J. ran his hand along Rio's sweat-dappled neck to his right hip, around his rump, and along his left side. Rio turned an ear and his eye followed, but he did not move his feet.

Someone at the rail quietly asked Wyker a question about training horses, what was so hard about it. Wyker spoke to the men lined up watching C.J. and Rio. "A horse is food to a predator, and their response to imminent death involves flight more than fight. So, it is huge for them to allow a predator to 'train' them, to let them get on their backs. It means they have to suspend their natural instincts. Their awareness of who and what's around them has much to do with their ability to 'see' behind them, as their eyes are more to the sides of their heads. And their hearing—the ears possess independent mobility. Of course, their powerful hindquarters and sharp hooves can buy them the time to escape."

The world outside the pen didn't exist to C.J. He felt completely in the moment with this horse. C.J. stopped at Rio's shoulder, tipped the horse's head, and put the rope halter on him. C.J. did not look to Wyker or to anyone else; his whole being was hooked up with Rio. Slowly, C.J. extended his left arm and sent Rio in a circle around him, disengaged his hindquarters, got his weight back, opened his shoulder, and sent him in the other direction also at the walk. Rio's head elevated a little, but his tail remained soft to his butt and there was no brace in his body. C.J. disengaged the hindquarters again and backed him a couple of steps, then stopped. He waited, and seconds later Rio worked his lips, took a deep breath, and swallowed.

C.J. went with care to Rio's shoulder, halter rope in his left hand as he touched the top of the neck and mane, coming to rest just at Rio's withers. C.J. turned and took the stirrup, rotating it to put a toe in. He stood for a second, his leg bent and his boot toe in the stirrup. The air held the shuffle of hooves and the whinnies of horses out in the pens, and a bird chirped somewhere. Time seemed suspended. C.J. put some weight in the stirrup, then transferred more of his weight until his right leg was off the ground a few inches...and he waited. Rio still hadn't moved his feet. Then C.J. put his whole weight in the stirrup and brought himself up so that if he wanted to, he could swing a leg and be in the saddle.

Wyker did not really say "go on" out loud, it was more of a whisper, but C.J. seemed to hear him. Rio's head came up and he shuffled his feet as C.J.'s weight settled into the saddle. C.J. reached down and stroked Rio's withers area with his free hand, then slowly reached back and stroked the top of his hip and rump. C.J. gently asked Rio to tip his head to C.J.'s left knee. Rio followed the feel, and did so smoothly. For a split second C.J. hesitated, at a loss about doing the same on the opposite side, as the lead rope was only on one side. He looked at Wyker, who said, "Let's not concern ourselves too much with that right now. Ask him to walk off."

Rio's walk-off was far from smooth. He wound up and went. It was C.J.'s quick grip with his legs that fueled the launch, and the death grip on the saddle horn stiffened his body and emphasized his imbalance as he worked to stay in the saddle. Rio churned around and back humped. Chunks of dirt flecked the side of the round pen walls, sounding like buckshot as they hit. The men scrambled backwards. C.J. tried to relax some and ride it out until it came down a notch.

"Easy, C.J., don't squeeze him with your legs, ease off with the death grip."

The guys laughed.

Wyker added, "That was more of a crow hop than a buck, huh C.J.?"

C.J. glanced at him with a raised eyebrow and nodded.

"Now ask again and just use a little pressure, release, and a little pressure. Find the feel that flows him at a walk around the pen. Watch that your rope doesn't get too loose there. Yeah, just take up a little of the slack in your rope. You don't want to take much of a hold of his face. Okay, now just stop 'riding' him and when his feet stop, gently touch him again. Good, there it is..."

Rio stopped moving his feet, licked his lips, and C.J. held the rope out to change direction. He opened his inside leg and gently bumped Rio from the outside to move him off. It wasn't much, but Rio launched and traversed the round pen. C.J. stayed with him, less awkwardly, both hands holding the horn, but not squeezing with his legs like before.

"Relax and go with him, just ride him...soften up your shoulders, trust you'll stay with him. Okay...it's a little fast...just ride it. Move with him, don't push him... he's trying to find what you want. You need to get clear with your intentions. Okay, yeah, that's better."

C.J. gradually released the saddle horn and with a light feel on the halter rope in his hand, they went around like that for a few laps until Rio slowed down to a trot. C.J. posted lightly to the rhythm of the trot, then he sat it to a walk.

"Good. At the walk, change direction again."

And C.J. did.

"That was good. Breathe. Okay, now gently guide him off the rail and to the center and stop. He's breathing a little hard and it was all good. Just sit there a bit and then step off him slowly."

C.J. eased his right leg out of the stirrup and momentarily held his weight over the saddle before he dismounted. Rio shuffled his feet some as C.J. lifted the fender to undo the girth. The halter rope was draped over his arm, tucked in the crook of his elbow, as he lifted the saddle off the horse's back. Rio shifted his weight, but didn't move away. Wyker smiled. C.J. walked the saddle to the rail. Rio hesitated, then followed the feel and moved with him. It was a big deal that C.J. trusted this horse enough to turn his back to him as he set the saddle, horn down, on the ground. And he took his time fixing the girth and setting the stirrup leathers before laying the saddle pad on top. Then he faced the mustang, stroked his damp neck, and slowly stroked his face. Rio dropped his head to the touch and let him. This impressed everyone, and looks were exchanged, but C.J. didn't notice. The moment was between him and his horse.

C.J. gave Rio a good full body grooming. He ran the soft brush down the long forelock repeatedly, brushed the damp spots by his ears, and the sides of his face. When C.J. stopped, Rio lowered his head and leaned his face against C.J.'s chest. C.J. dropped the brush in a plastic tote, untied the lead rope, and led Rio down the alley between the pens. The other inmates had moved off to put the gear away. Wyker watched C.J. and Rio make their way down to the holding pen. The sun cast a long shadow behind them. Both seemed relaxed and the feel looked right and light. It was a good day, a really fine day—the kind of day that would stay with him. C.J. had achieved his goal. It was done, and he was to be paroled.

Rio moved easily into his pen, turned, and stared at C.J. They seemed to look at each other for an eternity, and then Rio went into the group. Wyker stood back a ways, one hand resting on the pipe panel. C.J. turned, saw him, and half-smiled.

"Thanks for that. Felt good."

As C.J. walked by, Wyker fell in step next to him. "He was yours to put the first ride on. I'm glad it happened that way."

Horses moved around in one of the corrals, and as the two men walked past, a lead horse set about moving a lesser one off, ears pinned, asserting dominance. There was a squeal and a halfhearted kick from the underling, but he complied.

Wyker broke the silence by saying he'd spend more time with Rio. "He'll make a decent working horse. He's not afraid. He's had an honest start."

A conflicted C.J. added, "I felt that." He kicked a rock on the ground with the toe of his boot, and then he started to pass the halter to Wyker, who put a hand up to stop him. "You keep it. Who knows? Might be useful someday."

C.J. gave him a dark look and tossed it at Wyker's hand. Wyker caught part of it, but the lead rope fell on the ground and Wyker stepped around it.

"Yeah, right," C.J. snarled as he spun and marched toward the parking area. He went straight to the yellow bus and banged on the door until the driver opened up. He boarded and moved stiffly down the aisle to the back. C.J. sank into the seat, took his cowboy hat off, and ran a hand through his sweaty hair. He looked out the window, an elbow on the dusty windowsill, and his mouth pressed hard into his knuckles. He stared at the closest corral, closed his eyes, turned away, and didn't look out the window again until they were almost back to the prison.

Wyker stood with Tammy near the barn as he watched

the bus disappear. He felt the paper in his back pocket and pulled it out. He unfolded the envelope and smoothed the edges with his fingertips. It was addressed to him in the clean script of a woman's hand. The return address read "Three Bit Ranch." He frowned as he looked down at it.

A screeching cry from the air above made him look up. For several moments, he watched a hawk circling. The sharp-eyed predator's wings were fully extended, his tip feathers spread wide, grasping each hint of an updraft, intricately guiding minute adjustments as his head moved back and forth. Below the magnificent bird the horses milled about, and as Wyker pushed himself off the barn wall, he noticed a white diesel dually hauling a big horse trailer pull into the compound. Another rig followed closely behind it. Wyker checked himself, put the folded letter in his pocket, and stood, watching.

A diminutive woman with short, frizzy red hair and snug-fitting jeans got out of the driver's side. She wore laced up Roper boots with a stacked heel, which made her short stride choppy, awkward as she approached the other rig and waited for the driver. He was fit in a wiry way, and was short as well. He had thinning hair and a dour expression. Wyker watched them look out over the pens of horses, discuss something quietly, then make their way to the main office.

Wyker coiled and recoiled the rope on the halter as his mind chewed things over. Moments later, Andy Bates, the supervisor, came out the door with his clipboard. He held the office door for the woman, said something, and she erupted into a loud laugh—an unfortunate braying tinged with a forced harshness. Andy, pleased with himself, got that "looky, I made the little lady laugh" expression on his face. He walked with the couple down to the horse pens.

The three of them made their way along the main breezeway, and the woman talked a blue streak, anxious for the importance her knowledge would give her. "I do this program where we train these mustangs to be bridle horses and teach people the true Vaquero method of making a bridle horse. The horses learn to properly carry themselves and keep the shoulders and rib cages lifted, and they're really light in the bridle. They can become real cow horses. It's incredible how well they do. I have this filly—well, she's four now, so really she's a mare—and the start I put on her! She's going really good in the bridle. This project gets amazing results."

She continued to talk seamlessly about herself, her horses, and what she knew. It was all about her. They walked down the alley between the pens. As they approached, they ignored the cowboy and the dog, for which Wyker was sincerely grateful. It dismayed him that a person felt compelled to be that seriously stuck on themselves *and* talk about it. It was an accomplishment, of sorts, and downright disappointing that she had anything to do with horses.

Wyker shook his head and looked at Tammy. "Sweet Jesus, what an insufferable creature."

Tammy, at his feet, mouth open and panting, seemed to look up at him with a grin.

"Yeah, girl, you understand us better'n we do, huh?"

They fell in behind the trio, casual-like, when they were well past.

The pens close to the office held horses that had had some handling, but this pair steadily moved toward the mustangs that had been there the longest, like they knew where to look for those least adoptable. Wyker stayed far enough back that he went unnoticed, but close enough to hear. He watched their body language. They'd stop and the woman would make a show of taking pictures with her phone. She pointed out several horses.

She was animated and her stiff hair bobbed awkwardly as she spoke. "I like these. I like them very much. Oh yes, these will do very nicely…see that one there?" She pointed one out to Andy. "He's got a nicely sloped shoulder; some call that a good top line. I'll take that one; that one over there, the bay; and that big red roan one to the right. He's put together very handsomely. Oh my, I really like him."

She looked up into Andy's face with an animated expression as she spoke, and he dutifully wrote down her list. She leaned over the clipboard to be sure he got it right. She took more pictures and glanced frequently at her partner, who said nothing. He was bored and looked like he'd rather throttle something than be there.

Wyker caught Andy's eye and stayed well back. The couple moved off to another pen and Wyker observed her turn to her companion and mouth the words, "Is that enough?"

Content to leave them, Andy approached Wyker.

"Hey, Andy," Wyker greeted him.

"Hey. How'd it go today?"

Wyker lowered his voice a little and continued, "Good. Real good. Who're the tourists?"

"Ah…some folks looking over some horses to adopt."

45

"Really? Why are they looking at these? Most aren't even started…they trainers?"

"They got some training program, some project/clinic thing that they're doing…I dunno, she says they make great cow horses. Hey, maybe you know, what is a bridle horse?"

Wyker ignored the question. "You saw 'em before?"

"Yeah, they took twenty or so head six months ago, no problem. Said things worked out well and that their project was a huge success. Higher-ups say help them, so that's what we're doing."

"Uh-huh. They pick that red? The red roan one there?" He pointed toward Rio. As if he knew he was being talked about, Rio lifted his head and stared straight at Wyker while Andy looked at his notes.

"Uh, yeah, she wants him."

Wyker looked at the couple, then he looked at Rio and sighed. "Life's kinda funny, did you know that, Andy?"

Andy exhaled a snorting kind of laugh. "Sure, hysterical. I'm laughing all the time."

"Tell her to pick another one. That red, he's not going with her."

"What? Why?"

Wyker settled the coiled halter in his hand and rested it against his hip. He leaned an arm on the corral panel and looked Andy square. "He's already being adopted by somebody else."

"Really? I didn't know. You sure?"

The woman made a point of catching Andy's eye, waved, and gave him a phony smile.

Andy turned back to Wyker. "She seemed sweet to

pick him."

"Take him off her little shopping list, Andy. She'll get over it."

"Okay, whatever, he's off the list. Move him outta there so I don't have to worry about it. I'll go tell her."

Wyker opened the gate and approached Rio. He stood quietly as the other horses moved around in the pen. Tammy dashed back and forth at full speed along the outside of the fence as Wyker undid the knot on the halter and slid the end up over Rio's muzzle. As he tied the knot, he looked up over Rio's neck and caught the cold stare from the redhead. He stared back and she looked away, then turned on her fake smile and harsh laugh as Andy led them to another pen.

"Well boy, you're not going with the killers today, or any day. Those two jokers couldn't train the sun to shine," Wyker said to Rio as he led him out and started down the alley. Tammy darted ahead happily, then stopped and looked at Wyker with that expression of love she always had for him. Then her eyes changed and looked past him. He turned his head to follow her gaze. The redhead's "partner" was watching them go.

So, the education of Rio began, and he was a challenge. Wyker got him going better under the saddle in the round pen and got him more freed up. Wyker had to have his intentions clear with this horse. He had to be honest in his approach and timing. Timing with Rio was everything.

Freeing up the forward in a horse like Rio presented a whole round of releases, which only a good colt starter would know how to properly manage. Rio's strength and fierce spirit were matched with a keen intelligence. Wyker was impressed by how wicked smart this horse was. He learned everything very quickly, and once he got the concept of a maneuver and understood that balance made things easier and better, he'd refine smoothly. Transitions smoothed out almost overnight, like he'd stood under the stars and figured things through, and then built on the lessons from the day before. He was like a sponge.

Wyker's saddle always had a coiled lariat tied to it near the horn, and with young horses he'd hold it in his hand and move it around so the horse would see it in the corner of his eye. Pretty quickly the horse would get used to new things. To desensitize Rio to surprise sounds and movements, Wyker would slap his own leg with it. As part of his training, Wyker would unsaddle Rio and leave him tied to the hitching post, then practice roping things nearby; maybe a fencepost, a garbage can, or an imagined target in the dirt. He got Rio used to the rope and worked it a lot from the ground, rubbing him with the coiled rope and dragging it around on the ground next to and behind Rio. He'd ride Rio, and when things were good he'd swing a rope off him—not onto anything in particular—and walk the horse while recoiling it back. Rio soon became accustomed to the feel of the rope moving around him. He learned quickly and seemed to enjoy the new stuff that Wyker presented him, like when he'd drag a tire behind him. The first tries were a bit frisky, but Rio would follow a feel and he got there. It became a game, and the horse would even play with the tire in the paddock when the day was done.

Early one morning, Wyker swung the saddle onto Rio and did up the cinches loosely. He put a breast collar across Rio's chest and reached for a bosal with a mecate. The bosal was not new to Rio, but it was a cold morning and he was fresh. Wyker led him down to the big round pen, checked the cinch, tightened it up a little, and rubbed Rio's neck. He worked him with a flag before he mounted up. Then he moved him off and worked him up to a trot, stopping and changing directions, stopping, backing, and opening his shoulder to roll back. He stopped and backed him, rolled back again, then moved him up into a lope. They loped around, Rio's neck hair flattened from a light sweat. Wyker slowed him to a walk and Rio aired up. He walked in circles, relaxed, head low and even with his withers, his eyes soft.

They went to the gate, opened and closed it from the saddle smoothly, and headed down the broad alleyway between the pens. At the end, Wyker opened a bigger gate and closed it the same way. There was a dirt track that went off toward some low hills and brush. Wyker and Rio started down it, picked up an easy lope, and made their way to a nearby ranch. The foreman was a good friend, and they'd often help him gather, sort, and brand.

SEVEN

The old man sat alone in his ranch truck, his dog Sonny's head in his lap. He gripped the wheel so hard with both hands that they had gone numb. Around him were outbuildings, the feed shed, a tractor under an open shed row, and the cattle chute with the pens. And beyond that were the sloping gray hills, lonely with winter. He looked upon miles and miles of his heritage; hundreds of acres that represented many generations of his family's collective hard work, that scrub grassland of the high desert that had produced a legion of fine cattle. The constant work of it hadn't been a burden to his father or his grandfather, but was clearly an overwhelming burden to this generation, his children. They fled the hard work of the ranch as soon as they could and it broke his heart.

He felt the tears roll down the worn leather that was his face. Several drops landed on the soft brown-and-black head of the dog. Sonny didn't notice and kept his head on his master's lap with half-shut eyes. Hank let out a huge breath, one he felt he'd been holding for years. Finally, he released his grip on the steering wheel and found the key in the ignition. When would his pain ease? He asked himself this question as if it were the last. All the others seemed to have faded away. He ground the old truck into reverse, and without looking, backed up. He knew where everything was on this land—he didn't need to look. He found first gear and headed slowly down the rutted road so as not to jar Sonny's head, which still rested on his right thigh. The cattle guards at the gate would rattle the tire suspension so much that Hank knew exactly when Sonny would get up and sit on the bench seat in an effort to absorb the rough ride.

Hank Larsen was making the trek into town for a cup of hot coffee at the tavern. Maybe he'd feel like eating something. He knew he should before his clothes just fell off of him for nothing left to hang on to. The truck was at the edge of the highway pavement, and though there was no reason to stop anymore, he did it out of habit. Then he turned left and made his way into town.

Behind the tavern, Shiloh Taylor got out of her seen-better-days pick-up. She slammed the door. It popped open. She tried again. Damn thing wouldn't close. *Shit.* It was friggin' cold out and colder with the wind. Her embroidered jeans jacket did very little except cut the bitter sting a fraction. One end of her scarf had come loose and swung wildly back and forth, half hitting her in the face each time the wind swirled. She wore a pair of old and faded jeans, but how they hugged her body could just about make a grown man cry. She had a way of looking good all the time—blond and blue-eyed with a perfect mouth, full lips, and a body that wouldn't quit. She could walk casually through a room, grab the attention of any male with a pulse, and it took no effort. It just came naturally to her.

Many relationships bubbled and boiled over in the wake that was Shiloh. At times, she'd passed herself off as a horse trainer, but it was hard for her to stay long at any established stable before she moved on to the next place. Maybe it was her special curse that men simply could not ignore her, and that knack of stringing quite a few of them along at the same time tended to burn up any female goodwill. She had a baby voice—cloying and breathy— and she called everyone "honey" or "sweetie," and would physically stroke their arms. She had few, if any, real friends and a history of using up just about everyone and every place she'd ever been. She was lucky that her looks would carry her well past the age when most women struggled to hang on to theirs.

Finally, the truck door stayed shut. Shiloh walked to the back door of the Pine Tavern & Café and went inside. Toby would be there already and the coffee would be made. He'd be getting the grill warm and setting out his ingredients for the morning's breakfast. She hung up her coat, grabbed an apron with the Pine Tavern logo, and tied it around her slender waist. She grabbed her chit book and clocked in. There was another chit book tucked in the outside pocket of her bag. Shiloh reached into the cubby and pressed it deeper in, then zipped it closed. She turned and walked into the main dining area and said a cheery good morning to the already cranky Toby. She grabbed the coffeepot and turned to the counter and topped up a truck driver's cup. He just stared at her as an errant piece of hash brown plopped out of his open mouth, missed the plate, and landed on the counter.

Pulling a rag from down under the counter, Shiloh

wiped it up efficiently and smiled at him. "May I get you anything else, sweetie?"

He nodded, but didn't say what he wanted. She saw old Mr. Larsen drive slowly by and she waved to him. He didn't see her.

Luis and Jorge had gone into Martin for supplies and breakfast. Martin Ranch Supply & General Store didn't open until 8:00 a.m., so they left the dogs in the cab of the truck and went into the café. They talked quietly about the missing cows.

In Spanish, Jorge said, "I think we missed at least two other places they might be."

Luis was quiet as breakfast came. After Shiloh asked them if they needed anything else and moved away, he replied, "If we missed them, perhaps the *ladrones* did too."

They finished breakfast just as the OPEN sign clicked on in the window of Martin Ranch Supply and the owner, Lyle Martin, unlocked the door. Luis paid the check and they got up to go. At the truck, the dogs were on their feet, cold noses pressed against the glass of the passenger's side window, happy to see Jorge. Luis backed out and moved the truck down the street.

Shiloh cleared dishes, collected money, and wiped down the tables. A voice from over by the window said, "Check please," and she nodded an acknowledgment toward it. She put the cash in the drawer and stabbed a receipt on the brass spike by the register. Shiloh went around the counter, put a check on one table, and cleared more empty dishes.

Del was doing his usual hungry stare. He'd sit at a booth, all the way in, and move his empty plate farther away so she'd have to reach for it. If he didn't try to touch or grab at her, he'd make an exaggerated show of looking down her top. The debris of breakfast was lodged in a deep crevice to the left of his front tooth. It was hard to discern because the plaque on the rest of the teeth was generally the same color.

"Nice front end," he leered.

Del Riggs did not have a face one wanted to see first thing in the morning, or any time of day. Beneath the brim of his sweat-stained cap, his eyes were black and hard. Doll's eyes.

Shiloh did her best to ignore the obvious, and said, "Sweetie, you better be leaving me a good tip." With a saccharine smile, she left his check on the table.

"Love you too, honey. Don't you forget my receipt, now." He tipped himself toward the window to pull his worn leather billfold from his back pocket.

A small group of men got up from the next table where they'd been in quiet conversation. Del had eavesdropped when they first sat down, but soon lost interest. They had ignored Del and talked of general things during breakfast. As they moved past him, a skinny buckaroo named Mattie was the only one to give Del a polite greeting. "Mornin', Mr. Riggs."

Del nodded at him. "Matthew." *Good manners,* he thought.

Mattie was a buckaroo at the Bitterroot Ranch, a big outfit in the Jordan Valley. He was a simple person; tall, pencil thin, and socially awkward. He used to talk to Del more often, about ranch stuff, until the ranchers had started comparing notes on the thefts. Del guessed they were keeping a tight handle on all their buckaroos these days, none sure who was behind the thieving. It came to be that everyone looked a little suspicious. And skinny Mattie had a terrible crush on Shiloh; actually thought someday she'd see how in love he was, that she'd run away with him and they'd get married. He talked openly about the life they'd make after a few beers at the tavern.

Fool, Del thought after they walked by. He knew the way he talked to Shiloh irked Mattie. Mattie would mutter something about it being disrespectful to the lady and Del would laugh at him. Del couldn't figure out why Mattie was kind to him.

Some of the buckaroos from the Rushing Springs Ranch came in with a foreman as the Bitterroot ranch hands were leaving. Shiloh followed them to their table.

"Good morning, fellas, pick any table. Coffee? Who'd like coffee?"

Del was done, he got his change, counted out a stingy tip, and put the receipt in the breast pocket of his shirt. Then he walked out, noticing that the ranch hands were enthralled with Shiloh and those tight jeans. She brought them menus they did not need. Coffeepot in hand, she asked them again if they wanted some. Del smiled as they asked for juice too; another trip. Oh, and some water please, after she'd delivered the juice. She'd oblige them; she knew how to get the tips.

EIGHT

C.J. walked barefoot across the faded, worn carpet to the narrow bed. A detailed tattoo on his toned bicep reflected in the mirror above the cheap dresser as he passed by. It was tribal in nature—a third eye discernable at the point of his strong shoulder. C.J.'s six-foot frame was inked on both biceps. There was a lizard over his chiseled right pec, and a larger tattoo was across his lower back. It wrapped almost to his hip bones and rose several inches horizontally above his Wrangler jeans in symmetrical patterns of red and black.

The small room wasn't worth the money the state paid to house him. C.J. lay on the bed, one forearm under his head, the other rested on his upper abs, and he stared at the ceiling. No jobs available, there was no one to call or go see, and he wasn't hungry or tired. He wasn't anything.

His P.O. had a list of possible jobs for him, and C.J. had dutifully shown up and completed the "one-time-onlys"—the odd afternoon of ditch digging or hauling boxes from one warehouse to another. He didn't have a current driver's license, no money for a car, and no reason to get one. Shit, if he needed a car... *Well, try not to need a car.* His priority was to ignore any opportunity to fuck up.

A few miles away, a frustrated probation officer, Jim Tosca, sat in his cramped office surrounded by stacks of files on his desk. He was stalled by bureaucracy and the reality that there were few options to offer. What was he supposed to do? These men had served their time, but now what? There was nothing out there, no resources, and scarce work for these guys.

He'd just gotten an odd call from a guy named Wyker, who'd asked how C.J. Burke was doing. Jim had been all rosy and positive, said things were good with C.J. He'd made an effort to really convince him that it was going well. It made him nervous, because he wasn't sure who was asking; was it someone from his department checking up on him? His caseload was huge. He wondered if someone had fallen through the cracks. Had he missed something? Calls like that made a wreck of his imagination. He stared at the phone, and then at a half-eaten sandwich he'd brought for lunch. The surface of the wheat bread had dried out and the crust edges had begun to retract and curl. He got up and stared out the dirty window at the parking lot—the dismal view from his office through wire-reinforced glass—his hands deep in his pants pockets. Glare reflected off an unmarked probation car and blasted his eyes. Turning back to his desk, he touched the paper with Wyker's number on it, opened the drawer, slid it inside, and closed it.

Wyker hung up and reread Kitzie Collins's letter. He

and Tuff had been friends for the better part of his life. He looked up at a picture of them packing into the mountains when they went hunting together. They both looked so young, though Tuff was by far his senior. Wyker smiled at the memory, then looked at the letter again. It was filled with the worry of a strong woman whose fear of the future was all-consuming. Her loneliness and frustration about the cattle rustling was detailed in the letter. Kitzie was in trouble. Tuff's eyes stared at him from the faded photograph, as if to say, "Help her if you can." The dog-eared letter went back into his pocket. Tammy stared up at him as they walked toward his truck in the parking lot.

It took a while to drive there, and when they arrived, he was too late to see Mr. Tosca at his office. Wyker booked into a cheap motel, and got a sandwich at a gas station quick stop next door that had a deli counter of sorts. He drank a beer and watched TV until he fell asleep. The next morning, he drove past tired storefronts with several "For Lease" signs and a seedy residential motel. He parked outside the building that housed the probation department, and found the door to Tosca's office.

A muffled voice inside barked, "What!" to his knock.

Wyker opened the door and stuck his head in.

Jim Tosca looked up and asked, "Who are you?"

"I spoke with you yesterday. I'm Wyker."

Mr. Tosca made a lame attempt at straightening his desk, tipping a precarious balance of papers so that they slid dangerously close to the edge. He barely caught them before they scattered to the floor, and clipped his bottle of soda in the process, which did make it to the floor.

"Oh, yeah…ah, shit! Oh, not you, sorry…what are

you doing here?" Tosca sputtered as Wyker walked in.

Tosca was on bended knee to wipe up the mess on the floor. In awkward haste, he left it, resumed his place behind his desk, and put on an officious smile. Wyker pulled up a chair and respectfully removed his cowboy hat. Once seated, he rested it over his knee. He did this slowly and carefully, like he was approaching a braced-up colt, and then looked directly into Mr. Tosca's cautious eyes.

"I would like to talk about C.J. Burke."

A short time later, he was back in his truck with Tammy. He thought over what had been said and stroked her head. "Well girl, that went well. Better'n I expected. Surely a man who hates his job."

NINE

Luis thought the truck and trailer pulling in was someone needing work done. Jorge looked up from a gate he was fixing, and his cattle dogs were on their feet and alert. The rig pulled into the area near the main barn and stopped. The engine went silent and a tall man stepped out. As he closed the door, one of the horses in the trailer stomped impatiently. The man looked at Jorge and said hello. The dogs moved toward him, hackles up, and Jorge smiled at the stranger.

"May I help you?"

"I'm looking for Mrs. Collins, is she about?" said Wyker as he reached his hand down for the dogs to sniff. "Hey there, fella. How ya doing? And how about you?"

There was a whine from the dog carrier in the back of the truck. Wyker opened the cage door and Tammy bounded out, hopping off the open tailgate. Jorge's cattle dogs and Tammy made quick get-to-know-yous before Tammy was off like a shot looking for something to herd. Wyker called her back and she settled down near his feet.

Jorge smiled. "Good dog. You use her around cows?"

Jorge's two dogs trotted back and plopped down as Wyker answered, "She's handy."

Luis had been wrenching on a tractor and he reached into his back pocket for a rag. He wiped his right hand a bit more thoroughly before extending it to Wyker.

"I'm Luis and this is my son, Jorge. We work for Mrs. Collins."

"Will Wyker, a friend of the family. I knew Tuff and Kitzie many years ago. First time I've been back since, well, since…it's been a long time. Is she here?"

"Yes, she's in the house."

At that moment, Kitzie came out the door, putting on her coat and smiling at Wyker. Her smile grew and she opened her arms wide to envelop him in an enormous bear hug. She gripped his upper arms, leaned back, and tilted her head up at him. She looked truly delighted that he was there.

"I'm *always* here," she laughed. "Boy, is it good to see you again! What a nice surprise. Come on in."

Wyker paused. "In a sec. I need to unload first. Is there a spot where I can put three horses?"

Kitzie took a sip of her coffee and held the cup in both hands, elbows resting on the kitchen table. She listened carefully as he talked. He told her about his life since he last saw her and what he'd been doing in Canon City. Talked about the Colorado Wild Horse-Inmate Program he'd been involved with since its inception in 1992, all about his work with the BLM and the mustangs. At the end, he told her about Rio and C.J., and proposed the idea of having C.J. come work on the Three Bit for a while.

Tuff once said Wyker was a natural horseman—a man with a gift around horses—and that he always had a kind, steady way about him. Wyker and Kitzie sat at the table and talked for what seemed like hours, and Kitzie felt a measure of relief from the burdens she'd been carrying. There was stew on the stove for dinner and the kitchen smelled delicious. It felt the way it used to at the Three Bit.

She stirred the pot on the stove and said, "You came all this way for a visit?"

Wyker responded after he placed his empty cup down. Out of habit, he stared at it and rolled the bottom edge around on the table. "I got your letter. I want to help out."

"We don't need any help. We're fine. This cattle thing may not be anything. It could be we just haven't found the herd yet. I got all worked up over nothing when I wrote you. I overreacted."

"Kitzie, they've been at it for about three years, and now there's more attention on this. Oregon's Department of Agriculture and authorities all over the state are teaming up to catch these guys. A buddy of mine—an ODA Livestock investigator by the name of Hy Royston—and his partner have been assigned to this. Filled me in. He said they're working on better brand inspection and the use of electronic devices to track the cattle."

"What...microchips or something?"

"He told me some ranchers are setting up cameras, doing counts when cattle move through gates, and some are even doing DNA testing to establish a calf's DNA to its mother's. Certainly won't be stuff everyone will do. If the rustlers have this well-oiled operation, it may be that they are feeling the heat, and they must have knowledge of the efforts to catch them. Could be they've moved farther out and that's why your cows became vulnerable."

Kitzie refilled her cup. "What you're saying sounds unrealistic for the cattlemen I know. I read the U.S. lost nine thousand beef operations from 2009 to 2010. Inventory of cattle is the lowest since 1952. Demand is high; it'll go higher because we export a lot of beef worldwide. And yet ranchers work harder than ever and struggle to survive." She leaned her hands on the edge of the counter and looked out the window. "A lot of grazing land has been lost to development or other farming. Then there's the high cost of feed and energy. We barely break even and it's damn hard work for little money. Land is getting harder to lease and the next generation has no interest in ranching. The squeeze is on from all sides."

Wyker got up to wash his cup out, but Kitzie took it and did it for him. He leaned against the counter, arms folded across his chest, and looked around at the warm ranch kitchen. It was just as he remembered it, and he felt comfortable being there again. "Lots of good memories for me in this room," he said. Then he turned toward Kitzie. "It's been hard for you, and I understand why you've held on."

"I don't know if I'd be happy anywhere else. And I still have hope Carson will come back someday. My memories are here, all my good memories." She paused. "Do you know why Carson left? She said she saw no future in it. She may be right. Then there's Luis and Jorge. I could not ask for better friends. They have stayed with me all these years." She paused again. "About your friend C.J. ...you mentioned having him come here to help out. How do you suggest I justify that to them?"

Wyker looked out the door, content to see that the dogs were getting along. "I don't know that you have to. It'll work itself out." And then he added, "This place made my life better, and I kinda believe it could happen again."

Kitzie feigned an incredulous expression, which made him smile.

"Okay," he added, "as a favor to me then, on a trial basis. I'd like to take a break from the Inmate Program. That door's open; I can go back when I want."

Kitzie softened and agreed. "No promises. We'll try it. Now, let's go see what you brought with you."

Kitzie and Wyker walked through the barn to the paddocks on the other side. Jorge hopped over a fence he had tightened up and followed them. He was curious. Wyker had brought three horses with him. The first one they came to was a big Quarter Horse, a sorrel with a flash of white down his face, and Wyker called him Johnny.

The three dogs became five as Wyatt and Lulu got into the act. They ran around and had a grand time. Luis joined his son at the rail and Johnny came over to say hello. Wyker watched as Johnny put his nostrils to Kitzie's hand, and then sniffed her arm as it rested on the rail. The horse's ears pricked forward and followed the rowdy bunch of dogs, who were panting from playing at full speed. Jorge's two found his side and collapsed happily on the ground. Tammy ran back and forth along the rail, and Wyatt and Lulu stood ready for more, then ran off to play by themselves.

Kitzie made a comment Wyker had heard before. "He's nice and big. Where'd you get him?"

Wyker ran his hand over Johnny's face and muzzle. "A good friend. Remember the Cordoni family? Old man Cordoni didn't need him and gave him to me. He was a little too hot for his uses, and I've had him a few years now. We get along."

"Who else do we have here?" Kitzie asked as she eyed the other horses.

"That one, the little bay, I have about sixty days on her and I'm pleased with her mind."

Tammy ran back and forth, herding the bay through the fence, her instincts not letting her rest. Jorge's cattle dogs watched with interest, but were not as manic, and only worked when told to. Tammy was in herding mode from the moment she awoke until the day was done, and she never strayed far from Wyker's side.

Kitzie stroked the mare's neck and said, "She's super nice, not at all what I picture a mustang to look like. I can see why you like her."

In the last paddock, a mess of red hair and pent-up energy galloped around the whole of the enclosure, ears forward, taking in all he could see, stopping hard, head up, and breathing in all the new smells. Rio lifted his head high and sent an explosive burst of air through his nostrils, then was off again, throwing a buck here and there, and striking once into the air as he pivoted hard and changed direction. He stopped a few yards off the fence as the small group approached. Rio looked at them and dropped his head to look between the rails at Jorge's dogs, then stepped a bit closer. He was hooked on to Wyker, but interested in them all. It was a few more moments before he was at the rail and sniffing them. Wyker moved his hand up slowly and touched the side of Rio's face.

Luis watched, smiling. "This one's a handful, huh?" he said.

Kitzie smiled and looked at Rio. "Now this is more of

my mental picture of a wild mustang, only bigger. Was he cut late? Kinda full of himself. Think he had his own band?"

"Wouldn't surprise me if he did. I've got about ninety days on him. One of the inmates started him. I've been roping off him some, and moving cows." He raised a brow at Kitzie. "He's smart and tough—just the kind of hard-ass to go looking for some lost cows..."

"And who's gonna ride that out into the backcountry. You, old man?" She laughed at him as he feigned a hurt look.

"I'm not as old as all that."

"I'd ride him!" Jorge piped up.

"No *hijo*, that's not for you," Luis cautioned his son. "Now, let's show Mr. Wyker around."

"Please, that sounds too formal. Thank you, but Wyker's fine."

Kitzie left Wyker with Luis and Jorge. They showed him the layout close to the house; the big barn, hay storage, the water system, and the office/tack room. It was a good bilingual conversation, one that laid a foundation for a solid working friendship. Wyker went over and uncovered a saddle that had been Tuff's. He knew it, remembered it, and smiled. His hand rested on the saddle horn. He looked up at the wall and saw the picture of Tuff on a big gelding and little Carson in the saddle in front of him. He leaned in to get a better look, squinting, at the faded picture.

"Kitzie barely mentioned Carson," Wyker commented.

"Not something we talk about," Luis replied.

For the next few days, Wyker was up early either helping out with the cattle or with minor repairs, and working the horses he'd brought. He worked cows off of all three, the mare to a lesser degree. He moved her around the smaller of the herds located in various fenced pastures on the ranch. There was doctoring, sorting, and some branding. Wyker's presence on the Three Bit was immediately welcome, and both Luis and Jorge took to him. Extra hands lightened the load, and Luis had time to catch up on the automotive side of his life. There were a few folks who'd been waiting on him, and he gave them all a call and scheduled the cars he'd not had time to work on.

Wyker went slowly and thoughtfully with the mare. She had a good mind, but she was worried and had her days. One day she'd be solid, the next she'd shut down, scared. He'd have to back up a little, go over things again, and give her time. He worked in the big corral and Tammy ran around and around the outside wall. Jorge watched from the rail and asked lots of questions. He hadn't had the occasion to gentle a young horse, and it was an opportunity to learn from a natural teacher. Luis was quietly pleased to see Jorge take so easily to Wyker, and Wyker obviously enjoyed sharing. He said it helped him to keep learning. His manner invited conversation, and Jorge found respecting this horseman an easy thing to do.

Rio took more time to settle enough to go to work. He was wound up and anxious, and Wyker knew getting him to work would be good. Rio needed to feel secure in any situation, so Wyker took the time to be clear and consistent with him. Wyker exposed Rio to a black tarp he'd placed in the round pen, and spent time getting Rio to stand next to it without shying off. It took time to get him to step on it, then it was mere hours before Rio would stand on it and tolerate having it picked up, flapped around, and dragged on the ground. After changing it up and working on something else, Wyker went back to the tarp.

Jorge laughed as Wyker pulled the tarp all the way up Rio's neck, over his head, and let Rio stand there covered by it. He looked like a giant black ghost. Wyker pulled the whole thing slowly over the horse's head and plopped it into a heap on the ground under Rio's nose. Rio stood there, quiet and unconcerned, head down, eyes calm, and he never moved a foot until Wyker led him over to the fence. Wyker smiled a big, shit-eating grin at Jorge. Jorge said it was like when he trained his dogs, and he respected the result.

"I won't count on that happening every time." Wyker thumped gently on Rio's neck with his hand. "He's about where I want him. I think he's ready to go out," he said with a touch of pride.

Jorge hopped off the fence and turned, smiling. "Sure, we need to move the smaller herd up the little canyon and that might be good for him. What'll happen if you come off him out in the backcountry? You think he'll be gone and leave you in the dirt, and head off into the hills?"

"Hopefully he likes me better than that," Wyker said.

"You can count on Tammy to pick you up," Jorge replied, and she wagged her tail at both of them.

TEN

The breakfast rush was over and the prep for lunch not quite started. Shiloh was refilling the napkin holders when she called to Toby, "Hey, I'm going into the bar. Empty the dishwasher."

The back half of the building that housed the café was the bar, and three nights a week the Tavern Bar was open. Shiloh waitressed there Thursdays, Fridays, and Saturdays. The Town Council of Martin, all three members, held their bimonthly meeting in there and it was important to Toby that the bar was clean afterward.

While Shiloh was in the bar, she checked her cell phone. There were several messages, but one in particular she wanted to hear. She glanced down the passage separating the bar from the café as she listened to the sound of the redial. She ducked farther back into the area near the storeroom. The phone seemed to ring forever before a voice answered. At first, it was hard to hear him clearly; the connection was scratchy, the reception dodgy, but she was relieved the call had gone through.

"It's me...yeah, I'm alone." She looked at the door to the kitchen again and listened before she answered his question. "Yes, he was here this morning and I gave him what I had. It's been kinda weird around here. No, I've been very careful...folks are worried, that's why. Huh? What's up?"

The voice on the other end talked some more. She nodded her head slightly and her eyes narrowed as she listened. "When? Does Del know yet? No, I won't say anything, he's such an asshole. Jumpy? Me? No, hey, I gotta go."

Voices came from the kitchen. She spun her head, heart pounding, and peered around the dark bar toward the door as she chewed the nail on one of her fingers.

ELEVEN

The message light flashed on the phone in C.J.'s room. He retrieved the message, which was to come by and see Tosca. It did not say what for. He put on a clean shirt, ran a comb through his hair, and headed over.

Tosca sat at his desk surrounded by the same files, his shirt wrinkled, no tie, and the top two buttons undone.

C.J. knocked politely on the door, and Tosca hollered for him to come in.

"Have a seat. There's a job for you. It will mean you leave the state and go to Oregon. You got any problem with that?"

C.J. replied, "What kind of job?"

"Does it matter? Ranch work of some kind…not sure exactly, but it shouldn't be something you can't handle. It does mean you will be changing probation officers; a roving officer will come and evaluate you. He'll have the same authority to drug test, and the same authority to pull you in as I do—that is, if you agree to make the move. You'll live in some kind of bunkhouse, nothin' fancy, and plenty to be done I'm told. These folks need some help and someone has suggested you for the job."

"Who?"

"Just a referral. If you want to go and you agree to the terms of your probation, I'll get to the paperwork allowing the transfer. You need time to think about it?"

C.J. looked past Tosca out the dirty window at the

lonely parking lot. There wasn't much keeping him there. "Sure, I'll go."

"Okay then, I'll make some arrangements and I'll call you later."

Tosca decided maybe he needed a break from the dreary office, so he put in to escort C.J. to Oregon. He called the probation department in Oregon and arranged to meet C.J.'s new P.O.

The drive from Canon City was pure hell. C.J. never wanted to know anybody this well. Tosca talked incessantly about his medical condition, his ex-wives, his ex-friends, his ex-jobs, his dead parents, and how the failure that was his life was someone else's fault. A shitload of exes was Tosca's legacy, apparently. The man had a bladder like a peanut; every gas station, fast-food joint, truck stop, and a few friendly bushes caused him to pull over to relieve that pitiful organ. C.J. kept his mouth shut most of the time, not one to be chatty, but after stop number forty-five at a 7-Eleven, he suggested Depends.

Tosca asked for receipts for everything, haphazardly tossing them into the mix of debris that was the back seat. The car was literally full of the detritus of a life, and it was clear this was a man who never cooked anything for himself.

Turning to C.J., Tosca proudly said, "I'm careful to get receipts 'cause they'll reimburse for everything on the trip."

At that moment, a piece of cream-filled cupcake, stuck precariously to his moving lip, gained the momentum to pop free. The offensive remnant bounced off C.J.'s leg onto the floor.

C.J. growled, "What the fuck? Hell, turn in all the fucking aluminum back there, probably fill the goddamn tank."

That shut Tosca up and a grateful C.J. spent time looking out his window. It felt good to see the world go by to the sound of the road under the wheels. In jail, he'd look out the window and watch the weather go by. This felt different; much better in the car. He was moving. Yes, that was it, he was moving and it felt good to be moving. Moving on, moving forward, moving to something totally new, and to someplace new.

They pulled into Meridian, Idaho, too late to see his new P.O., so Tosca got them a motel room with hard double beds. Dinner was crappy fast-food burgers eaten in the room. C.J. had pretty much shut down. Spending the night with Tosca was worse than being in jail.

The next morning they met the new guy, Dale. Dale was a big man, tall, fit, and wore an expensive cowboy hat. He had nice boots and a truck in the parking lot that anyone would have admired. It was big and had a gooseneck set-up in the back—for his horse trailer, he said. Dale made Tosca look like the grunt office dweeb that he was. The three of them went to Dale's office, where there was paperwork to sign, and rules and regulations to go over.

When he was done, Dale rose and suggested that he take C.J. the rest of the way himself so Mr. Tosca could head back. It was not really a request; he said it in a drawl and good-old-boy way that basically dismissed Tosca. Tosca was ambivalent for a few minutes, saying that he had a professional obligation to see his duty through. But Dale clapped his hand on Tosca's back and guided him out of the office and to his car.

"When I check in with the office, I'll tell them you went with us; you get another day, maybe two. After all, you deserve it. You've done a heck of a job, Jimbo!"

C.J. watched from the doorway and marveled that the scene reminded him of a car salesman leading a buyer to just the right car. While he waited, C.J. moved about the room, stopping at a wall dedicated to Dale.

"Man sure is stuck on himself," he murmured.

There were signed pictures from celebrities and politicians, various awards, and certificates of support for local Little League teams. Pictures of Dale on horses and of Dale riding in parades and at rodeos crowded the wall. There were old pictures of county fair events with cattle, prized bulls, and heifers. Some of the frames were ancient and surrounded faces that were not of this time. This man had history. C.J. peered at these and noticed the background details; the folks in the stands were cheering and clapping, smiling proudly at the next generation learning their livelihood. The women were thick and practical. The men had the faces of hard living and permanently stained fingers on their clasped hands.

He was halfway around the room looking at the photographs when Dale returned.

"Got your file, took a quick look, and we'll get started. I see you like history."

C.J. nodded but said nothing. He picked up his things and headed for the door.

The truck was extreme. It had custom paint and lots of chrome. It had all the goodies on the inside as well; apparently, Dale never met an upgrade he didn't like. The hat rack in the back of the extra cab cradled a veritable collection of cowboy hats, each with a plastic cover.

Dale's personality filled the vehicle to overflow, but C.J. observed that this guy noticed everything. Dale talked like a cheap used-car salesman, but there was steely-eyed shrewdness beneath the bonhomie.

He knew that C.J. had taken stock as he drove out of the office parking lot and headed for the intersection. "Yup, I got me some hats, love 'em. Can never have enough good boots, good hats, good horses, good cows, or good women." And he laughed at his own humor. Dale did that a lot.

C.J. said, "In that order?"

Dale ran past that and talked about the Three Bit, said he never could figure out what the name meant. He talked long about Malheur County, the Jordan Valley, the small town of Martin, and how it used to be bigger. He talked about the geography of the Three Corners region where the states of Oregon, Idaho, and Nevada met. He told C.J. about how he used to ride the whole area on horseback moving cattle, and had gotten to know just about everyone that mattered. "I considered running for public office. Some powerful friends thought I'd make a fine senator. I know more than the asshole who holds the office now."

He talked steadily for the first hour, with not a thing mentioned about C.J. C.J. did what he did best—kept his mouth shut and listened selectively. It seemed that the perfect companion for ol' Dale was Dale. He just loved the sound of his own voice and his own stories. Mixed in with that, Dale was a treasure trove of information about the country they were going through—who grew what, who had what in terms of land and leases to government lands, and who got what by marrying whom.

C.J. liked the vista, the openness of the high desert, and the tough beauty of the country. To each side were outcrops of rock and broken ground where, in summer months, there would be grasses and bracken, but where now only the dead and frozen stalks ran wild. He silently wondered whether, if he'd ever had the opportunity to homestead a place, he would've been happy.

The one true blessing of driving with Dale was that he drove—he didn't make fifty stops, and in fact, they drove straight through. The only stop they made was in the town of Martin. Dale parked in front of Martin Ranch Supply & General Store. C.J. got out and stretched as Dale waved him inside. They walked to the back, to a private office, and Dale stuck his head in the door.

"Howdy, Lyle! You busy?"

Lyle Martin was a good-looking, well-built man in his mid-fifties. His office spoke of a well organized and thoughtful man. The whole building was neat and clean. He looked over the computer monitor on his desk, rose, and crossed the room to shake hands with the ebullient Dale.

"Hello, Dale…long time. Good of you to stop in."

"This here's C.J., going to take him out to the Collins place."

C.J. shook Lyle's hand and looked him in the eye. Lyle Martin had a solid handshake and his eyes were the same. C.J. immediately liked him.

"Pleased to meet you. Three Bit's good people." Then he added, looking at Dale, "Didn't know Kitzie was looking for help."

Dale continued to dominate the room. "I don't know how it worked out. He was asked for; a temp thing. So, how are things with you?"

C.J. politely excused himself and found the men's room, where he splashed water on his face and ran a comb through his hair. When he returned, Lyle and Dale were out on the main floor of the store by racks of clothes and close to the door. Lyle said something about a rancher, an old man who'd lost his ranch, and that it had been that family's for generations. He talked about business being down from the recession.

"Things are very hard for many people. Don't know how some are going to make it through. There's a lot of tension...awkward catching up with old friends here in the store. Rangemen are nervy from the rustling that's been going on. No denying it, trust has become an issue between old friends. Very sad."

They were standing by a rack of Western shirts and Dale parted two hangers and pulled a shirt out for a better look. "Yeah, I heard something about that. That bad, huh?"

"Oh yeah, the investigations are getting serious. The losses are staggering."

C.J. stood patiently near the door as the two men wrapped up their conversation. Dale shook Lyle's outstretched hand vigorously, just shy of too hard. "Glad you were in, must not be too long again...good seeing you."

As C.J. turned to open the door, he paused and said, "Nice meeting you, sir."

Lyle looked him in the eye. "If you are a good friend

to Kitzie, then you'll be a good friend of mine. Call me if you need anything."

Dale pushed the door open and was out in the street.

"Yes, sir, I understand. Thank you, sir."

Lyle added, "C.J.—it's Lyle…okay?"

C.J. nodded and followed Dale, who told him to wait by the truck.

C.J. watched Dale head across and down the empty street to a large building with a sign on it that read "Pine Tavern." There was another painted sign with a large arrow that pointed down the side of the building to the tavern's bar entrance. C.J. figured it was a dual-purpose place. He leaned against the truck, his arms resting on the side of the bed. He stretched his back and turned his head enough to crack his neck. Dale was visible through the glass door, in what seemed to be a serious conversation with a petite blond inside. C.J. frowned at her body language. It struck him as fear, as though she felt intimidated.

"None of your business, pal," he said to himself and shook his head. He looked down the street. Not much to see, so he found himself staring at a wheel on the truck. He pushed off and checked out the other one. They were brand new rims, shiny chrome, paired with big, hefty tires with little cowboy boots linked together as a pattern on the entire circumference of the sidewalls.

Dale returned and got behind the wheel. He held out a paper bag. "Here, have one of these…Toby made sticky buns this morning and there were a few left. They're the best!" He garbled the words as he had a mouthful of one.

They headed out of town just as it started to rain.

TWELVE

Hank sat alone, hollows sharp under his cheek-bones as if something had eaten him empty from within. He had nowhere to go, nothing to do. It had been a couple of days since the eviction and he needed a shower. When Spence had knocked on the door, he was polite, professional, and he did his best not to show how sorry he felt. Spence had asked if Hank would head to Portland, but Hank was too stubborn to freeload off his son and daughter-in-law. Hank had lived one life and there was no other place on this earth he wanted to be. So, he loaded his truck with all he cared about, drove into town, and sat in it in front of Martin Ranch Supply with Sonny, his old shepherd mix dog. That's where Spence found him today.

He came around to the driver's side window. Hank did not look at him.

"Hank? You know, the bank has no immediate plan for your place, and they're not likely to anytime soon. They've done their due diligence I guess."

Hank said nothing. He stared straight ahead, though he could see Spence's police uniform, heavy belt, the black leather holster, and the gear on his waist. Hank was think-ing what a good job Spence did keeping that gun clean and oiled.

Spence rested an arm on the cab and roof. Hank could feel how big a man Spence was. Fit, too. *Good for him.*

Spence continued, not waiting for Hank to say anything. "You still got that good generator in the shed out there, Hank? You might want to go back out and get it....never know how something like that might come in handy." Spence shifted uncomfortably. "You know, there's plenty of good equipment too. Things that need looking after."

Sonny yawned, changed the position of his head on Hank's thigh, and rolled an expressive eye up at him. Hank looked down at the old dog and stroked his head.

Spence felt awkward. He shuffled a foot as if kicking a pebble out of his way, and shifted his stance. He wanted to find a comfortable, good place between himself and a man he deeply respected. "I've heard that folks who've been evicted off properties just move right back in. Seems those banks forget about 'em. They might ask us now and then to do a drive-by and look for squatters...but I'm shorthanded."

Hank turned his head and looked up at Spence. Spence tried to smile and then looked at his watch. "Well, Hank, please let me know if there's anything I can do for you. You take care now. I'll be seeing you around. Be my pleasure to buy you coffee at the tavern sometime." He stepped back from the truck, turned, and began to straighten his patrol belt out of habit when Hank's voice stopped him.

"Spence, I hold no grudge against you for doing what you had to. Got a load of hate for the sons-a-bitches who stole my cows. Ruined me. Them I hate with a fierceness I don't recall having before in my life. It's a hurtful thing to want to harm someone who's taken all I have. I never felt this way before. Always liked and trusted people. And the worst of it is, I look at everyone now as my enemy." Hank paused to get his breath and calm himself. The hate he felt was the caustic kind, the kind that, just speaking of it, ate parts of a person away. He gathered his words and finished. "But there is one thing I do believe with all my being—that you are my friend. And I'd be real glad for that cup of coffee right now...if you got the time."

The two of them crossed the quiet street and went into the Pine Tavern, where Spence bought them both a hearty breakfast.

THIRTEEN

The windshield wipers had been on full blast since Dale and C.J. left town, and by the time they turned into the entrance of the Three Bit, rivers of water were running on either side of the gravel road. It was hard to see exactly where they were going with the poor visibility. They negotiated one last curve and found an open stretch where the road skirted a big pasture area. C.J. saw a couple of horses had taken shelter in a three-quarter shed. Beyond, he saw the outline of buildings and a turnaround area in front of the house. There was a large structure, probably a big barn, off to the left.

Dale parked the truck in front of the house and reached behind him for his briefcase, its new leather smell still clinging to it. C.J. got out, grabbed his gear from under the tarp in the back of the truck, and jogged through raindrops to the small porch. He stood there and waited for Dale, who carefully adjusted a plastic cover on his ten-gallon hat. He tried to work the briefcase under his slicker, but it wouldn't cooperate.

At the door, Dale had barely knocked when it was opened by a woman. C.J. guessed she was Kitzie Collins. She fastened the buttons of a long duster and peered up at them from under the brim of an Aussie duck rain hat, which was made of an oiled fabric famous for its ability to let the water roll off. She pulled the storm tie snug, then extended her hand and shook C.J.'s hand firmly.

"You must be C.J.," she said, then she quickly did the

same to Dale. "And Dale? Got a call from a Mr. Tosca. Kitzie Collins."

Dale started in, friendly, like he had it all goin' on. "Yes, Ms. Collins, pleased to meet you."

Kitzie focused her attention on C.J. and asked if he had any rain gear. She bent over and pulled on a pair of high rubber boots, then stood up. She pushed between C.J. and Dale and looked at C.J.'s scant belongings. "Guess not. Okay, please go just inside. Behind that small curtain is an alcove. You'll find a rain jacket, a hat, and I think—I hope—there's a pair of rubber boots in there that'll do. We have to go."

C.J. ducked past Dale and Kitzie and rummaged through the clothes and boots until he found what he needed.

Dale tried to position himself in Kitzie's way, to guide her inside to get to business. "Go? Go where?" he said.

Kitzie stopped him. "Is there some paperwork I need to sign or something?"

Dale held up his briefcase, streaks of moisture dark on the leather—a new threat to it, which caught his worried eye. He brushed his momentary dismay aside and his tone changed from good-old-boy to administrator. "Yes, there are some important things we should go over."

"Let me guess; I agree to take C.J. on here and you agree to monitor him," she said as C.J. pulled on a pair of boots and put on a raincoat.

The big man looked puzzled. It never occurred to him that he'd lose control of the situation to this woman. He tried to reassert himself and took on a more authoritarian tone.

"Ma'am, this is very important and I need to go over it with you. It's more than just your signature, there are conditions you'll be agreeing to..."

She ignored that too and raised a hand to stop him, making it very clear that he'd be no match for the strong-willed Kitzie Collins. C.J. smiled and watched the show.

"I agree to the conditions. There, done. Dale...I can call you Dale, right?"

He nodded and she forged ahead.

"Here's the deal. We have an emergency. I'm gonna sign your paperwork, you and I agree you did your thing, and I am all informed. Then we're done."

She produced a pen as she told C.J. to take some keys and go get the ranch truck, a blue one parked near the barn. "Oh, and C.J., in the breezeway there is a coiled nylon tow strap about three inches wide, and about a hundred feet of nylon rope hanging just above it on the wall. Throw both in the back of the truck. Thank you."

C.J. jogged out into the rain to find the truck, found it easily enough, and after he jiggled the key in the ignition, the motor caught with a roar and settled to just loud. He guessed the exhaust manifold was developing a crack. He drove it closer to the barn doors, hopped out, left the truck idling to warm, and went inside. The barn was stunning. He froze for a moment as he looked up into a design of rafters. The space reverberated with sound as rain thudded on the roof and muted natural light came through the cupola's windows. He reached for the coiled nylon rope that hung on a hook. The wide nylon strap was there, just as Kitzie had described, and he bent to pick it up, lunging for the barn door at the same time. The coiled strap weighed more than he thought. Its heft caught him by surprise and what should have been a manageable load stopped him like an anchor caught on a reef. Off-balance, he tipped over, put a hand out, and caught himself from falling against a wall. At the same time, he half lost the rope that he had over his shoulder. With a grimace, he looked around in case someone had seen him, but he was alone and no one was there to see his face-plant near miss. He quickly dragged the strap outside and hauled it up onto the truck, tossed the rope in on top of it, and closed the tailgate.

He hustled back into the truck. He was a bit fresh on the accelerator—no surprise as he hadn't driven anything in a very long time—and the tires spit mud at the barn wall, missing the door, which he'd not completely closed. There was an emergency, he was thinking, and while it may be out in a field somewhere, he also wondered how long Dale would survive in the whirlwind that was Kitzie. He guessed right on that as he watched her body language through the smears the tired wiper blades made on the windshield. What he could see through the windscreen made him smile.

While C.J. was gone, Kitzie had turned her attention back to Dale. "So, let's get this done. Time's a-wasting. Those the papers?" She took the file out of his hand, opened it, scanned the pages quickly, and scrawled on them in each place marked with an arrow sticky. She noticed a stapled copy of the documents, took it, and slipped it onto a shelf near the door. She closed the file folder and handed it to Dale as she guided him out through the short mudroom. The new briefcase teetered and began to slip from his grasp. With Kitzie all but pushing him out the door, he half caught it before it hit the wet porch.

Dale wasn't pleased to have completely lost control of the situation. He started to say, "Ms. Collins, this is not how we do this. I can wait for you here and we can go over this when you get back..."

But Kitzie stopped him again. "Oh, I wouldn't hear of it! Besides, it's not rocket science. "We're good," she said as she closed and locked the door. "Besides, it's been such a pleasure, and we wouldn't want to overdo a good thing now, would we?"

Dale had been quite thoroughly outmaneuvered, and he wasn't sure he cared if she was being sarcastic. She did it so nicely.

She was finished with him when C.J. pulled up on the other side of Dale's big truck. C.J. saw her hurry him into his truck and watched him flinch as she slammed the door. Numbed, Dale watched her jog around his truck and get into the blue one with C.J. With a wave to Dale, he floored it and spun a little more indignity along the side of Dale's rig. Dale watched them disappear in the heavy rain as he clutched his rain-streaked briefcase.

Kitzie instructed C.J. to drive past the barns, past the cattle pens, and across a pasture on a track that went to a gate. She asked C.J. to get out and open it, and then close it behind them. She slid across the bench seat to the driver's side. It was slow going along a rutted and sodden track. The sound of heavy rain on the truck was almost deafening, and little was said. Kitzie drove too fast for the conditions, and C.J. wondered silently what was up as he grabbed at a partially attached door handle, his other hand braced on the roof so he didn't get knocked out as the truck lurched hard in and out of a water-filled hole. C.J. saw the outline of an ATV in the far part of an open field.

Kitzie pulled up, put the truck in park, and said as she hopped out, "We have a horse down in the creek. Turn the truck around and back up to the right of the ATV. Don't get any closer. The banks are apt to be dangerously broken or even washed away."

She marched to what was the edge of a swollen creek bed. C.J. couldn't see much, as the heavy rain had made a streaky mess of the old truck's back window. He thought he saw the body of an animal lying in the muddy, rushing water as he scooted over to the driver's side and swung the truck around into position. The animal seemed to be held fast by the current and wedged so that it could not get up. Its head seemed to be perpendicular to the bank and there was someone in the creek who held it above water. He surmised from the churned-up ground that animals traversed the area regularly; there was a deeply worn spot where it appeared they crossed the actual creek bed.

Kitzie signaled him to stay put as she returned to the bed of the truck, grabbed the tow strap with one hand, and the coiled rope with the other. She bent down and hooked one end to the hitch. When she stood up, the wind blew her hat half off, but the storm tie saved it. She ignored it and moved down into the creek.

The rope snaked a path as Kitzie fed it out. She returned, showed C.J. how to put the truck in heavy low four-wheel drive, and handed him a wet hand radio. From the bed, she took a metal pole with a T handle on one end and a loop on the other, and carried it down to the men in the water. They worked to get one end of the strap under the mare's head through the mud, rushing water, and rocks, and up around near her withers. The handle was long so that whoever used it could stay clear of the horse's legs. They dug with bare hands in freezing-cold water to create a pass-through for the strap under the horse's body. The taller of the two men took the pole, got on the belly side of the horse, and began working the pole under its body. Kitzie held the horse's head and neck as the smaller man, down in the water, worked one end of the strap under the back of the horse. The icy water rushed up his arms, then to his neck as he got down lower, trying to work the strap to the hook. The water, churning with bits of gravel and debris, rushed up and over the collar of his coat and down his back.

After a few minutes, they were successful and pulled the hook out with the strap. They fixed the strap so that it encircled the horse and the two ends came up through the front legs. They held each side, making an effective hammock to hold the horse's head. Kitzie spoke into the radio loud enough to be heard over the rushing water as she backed away from the horse.

"Ready, C.J. Take the slack out...*slowly.*"

C.J. eased the clutch as he released the brake. The truck inched forward until the slack was out of the line. There was a second before the truck re-established a purchase on the ground, the weight of the horse fully felt. He could see the rope go taut and lower onto the muddy slope, then disappear.

Kitzie's voice crackled through the tiny speaker, "Easy...okay, more...give it a little more. Keep going..."

The back end of the truck swayed back and forth a little when it hit a slippery spot, then held and moved forward again.

"Good," he heard her say.

The horse's head, neck, and shoulders were cushioned by a blanket and tarp. The horse was still, she did not thrash, exhausted by the ordeal and the cold. Kitzie signaled him to stop. C.J. put the truck in park and opened the door, but Kitzie waved him to stay in the truck. The men undid the rope and pulled the canvas strap out from under the horse's body. Kitzie walked the end of the nylon rope to the back of the truck and tossed it in. C.J. moved over and she got into the driver's seat. The heater blasted blessed warmth, and Kitzie and C.J. watched as the men coaxed the mare to get up onto her feet. When she was up, the taller of the two men stroked her face. C.J. thought there was something familiar about the way the man touched the mare.

Kitzie was done; she put the truck in gear and started back to the ranch. "There must be a downed fence somewhere and that little mare must have gotten stuck in the creek when she followed the herd across it. There was another horse. There were two out here with the cows. Almost thought of giving up till tomorrow, when Jorge had the idea about the creek."

Back at the barn, she showed C.J. where the lights were and she pulled out some towels. "You know how to make a warm mash?"

C.J. answered, "No, can't say that I do."

They heard the ATV as Luis drove it into the barn and shut it down. He removed his hat and took his hood down, then smiled at them.

Kitzie asked, "How's she doing?"

"Better. Stiff at first. Took time to walk out; she was pretty shaky. It will take them a while to get here," Luis explained.

Kitzie did the introductions, then said, "C.J., let's go to the house and I'll make us some coffee and look at what I just signed."

They dodged raindrops from the barn to the house. Wyatt and Lulu enthusiastically met them at the door, all wiggles and happy energy. They checked C.J. out and gave him their seal of approval. In the kitchen, Kitzie showed him where the coffee was while she went upstairs to get out of her wet clothes. He saw the coffee maker on the counter. It was a familiar machine. He thought, *This I know how to do.*

Kitzie was quick and returned in jeans and a fisherman's cable sweater. She looked at C.J.'s progress, said nothing, and then leaned over the sink to look out the kitchen window toward the barn. She pulled her hair back into a ponytail, then pointed to a cupboard where C.J. found coffee mugs as she grabbed the milk from the fridge. The coffeepot began to gurgle and she looked out the kitchen window again. It was now almost completely dark.

C.J. watched her from his seat at the well-worn farm table. "You do that a lot."

"Do what?" Kitzie pulled the pot from the coffee machine and filled two mugs, then returned it to continue brewing. She handed a mug to C.J.

"Look out that window," C.J. said, gratefully accepting

the cup. "The counter there is smooth, the linoleum's just about worn off."

He looked to his coffee and drank as she turned her back against the counter, one hand leaning on it, the other with the cup held tightly. It was as if she was still fighting off the chill of the afternoon's activities. Her grip eased as she sipped the warm brew.

"We hit the ground running; usually pretty dull around here." She tipped an ear toward the ceiling. "Oh, I think it has stopped raining." She took another sip and looked at the large manila envelope on the kitchen table.

The dogs were on their feet at the door. They heard Luis come into the mudroom, and he stuck his head into the kitchen. "They're back."

"We'll talk later," Kitzie said to C.J.

Kitzie grabbed two mugs and filled them three-quarters full. Luis held the door for her. Wisps of steam rose from the cups' rims as Kitzie carried them to the barn. C.J. carried his small duffle with him, and as they went through the big sliding barn doors, Kitzie pointed to a small door he'd barely noticed earlier. He opened it and discovered a tiny landing with a funky narrow stairway.

"Please put your bag there."

By one of the stalls, C.J. noticed wet gear draped over a blanket bar. A young man was standing by a stall door and C.J. heard Luis say, "Jorge, *hijo*, you are *mojado*, wet." Louis handed him one of the many clean, dry towels he had in his arms. "We got this, go change."

Jorge looked cold and was grateful when Kitzie handed him the warm mug. He wrapped both hands around it, sipped some, then extended his hand and introduced himself to C.J. Through chattering teeth, Jorge managed a crooked smile before he disappeared out the barn door.

Luis had more towels for the mare and he set about drying her. There were warming lamps high up on the stall walls and Kitzie turned the timer dial to the maximum time. The powerful heaters clicked as a glow grew along the coils. C.J. looked up at them.

Kitzie said, "Foaling stall, sometimes we needed this." She looked at the mare and softly added, "Back in the day."

The mare was trembling and Luis used his hands to rub her back and sides to warm her. On the other side of the mare C.J. could see the top of a black hat and another hand reaching under her belly with a towel. Then the person stood up, looked over the mare's back, and smiled at C.J. At the same moment the wiggly, wet mess that was Tammy ambushed C.J. with her own brand of hello. C.J. patted her, and then looked up at Wyker as he came out of the stall. They shook hands. C.J. followed Wyker into the open area of the barn and covered his surprise with a stone-faced expression.

Wyker knew that face—the emotions buried deep— and didn't mind. "Glad you decided to come. Hope we didn't take you away from anything special."

C.J. shook his head. Kitzie had retrieved her vet bag, gone into the stall, and pulled out a stethoscope. Wyker had put a sheet and a blanket on the mare. Kitzie lifted the edges and listened to her heart, lungs, and gut sounds. The mare was a little bothered as Wyker reentered the stall and took her temperature. He knew that mares tended to be funny about their back ends, so he was cautious. She pinned her ears but, thankfully, didn't kick. Kitzie read the thermometer and saw the reading was close to normal.

Wyker changed out the first sheet. It was soaked through. The ticking of the heat lamps subsided to the warm glow of radiated heat, which had raised the temperature in the stall considerably. Kitzie commented that it felt good to her too.

C.J. brought warm mash in a shallow rubber bucket. The mare's shaking had visibly subsided, and she slurped it up.

"That's a good sign," Kitzie said.

They went to the tack room. Jorge came in and stood at the door as Kitzie closed the vet supply cabinet. Wyker had hung his wet outer gear on a hook in the main area of the barn, and below it, a sizeable puddle had formed. Wyker shuddered and put on a heavy coat he'd taken from a hook near the saddles. It was one of Tuff's old barn jackets.

Kitzie stared for a moment, then looked at the floor before she turned to Jorge and said, "Please show C.J. upstairs."

Jorge led the way across the breezeway to the entrance and went up the stairs, turning the lights on as they went. "It's a nice room, easy to figure out," he said, and he pointed to a baseboard heater. "That's it for heat, so turn it on soon if you want the room comfortable."

It was a tidy space and C.J. dropped his stuff. They followed Kitzie's voice back downstairs when she called them to dinner. He started down the stairs behind Jorge, hesitated, and doubled back to turn the baseboard heater on.

In the kitchen, Kitzie looked happy. Her garlic bread was really garlicky and warm in the oven. She grated a bunch of fresh Parmesan and made her signature salad full of fresh vegetables, her terrific dressing, and the garbanzo beans Tuff had been so fond of. There were hungry men around her table, and Kitzie welcomed everyone to sit and dig into the delicious stew. The pieces of French bread sopped in it were fantastic, and there was not much in the way of conversation for many minutes. Then there was talking well into the night.

Later, C.J. reflected on how he had gone from the crappy "no-tell motel" to where he was. He hadn't said much most of the meal, but was surprised at how much he had laughed. The conversation included exaggerated stories and hilarious tales of people and their animals. Everyone at the table laughed until they were goofy. It was so easy that C.J. forgot to be uncomfortable. He'd been so guarded for so long that genuinely laughing out loud felt new. He had trained himself to ignore the spontaneous, to deny the urge to join conversations. In his experience, it was best not to.

C.J. replayed the rest of the evening over in his mind as he lay in another strange bed, arm under his head, and watched the stars through the skylight. He felt safe. He drifted off to sleep and dreamed about Rio.

It began with Rio defending his herd. He pawed the ground, his thick, powerful neck arched, ears flattened, his body inflated by the challenge. His wild mane and forelock flew about as he moved aggressively, looking huge and dangerous. Rio showed no intention of backing down as he faced up to the threatening palomino before him, and both were ready to fight. They moved around each other, gaining ground, and dust rose around them. There was no wind. The billow of dust increased as the hooves of the other horses stirred. Yearlings and mares jockeyed for position to stay close, but not too close. More dust. It grew larger and swallowed them all.

FOURTEEN

The Sacramento River flowed peacefully by her hotel room window on the *Delta* riverboat. The furnishings were vintage and the restorations to the historical craft had been thoughtfully done. The bathroom had a toilet with a quaint pull chain. The light fixtures were antique, and Carson thought the low-energy bulbs looked out of place in them and ruined the look. But, in spite of the modern amenities that had been installed, they'd left enough of the old girl alone, and she sat on the river like the queen she was. Carson liked the classic atmosphere, and as she left her room to walk the deck, she felt as though she'd stepped back in time.

She leaned on the rail and looked at the river. The bright-orange hull of a lone kayak sliced its way through the mellow surface current. Were it not for that, it might have been another era. The present paddling by the past jarred her senses, and she retreated to the dining area.

Later, after an amazing dinner, Carson brought a bottle of wine back to her room and was soon halfway through it. A wing chair faced the bed and she rotated it to look out the window on the river side of the boat. Strategically placed lights lit up some of the river, and aside from the occasional noise of distant traffic, it was quiet. But inside her head, certain voices would not be silent. Her spirit had abandoned her and inside her chest, her heart felt broken.

The first part of the drive had been smooth and she

had felt strong with her decisions, wonderfully liberated. Then today, all day, she'd been in the throes of guilt and shame. She'd walked away from huge financial obligations and legally binding contracts. She'd left no forwarding address, said no goodbyes, and had jettisoned her life almost as if it had never happened. She'd wrapped herself in a delusional bubble, convinced there'd be no consequences. But there were always consequences.

"Could I just walk away?" she asked the darkness.

Negative thoughts carnivorously consumed her brain, and she slipped again into the trap of self-inflicted punishment. Carson leaned her head against the back of the chair and begged the hateful voices to take a break. She thought about calling him. She imagined the tone of his voice, what he'd say, and how he'd say it. The code he'd use if he couldn't talk openly. She wrestled with what clever things she'd say, what she really wanted to say, and what lie she'd tell if the wrong voice answered the phone. It would quickly become a complicated exercise, and Carson knew where it would leave her—frustrated and miserable.

Her emotions swung wildly the other way, in a harsher direction, one of blame. It wasn't *her*, it was *him*. She could blow a huge hole in his world. She could reveal things that would balance the emotional books. Not only could she burn a bridge, she could blow it to smithereens. That warped thinking provided a sense of power, but Carson knew in her heart she wouldn't do it. She told herself she was too decent to ruin his life for her ego. Their mutual friends had the idea he was this great guy, and not a consummate liar. The truth? He was an ethical man, but not a moral one, and not a soul in that community would know the difference, nor would they care.

She knew that she would be the one blamed and vilified. The vagaries of human tribal behavior made her mind spin with anger, churning up the desire to break something. She'd read somewhere that a kind of power and energy suffused angry people, and that it was seductive. Carson knew that some of them held on to their anger for years, and she didn't want to be one of them. She felt it in the pit of her stomach...but who was she angry with? A story would get spun that the guy was always the victim, manipulated by a woman's feminine wiles. In short order, he'd be forgiven his indiscretion; he'd get a pass. And just as swiftly, she'd be shunned and discarded.

Once more Carson had taken the ride her imagination spat out, twisted herself in knots, and the tears flowed. When she stopped crying, she was annoyed that she'd wasted precious energy thinking about it at all. She decided that it was only an impulse, best to forget the idea completely. Like the river, the only way from here was to move on.

Carson refilled her glass and continued to stare at the river. She felt that she could stay right there and watch it meander by forever. It flowed slowly, almost imperceptibly, past the riverboat. The river was broad, deep, and silent, but there was a powerful current just beneath its deceptively smooth, brownish-blue surface. Swirling patches of upwelling water erupted into irregular, somewhat circular shapes, and the riverboat's lights made the changing patterns visible down the length of the boat. They'd start small and swell into larger and larger concentric patterns as they swiftly floated past. Occasionally, the silence was broken by the low-decibel putt of a motorboat.

In the dark of her room, Carson took another sip of wine, put the glass on the table, and pulled at the blanket that lay across the bottom edge of the queen-size bed. It draped over the arm of the chair and she wanted to disappear into it. She wrapped it around her shoulders and fell into a dreamless sleep.

FIFTEEN

Dawn breached the night, and the skylight above the bed had begun its transformation. The room brightened. Half asleep, C.J. heard singing in Spanish. It was melodic, wistful, and far away, but then it got closer. There was a drumbeat on the skylight, like heavy rain or hail. He thought, *Rain?* And he wondered, *Am I awake?* The singing became drowned out. He sat up in the darkness and looked around through sheets of rain that now fell on him. He looked up and saw there was no glass in the skylight. He wanted the singing. He felt he must find the song, the music.

Then he was no longer in bed, and he walked. He walked faster and faster until he was running. The slap-slap of his bare feet in the water on the wet ground was all he heard. The singing was gone and was replaced by loss—an overwhelming sense that something had gotten away. He was soaking wet. The rain stung his eyes and blinded him. He held up an arm to block the onslaught. The rain was deafening. It roared like an angry beast in pain, and he realized he was afraid. He turned to look back and ran harder. He wasn't running toward something, he was running away from something terrible...and it was coming for him.

C.J.'s heart pounded and his open mouth found little air. The ground was hard on his heels, and though he was a naturally fast runner, whatever this was, it was faster. It gained on him. Its presence overtook and enveloped him.

He couldn't breathe anymore. He tripped and gasped for air as he fell. His eyes were wide with fear and he could hear the beating of his heart, just like the rain. He lay on his back in rain that was so hard it was like bullets beating his body into the soaked ground. The well-aimed drops shredded his clothing. The rain pierced his naked body, submerging it into the ground. The earth, sodden with his blood, buried him. He was dead and Rio stood above him. C.J.'s being was in the horse, and through the horse he looked down on his own cold, unseeing eyes.

C.J. awoke with a start in a cold sweat. His heart was beating so hard it felt as though it would leap out of his chest. He put his hand over it to hold it inside. He didn't know where he was or what day it was, and the sense of not being able to breathe confused him.

Above, dawn colored the small skylight, and he heard singing. Spanish. It came from below in the barn some-where and it was real, of that he was sure. It helped him focus and remember. The realization was aided by the footfalls of a horse and a soft snort from its nostrils. He heard one of the horses take hold of some hay from a feeder and pull it out onto the floor of its stall. He im-agined lips seeking favorite bits.

C.J. took several deep breaths to calm himself. He pushed the covers off, slid his feet to the floor, and sat at the edge of the bed. The chill of the room hit his chest and he felt goose bumps rise on his arms. He rested his elbows on his knees, his face in his hands. Then he ran his hands up over his head through his hair, physically rub-bing the images of the dream away. C.J. looked around the small bedroom, then stood up and stretched. He stepped into the bathroom, tossed water on his face, and looked at his image in the small mirror. The person looking back at him was different. His eyes had lost some edge, and the deeper creases had faded, revealing the still-handsome features. As he brushed his teeth, he noticed his chest and arms still had the tone of his youth, and as he rinsed the toothpaste suds out of the sink and wiped it clean, he considered his age and wondered when exactly he'd thought he'd become "old." Thirty-two wasn't old...was it?

He got dressed. The door at the bottom of the stairs was closed and it grew colder as he approached the ground floor. When he opened the door and entered the main barn area, he could hear humming and soft singing. As he closed the door behind him, C.J. pinpointed the singing as coming from a stall to his left.

The rain had stopped, and sunlight filtered through the trussed ceiling from the barn cupola. The barn was beautiful and C.J. admired the design. There was a spatiality to it that pulled his gaze upwards until he saw a pair of eyes staring down at him. A magnificent barn owl was perched in the beams, his mate close by. C.J. thought they were both quite marvelous.

A voice brought him out of his reverie. "Their home."

Luis looked over at him from the mare's stall and pointed toward the owls.

C.J. walked over to where the bay mare ate contentedly, a heavy quilted blanket on her and the sweat sheet drying on a rail nearby.

Luis looked into the automatic waterer, judged it didn't need cleaning and said, "*Buenos dias,* amigo…you sleep well?" He finished cleaning the mare's bedding, picking out unwanted debris with an apple picker and putting it into a wheelbarrow.

"Yes. I heard singing," C.J. answered.

"My father used to sing to us all the time. He was an accomplished musician and singer. He taught us many songs. He sang when he worked. As children, we loved to hear him sing. I like to sing when I am with the animals."

C.J. looked around for another tool so he could help, but Luis stopped him. "No, I got this. Thank you. There's coffee and Kitzie made fresh biscuits. I like biscuits and coffee. She makes good jam too. You should try it."

Luis pushed the wheelbarrow through the stall door, and C.J. slid the door closed and latched it behind him. Luis wheeled the cart to the big door and placed the apple picker on a hook by the door to the tack room. C.J. liked that the barn was so organized. They went into the house and Kitzie looked up from the table where she sat with Wyker and Jorge.

"Good morning. Was everything okay in your room?" she said.

"Yes, thank you, very comfortable," C.J. replied.

"Grab a cup and the biscuits are fresh…maybe still warm. Have a seat. We were just talking about you. Your ears burnin'?"

"Should they be?" he said as he got coffee and sat down at the table.

Luis refilled his cup and took more biscuits. It was a good thing Kitzie had made a lot of them.

Wyker nodded good morning and said, "We've been talking about what we need to get done today. I have horses to work and we have some barbed wire fencing to check in that pasture. You have any experience pounding T-posts and stringing barbed wire?"

C.J. swallowed. "I'll learn."

Kitzie smiled. "Good. Luis, we have some lights out in the barn, and the float in the trough in the far left outside paddock needs attention. I think it froze and broke or something. You working on that truck today?"

Luis nodded as he chewed his biscuit. Then he added, "Almost done, and then I'll see to those. Jorge will help C.J. with the fencing."

Kitzie smiled. "Okay, anyone want eggs? Yes? Scrambled okay?"

After breakfast was cleared up, Wyker and C.J. walked toward another outbuilding and Wyker asked him about getting back in the saddle.

C.J. said, "Sure."

Wyker stopped for a second and looked at C.J. "Good. There's something I want help with."

C.J. shook his head in a "whatever" kind of way, but didn't ask what.

They walked together to the right of the main barn and went around the building. They passed between empty paddocks, the cattle barn, and around behind Luis and Jorge's cottage toward a small barn. It looked to hold a few tons of hay and there seemed to be more toward the back of the structure. C.J. saw there were a couple of stalls with some narrow paddocks that extended out the back of the weathered wood building. There were signs of some recent shoring-up and repairs.

There was a small door to the left that looked like a tack/grain room entrance tucked under the overhang.

They walked between the stacked hay that created a kind of breezeway and turned to the right, where the path became wider. The top door of the first stall was latched open and through it, C.J. saw that a new piece of three-quarter-inch plywood sheeting had been recently put up. The section next to it was bare; a rotten piece had been removed and the area readied for a new one. The floor had been scraped clean and was laid with fresh quarry fines. A tamper stood in the center of the stall, and C.J. saw signs that compressing the fines had been started.

"Going into Martin tomorrow to get more plywood and mats. I need some parts for the stock waterer, a float, and a heating element. The hay feeder seems okay, though I like a bin better. Really just want to put them out, but Kitzie wanted it this way for now," Wyker said as he leaned in to take stock.

There came a thump and a thud from the other stall and the sounds of a body shaking off dirt.

"Ah, I think someone's awake. Damn thing sleeps like a rock star," Wyker said.

A face came to the door of the stall and looked out at them. Rio tipped his head toward C.J., and Wyker patted the side of the horse's face.

"Surprise."

Wyker moved back, leaned against the hay bales, and waited. Rio nuzzled C.J.'s hand as C.J. took in those familiar whiskers, the line of Rio's muzzle, and the light-red hairs that traveled up the sides of his face to those big, expressive eyes. C.J. moved to rub that spot just in front of his right ear, and Rio leaned into his hand with a kindness that C.J. figured he'd never see; a kindness he'd not expected to feel—no curtain of self-protection, of self-defense. Those had come down in the both of them. Embarrassed, C.J.'s eyes swam as he focused on his feet. The leather over the left toe was really thin, and his toes were cold.

After a few awkward moments, C.J. looked at Rio but spoke to Wyker. "What's he doing here?"

"Waiting for you," Wyker replied as he pushed himself off the hay bales, handed C.J. the halter he'd once turned down, and left the two of them alone.

C.J. was unsure about this development. It changed things. His world shifted around what he thought he was doing there. He hesitated before he slipped open the latch on the door and walked into the stall. His back was to Rio as he reached over the door and latched it. He half expected Rio to charge out and down the forty-five-foot paddock, but Rio didn't move off in a blowing huff. He didn't leave. C.J. was stunned. Rio stood quietly as C.J. walked to his neck and gently ran his palm down Rio's side. Rio dropped his head, one foot cocked and rested. As C.J. ran his palm around and over Rio's butt, he brushed away pieces of wood shavings off him. He went up the other side and stroked his neck. Rio took a deep breath, exhaled, and blew his nose, clearing a little dust. Then he lowered his head, and with those sensitive lips, examined the floor of the stall for any leftover bits of hay.

C.J. stood in the stall with Rio for a long time, and when he let himself out, he leaned his elbows on the top edge of the door and just looked at Rio. He shook his head in disbelief. This was without a doubt the nicest gift he'd ever gotten.

When C.J. retraced his steps to the barn entryway, he saw that Wyker had gotten his saddle out. "I can't pay you for him," he said.

"Don't have to. He's yours."

And that was all that was spoken about it.

The next few days were full. C.J. helped with carpentry in Rio's barn, with fence mending, a gate latch frozen with rust, a seized lock, and myriad chores that kept him busy from dawn to dusk, and it was glorious. Though he wore his usual emotionless face, his heart felt light and the hard work filled him with purpose. He began and ended his days with Rio. He rode him and practiced on him. He watched Wyker when he worked Johnny with the cows. He learned to check the recovering mare, and learned what "good gut sounds" meant. He also, much to his chagrin, learned how to ascertain that her temperature was normal.

When C.J. was first given the task of taking the mare's temperature, Jorge wasn't forthcoming on technique, and like many mares, she was nervy about her hindquarters and spun away from C.J. He was none too thrilled about putting the thermometer inside her, and the strange dance they did in the stall seemed to be very amusing to Jorge. C.J. held the thermometer in one hand and had hold of the mare's tail in the other, and she was dragging him around the stall. It resembled a demented "pin the tail on the donkey," which was hilarious until Jorge heard Kitzie coming. By the time Kitzie was at the stall door, Jorge had the mare's halter rope in hand and had steadied her while C.J. dutifully inserted the thermometer. He turned his head away and wore a grossed-out expression on his face as he did it. There was a string attached to the thermometer and a clip at the end of the string, which Jorge instructed C.J. to clip to the mare's tail...and wait. C.J. asked him what that was for, and Jorge said it was to make sure they didn't lose the thermometer.

C.J. mouthed, "Lose it? Lose it...where?"

Kitzie asked, "How's she doing?"

Jorge looked up, "Fine. She could be turned out later."

"Okay then, that's good. Hurry up, day's a-wasting. Hook the wagon up to the mule and take supplies along. Check all the fences in that pasture. One must be down. She got into that creek somehow."

C.J. asked where they kept the mule; he didn't recall seeing one in the paddock. Kitzie hesitated and looked at him with a quizzical expression on her face. Then she smiled when it dawned on her. She pointed to the ATV and C.J. nodded that he understood.

She added, "Somebody should grab a horse and ride, save some time."

C.J.'s eyebrows shot up. "I'll ride."

Kitzie noticed his obvious enthusiasm and answered, "Okay, find Wyker. I don't want you running like crazy out there on your horse. It's still mucky and you could go down. Stay safe. I want everyone back where they belong by the end of today if possible."

C.J. noted that she had said "*your horse.*" He left the barn, rounded the corner, and was thrilled to see Wyker ponying Rio off of Johnny.

"Saddle up. I'm gonna help Jorge. You'll find some gloves in the tack room. There's always pairs lying around."

They prepped the ATV, topped the tank off, and loaded the wagon with supplies. Then the three of them—C.J. and Wyker on horseback, Jorge on the ATV—headed out to fix fences. At the gate, Jorge and the ATV turned left, and Wyker and C.J. moved out along the right looking for the broken fencing. They'd use walkie-talkies to communicate.

The riders and Tammy moved off at a trot, then picked up a gentle lope. Despite his recent practicing, C.J. struggled, and his timing felt awkward. He bumped around in the saddle, and took a little while to find consistent balance and to get reconnected with riding again. The scrub grasses were soft from the rain, and Wyker picked a path with the most solid ground. The air smelled crisp and clean. Remnants of the morning ground fog clung to shadowed, low-lying ground. Light played on the surrounding hills, with views of snow-dusted mountains in the distance. C.J. couldn't help but feel this was the best job he'd ever had.

Jorge found the break in the fencing and he called them on the radio with his location.

"Wyker, I found it and it's a good-sized hole. Probably six stakes."

When C.J. and Wyker found Jorge, they saw that a wide gap had been opened up and the tracks that went through belonged to about ten cows and a couple of horses. The tracks angled off to the east. Jorge had pulled the jack out and set a flat piece of wood to steady it. He had the chain in hand as Wyker said, "Looks like you have this, Jorge. We'll go get them."

Jorge said, "These are in deep, but the ground is saturated. I'm good." He nodded and set up to pull out one of the bent stakes.

Wyker and C.J. rode along the fence line to the area where they'd pulled the mare out of the creek. As they traversed along it, it was dicey as to where to safely cross. The bank's edges had been carved away and there were sharp mud cornices. The churning currents created unstable areas where big chunks had broken off and spilled into the creek. It was in areas like this that an animal could easily bog down. It was like quicksand, and foundering would be easy. Even along the edges, where the water had barely begun the process of being absorbed into the ground, one could still become stuck.

They rode past the area where they had rescued the mare, looking for a shallower angle, a more solid place to cross. They found a spot where the creek opened up, had a pebbled bottom, and the water ran clearer where it ran shallow. The section of the creek was broad and flattened out. Carefully, they worked the horses down into and across the creek's receding waters. Rio was confident where C.J. might have been hesitant. To C.J., it felt like Rio knew this kind of ground could be dangerous. His solid hooves carried them both through the current. In a deep spot, the water flowed around the horse's legs. It splashed up and soaked the bottom of C.J.'s jeans. Tammy bounded across easily and waited for Wyker on the other side, panting happily with her tongue hanging out. They found a way up the other side of the slippery bank and backtracked along the creek, easily picking up the trail of the missing herd.

They followed the tracks to a thick stand of low-hanging trees, which on horseback necessitated a detour. Beyond that, the cattle had meandered, grazing past small patches of trees dotting an open expanse of low brush and scrap. C.J. and Wyker had no visual of the animals for a good thirty minutes of riding, but soon came upon fresh cow manure and some horse manure, which meant the ranch horse was staying close to the cows.

They saw some deer, and farther along a thick-furred bobcat stood focused on hunting a gopher or a mole. As they rode by, he watched them, but made no move to leave potential food. Tammy ignored him and trotted beside Johnny.

They went up a rocky bluff, traversing back and forth to a point where they had a commanding view of the valley. To the north, they could see a distant set of mountains capped with snow. The colors of the high desert were everywhere—browns and grays, varying shades of faded green, and tufts of grasses sticking up through and around volcanic rocky sculptures. Long wisps of high stratus clouds played across the sky and thickened to the west.

Wyker pulled his binoculars out and focused them on an area of trees a few miles off. "They're under those trees in the center over there. Looks close, but it's a few miles."

They picked their way down the face of the hill, winding through a scattered field of boulders and rocky promontories. Though they no longer had a line of sight on the herd, signs were frequent that the cattle had been grazing along this route. At the bottom of the hillside, the ground leveled off to a grassy plain and the cattle were about a thousand yards off—twelve cows, most lying down napping, with two standing to the left of the trees, and the ranch horse beyond that.

Tammy hooked on, and Wyker looked down at her before he gave C.J. instructions.

"Slowly now, and as we get close, I'll swing around the left and you to the right. I'm going to get behind the two standing and gently push them back this way. You watch those branches; don't get hung up under there. Follow my lead, do what I do. I'm thinking that horse will come along when we start moving the herd."

They moved their horses into a slow, calm walk toward the group of trees. The cows seemed unconcerned. The two standing cows had eyes on the approaching horsemen. The ranch horse grazed off a ways, and paid attention as well, then dropped his head and continued foraging.

As they neared the trees, Wyker and C.J. split apart. Wyker walked a wide turn around and behind the standing cows, and as he got into their comfort zone, they instinctively moved away from the pressure of his presence. Wyker kept Tammy on his left. Four of the cows that were lying down got up, and the others soon did the same. C.J. and Rio moved into position at the edge of the trees on the right side. The branches that hadn't looked low from a distance were indeed enough to hook him off the saddle if he got in the wrong way. He changed his line and found a better opening between them.

All the cows were now on their feet, and C.J. glanced over his left shoulder, checking on the loose horse. Rio was calm, focused on the cows, and C.J. found that he barely had to lift the reins. To stop Rio's feet and hold, he just opened his legs a little and Rio stopped. The cattle faced up to the riders. Wyker and C.J. needed them to turn and start back the way they had come. Going very slowly, they moved into the cattle's comfort zone and the animals began to move off. A couple of them turned their heads, their big, ponderous bodies following, as they came out from under the trees. The two over by Wyker took a couple of trot steps and joined up. The horse behind C.J. had taken a couple of steps toward them, but then stopped and watched.

C.J. inched forward and leaned way over the side of his saddle to dodge a group of wispy lower branches. As the cows cleared the trees, those at the front started a slow walk back toward the hill. C.J. looked at that rocky hill and wondered which way they'd push them up and over it.

The men fell into position at the rear of the herd. Wyker was off to his right about twenty-five yards, moving slowly. One cow stopped momentarily. Wyker had his coiled rope in hand, and he raised it to move the cow off to join back up with his buddies.

C.J. looked again at the ranch horse, still frozen in place and watching them go. The space between them expanded. Tammy was between Johnny and Rio, and she went back and forth, not getting in there but working the edges. C.J. looked ahead and watched his distance to the cattle. He did not want to get too close and push them too hard. Slow and steady was the pace Wyker wanted.

C.J. had forgotten how good it felt to be on Rio's back. Rio amazed him. Their connection felt almost automatic. C.J. barely gave him cues. It was as though Rio watched the cows and knew where to be—how close, when to stop his feet, and when to move on. C.J. actually smiled as Rio put his ears back at the rear end of one cow that thought stopping and turning was a good idea. The cow changed its mind.

The squeal of a whinny came from behind, rattling C.J. out of his reverie. The pounding thud of galloping hooves approached fast. Rio's head and neck elevated and he began dancing around, throwing a few hump-backed crow hops. The lone ranch horse had reached his limit of separation and had bolted into a full run to catch up. Rio flagged his tail and held his head high. C.J. gripped the horn, and forgot all about the cows as the herd startled into a jog and began splitting apart. Several cows stopped, looked at the commotion, decided they didn't care, and kept walking. Wyker called over to C.J.

"Ride your horse. Don't pull on his face for that. If you have to, make a full circle… there, tip his head, and when he weighs nothing on your hand, walk off and do what you were doing before. Don't make a big deal out of it and it won't be a big deal."

C.J. followed the instructions as the ranch horse ran past and hooked up with the cows. The horse whinnied some more, eyes and nostrils wide, and then broke to a trot. He circled and found a place just ahead of the cows, where he slowed to a walk. Sweat flattened the long hair on his neck, making it darker than the rest of him, and he settled down.

Rio jigged sideways and C.J. felt the horse's heightened energy beneath him, which reminded him of how strong Rio was if he chose to be. He tried to breathe normally and hoped the hammering of his heart would chill out so he could manage the surge of adrenaline. Rio calmed down, quickly reconnecting his focus on the job at hand and softening beneath his rider. C.J.'s post-adrenaline rush, with its undesirable numbness of the extremities and faint nausea, took more time to dissipate.

"Always look for a place to reward a horse. Acknowledge the smallest try. Give yourself the same. Breathing is good, too," Wyker encouraged.

C.J. looked at Wyker and laughed, realizing he had stopped breathing. He reached down and stroked Rio's neck. Then he leaned back and patted his rump. Rio's ears flicked back at him, then were forward on the task at hand.

Tammy was useful in their efforts to move the herd. Wyker and C.J. steered them forward up into the craggy slope, which had not looked so steep when they first came down it. From this side, it was a climb and was broken up by boulders in places. It looked different to C.J., and where there seemed to be a clean way up from the bottom, it would dead-end. Wyker had a good bead on the cleanest way up. Here and there he'd call to C.J. to hold and change trajectory, and C.J. would see he was not looking far enough ahead. Tammy was making up the distances and keeping the herd together beautifully. C.J. had never seen her work like this…really work. Nothing distracted her from her task; she was a working dog, sensitive to Wyker's almost imperceptible commands and the ebb and flow of the herd.

It took a while to get all the way up and over, and it was getting later in the afternoon.

"Will we make it back to Jorge before dark?" C.J. asked.

"Probably just at dark," Wyker replied. "Best to cross that muck of a creek with enough light to pick a good place. No need to get wet and cold again."

They made good time, and did reach the creek with more than enough light. This time Tammy and C.J. held the herd while Wyker picked a crossing spot he liked. He walkie-talkied Jorge and told him where they were. Jorge came and his two dogs joined in. Three working dogs were a wonder to watch. C.J. and Rio became spectators, as they were not needed to finish the job. The dogs got the herd and the ranch horse back through the fence opening by themselves. The herd moved comfortably into the pasture, and the three dogs found a spot in which to lie down and catch their wind.

C.J. got off Rio and gave Jorge a hand closing the last gap in the fence with barbed wire. Soon it was dark, and they followed the headlight of the ATV across the big pasture until they saw the lights of the barn and house.

SIXTEEN

Hank was at his stool. He'd become a fixture at the tavern most mornings. He'd watch the comings and goings of the ranch owners, hired hands, and buckaroos as they came in and ate their meals. He'd study them, looking for "tells" like he'd seen in the gambling movies. He paid careful attention to their moods, and eavesdropped as much as he could on their conversations.

At night, he'd settle into a section of his house. He was more comfortable there than he thought he'd be. He preferred oil lamps for light, and he used the generator to power the circular saw, which he used to cut up scrap wood. He was not strong enough to use the hand ax for more than a piece or two, so he hauled in gas, a gallon at a time, for the log splitter so he could split wood for the fireplace.

He made notes of the comings and goings at the café each day, and had 3x5 cards with the names and descriptions of everyone who frequented the place spread out on the kitchen table. He knew it was foolish, but it filled the empty time. And it made him forget how he felt. He seemed to feel cold all the time. Piles of wood that once littered the property steadily shrank as he used them for heat. The added bonus was that the place was looking better and it made him right pleased with his efforts.

He holed up in the kitchen and family room, managing to drag one of his son's twin-bed mattresses and box springs near the fireplace. His life revolved around the kitchen table with his hand-scrawled lists of people, ranches, and missing herds. He had maps with certain areas marked out on them. But most every chance he got, he was at the café and he watched. He watched everyone. Hank looked for something, some kind of clue as to who'd taken his life from him.

He knew he was old, probably sick, and he had to find them. He had convinced himself "they" were there among them. He never talked about it to anyone, not even Spence, who'd become his only friend. Deep down, he knew Lyle Martin was a friend too, but he did not want friends now. He wanted his enemies.

The next morning, Carson sat in a small Sacramento coffeehouse near the railroad museum, compulsively reading the legal notices section in the *Sacramento Bee*. It was a depressing habit she'd developed and she was not surprised to see two full pages, front and back, of notices of default. She saw a smattering of petitions to administer estates and one notice of public bid to the city for a construction project. Some people looked at the obituaries; she'd taught herself how to interpret the semantics of the legal notices. Carson circled addresses and amounts on the defaults and noticed the dates of sale.

"God, there're so many." She flipped the paper back to the front page and took a sip of her latte. Then she scanned the stories above the fold. Foreclosures statewide

were down, one article said. And farther down was speculation that the banks were manipulating the process to
hide the true enormity of the meltdown.

She murmured to herself, "No way is this anywhere
near the bottom. These people are dreaming out their
asses. The whole system needs a reset." She looked around
self-consciously and was relieved to see no one had heard
her; the place was pretty much empty. She flipped to the
weather section to see what the conditions might be where
she was headed, and saw that things looked pretty clear.
She'd be in Nevada that night.

Then, in the Lifestyle section, she read a story about
the rise, crushing fall, and rise of a once-successful currency trader who went from a mansion in Pacific Heights to
jobless in the Tenderloin. He'd made some better choices
and now moved in even more elite circles with a new ca-
reer. Instead of being embarrassed about the humbling
experience, he felt enriched by it. "It fundamentally
changed my values and how I looked at my life," he was
quoted as saying. "Before, I had taken my success for
granted. You learn to be grateful—without that, you'll
never be happy no matter how much or how little you
have."

Carson stared at the words and felt small and childish.
She was embarrassed and a little jealous of his clarity, his
maturity, and...what? How did he forgive himself? How
did he find a way to get back to feeling good and strong?
Exasperated, she tried to fold the paper neatly for the next
person who might sit there, but it frustrated her and instead she mashed the sections together haphazardly. She
tossed a small tip on the table, and the dollar bill slid off

and fell to the floor. Her patience shot, she bent to pick it up, and the paper fell too.

Back in the truck in the parking area, Carson looked at her purse on the seat next to her. She knew that her gas card was paid up enough to get her there, and beyond that, she had three hundred dollars to her name. She didn't want to use her credit card anymore. She looked at her hands on the steering wheel and her eyes filled with tears. Gripping the wheel, she dropped chin to chest and began to sob. Her mouth was open in a silent scream, her arms taut, and her body frozen in the anguish that had been building for a very long time. She took in a huge breath and sobbed painful waves of frustration and frightened grief. It was a racking crest that, once started, could not be stopped, and the tears fell from her eyes, landing a pattern of drops on the top of her thighs. Finally, she closed her mouth, her head still hung, and more tears silently dropped where the others had begun to feel wet through her jeans. Though futile, she wiped at the fabric, then leaned back against the seat. She wiped her face with both hands, started the truck, and said to herself, "Okay then, enough of that. Let's go."

SEVENTEEN

L ight from the barn cast a shadow on the dark ground as Wyker opened the last of the gates and Tammy ran through. C.J. dismounted and loosened the cinch, and began to lead Rio toward the barn. He checked himself and turned to Wyker.

"We putting them in here tonight...or back in the small barn?"

"No. In here, it has lights. The small barn's only working light is in the tack room."

Wyker finished by dismounting and led Johnny inside. At the far end, Jorge was beginning to throw dinner. After haltering Rio, C.J. lifted the bridle headstall off the horn and walked into the tack room. "Hang this in a specific place?"

Wyker looked up. "Find a spot next to an open rack so we'll keep the gear together."

C.J. came back out and finished unsaddling Rio. He lifted the saddle and pad off, and went into the tack room to hang them up. As he did, Kitzie appeared from the house and asked how things had gone.

"It went smoothly. C.J. did just fine."

Kitzie smiled at C.J. as he put the saddle on a rack and piped up, "I think the dogs did most of the work."

She nodded. "They usually do."

Jorge laughed and came back with, "Hey, what about me? I wasn't just sitting there while you two were off on a nice trail ride enjoying the sights."

121

Kitzie was quiet for a moment. Then she told them she'd just gotten a call, and forty head were missing from the Sanders ranch. "Or at least they suspect they're gone. They're still looking. Come on in when you're done and we'll talk about it."

Wyker stared at her. "You okay?"

She lifted her eyes to his and he could see clouds of worry in them. She cared deeply about her friends and neighbors. What hurt them, hurt her. She felt selfish because her own loss was not far from her thoughts either.

"We really need to do something, don't we?" she said.

EIGHTEEN

Outside the Pine Tavern Café it was not as cold, and as Del finished his coffee, he felt invincible; heck, maybe even handsome. Getting up from the table and moving toward the door, he made sure his hand brushed up against Shiloh as they passed each other. She was carrying dishes and the half-empty coffeepot, and she effectively dodged a more invasive grab. She ignored him and did her job.

Del walked to his beat-up Chevy Malibu and got in. He pulled out the receipt that Shiloh had given him and unfolded it. He read the combination of numbers and letters, then opened the glove box and pulled out the cell phone and the charger adaptor thing. He pulled the cigarette lighter out and inserted the plug, then started the engine. He was impatient to see whether the phone had a signal. It didn't. He backed out and drove slowly down the street. He saw the bars spike and pulled over to the side of the road just past the last building at the edge of town.

Hank had been watching. This time, he latched on to Del trying to play a bit of grab-ass with the slut. Del was such an ass, so obvious about it that Hank mostly ignored him. But today there weren't many people left in the tavern and Del was about the only thing to watch. Hank had watched in the mirror when Shiloh was clearing and giving Del the receipt for his breakfast. Wait a minute; what had he just seen? He watched her with a few other patrons, writing up two more receipts for breakfasts. She had the book in the right pocket of her short apron. Wait a minute; what had she done there? With Del, he got one she pulled from the *left* pocket, he was sure if it. Then, as she turned, he saw the outline of two separate books in the apron's pockets.

Hank rubbed his rheumy eyes. They watered almost constantly nowadays, and it often looked like he was crying as the ducts had gone a bit native on him. Damned eyes. He took his glasses out of his shirt pocket. The prescription was an old one, but they did help a little. He watched some more.

Del had left the money on the table and the receipt wasn't there. Okay, so he took it...most did. He then watched Del get into the crappy Nova...*No, it's a Malibu*, he thought. He watched Shiloh pick up the money, then clear and clean the table.

Hank took a sip of his very cold coffee, never taking his eyes off her. Then he saw it. It was a slip of the hand, a switch. He'd seen it before, and now he was sure. Did she only do this with Del? He watched her pull the diner's copy of the receipt out of her right-hand pocket and slide it onto the spike. Something about this energized Hank and he turned to look out the window. Del was still sitting in his car. He leaned over and did something. He started the car, and a puff of black smoke belched from the tail end. The car shuddered in a fragile idle and he sat there messing with something for a minute.

Hank got up and dug a hand into the depths of his pocket for some change for his coffee, his pants staying on only for the ragged, worn belt he had cinched around his waist. He shuffled over to the register to put the money down and he reached across the counter to place it. He did so on purpose to get a look at the top receipt on the spike. It was Del's, but it was wrong. That's not what he'd had to eat. It was wrong. It was subtle, but something about it was wrong.

Hank said no thank yous or goodbyes, and no one tried to say either to him. He'd become invisible over the past months; the shuffling, teary old guy. He was oddly excited, and he didn't want to reveal the sudden burst of purpose he felt by changing his routine, so he shuffled out the door and headed to his truck. The Malibu was gone, but he noticed it was parked off to the side of the road down a ways. He got in and Sonny sat up from his nap across the truck's bench seat. Hank didn't need to go out of town that way. Home, what was left of it, was the other direction, but who would pay any attention to the old man if he was confused and had to turn around? He pulled out and went down past Del.

Del was busy and didn't notice Hank looking at him as he went by. But Hank observed Del reading a small piece of paper and talking into what looked like an expensive cell phone plugged into his dash. Hank watched in his side rearview mirror as best he could. Del was sure deep into conversation, he thought. Down a short way, Hank made a sloppy U-turn—more like a four-point turn. His old Ford long bed turned like the *USS Enterprise*. As he came back by the parked Del, Hank saw enough to know that the paper was a kind of receipt.

That's when it clicked for the old man. It was the same color as the one Shiloh had handed Del in the Tavern. *The receipt books are identical? Except she does something different with him, and it is subtle, perhaps so she won't make a mistake.* That was what caught his eye, the color. Hank almost laughed out loud.

Del turned his eyes to Hank's slow drive-by, interrupted his conversation, and noticed the old man's truck. He realized too late that he'd been holding the receipt up too high. He immediately dropped his hand to below window level and looked around, but something in his gut told him it was too late. *This is crazy,* he thought. *That's just a stupid old man.*

He missed a beat in the conversation and an impatient voice at the other end barked, "Del, what? Read it back again."

Del stammered, "Um…uh…I think the phone cut out or something."

Del felt sick and dark clouds crept to the edges of his previously invincible day. The voice at the other end was having none of his excuses.

"Bullshit, there's nothing wrong with the fucking phone. Where are you calling from? What the fuck are you doing?"

Del cleared his throat. A splash of spit dotted the phone, and he wiped it on his pants leg, brushing the phone buttons. He could hear the tones coming out of the earpiece, and he quickly said, "No one's around. Wait, the adaptor thing got loose in the socket. It's old and…there, I have it in there good now. No problem."

He repeated the last part. He smiled as he finished. He was confident they had gotten some good stuff this time and said as much to the voice on the other end. But the line had gone dead.

NINETEEN

Carson's hands were on the wheel, but her mind was not focused on the road. Thankfully, it was lonely, straight, and flat. Her thoughts drifted back to stolen moments. Part of her enjoyed the memory, but the bigger part of her knew that none of it was real. It wasn't real, yet she felt it was hers. It was the only secret she'd ever kept, and no one ever suspected.

Time ticked beneath the wheels, more distance from so many things she had firmly embraced and foolishly thought would never change. It was a funny kind of relief. No more pretending. No awkward attachment to something that was never hers.

"Know what is yours and what is not yours." She wondered who'd said that to her. They were right.

Hours later at the motel, Carson awoke in darkness on a double bed on top of the bedspread. The TV was on and a ghastly infomercial pitched away. She turned the face of the clock toward her and worked a moment to remember where she was.

Two empty bottles of cheap wine were on the dresser next to the TV; one must have tipped over, depositing its last drops on the carpet. On the edge of the bed, legs dangling, Carson looked to the growing dawn as it peeked at the edges of the drawn curtains. *Susanville, yeah, that's right.* Then she recalled the motel entrance and the 7-Eleven next door. She'd bought the wine there, and she scanned the cramped room from her perch to see if she'd bought any food. She hadn't.

The screen flickered and she wondered why anyone would buy that shit, and she felt sick. She hurried to the bathroom and knelt just in time to get the lid up. Afterward, she let go of the toilet, slid across the tile floor, and coiled like a small snake. She rested there, absorbing the coolness of the floor, grateful that the staff at this place actually cleaned well. Convinced she'd gotten the worst out, she propped herself up against the wall between the tub/shower and the toilet. After a moment she reached up, flushed, and listened to the water swirl and swish the porcelain bowl. Her imagination followed it down through the floor. The pipes rattled so loud that its journey through the building could have been traced by a blind man. She then realized she was on the second floor.

"That's funny, I don't remember stairs..."

She laughed as she pondered the irony of where she was. She'd retched out one life, unceremoniously flushed it, and hoped it was a cosmic sign that something positive would replace it.

The Three Bit kitchen table was full and they ate family style. Plates of food were rotated on a Lazy Susan in the center, and they served themselves generous portions. Kitzie had made a huge pot of penne pasta with lots of bacon and fresh Parmesan cheese. The steaks were tender and very tasty. And Kitzie loved her big bowls of salad. C.J. and Kitzie had soda; Luis, Jorge, and Wyker had beer.

Jorge asked, "What does C.J. stand for?"

"That's it, just C.J."

"Really? I heard some people do just initials for names. Really, I did," he said to the amused looks from his father and Wyker.

Kitzie said, "C.J. is short for something. Christopher? You don't look like a Charles. Chuck, Chucky? Charles Joseph? Clues?"

C.J. shook his head and tried to change the subject by complimenting the meal. Kitzie appreciated that, but pursued a couple more guesses, then remembered she could find out by looking at C.J.'s paperwork. Someone said that would be cheating, which is when Wyker said he knew, and with a big smile said, "Crazy Joe."

"That's it. How'd you guess?" C.J. said.

"Just figures after seeing you ride."

They laughed. The teasing continued until Kitzie got up and made a start to clean the dishes.

C.J. stopped her. "Please. I'll clean up."

Luis was ribbing Jorge about the less-than-perfect job he'd done cleaning up the ATV after the other night, and they laughed about what he'd used to do it. Kitzie sat quietly, both hands wrapped around her glass of soda. She gave it a little shake and watched the ice cubes resettle in the glass, bubbles finding new paths to the surface.

Wyker watched her. "If the herd is gone, we need to go after it."

There was a long silence.

Jorge looked to his father, who said, "I'd like a chance to go back and look again. Maybe we missed them. How about the four of us go, begin where we left off, and bring gear to pack out after the herd if it has been rustled?"

Jorge perked up at the idea of getting the bastards. "Track 'em down, like in the Old West, like in the movies."

Luis looked at his son and shook his head. *"Hijo,* we talked about this. No crazy ideas. This is serious business."

Wyker went on, "I'd like to see where you looked, and four would cover more ground."

Kitzie rubbed her eyes and ran a hand through her hair. "I'm too tired to talk about it anymore tonight."

Later, C.J. stood alone in the dark breezeway of the barn. Soft light penetrated the vastness of the area from a fixture over the barn doors. A breeze came through and he felt a chill. His hands pushed deeper into the pockets of his coat and he pulled it close. He felt something in an inside pocket. He opened the jacket and found a picture. He angled to see it in the available light. It was an old picture, and at first, he was confused because he did not recognize the girl. Then it struck him. It was a borrowed coat. This was a picture from Kitzie's pocket.

C.J. turned the picture over and saw the name "Carson" written on the back with a faded date. He turned the picture back over and saw how bent and cracked it was. Years and years old, a lifetime ago. She must have been a teenager, or just barely, and was very pretty. He looked up into the trusses of the barn roof and heard the owl rustling, then call. A breeze of cold air found his face. It touched his cheek and he felt the fingers of another memory. This one colder, and his own. C.J. put the picture back where he'd found it, and pulled the jacket close again. He shuddered, and the tightness in his chest told him he would not sleep well that night.

The dreams would always start the same way. It would begin when they were happy. He used to carry a photograph in his pocket too—one of them at the beach and there were big waves crashing white froth against the rocks. There was an overlook, a little bluff, where they'd sit and watch the edge of the world from a railing. The memories of his childhood in Australia were fun and happy; memories of how it felt to be so golden in everyone's eyes, to shine brightly with hardly any effort, to be good at just about everything. In the picture, young C.J. looked up over his right shoulder at the camera with that impetuous grin and those mischievous eyes. He had been a good-looking boy. The younger, brown-haired boy with him was Richard, his serious and pensive little brother. The world frightened and challenged him almost constantly. Richard adored and worshipped his big brother C.J.

Richie tried to do all the things C.J. did, and got scraped and bruised a lot in the process. Being naturally gifted, sports in school were easy, and C.J. never tried on purpose to stand out. As much as Richie would practice to be as good, it never seemed to matter. Richie heard all the tales of his older brother's athletic feats in school, and tried to measure up to him, although C.J. had graduated a few years before. Richie craved his big brother's approval, his unconditional love, and C.J. always gave it when he was around.

C.J. grimaced at the thoughts. He hated this time, when it was quiet and the thoughts came. Time to walk. Maybe down the drive a ways, until the pounding in his ears subsided, and until the image of his little brother's heartbroken face faded back into the shadows of his memory.

"Damn it!" He spat the words, went back out the barn door, and walked. His pace quickened down the driveway along a paddock area and past a fenced pasture. He hadn't thought of those horrible moments for a long, long time. He felt nauseated. He never meant to harm Richie. He started to run, the cold air catching sharp in his lungs until he caught a rough part in the dirt and almost fell. He doubled over, gasping, then looked up into the black and spoke to his brother: "Oh God, Richie, I didn't know you'd fallen in love."

He glanced back at the lights glowing from the house, and thought maybe sitting around the table with the others had brought the memory back. It was Thanksgiving when it had gone down, and because his mum was American, every year they celebrated. Thanksgiving was C.J.'s favorite holiday; better than Christmas. Richie had brought a friend with him, said it was casual, nothing special, and it never occurred to C.J. that Richie was in love with her. C.J. was just fooling around, being himself, and he did nothing he didn't normally do. But like most girls, Richie's friend noticed.

C.J. marched on the gravel and could hear bits of frost crunching under his feet. That time was supposed to be wondrous, magical, and he hated it. Richie had come looking for her, caught them together—not that they'd been doing anything really, but it was bad enough.

Richie had never stayed mad at him for any real length of time, but it all changed when he saw C.J. with her. For C.J.'s kid brother, this girl was it—she was special. He had invested himself and she loved him in a way that was untouched by his magnetic older brother. The betrayal was total. Richie never uttered a word, but the look, the last expression that C.J. ever saw on his brother's face, was something he had never forgotten. Its tinge remained in everything he did.

C.J. had pushed her away the instant he realized what had happened. For her part, she must have cared, because she ran after Richie. Minutes later, C.J. heard the car start and roar away. And then, not long after, the flashing lights outside the house. His mother collapsed at the news, and his father shut down completely. Afterward, his father's health failed and he remained silent forever. It all fell apart. Nothing worked after that. Nothing was left. It all changed.

It was an hour later when C.J. returned to the barn. He closed the barn door behind him, gripped the frigid metal handles, and pressed his forehead on the cold metal frame. Finally, he turned. His eyes adjusted to the dark and he found the door to the stairs. Somewhere outside he heard the owl as he trudged to his room.

With one hand on the sink, C.J. brushed his teeth, spit, and rinsed. This time when he stared at his reflection in the mirror, he saw the grayness around his eyes, the old pain. Nothing good ever came from revisiting the pain. It was always better to shut down before it grabbed hold and wrecked everything. He shook his head and turned away, stepped to the only window and looked out into the night. The stars were amazing. The cloud cover had brushed past and there was a ceiling of twinkling lights. He loved Rio, loved being near him again. He felt redeemed around Rio, like they both had a chance, and he liked these folks. It felt good, the work felt good, even the bumps and bruises didn't bother him. Part of him wanted to forget his past and embrace where he was in that moment. Here was a turn in his road, as he saw it, and it frightened him. He bargained with his hard heart to stay close.

"Be careful, this could go south too; watch yourself…don't get to counting on all this."

He went to bed and hoped the dreams would leave him alone.

Miles away in the darkness, a nondescript, short-distance cattle truck had a full load of stolen cattle. The truck slowly pulled away. The pipe panels they'd used to construct the cattle pen and chute for loading had been quickly reloaded on a bobtail. The two guys, whose names were never mentioned, hopped in without a word and hauled ass down the gravel road. Once they reached their destination, they'd drop the truck and head to their real day jobs. Stiles had seen the drill and the guys before, and he made a mental note that next time they'd need a few more panels and a bigger truck for the cows he and Ramos had stashed.

It was starting to get light, and the guy from the Bellamy operation was putting some fancy gizmo back into its case. He'd waved the thing over all the cows, said they were clear, and away they went. This guy was new to Stiles, and Stiles hadn't said more than two words to the man.

Ramos had their horses off a ways and was tired and very cranky.

Stiles watched the cattle truck brake for a divot in the rough road, then the taillights faded and the truck vanished into the valley around a hill. As he turned to go to the horses, the new guy called to him. He was standing at the truck he'd come in. The ranch logo had been painted out crudely but effectively, and Stiles could see the plate on the front end was sporting well-placed dirt that completely obliterated the numbers.

The man waved a phone at Stiles and said, "Untraceable. He wants you."

With a gloved hand, Stiles took the cell phone from the man and spoke into it. "Yeah?"

"My man says this bunch is fine."

"Of course. No reason they shouldn't be."

"We need to talk. I'm sending a trailer to get your horses; they'll rest up a day or two. Ramos can stay at the motel and get a break. You come with my guy now."

Stiles turned and looked toward the impatient Ramos. "Okay."

He handed the phone back and told Ramos what was up. "We're getting a break…couple days. A trailer is coming to get you and the horses. I'll see you later."

They heard a truck and both men stiffened. Stiles looked over at the Bellamy man and he seemed unconcerned, so Stiles relaxed a little. Otherwise, he'd have been gone before anyone could get a clear look at them.

"He said he'd sent someone, pretty quick about it. Must be them now. I'll be there shortly."

Ramos didn't say anything. He spat and kind of

grunted something, which was his answer. After so much time living hard in the backcountry, Stiles could understand Ramos's collection of grunts and guttural sounds. Speaking was just too much trouble.

TWENTY

The next morning proved fresh energy had grown on the idea to pack into the area where the cattle should have been, and preparation began in earnest after morning chores. C.J. knew that his input was not necessary to the success of the plan, and he understood his role in it. He practiced roping off of Rio. He roped the dummy, the fence posts, and Jorge, dropping a loop on him as he walked away. Jorge feigned annoyance.

After returning to the house, C.J. used the boot jack to take off his muddy boots and looked through the door's window. He left his boots in the mudroom, padded into the kitchen in stocking feet, and poured himself a cup of coffee. He leaned against the counter and listened to the others as they made plans. Wyker and Luis had marked out a large area. Luis thought a spot near the creek was a good place to camp for a day or two while they reconnoitered in circles outward to search the canyons and small bluffs. They'd separate, Luis and Jorge, Wyker and C.J., and keep in touch using the radios. Communication would depend on line of sight, so they'd work out when to talk to each other in four-hour intervals from high points. And they would be armed. Jorge wanted to bring a pistol and Luis said he'd think on it. C.J. knew that a weapon would be a violation of his probation and the subject was avoided. He had a small folding knife, which held a number of utilitarian blades—a hoof pick, pliers, an awl, and screwdriver, among other accouterments. He did not want to know if that was a violation, and he did nothing to conceal it as it was in a leather pouch that hung on his belt. It was decided to get the necessities organized as quickly as possible.

Later, C.J. and Wyker were in the small barn to put the tools and debris away from repairs they'd completed. Everything looked good, but Wyker was distracted. More than once he'd put something down and forgotten where. His thoughts were focused on possible best- and worst-case scenarios. Finally, he told C.J., "I'm going into Burns to talk to an old friend of mine; he's an agent with the Oregon Ag Department. He'll give me an unofficial update on the investigation."

C.J. grabbed a broom and began to sweep the breezeway. "What for?"

Wyker pulled his heavy work gloves off and laid one over the other. "There's potential for a situation. The backcountry can be unpredictable."

C.J. nodded and walked to Rio's stall. Rio lifted his head from the hay and looked at him, came over, sniffed his arm, and then went back to munching hay.

Wyker watched him.

C.J. said, "I've been in situations and shit has happened. Maybe, well, I did the wrong thing. I don't want to do wrong by him." C.J. nodded toward Rio. "When it was bad, it was just me; there wasn't anyone else to think of. What I need you to know is that I won't let anything happen to him. I won't allow it."

The next day, as Wyker left to go to Burns, C.J. worked with Luis and gathered supplies. Kitzie watched from the kitchen door as they went into the big barn together. Wyatt and Lulu stood by her at the door. They looked up at her, then realized she wasn't going out and settled back down. She sat at the table and went over her list. Her vision blurred, and a big tear fell on the paper. She wiped the trail off her cheek. She just wanted everything to be okay.

Kitzie leaned back in the chair and recalled the memory of a fight with Tuff. It was a stupid disagreement over Carson. Tuff saw Carson's future as her being the one to carry on the family legacy, but Carson wanted other things. She yearned for a bigger world, had her own dreams, and being married to a rancher in eastern Oregon wasn't one of them.

Kitzie had argued, "Sure she could do it, and maybe she would do it. But would she be happy?"

That had been their only real disagreement with each other; the struggle over whose plan was better for Carson's future. Kitzie had saved money for Carson's education, although she knew that might be a point of contention when the time came. Tuff was fiercely protective of his only daughter, and at the same time parochial in his views of seeing her married off properly.

Tuff struggled to understand the images of fashion, fame, and wealth shaped by television shows and magazines like *People*. Celebrity and fame were much more appealing to his daughter than the harsh weather and endless work of the ranch. In the end, she rebelled, and it broke Tuff's heart. Kitzie's too, and she shook off those memo-

ries, scooted the chair closer to the table, opened her laptop, and went to work.

Wyker pulled up to a parking lot where he'd arranged
to meet up with Hy. For whatever reason, Hy did not
want a public meeting. Wyker, engine idling, watched as
Hy got out of his state vehicle and came around to the
passenger's side of Wyker's truck. He got in and pointed
down the road. "Let's take a drive."

"How ya been, Hy? Appreciate the time."

"Good, and you? Thought you were in Colorado."

"I was. Didn't feel like work. Never get tired of the
horses, just the people."

Hy made a short laugh. "Well, that doesn't sound like
you. So, what's up? You getting cynical in your old age?"

"Hope not old or cynical. Got a friend who's missing
some cows."

"Who?"

"Collins Cutting Horses, the Three Bit Ranch. Remember Tuff Collins?"

"Never forget him. Biggest hands I ever saw."

"Yeah, I can still feel his grip. His widow's running the
place now. Going okay until lately."

"Oh, Tuff passed? Too bad. Good man. Seems to me
I remember her, good-looking woman, and they had a
daughter, too, yeah?"

Sensing Hy was buying a little conversational space
before getting to business, Wyker was patient and kept

driving. "Yeah. Kitzie's held it together out there. I'd like to find those cows."

Hy looked over at his old friend. "I see. What do you want from me?"

"Got a guy with me, from Colorado, one of the ones from the program."

"From what part of the program?"

"The bad part, an inmate. He's now on parole."

Hy had turned his head to look out the window at the passing countryside. "What are we talking here?"

"He has some past bad behavior, paid for it. I trust him. Kitzie's guys went looking and didn't find the herd. We'll go out again tomorrow, or the day after, and look a little harder."

Hy motioned for Wyker to turn around, and Wyker did a U-turn and headed back. Hy said, "They're probably already trucked off by now. I haven't seen a report on cattle theft from there. Who's investigating?"

"No report. Guess I'm investigating."

"I can't endorse that officially. She needs to make a report. If I were having this conversation with anyone else, I'd be obligated to insist. You know?"

Wyker nodded.

"So, what do you want?"

"I understand it's a priority for you, and I wanted to get the lay of the land and inform you. With the reward and all, I felt it important that you know I'll be out there."

"Two hundred thousand and climbing. Brings out all kinds of rumors."

"I came to help a friend. I'm straight with you, and reward's not the point. What I want to know from you is…what's going on out there?"

"No offense intended, it's just this thing has gotten very ugly. Off the record, people are angry and frustrated. They're sure it's someone they know and that pisses them off. Not knowing who to trust, if your own people are setting you up…" He paused before adding, "Be sure your friend isn't carrying."

"He won't be, but I will."

Hy let out a long sigh. "I got a guy out there, kinda undercover, but he knows the rez. I don't know if he'll check in before you go, but if he does, I'll tell him."

"Appreciate it. The number I have the best way to reach you?"

Hy pulled out his business card and scribbled a couple more numbers and a name on the back. He handed it to Wyker, who gave it a quick glance as they came within sight of Hy's vehicle.

"Okay, who's Dave?"

"My partner in the investigation."

"What happened to—"

"He retired and I talked an old friend from my days in the Bay Area into coming out here. Good guy. He retired after thirty years on the force and loved this country. Name's Dave Clancy. You need to reach me, those numbers will be the fastest. If you can't, call Dave."

Wyker parked, and both men got out and went to Hy's trunk, where Hy pulled out a topographical map of the Three Corners region and spread it out on the trunk lid.

Wyker returned after dark. Everyone had already eaten, and his dinner was on a plate warming in the oven. He sat down with Kitzie, C.J., Luis, and Jorge and they went over the preparations for the trip. Though it was late, the men went out to the barn to organize and prepare to pack. The cross-buck pack saddle with all-leather rigging and the large, heavy-duty pannier were set out in the center area of the barn, and items were set in groups alongside them. There were two sets of panniers, one a box set, and there were two liners. These would be harnessed onto two extra horses that were accustomed to packing. It was important to balance the gear evenly over the horses so as not to sore and blister a horse's back. Any part that was not correct was just a bad way to start any trip, so each container was first packed on the ground and then unpacked. They made sure the harnesses and rigging were correct. The following morning, they'd fit each horse to its own pannier, load, and go.

Kitzie had pulled out a collection of bedrolls for the men to tie to the backs of the saddles. Jorge had unrolled one and was pretending to nap, his arm under his head. He opened his eyes to an upside-down Wyker.

"Test driving the accommodations?" Wyker said. "Is that the one you have chosen, or are you trying them all?"

"They're probably all the same, huh?"

"Yup."

Wyker and Kitzie had discussed which ranch horses were going, and decided whether any needed trimming or shoes before they left. Earlier she had set out some Easy Boots—thick-soled rubber boots that fit over a horse's hoof in case they lost a shoe or became stone bruised—

along with a large tackle box filled with vet supplies. Wyker now looked through the box and took what he needed. While he did so, Kitzie wandered in from the house carrying a cup of tea. She spun the desk chair toward Wyker and sat down.

"You have any bute paste?" he asked.

"In that drawer near the sink should be some." She pointed. "Take the small pack of Previcox tabs too. You can quarter them easily, it says it's for dogs, but I like those when I don't want to use bute."

Wyker found both, and asked if there was any Banamine paste, along with injectable Banamine, needles, and syringes.

"Over there. Tuff used to say 'better to be prepared for a situation and not have one than have a situation and not be prepared.' Or something like that."

Wyker glanced up to see her gaze touch reminders of Tuff all around the desk. It almost seemed as if he'd left it just yesterday. Wyker let the silence be and got a satchel off the floor by the door. He opened the bag and pulled out ammunition, gun-cleaning materials, a small headlamp, a .40 caliber six-shooter, and an elaborate leather holster. Though he wouldn't take more than was necessary, he usually checked and rechecked that each weapon was empty and in order.

Kitzie watched him and stood up to get a better view. "You're kidding."

"My dad's favorite, and I also brought the .40 caliber rifle with his scabbard." He picked it up and showed it to Kitzie. "But I'll probably take the 30-30 lever action."

"Don't you want something more powerful? There's a

gun safe in the house and you can pick out what you like." She hesitated, "Are you going to give C.J. a gun?"

"No, and he's not asking for one. It would violate his parole." Wyker didn't look up. "I learned to shoot with this; with both, actually. And the handy thing is they use the same ammo. Not to mention how cool it feels to wear this."

Wyker held up the Badlands leather chest harness with its custom shoulder holster. He put one strap of the rig up over his right shoulder, straight up from the top of the holster; another strap parted from the butt end and went around his back to his left side, and the back strap attached to the nose tip of the holster. The holster was comfortably positioned below his chest and above his belt, giving perfect access on the fly. He'd had it customized with small tubular slots on the shoulder strap to hold extra ammo. Along the top of the leather holster was a thin sheath for a fine-tipped blade. Leather hammer locks—pieces of leather that snapped across hammer area of the gun—held it firmly in place. The knife had a specially designed handle with a notch in the top for the separate keeper to hold it in place. The knife keeper went along the top edge of the leather holster and the gun keeper along the front. With one motion he could free the gun and fire, and do the same with the knife. It was beautifully designed.

Kitzie asked where he'd found it.

"An old friend of mine, a backcountry horseman I knew, had a guy in North Dakota make one like this. I admired it and I contacted the same people to make me this one. It's super handy."

"Made in the USA. You boys and your toys." She smiled. "It is very nice, and wicked serious looking."

Wyker took it off, wiped the leather, and set it aside. Then he picked up the firearms, dismantled everything, and thoroughly cleaned and checked each piece. With the bright beam from the headlamp and some magnifier glasses, he looked down the barrels very closely.

Kitzie sat and watched him. He felt her smile when he put the magnifiers on.

He wiped the barrel with the gun cloth and said, "Okay, I admit it, I need these now."

"Don't we all..."

Something in her voice made him glance over and he saw her staring up at an old picture of Carson. She got up and headed for the door.

"Why don't you call her?" Wyker asked.

"I don't have her number."

TWENTY-ONE

Tiny Bellamy was anything but tiny, though he did carry his measure with a sense of humor that surprised many. He was an imposing man with a florid face and the neck jowls to match, and wore aviator sunglasses all the time, even inside. He missed nothing and was usually several paces ahead in any situation. He planned, paid well to get things done, and had built an impressive collection of ranches located in three states. He had several thousand head of cattle at Villa Del Sol Ranch, a huge breeding program, and was a respected member of a dozen associations and organizations.

On this particularly fine morning, Tiny was humming to himself in his extreme kitchen surrounded by top-end appliances, brick details, granite everywhere, and he was cooking up eggs, bacon, hash browns…the works. He glanced over at the out-of-place Stiles. "Want a latte? Maxie over there'll make you one."

Stiles was never sure how to treat Maxie, and Maxie didn't act like a servant. It was so confusing. Stiles felt a busy Maxie was a good thing, so he said, "Um…sure, I guess so."

Tiny smiled as Maxie moved to the machine that ground the coffee to a perfect espresso grind. There was a deceptive quality to Maxie. He had a controlled strength to him, and the white kitchen coat fit snugly across his well-muscled back. Clean, pressed business slacks finished to polished black leather shoes with thick, soft soles. He moved silently, with an underlying quickness easily called upon to do his master's bidding with no questions asked.

"I'll let Maxie finish cooking and we'll go sit in the breakfast room. OJ, too, Maxie."

Maxie, wordless, nodded affirmatively, and smoothly divided his attention between the latte machine and the stove.

Tiny led the way to an adjoining, octagon-shaped breakfast room. A bench curved under the windows, and a huge, round table with luxurious chairs filled the open side. It could easily accommodate a casual meal for fifteen. There were rich pillows in the window seat—about ten of them—and Stiles guessed each pillow was easily a car payment. Stiles followed Tiny and politely waited for him to maneuver his girth down and over onto the bench. Stiles looked out at the stunning view of the manicured gardens, which surrounded a custom infinity pool. A pool guy was out there doing his job. Everything was immaculate, perfectly trimmed, and the stamped concrete paths that wound throughout the gardens glistened from the early morning wash-down by the groundskeeper. A handsome fountain splashed just outside the windows and sent brilliant reflections throughout the room.

Stiles didn't care that he was filthy from the trail. He sat down in one of the plush chairs and dropped his well-worn hat on the table.

Through heavy-lidded eyes, Tiny caught the hat bit but said nothing. He could tolerate a little disrespect to the otherwise perfect room, as Stiles was very useful to him. He could overlook the small things.

Maxie brought two plates of food.

Stiles found watching his boss eat an exercise in selective hearing. Tiny, his mouth full of food, pointed with his knife (which had a glob of red fruit goo on the end) and said, "You should try this jam on your toast…it's incredible."

Stiles did his best to be polite, though the loud popping sound of Tiny's dysfunctional jaw made eating with him next to intolerable. Tiny was oblivious as he chewed his food. Stiles nodded in agreement as Tiny spoke, but couldn't care less about the fucking jam, and he wasn't all that hungry.

"Okay if we skip the pleasantries and get down to business?" Stiles said.

His mouth still full of food, Tiny talked on. "Sure, of course. I have the books for you. We'll go over it like usual. And I have your cash, as always, in small bills. Sure gets bulky that way. What do you do with it all?"

Stiles ignored the chatter.

Tiny went on, "Oh hell, who cares? All that matters now is that we are going to stop this little gravy train. We're done."

Stiles gave him an incredulous look and Tiny hurried on.

"I believe in quitting while I'm ahead—while *we're* ahead. The stock has fit nicely into the breeding program, and it self-sustains. It'd be near impossible now to pull them from my stock without DNA matches, and even then, we've been busy. The markers would be faint at best."

Stiles asked, "What happened? Is there something

else?"

Tiny pointed his dirty fork toward Stiles. "We both know that that reward is getting high enough that some of your friends might get greedy. That's why we just fade away, toss the untraceable cell phones, and disconnect from the little network that has worked so well for us. Roll it up. We're done."

"Okay, but I have a very nice herd tucked away, and *then* we walk. I need the truck near Running Horse Lake. I'll let you know where and when." Stiles took a bite of his eggs and reached for the latte Maxie had set on the table for him.

Tiny was not happy about being told what to do. He stopped eating and took a sip of his fresh-squeezed orange juice. A piece of pulp stuck to his lip as he said, "Leave 'em."

Stiles wanted to finish on his terms. "They're too nice to just let 'em go."

Tiny, elbows on the table, stared at Stiles. "We don't need them. I know when to quit and it's now. We stop. Cut those little pea-brain snitches of yours loose and walk away, Stiles."

"One more load and then we stop. I already have them. I'm not just leaving them out there. No one will find them where I have them, and it's only a three-day ride to the rez haul-out. Another week or so, you have a tandem rig waiting there, and we go off into the sunset like you say."

Tiny's face reddened, and in the sudden glare off of the polished table, he took a moment to put his aviator glasses on. Stiles sensed he needed a moment to compose himself, so he calmly sopped up some egg yolk with a dry piece of toast.

Maxie watched Tiny from across the room, and they stared at each other as Stiles picked up his juice and drained it, then wiped his mouth with a linen napkin. Maxie stepped silently closer to the table behind Stiles. Tiny cracked a broad grin and laughed out loud.

"You always were one stubborn son-of-a-bitch. What the hell? It's just one more week. But a day past—and you'd better hear me loud and clear—there'll be no truck. You finish quick, cut that nasty Mex of yours loose in some shit bar, and disappear. You hear me, Stiles?"

Stiles reached over and put his hat on. "Then pay me now. We wrap it up and we never see each other again."

Tiny glanced at Maxie. "Done. And we're done."

Maxie disappeared, and moments later came back with a bag and set it on the table in front of Stiles. Stiles, still extra cautious around Tiny's "help," waited for Maxie to back off. When he heard him busy with the dishes, he opened the bag and began to count.

TWENTY-TWO

C.J.'s face was in the dirt. He was conscious but stunned, and he heard all kinds of hell breaking loose around him A piece of something popped him on the head and he felt a warm trickle roll down his cheek. He cursed the fact that he'd ruined another shirt with blood.

He'd thought he'd try the pack saddle on the mule, loaded the empty panniers on it, and tied them down as Wyker had shown him. He then mounted up on Rio in the big arena to practice ponying. The lead rope got on the wrong side, and the mule got stuck, turned the wrong way, and wouldn't move. C.J. tried to reposition Rio, but the rope got up under Rio's tail. Rio clamped his tail hard on it and C.J. held on to the rope. He knew he should have let it go, but instead, things came apart and C.J. was in the dirt.

He had just missed the fence, and he now used it to steady himself as he stood. He leaned on a rail and surveyed the wreckage of the pack gear strewn across the arena. He tasted blood in his mouth and touched a split in his lip. *Shit!* He collected the debris of the rigging, the broken pannier box, and a piece of rope that looked like it belonged to what was left of a rope halter. Rio and the mule stood off near the gate all quiet, like kids in church. Hard to tell anything had happened to look at them. C.J. checked them, let them stand, then grabbed a cart and loaded the gear into it.

Wyker found him near the barn and asked him what had happened.

C.J. told him, "I'm not hurt, just pissed. And they didn't get hurt at all. Not fond of that fucking mule."

Carson sat in the truck. In some ways, she could hardly believe she was back. Martin Ranch Supply had gotten a new coat of paint recently, and the Pine Tavern seemed to be in business still. The same small-town dullness she remembered growing up hung over the area. There was a little light, but mostly the sun had gone down. She tilted the rearview mirror toward her face and stared into her own eyes. She didn't know what she was hoping to see staring back at her, and she didn't know what to feel. Didn't matter. She was going into the bar.

Carson adjusted the mirror back into the correct position and got a hairbrush out of the glove box. As she ran it haphazardly through her hair, it caught in the knots the open window had made in it. She fished a tube of lip gloss out of her jacket pocket.

She locked and closed the truck door, and as it swung shut, a more complete reflection of Carson Collins appeared in the glass. She was certain no one would recognize her, or care. She wanted to be firm in her resolve to finish this journey. But first, she might as well drink away the last of her money.

It was early in the Pine Tavern, yet the two pool tables were busy, quarters lined up for the next few games. Del was sitting at the bar, and it was the usual faces in the usual places. He'd tried half-assed flirting with Shiloh, but she was having none of it. He saw a couple of young buckaroos that C.R. Ketrick had brought in from outside the area. He had a good-sized place and could afford to import new help.

Shiloh was paying them all kinds of attention. When they first saw her, the disbelief on their faces was priceless. One of the young bucks made the effort at not noticing her, looking all serious and responsible, but when he thought his new boss wasn't looking, his eyes followed her every movement just like the others. Only the patriarch, the very serious C.R. Ketrick seemed to be immune.

The scene was mildly amusing, Del thought, but he was more curious about where C.R. had moved some of those Angus of his. He looked down into the last of his drink. Still an opportunity there with so many cows, and it did take a while to count them.

A woman had come in and taken a seat at the end of the bar, well away from the nearest occupied stool. Del considered himself a keen observer of human nature and decided that she wasn't there trawling. From the angle he had, he thought she could give Shiloh some competition if she wanted to. A couple of the guys tried buying her a drink or chatting her up, and they got a polite, "No, thank you," for the try. She ordered a bottle of wine and killed one glass, then another. Her solitude deepened. Had the stool been a hole, she'd have disappeared entirely. But there was no denying it—there was something special underneath the sadness surrounding her.

Eventually, Del tried to impress her, but she blew him off, though less politely. He told himself he wasn't really in the mood anyway. He was preoccupied; something nagged at him. Bored, he nursed a beer, watched the game on TV, and half watched a game of pool. Del had noticed the old man watching him. It had mildly annoyed him before, but now it was beyond annoying. It was like the old bastard was fixated on him. Del had seen Hank again that day, when he drove by Del's parked car, then turned around and came back, staring. Del was bothered by it, and the more he thought about it the more it troubled him.

He knew old Hank was holed up at his own homestead. He knew the old man was all alone out there, just him and that old dog. An uneasiness plagued Del. He was more paranoid these days. Things felt weird as the whole community eyed each other with suspicion. He glanced at the now empty table where C.R. had held court with his new guys. Maybe that's why he'd hired out, and not local. Del half wondered about the looks he got when he walked into a place. Had he been made? Did they know?

A commercial came on. The dregs of his beer were nasty, and he signaled for a fresh one. He stared at the woman at the end of the bar. He wondered what she was doing there. Then a chill came over him. Could be someone there to investigate? Was she looking for the rustlers? No, she was pounding it down good. Nothing furtive about that.

Shiloh tried to engage the woman with small talk and the woman ignored her. Not one to give up, Shiloh was back again to clear her tray and put in drink orders. While she waited for the drinks, Shiloh touched the woman. It was a benign gesture, one of friendly affection to break the ice and start a conversation. Perhaps it was that "petting thing" Shiloh did, or maybe that little-girl voice that startled her, but the woman recoiled, surprised by the contact. That it annoyed the woman was completely lost on Shiloh. After all, everyone loved Shiloh.

Del saw the set-up from twenty feet away. Shiloh apologized for startling her and opened, "You know, these guys, they don't mean any harm, they're all friendly here. Would you like me to introduce you?"

The woman shook her head and refocused to finish her umpteenth glass of wine. When Shiloh walked away with her tray full, the woman signaled the bartender. Del couldn't hear what she said. The bartender pulled up another bottle of red wine, opened it, and placed it in front of her while removing the empty one.

Del looked over at the pool table and realized he was not the only one watching her. Lyle Martin had lost his concentration on a game of eight ball he'd been sure to win. He lost the game, handed his cue off, and returned to his small table. He sat with his back to the wall, facing the end of the bar where the second bottle of wine was getting used up as quickly as the first.

The woman slouched a little and rubbed her temples, as if trying to smooth her thoughts away. She leaned her cheek into her right hand and fixed a blank stare at the wall of bottles behind the bar.

Shiloh returned to the woman's left with a tray of empties and made another attempt. "That's a nice red, huh? Folks like it around here."

"Whatever," was the woman's reply.

"Oh, sweetie, is something bothering you? What you need is a friend to talk to." And Shiloh touched the woman's arm again, a gesture between a pat and a stroke.

The woman jerked away from the contact and swore. "Jesus, stop petting me! What the fuck!"

Shiloh had half turned toward the woman, the empties balanced on her left hand as she held her right hand to touch the woman's arm again and calm her. "Sweetie…"

"What is with you? Are you too stupid for words?" the woman growled as she swung her right arm up to dislodge Shiloh's patronizing hand.

It happened in an instant. It could have been that she tried to get up off the stool to leave. Tough to say for sure. As drunk as she'd gotten, she lost her balance, and her arm swung wide and caught the edge of the tray Shiloh held. The tray spun hard, its edge came up in a perfect trajectory, and everything on it flew. Shiloh turned her head just before a shower of tray, glasses, ice, and alcohol hit. A heavy mug hit Shiloh on her upper cheek and eye, and the rest of the tray's contents bounced away.

The woman's stool tipped over with a crash and she staggered back. Her composure was completely gone as she hissed at the stunned Shiloh before the tray finished its reverberation on the floor and ice cubes scattered everywhere. Del watched, thoroughly captivated, while she continued to berate the wet and disorganized Shiloh.

Toby hurried to Shiloh's side and tried to pry Shiloh's

hand from her wounded eye. He turned toward the woman and said, "Hey, you settle down now!"

The woman wobbled back and forth and stared at her wine. The wine bottle lay on its side. She struggled to track the red rivulet as it finished its course along the curved rim of the bar's edge. "That's not my fault. She wouldn't stop touching me, for Chrissssssssakes." She slurred the last part, swayed, unsteady on her feet, and her face looked flushed.

Someone touched her elbow, and she swung around toward the offender. He stood close to her. Uncomfortably close. But his eyes were familiar somehow, and they weren't angry eyes that stared into hers. She blinked furiously and tried to free her arm, but his hold was firm and he took her by her other elbow. She tried to shake him free and felt the urge to run.

"Son-of-a-bitch, what the hell…lemme go!"

She struggled against the man, who took her hard by both upper arms. She cried out in pain. He leaned in and spoke quietly in her ear, "Carson. Come on."

She squinted through disheveled hair. "What the fu…"

He pulled her in and whispered directly into her ear, "Carson Anne Collins, if Tuff were here he'd kick your ass."

Her head jerked back. She visibly deflated and the fight went out of her like a strong wind blowing out. She looked into the man's eyes, shocked and speechless as the tears welled up.

"Time to go," he said.

The bartender said something to the man. Carson thought she heard the man reply, "I'll take care of it, put it on my tab."

He walked her past the silent, staring people at the bar; past the pool tables where the games had temporarily stopped; past the scattered whispers of, "What'd he say to her?" and "Who *is* that?" He walked her past everyone, not looking at any of them.

She trembled as he took her outside. She was just about done.

The brisk, cold air caught in her throat, and the night pitched and spun furiously. They stepped off the curb to cross the street and he held her up as she stumbled. The "whirlies" rotated her, her body bent over double, and she threw up on the street.

Giving her space, which kept his favorite Heritage Roughstock boots clean, the man fished a set of keys from his coat pocket. Her first round of nausea over, he guided her across the street and leaned her against a store window. Carson let her head bump the glass with a slight thud. He opened the front door, disengaged the alarm, and guided her inside. The man walked her through the dark aisles toward the back office, then sat her down in the armchair in front of his desk, grabbed an empty trashcan, and placed it between her legs.

Across the room, he made a pot of strong coffee. Carson stared into the garbage can and leaned on its cool edges. A memory stirred. She knew this place. She once had to be sure the cans were empty at the end of the day. The can blurred as a large tear finally broke free of the lashes that held it back. It was a solitary sign of her distress, and it rolled slowly down her cheek, sped up, and made a hollow sound at the bottom of the can. Through a curtain of hair, Carson spoke to the can, "Empty the trash. At the end of the day, empty all the cans. So they'll be clean for tomorrow..."

"That's a good sign. You remember," was the reply from the man's back as the coffeepot gurgled to life.

She lurched to stand, hand braced against the heavy desk, when the roiling in her stomach urged her to get to the bathroom. Hand over her mouth, she propelled herself out to the short hall to the bathroom and heaved again. She left the stall door open as she rushed to void the rest. She cleaned up and stumbled back to the office, where she sat on the small sofa against the wall.

He sat at his desk with bottled water in his hand. He took a sip, and Carson stared at the broad, clean wooden surface between them. It was a familiar barrier. She blinked and the surface blurred with tears. She looked into Lyle's face, and tears that betrayed containment rained down her cheeks. It was quiet. Her sniffling sounded so loud, and Carson felt very small. She struggled to stifle herself. Lyle slid a box of tissues across the desk. She blew her nose and gained some composure.

"You ready for some coffee?"

She nodded. He rose and poured her a cup. Carson stared at the steam tendrils that rose from the surface as he handed her the cup. She tried to think of what to say. She was suddenly seven years old and it wasn't Lyle's desk she sat in front of, but her father's. Tears, unbidden, resumed, and she gave in to them.

"Does your mom know you're here?"

She shuddered an inhalation. It was the edge of hysteria, and she knew it. To steady herself, she looked up to the pattern on the ceiling, the old-style acoustic tiles, and studied the perforations for images. Like looking at clouds, she imagined faces or animals. Then she wiped her eyes again and shook her head. "Not yet."

"I turned the heat on in here. The sofa's okay, not great. It's late and I'm going home. There's a bottle of water on the table. Try to rest."

And Lyle left.

Back across the street, Del replayed what had happened. He was curious how Lyle seemed to know the woman. Shiloh sat at a table surrounded by doting cowboys. One had some ice, from his drink of all things, and tried to put it on her eye. Funny thing, Shiloh was cool and calm, not really upset. She soaked up the attention while the few women in the bar hated that, once again, Shiloh had sucked all the air from the room. They were simultaneously annoyed, but felt a sense of gratitude to the stranger for the show.

The bar-back cleaned up the mess and the bar manager stood at the end of the bar, a towel in hand, his mouth a tight-lipped grimace. He wanted to get back to work. He wanted to bust up the pity party and finish the night. Reluctantly, he waited the tables, cleared empties, and took drink orders.

Del watched him and thought of a pebble hitting a pond. Had Shiloh picked out that woman for a reason? If so, it worked. Shiloh wouldn't have to work for the rest of the night. She got up and looked into one of the mirrors that lined the room above the faux wainscoting. He caught that she posed in a natural kind of way that was pure Shiloh. Del surveyed the room further. He thought there might have been more to her tactics; there might be something else he had missed.

C.R. Ketrick's young nephew was over at the pool table. He'd been drinking pretty good all night, and he was high-fiving after winning another game. His color was up, but not from his drinks. He'd zeroed in on the Shiloh show in the reflection in the Budweiser mirror. And she had looked back. Del looked at Shiloh again and did the math. He was maybe fifteen years younger, but she had him with a look. She would work the table of dumbasses that fawned over her for a bit more attention, and then get to playing with a new toy.

Del swiveled his stool back around, planted his elbows on the bar, and finished his drink. He fished money out of his pocket, set that and a very small tip on the bar, and headed out the door without looking back or saying goodbye.

Del sat in his car in the lot behind the Pine Tavern for a while. He was still bothered about the old man. Why was Hank Larsen still on his mind? Because there was something there, that's why. The more he dwelled on it, the wilder his thinking became. And then Del struck upon a course of action that, though perhaps unwise, was something Del felt was totally necessary. He'd have to have a talk with the old man. Private like.

TWENTY-THREE

The sun cleared the low hills to the east and long beams of gold kissed the roof peaks of the barn and covered arena. Kitzie was up when Wyker, C.J., Luis, and Jorge left. Afterward, she puttered around in the warm-ups she sometimes slept in. She enjoyed mornings—something about that early light made the world feel new and beautiful.

The laptop was on the kitchen table with the adding machine, and her file box was open on the chair. She'd been at the computer checking the accounts and had done some online banking. She thanked Tuff for being the smartest man in the room. She spoke to the computer screen, "The annuity was probably one of the smartest things you did, my darling. It's carrying the ranch."

But the margin was thread-thin. *Some people live paycheck to paycheck,* she thought. *We live cow to cow.* She heard one of the barn cats at the door, claws raking her beleaguered screen. Her dogs slept at her feet and only Wyatt lifted his head to look toward the noise.

Kitzie spoke to Wyatt as though he were a person. "I hear her, Wy, she's begging, isn't she? Okay...it's time for your breakfast too."

His ears went up and he looked excited, and both faces stared intently at her. They hopped and wiggled around as she filled bowls and placed them on the floor. She got a scoop of dry cat food out of a plastic tub and went to the door. A blast of cold air raised goose bumps when she bent down to pet the tabby barn cat.

"Here you go, Tigger. Good stuff, huh?"

Tigger rubbed and purred around the bottom of Kitzie's legs. He settled in on the little pile of dry food. Kitzie folded her arms across her chest and looked around. It was a quiet morning—so still that one couldn't tell where the low-lying mist ended and the sky began. It was bright and she squinted. The cross-fenced pastures on both sides of the drive looked ghostly as the sunlight began to penetrate the light ground fog. One of her oldest broodmares was in the pasture closest to the house. Fiona, or Fi, was twenty and her latest foal, now a yearling, was in the barn. This morning she was out in pasture with one of her older daughters, a six-year-old Quarter Horse mare, and an old ranch gelding. Kitzie liked seeing them there first thing in the morning.

Kitzie shaded her eyes with her hand. There was a truck down by the pasture. It seemed to be empty, and badly parked in the middle of the driveway. She scanned to the left of it and saw someone in the pasture with the horses.

"Shit!" Kitzie whispered and spun into the house. She looked left and right, and under the chairs in the kitchen for her shoes. Her slippers would not do, and she kicked them aside in frustration. She grabbed a pair of rubber boots and pulled them on, no socks. She ripped a coat off the hook by the door, and realized too late that it was one of Tuff's and was way too big. She didn't care. She hesitated a second, then grabbed the closest thing to a weapon she could think of—a heavy Maglite.

She ran down the gravel drive. Wyatt and Lulu had made it through the closing door and jumped around her. She practically tripped over Wyatt and she let out an exasperated, "Wyatt!"

She was almost to the corner of the pasture fence. The sun had cleared the mist and now glared in her eyes, making it difficult to see who the trespasser was. Whoever it was, he or she was still a hundred yards out. Lulu spotted the person, slipped in under the bottom pasture rail, and raced off at a dead run. Wyatt realized she was going, and as he was faster, caught up to her and passed her.

Kitzie climbed the fence, which would have gone better had she had her own coat on. She got a little hung up and tumbled as she tried to leap off and run at the same time. She scraped her arm and swore. She sorted herself out and began to run as best she could, but not as fast on the uneven pasture ground as she had been able to run on the gravel.

Whoever it was, the horses circled them and Fiona was in the middle.

Shit, shit, shit! Kitzie could not go any faster without badly turning an ankle, and she looked down at the ground to avoid doing just that. She didn't realize how much ground she'd covered until a voice brought her up sharply.

"Hi, Mom."

Kitzie was out of breath, stunned, and couldn't think of anything to say. Carson stared down at the ground, recalling the countless times she'd eaten some of it playing or coming off a horse. She smiled as she thought that the dirt felt like an old friend.

Kitzie's mind raced and desperately hoped that the

right words—the best words—would be the first ones out
of her mouth.

Carson was intensely uncomfortable. She ran a hand
over her forehead, through dirty hair, brought her arm
down, and then crossed her arms in front of her chest like
a shield. Her hair was backlit by the sun and it fell perfectly around her shoulders. It was one of her gifts, and a
mannerism Kitzie instantly recognized. Carson could be a
mess, and with a swipe of a hand, could look up at you
and be beautiful.

Fiona nudged her on the shoulder, and Carson had to
take a step to keep her balance. "Hey, Fi, don't get pushy."
She didn't really mind, and affectionately stroked the familiar face.

Kitzie stepped closer and ran her hand across Fiona's
neck.

"She looks good," Carson observed.

Carefully, mother and daughter tested the ground between them. Both wondered what the next move should
or would be. It was Kitzie who crossed that threshold and
took the chance. She moved toward Carson with half-
open arms and expected her to back off. When she didn't,
she tentatively embraced her. She tempered the urge to
hold her tight until she felt Carson's arms around her.

Carson closed her eyes and willed herself to hold still
as the distance closed between them. Her world blurred
and swam as a tear broke free. She was grateful her mother had taken the steps; she wasn't sure she could. She
wasn't sure of anything except for her mother's love.

Kitzie held her daughter. She didn't want to overdo it
or become too emotional. There was the briefest hesita-

tion, one that could have been a pull-back, but instead, Carson's arms were around her mother in a tight embrace. And before Kitzie knew it, her daughter sobbed in her arms.

Time became irrelevant and Kitzie wasn't sure how long the moment lasted. Later, when she followed Carson through the side door to the kitchen, both were back to the uncomfortable place and each searched for the right words.

Carson stopped just inside the kitchen and took in the room. It had hardly changed, and she felt some of the tension in her eyes and forehead melt a little. The coffee smelled good and Kitzie poured each of them a cup. Carson sat at the table and saw sky out the window over the sink. Kitzie fried up bacon and eggs. The dogs settled under the table at Carson's feet. Kitzie resisted the urge to ask how long Carson would stay. She could see that Carson was tired and ragged. Carson mentioned she'd seen Lyle Martin in town last night and that he had helped her, but she didn't elaborate.

Kitzie surprised herself. She had the patience to wait until Carson was ready to talk. They ate a little breakfast; a meal sprinkled with a minimum of conversation, a smattering of benign pleasantries, and no hint of what had brought Carson home. When she was through eating, Carson asked if she could lie down and sleep, and if her old room was okay. Of course it was, Kitzie said, and let her go up as she cleaned up the dishes.

Carson glanced around as she headed for the stairs. Her dad's old recliner sat lonely in the living room. She wondered why it was that places from childhood had a memory smell. She thought if she were blind and deaf and breathed this air, she'd know exactly where she was.

Upstairs, it was the wallpaper in the short hallway she noticed was the same, but the carpet seemed newer. It was still a small second floor, just two small bedrooms and a bathroom. Carson opened the door to her old room and she felt tears close to the surface, but she was too spent to cry. She was home. She'd gone to sanctuary. Carson sat on the edge of her old twin bed. Then she got up and went to the closet and pulled a light blanket off the top shelf. Carson curled up on her left side and fell instantly asleep.

A short while later, unable to resist the urge, Kitzie came up and gently tucked the blanket around her daughter. She remembered that as a child, Carson always wanted the door open at night so she could hear her parents talking. It made the little girl feel secure to know they were close by. When Kitzie walked out, she left the door open, looked back at her daughter, and hoped that a door was opening between them.

Carson slept, but then began to toss. Her sleep became fitful and shallow. She felt like she was sinking through the bed and down into nothingness far below. She was on her back, on a small wooden raft about the size of a door, her eyes wide open, and turning her head from side to side. She found herself washed up on a deserted beach. Each wave that lapped at the raft splashed water at her feet. She felt the waves nudge her tiny craft. Then the raft moved on its own into an endless, flat body of water. She wasn't sure it was the sea. It had no smell, and as she trailed her hand in the water, she lifted a finger to her lips and tasted nothing.

She looked around, confused. Why was the raft moving? How was it moving with nothing to propel it? There was no wind, the water was calm, yet the raft was moving quickly to nowhere. She scanned in all directions for some sign of land, but saw none. She rolled onto her hands and knees and stared at the wake behind the raft. What was that in the water? She saw... *things*...in the water. A little panicked, she looked around again. That empty, frightened feeling enveloped her—the realization that no one knows where you are.

She looked back at the wake reluctantly. Maybe, if she didn't pay attention to whatever was in the water, it wouldn't notice her. But she stared at it anyway. Then she saw the faces. The water had morphed into the faces and bodies of people she knew, both alive and dead; she'd grown up with some of them, worked with some, dated, loved, and hated some. But each one was familiar and they did not just wash by—they roiled around, turning face-up repeatedly as the water spun them. She saw her dad, her mother, every family pet. Even her favorite rooster, Foghorn, made a macabre swim through the wake. They had no eyes, and she shut hers tightly to avoid seeing them.

Then there was violent shaking. She had to look. She opened her eyes and saw that the people were gone. There were huge waves, yet still no wind. The violence that ripped at the raft had her sitting up, holding the edges. The waves became things. All the things she'd had. One wave was her job. Pieces of it composed the wave's fluidity. The things weren't sharp-edged or defined, they were soft and squishy and distorted. They rose and fell around her. In their rising and falling, there'd be a frozen moment, a suspension of motion, where she could make out what the object was through its distortion. Office-supply white caps, waves of smooth pieces of paper, files, paper clips, envelopes, desk blotters, and cash. Fabulous cars, clothes, expensive shoes, jewelry, make-up, and her beautiful furniture…

The waves grew like a roller coaster. Her raft dropped into a trough and then ascended a huge face. The raft balanced for a second, level at the crest, then tipped forward and plummeted down the other side. The next wave appeared in succession. Carson's fingers clutched the edges of the raft as her body was thrown violently from side to side, her mouth open in a silent scream.

The items separated and objects rose from hidden depths. The corner of her former house appeared. The raft bucked and she held on, then it surged forward. The things in the churning ocean began a slow rotation around the house. The house was in the center, and by shifting her weight, Carson maneuvered closer to it.

She realized that the house was a reflection in the water and wasn't real. She heard her own voice say, "Whoa," and the raft slid to a stop. The reflection sank and pulled the whole mess with it. She was caught in a vortex. The house below sucked her down. Then she was in the wall, part of it, and she couldn't breathe.

Carson sat bolt upright in her old bedroom, gasping for breath. Had she been holding her breath in her sleep? Who cared? She knew she'd almost died.

Kitzie tapped on the door and said, "Carson, are you awake?"

Carson answered and her mother came in. The expression on Kitzie's face was a mixture of concern and caution.

"I didn't want to disturb you. I need to check the calves in the far pasture and I'm gonna ride out and take a look. Do you feel up to going?"

Carson shook the dregs of the bad dream off and thought that sounded good. In fact, she felt her spirits lift at the thought of it. "Sure."

"I talked with Lupe and he'll feed tonight. He's Luis's cousin. Works at the Running Horse Ranch. Luis arranged for him to come help out while they're gone. They went to look for our missing cows. He's a hard worker, though not that savvy about cattle, but he's good with horses."

Carson sat up. Her legs dangled off the edge of the bed, and she noted the bed was about the same size as the raft in her dream. She hopped off it quickly and asked, "What missing cows?"

Kitzie either didn't hear the question or chose to act like she didn't, and Carson let it go.

"I'm gonna saddle up, how 'bout you?" Kitzie said.

She saw a smile on her daughter's face for the first time in years.

TWENTY-FOUR

Every time Del turned around he'd see old man Larsen, his shitty truck, or his all-but-dead old dog. *Jeez*, thought Del, *how can he stand the smell of that animal?* A few times Del could've sworn he saw Hank's truck behind him on the open road. He'd pull over, wait to see, and it'd be someone else. On one such occasion, it was someone he knew—Spence, the sheriff, done with his shift for the day and on his way home. Spence stopped just past Del, turned on emergency flashers, and walked back to Del's car to see if everything was all right.

Del tried to look casual, and failed. "Hey there, Spence."

"Evening Del…everything okay? You broke down or something?"

Del was embarrassed that he'd let his paranoia play on him so much. The thought crossed his mind for a second that Spence might be following him. "Aw, heck no, lost the cherry on my smoke…was 'fraid it might burn a hole in these jeans…only clean ones I got left, ya know?"

Spence nodded affirmatively and looked around for the bigger picture. He took mental notes of location, time, place, and finished with a not-so-subtle glance into the back seat. "You don't have an open container, do you, Del?"

He leaned in a little closer and Del eased back from

the sheriff. He laughed uncomfortably and tried to re-member how long ago he'd downed his last couple of beers.

"Course not. I drove out this way to clear my head. Got nowhere to be, ya know?"

Spence straightened himself and stepped back a little from the car, satisfied that Del was not in any trouble at the moment. He smiled an official cop smile and rested his hands on his belt. "Wouldn't want to intrude on thinking. Goodnight."

"Thanks for checking," Del said politely, though it sounded hollow and phony.

Del sat there and watched Spence disappear down the road. He pulled out a fresh pack of smokes and began the ritual of smacking one end of the pack against the palm of his hand to compress the tobacco, then pulled the little plastic string to open the sealed pack.

TWENTY-FIVE

The sun came with faint warmth. C.J. squinted into the dawn as the cold air hit his face. He held the rope reins in one hand and felt the movement on the lead rope of the packhorse he ponied. They had left well before first light. Luis and Jorge knew where they wanted to be by day's end, and talked of being two-thirds of the way to the site where they hoped to find the cattle. He'd overheard them talk of circular patterns they had ridden last time as they searched. Wyker hadn't said much in hours. C.J. was quiet too. Luis hummed something, which occasionally became a Mexican ballad; a sweet, mournful song of some kind.

C.J. was at the back of the string and caught sounds the retreating night made as it breathed its last breath before the light. His mind drifted to the clip-clop sound of hooves on hard ground, and a memory of Australia filled his thoughts. When he was twelve, he'd stayed out all night, enacting a fanciful version of an Aboriginal test of manhood. He'd freaked his parents out completely when he disappeared into the bush near their home. He'd heard the dingoes and the night calls of strange animals. By midnight, he pretended he'd gone through a rite of passage and thought he'd sneak home undetected. Instead, the house was awake and he got into trouble for scaring everyone.

A nearby voice said something to him. C.J. didn't hear,

so Jorge said a little louder, "Hey, you asleep back there?"

C.J. responded that he hadn't heard him, and Jorge asked if he'd remembered to check the cinches before they left. C.J. tried to remember. That was several hours ago. He ran a quick recollection of sequence and could not, for the life of him, remember exactly what he'd done or when.

Wyker called for a short break, and C.J. was grateful the second he slid his hand under the billet. It was loose. The first steep incline and it would've been a bucking strap, not a saddle. Rio stood quietly while C.J. checked the pack animal. Those cinches were decent. He heard a stifled laugh and realized there'd been a friendly bet, which might have become interesting had they not stopped and checked.

They mounted back up and set to moving through a long, flat valley. The two-track road was clear in the morning light, and the sun glided across the rocky surfaces, throwing slanted blue shadows across the frost from the scattered boulders nearby.

TWENTY-SIX

Shiloh was not happy. Uncharacteristically, the face she saw in the mirror that morning needed work and she wondered how to minimize the damage. The tray had acted like a catapult when it propelled the beer mug. The mug had risen like a missile off its launch pad, and she'd had no time to properly dodge it, though she did manage to deflect its trajectory to her left eye socket.

Leaning closer to the old mirror, she probed the tender area with her index finger and flinched. She leaned against the tiny sink on stiff arms. She was tired and looked to her make-up bag for some porcelain camouflage. The bag was on the tank lid of the toilet, which doubled as her bathroom counter. She dug around for concealer. She hardly ever used the stuff and it was dried up and ancient. She wet her finger and that helped some.

Toby had just pulled supplies out for breakfast when Shiloh arrived. His arms full, he looked at her and nodded his greeting. She had her back to him as she put her bag and coat in the cubbies designated for employees. Toby's eyes lingered on her back. He'd heard rumors already that morning, but she took her time turning so he could see. At the moment she turned, he decided against staring, did a rather graceful pirouette, and closed the refrigerator door with the side of his foot. Shiloh followed him into the prep area, where he caught a full-on view of her facial injury management efforts.

"Sweet Jesus! What the hell happened to you?"

"Oh, just an accident last night in the tavern," she replied.

He got things ready as she continued with the story.

"I had my tray of empties and somebody got up, caught it just right. One of the mugs nailed me."

Toby stopped and peered closer at her face. Shiloh tried not to back away from the uncomfortable scrutiny. She grabbed her apron and her chit books, and moved off into the area between the customer counter and the pass-through from Toby's kitchen. She went to set up the register and turn on some more lights. Though one or two early birds had been let in, the café wasn't officially open for another twenty minutes.

TWENTY-SEVEN

He was in the saddle again, and cold again, and all the beauty had gone out of this country for him. Riding out was for a purpose. It had been so long since he had done anything just for the pleasure of doing it. One of Stiles's goals was in reach, and he would never do this shit again. He hoped maybe someday he'd return to his love of riding and horses—leisurely, the way he used to do it, maybe as a hobby and for pleasure.

What was gnawing on his brain was the resolution of the other thing, his reason for setting things up the way he had. He was not concerned about how the cattle thing wrapped up; he had to figure out how to get *her*. Would she drop everything and leave with him? Would she understand why?

His reverie was stopped in mid-thought by Ramos's hacking cough as he came alongside Stiles. "What did the *gordo* say?"

"He stuffed his face. We're taking that route going south and he'll meet us on the rez, the Nevada side."

Ramos spat on the ground and grunted.

Stiles added, "I haven't heard from my people in Martin."

They headed north and were a two-day ride from where the cattle waited. Stiles knew that Ramos was his own creature and that he owed Ramos nothing. Ramos sent the money he made to his family in Mexico, he kept very little, and Stiles didn't much care what happened to him. Stiles felt that wasn't an issue, but the thing that stuck in his craw was the meeting with Tiny. That meeting felt different from the other meetings. Something about it irritated Stiles, and he had trouble fully grasping what it was. And it bothered Stiles. For many miles, he considered the existence of another influence on ol' Tiny. Perhaps an invisible, important stakeholder. Stiles finally concluded there was another partner—one he didn't know about. He rolled the thought around in his head as they trotted out to cover some open ground of flattened dead grass.

Maybe he was being paranoid, but Tiny had never been so on-edge. He always let Stiles run the operation and handled his end. He was usually a cheerfully greedy fat guy, only he hadn't been at that last meeting. Maxie seemed ready and able to act. For the first time, Stiles felt expendable. From the word go, this was something he knew to be true, but it was the first time he felt threatened. Maybe that gardener had planted more than bulbs and bushes on the estate.

Some twenty miles off, the ground fell away to a squat valley. Wyker dropped the reins on his horse's neck and used powerful binoculars to scan the area. Satisfied the coast was clear, the group continued on the track and moved out for the better part of an hour. The horses traveled well. Breaths plumed out of their nostrils, dissipated quickly, and there was no drama. Rio picked up a slow, three-beat lope that was like heaven to sit, and C.J. felt himself easily ride each stride. Behind him, C.J. felt the packhorse easily keep up in an extended trot.

C.J. called to Luis, "Hey Luis, this country is so open, how do you think they do it?"

The string slowed to a walk as the ground changed and they picked their way through fallen boulders tufted with dead and rusty grasses.

Luis's voice came clearly. "There are a lot of men who have worked these ranches out here, moved around working for different people and know this country well."

"You mean they have some way of knowing where the animals are?"

"Seems so. The ranchers think it's someone who knows them. The rustlers ride like shadows. They were seen once. The story is the guy lost them when they jumped their horses off a rimrock and vanished."

TWENTY-EIGHT

Ramos snored, head drooped on his chest, as he rested his back against a rock, his ratty poncho wrapped tightly around him. Stiles slipped away without waking him or stirring the horses. He walked about half a mile to a rocky outcrop and knelt to move a pile of small rocks that covered a carefully dug hole. From the hole, he lifted a metal box with a locked lid, spun the combination dial, and opened it. There was a small hole drilled through the backside of the box, and a small rubber plug kept moisture from seeping into it. Stiles unhooked the wire that went through the hole. Leaving the box on the ground, he stepped up onto the rocks and looked to the top, where a small solar panel was set up. Stiles undid his neckerchief and wiped the surface. It surprised him that it was pretty clean. Ramos had never caught on that one reason Stiles picked this particular route was because of the box.

Stiles climbed back down, reached into the box, and found the batteries. He had one he left on the solar-powered charger and one charged in the phone. Also inside the box were two SIM cards for the phone; one he used to call Del, and the other one was for her. He put the card in to call Del and turned the phone on. He moved around the area a little to find the strongest signal, then dialed the number.

Half asleep against the headrest in the car, Del stank of smoke, sweat, and alcohol. He'd been drinking when he realized he'd left his cell phone in the glove box. He was tired, cranky, and annoyed that Shiloh was ignoring him, and the quiet of his car was a break from the heat and noise of the tavern. He felt the least she could do was be nice to him. After all, he was a customer too. He'd not heard anything for too long and he was uneasy. Everything made him jumpy. Hank had been following him for the past several weeks and that pissed him off. Damn old man watched him eat every morning. What made him want to watch him eat? Del suspected why, and it worried him that the old fucker had figured something out. Hell, even if he hadn't, it was time it stopped.

Eyes half closed, Del had just begun to consider ways to stop it when the glove box rang and startled the hell out of him. He'd distracted himself to the point of forgetting why he'd come out to the car in the first place. He jerked up and leaned over to unlock the glove box. His fingers fumbled and he impatiently ripped the glove box open, which broke what was left of the flimsy lock. He seized the phone and pressed the green button.

"Yeah."

Through the phone he heard, "About time."

Del looked around at the other cars in the parking lot by the bar. "Couldn't find the fucking key to open the stupid glove box. I'll fix it."

"Don't have to. It won't matter," was the response,

which redirected Del's attention from gathering the broken pieces of plastic off the floor.

Here it comes, he thought as his stomach turned. "Whaddya mean, it won't matter?"

"Because this is the last time," the voice replied calmly.

Del gripped the phone, did a quick calculation of how much money he had, and got mad. "Like hell."

"It's done. Over."

"Aw, come on. Why? Has something happened? What's happened?"

"Nothing."

"You can't stop! I need money."

"What you have or don't have is not my concern."

"But this is my only real job. There's no work anywhere. You have to give me more time. I need the money."

"You've got all you're gonna get."

Del's voice sounded pinched and he raised it enough to be heard several yards away. "NO! You can't do that to me! I have some really good information, and you'll want these..." He stammered. "These are really nice...from...from the Running Horse. You always say they have some of the best."

There was silence and Del became more aggravated. "Come on! What about that prick-tease little bitch? I'll bet you're not so done with her...what's she get? I swear to God I'll burn her if you cut me off."

The voice was calm and deadly serious. "That would be a very bad idea. We're done. Throw the phone away. Destroy the SIM card." And then it seemed the line had gone dead.

Del held the phone away from his ear and looked at it, put it back up to his ear, and yelled into it, "Wait, I didn't mean it! Don't hang up. Let's talk about this! You have to give me a little more time to make a plan. This economy is killing people out here and I have nothing!"

There was silence, but Del thought the voice was still there. He deserved more. He hissed, "I'll hurt her..." He listened, trying to hear anything on the other end. He cocked his head and pressed the phone hard to his ear. He heard what he thought was the sound of breathing on the other end of the line.

"Make your plan. If anything happens to her, there will be no money," the voice said.

Del's mind churned. So, she *was* important to him. He thought he could make this work to his advantage and he felt confident that it wasn't over. "There, see? That wasn't so hard. We can be reasonable people. No need to be un-friendly, not when we've been partners for so long."

The line was dead; the voice had gone. Del held the phone in his lap and leaned his forehead on the wheel. He didn't turn the phone off; he simply tossed it into the broken glove box and got out of the car. He decided he was thirsty, and unsteadily bumped off the rear quarter panel of his car as he said to himself, "Can't get rid of me."

Hank watched Del make his way back to the door of the bar, open it, and go in. Then Hank moved across the lot from the corner of the building. He'd parked his old truck back there, out of sight, since Del had been acting spooked. Old Hank smiled at the thought that he'd rattled that fucker. The thought actually made Hank laugh—a bright spot of sarcastic humor in his otherwise miserable existence. What an asshole that man was. Hank knew he was right. He just knew it.

Hank got out of his old truck and left the door ajar. He wanted to be quiet, and that old door required a vicious slam. He had his old hammer hanging off his overalls and he fingered the handle as he slipped between a couple of ranch trucks. He'd been thinking he'd break the window of Del's car to get in, and almost did until he thought to try the driver's side door. Amazed that it opened right up, Hank leaned in and looked around. He'd heard Del yelling at someone, so he hoped that phone Del had was in there somewhere.

Hank lifted up some old newspapers and glanced at a pile of empty soda cans, plastic cups, and straws protruding from plastic lids. There were bags from fast-food chains he'd never heard of and the old man suspected Del covered more ground than he originally thought. The whole area behind both seats was stuffed with empty cigarette packages and garbage. The car was a mobile trash can. Almost immediately he spotted the broken glove box, and he pulled it open. The phone fell out and dropped onto the floor. Hank was reaching over for it when he heard a voice behind him. Hank's fingers grasped the phone and he stood up, startled. It was that skinny kid, that ranch hand that came in and was so heartsick in love with Shiloh.

"What ya doin' in Del's car?"

185

Hank felt his face redden and he said, "Shouldn't startle an old man like me, could kill me, ya know." And he straightened up and held the phone out in his hand for Matthew to see. "Del found my phone and told me to come get it. My son sent it to me; he's worried for me. No other way to get in touch. I'm not used to it and I left it at the diner this morning. Heard Del had it and wanted to get it back to me. Don't want to bother him in the bar, got it myself, and I'll be going home now."

Matthew knew this did not sound like Del. He'd help no one but himself. The old man did have a son, he remembered that much. And as Del was no friend, Matthew didn't care what the old man was up to in that shit's car.

"Well, that's a good son you have there. I'm glad he's concerned for you."

Hank looked up into Matthew's face with red eyes, and they misted at the thought that his son had not been in touch at all; hadn't even tried. "Yes, Matthew, I am *very* lucky. Well, I'll be going now…see ya."

Hank moved off into the darkness. Matthew proceeded to one of the ranch trucks where he'd left an almost-empty bottle of Stetson cologne in the door. He'd watched Shiloh all night as she worked. Maybe he'd freshen up a bit and see if that helped. He had a comb on the dash and he ran it through his hair, then decided to leave his hat in the truck. He smiled at his reflection in the rearview mirror, felt more hopeful than he had any right to be, locked the door, slipped the keys in his jeans pocket, and went back to the bar.

In the half-moon darkness, Stiles stared at the phone. The power reserve had dimmed the screen, then brightened when he dialed the number. It rang until voicemail picked up and Stiles listened, then made his decision. "I need to talk to you. Things have changed and you have to call me immediately." He knew he shouldn't say more, but plunged on anyway. "Avoid Del. Can't tell you more than that here. I'll have some important instructions for you…and I don't know when…" He stopped to think, and before he could finish, he heard the beep of the voicemail and the line went dead.

Stiles always thought better when he was moving, and his whitened knuckles gripped the cell phone so hard, he thought he had cracked it. He paced for several minutes, then stopped and sat down on one of the small boulders. He looked at the phone and knew that what he was about to do could ruin all his careful planning, but to take the phone with him wasn't what he wanted to do, either. There was so much to tell her, and he'd put it off until the right time. He hoped she'd understand. He redialed the number and waited.

Shiloh was pumping and had no chance to go near her locker on her break. Her purse was in the locker with two cell phones. One was her regular phone, the other was the "special" one, which she kept in a secret compartment in the bottom of the bag. The noise in the hall from the bar made it impossible to hear the vibration of the bag against the cheap, hollow metal wall of the locker. The bar was busy with people playing pool or dice, and talking over the piped-in country music. The bartender moved humorlessly as he filled drink orders. Shiloh grabbed her full tray, caught an annoyed glance from a customer, moved smoothly to a far table with a smile, and distributed the drinks. She went past Lyle Martin, leaning lightly on his pool cue, and she smiled at him.

"How's the eye?" he asked.

She stopped and tilted her head so he could get a better look.

Lyle looked at her, carefully maintaining a gentlemanly personal distance. He was always polite, she thought, as he said, "Doesn't look too bad. I'm glad you weren't seriously hurt. I want to apologize for...that. Sorry she behaved badly. I'm sure she didn't mean it."

"Oh, that's okay, part of the job I guess. She was having a bad time," Shiloh said over her shoulder as she moved to the rail along the wall and collected some empties. "Can I get you anything, Lyle?"

"Yes, thank you, another beer, on tap please."

"Coming up." She worked through the bodies hanging around the pool table and saw that Mattie had returned. He smiled at her as she walked through the cloud of cologne that wafted around him. Shiloh turned, spied a few empties, and veered off to grab them. She felt Mattie hard on her heels, and as she turned with her full tray, she almost crashed it into his midsection. Embarrassed, Mattie caught the first of the tottering load.

Shiloh was as sweet as could be. "Whoopsie! That was close. Thanks, Mattie…may I get you a drink?"

Mattie stammered yes and watched her walk away.

She went past a table full of wranglers from the Running Horse. One of them reached out as she went by and touched her. She swung her hip to avoid the offending hand, but he caught a brief touch on the back pocket of her jeans and she gave him a friendly look of admonishment.

Mattie watched those faded blue jeans, that beautiful back, the curve of her shoulder blades under the skimpy T-shirt, and the blond hair. He was pissed that that act had blurred his retreating picture of perfection. He wanted to get up in that guy's face about it, but he felt a hand on his arm and a soft voice ask him if he'd care to play a game of eight ball. Mattie whipped his head around and saw Lyle Martin's kind eyes smiling at him. Mattie expelled a short burst of air out his nose, dropped his head, then nodded and smiled a bit sheepishly. "Sure, Mr. Martin…thanks."

At the waitress station, Shiloh handed off the empties, put in the orders, and grabbed a fresh supply of little bar napkins. While she waited, she felt someone. At the other end of the bar sat Del, and his eyes bored a very uncomfortable hole into her. Shiloh did a half-smile at Del and looked back to her tray as the drinks and bottles came within reach. She cast another quick look in Del's direction and saw him sipping on an almost-empty highball. He stared at her over the edge of the glass.

TWENTY-NINE

Darkness was falling when they had reached a spot where Luis and Jorge had been before. They hobbled the horses and pack animals, and off-loaded the gear. They set up camp and ate the sandwiches that Kitzie had made, and discussed whether to make a fire. They were in an area with lines of sight, and a fire might be seen. Ultimately, they decided being cold for a while was worth it if they were to succeed. So, they sat together and talked. Much of the conversation revolved around the country they were in, specific landmarks, and how they would organize their search patterns.

C.J. listened and said little. He was feeling rather good about how well he and Rio had gotten on that day. And like any overprotective "parent," he continually left the group to check on him.

He had just started to do so again when Jorge said, "He's fine. If I were a horse, that would annoy me after a bit."

C.J. nodded. His eyes had adjusted to the dark, and he saw the smile from Jorge, his dogs on the ground beside him, and he was about to say something when a group of coyotes called from nearby. It was a magical sound to C.J. With each call, C.J. strained to hear the next. It was like watching shooting stars in the night; you'd see one and search the heavens for more. Their conversation moved around, yipping and short barks, then silence. The silence lasted a long time and C.J. felt himself willing them to call again.

A voice interrupted his reverie with a phrase from a popular science fiction series. "Space...the final frontier..."

C.J. laughed at himself. He had totally checked out. "Yeah, right. Okay. Today was amazing. I love this country. Not like back home, but big like back home. I see why the cattle rustlers have been so hard to find. At first, I thought no way, you can see for miles, and then not see a mile after traveling half a mile. The land's unevenness and color make it all blur together. The only thing I felt completely aware of today was Rio. I felt each footfall and every breath. I guess that connection is what I've been working toward."

They smiled at him in the dark and Jorge reached over and petted both the dogs. Then they talked briefly about the next day's search. They'd be separated most of the day and would join up again the next night. With that decided, they turned in.

At the tavern, Mattie was in the head when a darkly drunk Del came in. He banged the door against the wall with his left shoulder, off-balance and irritable. Mattie looked over and nodded an acknowledgment. Del did his business, then stumbled to the sink. Mattie washed his hands and threw the paper towel he'd used in the trash.

As he left, Mattie said, "I saw Mr. Larsen. He got his phone from your car. Nice of you to get it back for him.

He said thanks."

Del's face went blank.

It was well past 2:00 a.m. The people were gone, the place was closed, and the manager was headed to his truck. Shiloh heard him start up and idle. She arranged her scarf around her neck, and realized the phone had a message as it vibrated in the bottom compartment of her purse. She pulled it out and looked, pressed the buttons with tired fingers, and put it to her ear. About halfway through the message, her eyes popped open wide. She took the phone away from her ear and pressed the button that replayed the message and listened again. Then she dropped her arm to her side, leaned against the building, and stared up into a starless sky. She'd been so absorbed that she was surprised to find herself alone in the dark parking lot. She hadn't even heard the manager's truck leave. Cold, she pushed herself off the building, lost in thought. The time had come for things to change. She shivered and felt uneasy when she realized why Del had been staring at her. She snapped out of herself and walked quickly to her truck.

With fingers stiff from the cold, she fumbled with the door lock. Without a sound, he grabbed her from behind. She let out a cry and swore, and dropped the keys and her purse as he whipped her around. He shoved her hard onto the hood. She was bent over, the side of her face pressed against the freezing-cold metal. His hand held her fast in the middle of her back, pinning her like a bug in a specimen frame. He pulled her jacket and shirt up her back and commanded her to undo her jeans. She recognized the voice, and her knees weakened with terror.

"Do it now."

Shiloh struggled. She tried to bend her knee to bring the heel of her boot up hard between his legs, but he was ready for her. He grabbed her by the hair, lifted her head, then slammed the left side of her face onto the hood so hard it stunned her and almost knocked her out. She groaned when he did it again. Her stiff fingers found the front of her jeans, but her hips were pinned hard against the front hood of the Toyota truck. He pulled her back off the hood so she could undo the top button.

Impatient, he grabbed the back of her jeans and pulled hard. The zipper didn't give, so he let her unzip them. She placed her hands and forearms against the front grille, hoping to somehow grab him hard and get away. She thought how best to hurt his dick if she could get a hold of it, maybe his balls...anything that was sensitive.

He ripped her pants down to below her knees and looked down at her ass in the half-light of the parking lot. He wanted to stare at it. It was perfect, and the finest ass he had ever seen. Better than in the magazines. He leaned in closer, his foul breath a ghastly cloud. "Hold still. Put your arms out on the hood."

She pulled her arms slowly, her fingertips touching the cold metal of the hood. He ran his hand over the right cheek of her naked ass. Shiloh shuddered from fear and cold. She heard him unzip and felt him fumble a bit, and in that second she put her palms back in a better-leveraged position and tried to push herself off the hood. He was ready for the try and shoved her hard a third time. Her left ear stung viciously from sharp contact with the hood. She felt bile backing up in her throat and the taste flooded her mouth. She hoped she wouldn't throw up.

He pressed himself against her and forced her arms above her head on the hood. "Move 'em again and see what that gets you."

Then she felt the head of his prick. It slapped at the back of her thighs and sluggishly grew harder as he rubbed himself on her. He slipped it up and down against the back of her thighs. He tried to force it between her legs, but she clamped them together as hard as she could to keep him out. He found this excited him, and he rubbed his swelling tip back and forth on her bare ass. It was hot against her cold skin, then she felt moisture tracking a pattern on her skin. She tried to struggle away from him and he spanked her hard. She screamed and he found the back of the scarf, which was wrapped around her neck, and pulled on it. She heard his breathing grow thick as he talked to himself. He tightened the tension gradually, arching her slender body against the hood and front end of the truck. She felt her throat constrict to the pressure. He reached around, held her against the truck, and forced a piece of the scarf into her mouth. He let her back down against the hood and gripped her reddened cheeks. Strangled pain welled up inside her. The bending her body was being forced to do took the air out of her. He released her so he could look down at himself in his own little bit of wonder, his stupid little island of pride.

"Damn, my cock looks huge on your fine ass. Do you

feel that, bitch? I can spank you with my dick. I see you walk this by me and now it don't matter, gonna get mine nice and tight."

He popped the head of his penis against Shiloh's exposed cheeks. He let go of the scarf, and pressed himself against her as he worked his prick in between her clamped legs…getting more excited as he did so. "You are going to let me in or I'll do ya dirty. You get me? Nod your head."

Shiloh nodded against the hood metal and said nothing. He stood up and she felt him grasp her ass and pull it open, and he freed his penis from her clamped thighs.

She struggled to free herself. She spat out the scarf and screamed, "NO!" She screamed it again and again.

But the Toyota gave him perfect leverage and he shoved his cock into her so hard that she screamed from the bottom of her throat. He lifted her off the ground with his first brutal thrust. The front of her thighs scraped the hard, top edge of the hood and hurt viciously. Del grabbed Shiloh by the top of her shoulders, pulled her back down so her feet touched the ground, and hammered into her over and over. The weak emergency brake shuddered, and the feeble, tired transmission gave way and the truck moved a fraction backwards with each assault. Each violent thrust brought descriptions from Del.

"Shut up, bitch, and take it. Goddamn…*agh, aghh. Oh yeah!*" he grunted into her.

He slid his hands down her arms, gripping them from behind and holding them like reins on a horse, using them like handles to get perfect leverage. Since Shiloh was so small, he had her more by the elbows than her wrists, and he managed to shuffle forward with each thrust as the truck gave millimeters of ground. Her shoulders ached in protest.

And then he came. And came and came. It was disgusting. She actually felt the burst inside her. She felt tears on her face and her cheek was wet from a small pool of her own saliva, blood, and tears mixed on the hood of the truck. He dribbled out of her and took a step back. She didn't move. Then, in a fit, he humiliated her by spanking her several times so hard that the sound of his flat hand on her skin echoed around the small parking area and off the back of the building. He hit and banged her battered hips and thighs against the truck. Numb as she was, it stung like hell, and she passed out. Her body crumpled and slumped down the front of the truck onto the broken pavement.

Del disappeared into the dark. Shiloh awoke in a panic a few minutes later and looked around. Terrified he'd come back, she lifted herself up onto her hands and knees, and rolled herself to one side of the pavement to pull her pants up. Before she could fasten them, she felt ill. Back on her knees, she retched on the ground and sobbed. She looked under the truck and saw where her keys and purse had fallen. She used the truck bumper, then the hood, to right herself, and she struggled to fasten her jeans. She thought she heard a car, scrambled for her purse and keys, got the fucking door open, and locked it behind her. Her body was badly bruised and her hand shook violently when she put the key in the ignition. Her mouth had stopped bleeding and she tried, without success, to ignore the wetness in her crotch. The truck needed to warm up enough to drive. She felt the moisture spread in her pants and knew she should be calm, but that was easier said than done.

THIRTY

Stiles and Ramos had covered a lot of ground in the dark. They were now in the opening to a small canyon, invisible from anywhere except directly overhead. The canyon was not deep, but the hillsides that formed it were steep enough that cattle preferred not to navigate them. Plus, as Stiles noted, there was still good enough forage on the lower part of the walls. They moved their horses up the canyon at a quick walk and spotted the first couple of cows about two miles in. They slowed to an easy walk to keep the cattle from spooking, maintaining as much distance from their sphere of influence as possible as they proceeded all the way up the canyon. Ramos was counting under his breath in Spanish. They hadn't made it quite all the way to the end of the canyon when Ramos grunted to Stiles, *"Toda aquí."*

Stiles turned and reversed direction, and the two riders spaced themselves out. They rode back down the canyon in the dark, and gathered cattle here and there. Ramos let out a short, soft whistle when one stuck. He removed the coiled rope that was tied to his saddle. With it in one hand, he lifted his arm and smacked the thigh of his rough-out leather chaps. The cattle formed up slowly. When an errant hoof hit a rock and made a thud, the closest cattle jumped sideways. It took an hour or more to gather, and Stiles checked them as best he could in the dark. He heard no sounds that made him think they were anything but healthy; there was no unusual coughing, and no obviously weak animals. They formed up well and as his eyes adjusted to their movements in the dark, his general impression of them was good, and he was glad of that. Trouble would only slow them down.

After an hour or so of gentle going, they saw the mouth of the canyon where the land opened up. By dawn, they had pushed the cattle to walk out a little more to cover a section where they were exposed. By midday, they were headed southeast toward the McDermitt Reservation and the meeting point in Nevada.

THIRTY-ONE

It was somewhere around 3:30 in the morning when Del pulled a warm beer from the pile of crap in his back seat, fishtail swerved to stay on the road, and popped the top. He drove out of Martin and had no other plan than to get that phone back. He drank. He drove, ignored his seatbelt, and convinced himself he was invincible. A legend in his own mind.

Hank had driven straight back to the ranch, Sonny's head in his lap the whole way. He parked the truck under a dilapidated wooden awning, bleached and aged from years and weather, attached to the old barn. He was not adept at newfangled things, computers and such, and he wondered, *What next?* He wasn't sure how to turn the phone on, let alone use it. All he knew for sure was that it was important to Del. And he was certain that somehow Del had had some responsibility in the disappearance of his herd last fall.

Hank looked out the windshield through the open end of the awning. Had it been light out, he'd have seen the hillside knoll where three generations of his family were buried. Then there was open land, which stretched as far as the eye could see, and it was beautiful country. But in the darkness with only a sliver of a moon, he saw only what the short, dim view his headlights provided. He had his memories, the old photo albums at the house, and his father's silver pocket watch. He sighed and looked down at the cell phone in his hand. He looked around the truck. No place there he wanted to hide it. He suspected that Matthew would say something to Del. Maybe not, but he guessed on the side of Del coming out there wanting the phone back. Where could he hide it so he could use it as leverage and get some version of the truth?

Hank got out of the truck. Sonny stood at the edge of the bench seat, and Hank helped him down. He closed the door to the truck, turned the flashlight on, and started toward the house. At the side door, Hank stopped. He looked at the potted plants his wife used to lovingly care for, and that funny ugly frog thing that she insisted stay in one particular spot. It was tucked back in between two clay pots that held only hard-packed dirt and decaying remnants of plants. He bent over and lifted it out of there, and turned it over. It was hollow. The heavy porcelain was cracked and chipped, and still held the awful green pigment as only that type of hideous garden art could. Hank put the flashlight on the porch rail, aimed where it would illuminate the bottom of the frog. He then pulled the phone from his pocket and tried to wedge it through the opening. At first, it wouldn't go, but he kept at it, changing the angle of attack until...yes! It went in and he could reach it with his fingers. He'd be able to get it out...good.

Flashlight in hand, Hank put the frog back exactly in its place. He noticed his hands had left marks, so he stepped off the porch, found a little handful of soft dirt, and went back to the frog and dusted it lightly. There— looked like it hadn't been touched in years. Then Hank turned and opened the door, and he and Sonny went into the kitchen/family room. He turned the old kerosene heater on and its tick-tick sounds and kerosene odor filled the kitchen end of the rectangular-shaped room. He set some kindling up and lit a fire. Sonny liked to sleep near the hearth and sat patiently next to Hank while he straightened his dog bed. Hank moved the bed off a little ways so the sparks didn't land on it, and placed the fireplace screen. Then, as the flames started to catch, Sonny settled on his bed and Hank lit the two lanterns on the old wooden table. He was fatigued, and the old sofa, with its shabby but neatly folded quilt, beckoned.

He sat at the table, stared into the flame of one of the lanterns, and took stock of his situation. The prognosis was grim. He was holed up in a house he no longer owned, and he was filled with a sense of foreboding. He looked over at Sonny, who watched him. Sonny would not shut his eyes until the old man was on the sofa, illuminated by the embers of the fire, and had fallen asleep. Sonny was the thread, the connection, Hank's reason for still doing anything; caring for him, sheltering him, looking after someone. Where had all the things he used to look after gone?

Del found the overgrown track that went out to what was once the Larsen ranch. The crooked, bank-owned For Sale sign was faded, its clarification crudely painted over with a large black X. Del turned down the track with only parking lights on, creeping along at a couple miles an hour. The track wound over low-lying hills, no more than bumps in a pasture. He didn't think the house was visible from the road. He took the last slug of flat beer and pitched the can out the window. The cold night air felt good on his face. He hit a deep pothole and all the garbage behind him heaved up and down noisily. "Fucking holes."

Del stopped when he saw the outline of a large building. It was an old hay barn. Didn't seem to be a main house, so he kept going. A fouled plug made the engine skip and it was running rough, at times threatening to die. Del coaxed it along until he was within sight of the main buildings and the house, then rolled backwards down the slope of the road to the lowest point and turned the engine off. Del opened the car door, and as he got out, some of the garbage from the back seat fell out onto the ground. He stepped over it and walked until he reached the crest of the rise, where he got a full view of the area. The cold wind hit him and he shuddered in his shirtsleeves. He stopped and looked back at his car, and wondered if he should get his jacket, but decided the cold kept him sharp. He walked toward the ranch house and Hank's truck.

THIRTY-TWO

None of this was real—a thin bedroll between him and the ground, his canteen for a pillow, the soothing sounds of Rio and the other horses nearby, and a partly cloudy sky overhead. C.J. never imagined he'd be where he was and that he'd be in search of stolen cattle. The night before, he felt sleep wouldn't come, but it did. The sound of Wyker's voice woke him in the predawn darkness, and he was surprised at how well he'd slept. Ground fog had moved into the low crevices of the surrounding area, and the dampness was everywhere.

Somewhere off to C.J.'s left, he heard Luis laugh. C.J. sat up, craned his neck to look, and said, "Huh?"

"You snore. Kept us all awake. Your horse too," Jorge teased.

C.J. muttered something that sounded like "bullshit," and rolled up his gear. Daylight was only promised, no light yet to the east, and he used his headlamp to do Rio's feedbag. For C.J., an energy bar and some water were breakfast. Coffee, though craved, was voted down as it would take time to make, and they needed to get going.

Luis had saddled up, his bedroll secure on the back of his saddle. As he checked his straps, he froze and listened. From somewhere nearby came a whinny. And then a few more. "Sounds like a band of wild mustangs."

C.J. turned off his lamp and looked in the direction of the sound. Rio stopped chewing and listened too. C.J.

204

wondered what he felt.

Put together and mounted up, the men made their way slowly down a steep hillside and across a wash. At the bottom, they maneuvered their horses and the dogs to go to the left along the gravelly bottom. They coordinated their wrist watches and separated. C.J. rode with Wyker, and Jorge with his father. C.J. and Wyker took both pack-horses so that Luis and Jorge could cover more ground. Wyker also cracked that C.J. and Rio needed practice po-nying. Both teams would skirt the Running Horse Ranch and would generally head southeast. They would meet at a prearranged location later in the day.

Wyker and C.J. rode single file with their packhorses in tow, and from behind C.J. asked what they'd do if they ran into anyone.

Wyker replied, "We'll deal with them."

Tammy trotted around the bunch grasses and rocks beside or behind the packhorses. Here and there, she'd jet ahead, wait, and fall in behind. The footfalls of the horses and the song of an early bird filled the dawn air.

THIRTY-THREE

Del found Hank's truck and crept along the driver's side and around the front, where he almost fell flat when he tripped over a pile of crap lying there. He reached down and steadied an old box so it didn't crash to the ground. Every footfall sounded loud, and he steadied himself with a hand on the cold metal of the hood. Images of Shiloh flashed through his mind. *Totally worth it,* he thought and he felt his nether parts stir at the fresh memory.

He shook that off and focused on the door handle on the passenger's side. As he pulled on it, its hinges screeched in protest and Del froze in horror. He heard nothing, so he pulled it open quick-like, and felt along the bench seat, the floor, and under the seat. Anything that wasn't the phone he tossed on the ground. Del ran a hand along the dash. Nothing. He dropped the visor—nothing there—and wished he had a flashlight. He touched the glove box latch. It opened easily and he emptied it. No phone. He reached across and searched the driver's side. He shifted more of his weight into the truck, and the truck's leaf springs groaned almost as loud as his heart thundered in his chest. Del willed himself to settle down, but considered the possibility that old Hank had a shotgun. He redistributed his weight, finished the search, and didn't find his cell phone.

Del eased himself out of the truck. Through an open

mouth, he sucked a gulp of cold air and looked around. He smelled rotted wood and stale hay. Out of curiosity, he lifted the edge of a small crate with the toe of his boot. Maybe he'd find the phone stashed underneath. A couple of critters scurried out and Del thought he'd have a heart attack, it startled him so. He dropped the edge of it with a thud. His head pounded, and a sheen of sweat formed along his temples and hairline. He pressed his palms against the old wood siding of the barn and forced himself to get a grip. He shut his eyes tight until it hurt, took several deep breaths, and felt the first bead of sweat let go down the side of his face. He wiped it away and slid between the truck and the barn wall. Exasperated, he walked purposefully to the house.

The old man lay on the sofa under a heavy quilt, his left arm under his neck and head. He'd been watching the fire slowly die. Its glow illuminated just the edge of Sonny's bed. He'd heard the noise outside, and guessed it to be somewhere near his truck. He watched Sonny sleep. Sonny's gray muzzle rested on his paws as he slept by the warm hearthstones of the fireplace. Time was Sonny'd be up barking his head off when he heard a stranger or animal outside. Hank loved to watch him sleep and have youthful dog dreams of the chase. Hank wasn't afraid, but he feared for Sonny. He knew that Del wouldn't find what he was looking for, and he'd be inside soon. Sonny didn't have the strength—maybe the will, but not the strength—to defend what was his. And Hank knew that he'd try. A heavy Maglite rested near his right hand and Hank hoped he'd get at least one good crack at the motherfucker. He knew he'd do anything to prevent Sonny from getting hurt.

There was a stepped landing by the door with empty clay pots piled to either side. The door wasn't locked, and Del shoved it open. The door hit something and bounced back and hit him, so he pushed it open again, swore, and held it to keep it open.

Hank smiled, knowing that door and how it hurt when it did that. Sonny was up on his feet and Hank hand-signaled the dog to stay. Sonny did as he was told, though every hair on his back was raised, his body tensed, and he growled. Slowly, Hank sat up, Maglite in his right hand, down out of sight. He figured to play like a sleepy old man, and draw Del close.

Del saw the table with its cards, scribbled lists, and Hank's maps. He said, "Been busy, have we? And you have something that doesn't belong to you."

Hank did not reply.

"You son-of-a-bitch, where is it?" Del barked hoarse-ly. He thought that what he heard inside himself, his own voice, was warped somehow. It was strangled by adrena-line, alcohol, and madness.

"I at least know who my mother was, Del, and she wouldn't take any sass from a common piece of crap like you. She'd-a met you at the door with the shotgun and shot you dead like the thievin' shit you are."

Del heard the growl by the fireplace before his eyes adjusted to the semi-darkness and he saw the animal crouched, ready to spring. He saw Hank signal him to hold back. Del moved to confront him and grabbed the old man's shoulder, but caught only layers of clothing. Hank's woolen shirt tore as Del hauled him off the couch.

The old man was skin and bones, and the force of the grab lifted him so easily that Del lost his balance. He'd expected some resistance, and it startled him. Hank used the force of being spun, every ounce of rage he possessed, and a well-timed swing of the heavy Maglite. It had perfect momentum and trajectory when it contacted Del's head. There was a sickening crack and the Maglite fell from Hank's hand.

Del's grip on Hank dropped as fast as Del's body did when it hit the floor. Hank whistled to Sonny and he launched with surprising speed and agility. He bit into Del's outstretched legs repeatedly, drawing blood with each strike, and snarling so fiercely that Hank was proud. Sonny's frenzy was backlit by the faint light of the fireplace. It cast a huge shadow and stretched the dog to demonic proportions. Del gripped his broken head, screamed, and kicked at the dog.

Hank made for the door and whistled for Sonny to break off and follow. Outside in stocking feet, he headed for his truck. He had no plan and he had no weapon. He heard a yelp from behind him and realized Sonny was not with him. A bloodied Del had come out the door with Sonny still on the attack. Del sent two vicious kicks to the dog's head and midsection. The second blow pitched old Sonny, rolling him off to the left, and he crashed into the pottery and debris. Next to the hideous ceramic frog was an overturned clay pot, which slid sideways and threatened to go off the lip of the step.

Hank turned and started back toward Del and Sonny. Hot with rage, he came at Del with balled fists. Del punched the old man and Hank doubled over and began to fall to the right.

Del grabbed him by the front of his torn shirt, pulled him up, and screamed into his face, "Where's the fucking phone!"

Hank had no air. Pain racked his skeletal frame, and the night swam bright sparkly flashes around him. But even in his old age he always could do one thing without thinking about it. In agony, he mustered one final act of defiance. He spat on Del. The disgusting projectile latched onto Del's gaping mouth and part of his chin, interrupting Del's screaming rant. There was a stunned moment and it was perfect. From the edge of consciousness, Hank smiled with bloodied teeth.

Disgusted and enraged, Del bellowed out guttural sounds that formed no words, and he hit Hank repeatedly. It was like hitting fragile glass ornaments from a holiday tree. Del's first blow caved in the old man's cheek and eye socket. The rest Hank never felt. When Del threw him down, he was dead.

Del staggered back a few steps, chest heaving from exertion and rage. He noticed that his hands hurt, the numbness from the cold not enough to quell the throbbing. Del turned quickly when he remembered the dog, but it was gone. Dazed, he wondered what time it was. He felt something trickle down his neck and he touched it and pulled his hand away. It was covered in blood. He fingered the area and found the source. Blood was pouring out of his ear. He turned all the way around and felt dizzy and sick. The sky in the east looked like dawn might be near. He looked at the body and shouted up into the heavens, "FUUCCKKK!"

He mumbled to himself and went back into the house to search it. He picked up the Maglite, and looked left and right for the fucking dog; he thought it might have retreated back inside. He checked twice, and then ransacked the place and didn't find the phone. Not knowing where the dog was made Del uneasy. His head hurt fiercely; a pain the likes he'd never felt before. And the blood was still coming. It soaked his shirt and he felt chilled.

His adrenaline gone, his defeat complete, he kicked over the kerosene heater and watched it leak fuel. He didn't know whether it would explode, so he scrambled out of the building. His head pounded something awful and blood from the blow crusted the side of his face.

"Goddamn Maglites," he muttered. The side of his head felt like shit, and the bites on his legs throbbed. Drying blood stuck the wounds to his pants, and the wounds pulled and tore open with each step.

Unsteady and dizzy, Del wondered about a concussion, or worse, as he walked past Hank's lifeless body. No sign of the dog. He guessed it had crawled off somewhere to die. He'd heard ribs crack when he kicked it. Every step toward his car was agony. He was numb from all that had happened, and it seemed to take forever to get to the car. His right ear rang, and he held it to make it stop. It didn't. He convinced himself his ear wasn't spewing as much blood as it was. He'd left his car door ajar, and the interior light had burned out. He opened the door wider and got in. He had to drive up near the house in order to turn around. As he approached the house, he saw flickering through the window. The house had caught fire.

Headlights swept over the inert form of the old man,

then the car accelerated down the little hill, gravel and dirt kicking a racket on the undercarriage. Del bounced uncomfortably in the seat as the car careened over the rutted road. The headlights were misaligned and dingy with dirt, but he was stunned to pick out the shape of a dog ahead of him. There was a bend in the track at the bottom of a low rise and there it stood, eyes reflecting red in the headlights. Like a devil out of the dark, it waited for him.

Del floored it and headed straight for the dog. Sonny seemed to be frozen in place until the last possible second, then he scooted away. Del wrenched the wheel sharply.

"Gonna run your ass down, you can't hi—"

And that was all he said. He'd focused so hard on the dog that he missed seeing the boulder. The dog's shadow passed between the car's headlights and the boulder—a big one, hood high—and Del accelerated hard into it.

The steering wheel fractured the front of his skull and formed a perfect impression on his forehead. When he stirred some minutes later, the world swam. One headlight cast its short beam on the high-desert scrub through steam rising from the wrecked front end. Del's door had popped open and he fell out onto the ground. He knew he had to get out of there, but he was badly injured. He felt panic and he used the left rear quarter panel to pull himself up. He weaved back and forth on uneven ground, and in the dark could barely see. He had walked about ten feet, which felt like a mile, when he heard something behind him. It was a growl.

Del panicked and tried to move faster, but tripped on something and fell over a small pile of painted rocks, put there long ago to delineate the edge of the track. His right temple hit the sharp corner of one of the rocks. Stunned, he lay on his side. Blood trickled into the dirt beneath him. He struggled to move as the life oozed out of him. His mouth gaped open. He tried to breathe as his body twitched and convulsed. Then he became aware of the dog close beside him. He could hear its ragged breathing, and he could do nothing about it. His eyes made out the dirty paws in the half-dark, and in the distance, he heard sounds of the burning house, which lit up the predawn sky.

Del's convulsions slowed but he still gasped for air. The dog turned and Del felt a tiny measure of relief. Perhaps he was too hurt to attack. Then he helplessly watched as Sonny lined himself up, balanced his broken body as best he could, lifted his leg, and peed on Del's bloody face and into his open mouth.

Dawn creased the sky. The sunbeams broke high through the lowest curves on the surrounding mountains, and penetrated the haze and smoke from the fire. It was so still, smoky ash bits hung in the air as Sonny's broken body made the half-mile journey back to the house. Every step was an effort. His head bobbed close to the ground as he made a beeline to his master's body. He sniffed and nuzzled the old man, then lay down next to him. He carefully put his head on Hank's chest, breathed deeply, and closed his eyes.

And that is where Spence Petersen found him an hour later. The sight of flames had alerted someone on the highway and Spence was first on the scene. He'd come across Del's body and the wreck first, then a mess of debris in the dirt and tire tracks he guessed would match Del's beater. Then he found Hank and Sonny.

There was no reason to check for a pulse. He removed his hat, held it over his heart, and said a prayer for them. He stood for a long time, then looked around, wiped his eyes, and fingered the brim of his hat. Finally, he put the hat back on and squared it evenly on his head.

The ranch house still burned in places. There was no one there yet to put it out, and Spence walked over to what was the door. It amazed him that the frame of the door still stood, charred, but intact. The concrete step was uncharred and Spence saw the shattered pottery. He saw one piece had survived—an ugly green frog—and it was upside down. On an unexplained impulse, he bent down to right it, and when he lifted it up, he found a cell phone inside. It was in perfect condition, unharmed from the night's events. Spence didn't touch it, he just stared down at it.

Spence replaced the frog as he had first found it, walked to his car, got his camera out, and retrieved his evidence kit from the trunk. He carried both back to the porch and photographed the frog, the phone, the area. Then he used a gloved hand to retrieve the cell phone and seal it in an evidence bag, and wrote the particulars on the label. He was about to put the bag into his kit when he stopped and rolled the phone around inside the bag. He knew that Hank didn't have a cell phone, and he wondered what this phone was doing there. It occurred to him that he'd seen Del with a similar make and model the other day by the side of the road. He put the bag in his kit. His mind was putting together a theory, one that provided a motive for Del coming out there. He couldn't be sure about the phone being Del's, but in that moment, it was what he suspected.

He stood up and rested the camera in the crook of his arm. He approached Hank's body to photograph the scene and it wrenched at his heart. He knelt beside them and looked at Sonny's peaceful face. Had he not known better, he'd think he was sleeping. Spence ran a light hand over the cold fur on the dog's head and said, "Good boy, Sonny."

THIRTY-FOUR

Carson looked at herself in the mirror in her old bedroom. She wore the jeans she'd worn in high school, boots she loved to ride in, a shirt she'd not seen in years, and one of her mother's warm riding jackets. She felt like the lost little girl she was. She turned to see herself from the side with a critical eye to detail, and considered how much it showed. She felt hollow inside, but the outside seemed redeemable. She grabbed her hat off the bed and a pair of warm leather gloves, adjusted the bandana at her throat, and skipped down the stairs.

She stopped at the bottom and cocked her head to look back at the stairs. She used to come down the stairs that same way when she was little. She could hear the echo of her father's voice saying, "That girl simply don't know how to walk down the stairs."

Kitzie heard her and asked, "You ready?"

Carson said yes and turned for the door, stopped, and added, "Dad always said, 'The best thing for the inside of a person is the outside of a horse.'"

From the mudroom, Kitzie smiled as she watched her daughter walk toward the barn, the dogs running ahead of her.

Inside the barn, the smell of horses, dust, sweat, and leather filled Carson's nostrils and she breathed it in as she walked past rows of stalls. Some of the happiest times of her life had been spent in this building. The barn was quiet now, not like it was when she was a kid, when it was a show barn. She'd watched the grown-ups busy with horses every day. Live-in rigs were parked for weeks at a time and there was a constant hum of energy. Training schedules were on everyone's mind and timelines between shows. It was either get ready to go on the road or unpack from being on the road.

Carson walked into the tack room where the warm smell of leather surrounded her. She walked directly to a three-tiered rack, uncovered the saddle on the middle rack, and knew before she touched it that it was her saddle. It was a good, working, custom-made ride with bucking rolls, turned leathers, and broad, flat stirrups. She uncovered her old friend and ran her hand over the leather seat. Carson knew the stirrups were her length, and that no one had ridden in it. She could also tell someone had been keeping the saddle clean and well cared for. She turned and met her mother's eyes. Kitzie had watched silently and said nothing.

Kitzie joined Carson and smiled when her daughter lifted the snaffle bit rig down from its hook, and her favorite mecate, precisely where she'd left it. Even the drool straps were clean and cared for. She found the matching breast collar and went to the saddle pad rack. She looked through them; there were two, and each held about five clean pads. "Dad was a fanatic about clean gear, especially pads," she murmured to herself.

She hauled the saddle off the rack and put it near the tie rail. Then she went back for her pad, collar, and bridle. In the corner, she spotted her old chinks, and her heart leaped. The leather belted part still fit her across her hips and she wrapped the rough leather around her legs, doing up the two buckles at the back of each leg that held them securely across her thighs. Three inches of leather fringe cut along the outside and bottom edges, and stopped just below her knee.

"I remember these. Loved them." Then to her mom, she said, "So, what's up with the calves?"

Kitzie said they'd have to go see, and grabbed a rope halter. She got one of her favorite geldings, pointed Carson to the bay mare next to him, and they saddled up. Outside, Kitzie checked her cinch and climbed into the saddle. She adjusted her rope reins and looped the mecate under the leather belt at her waist. She set it so it had a nice length to the bit and was looped properly under the belt. Comfortable, she watched Carson mount up for the first time in more than ten years. It was good to see. Carson settled, picked the reins up off the horn, and dallied the mecate several loops around it. Kitzie looked at her daughter and smiled.

"You look better than I thought you would up there. Let's go."

They moved off at an easy walk toward the big covered arena. Kitzie side-passed to the gate, opened it, and they both went in, the sounds of their movements echoing off the high roof. The bars and tresses with the skylights filled the space over their heads, like pick-up sticks holding the world up. Carson moved off to the center and walked some circles to get her "feel" back. She stopped and backed a few paces, then opened the horse's shoulder and moved off in the opposite direction, soft and easy. She walked a larger diameter circle that put her along the walls, then did the same maneuver. She felt the lightness she wanted and smiled. Then she backed a few steps, opened the shoulder, turned her mare, and repeated this in both directions. The horse moved easily, and Carson said, "Very nice. I'll bet she's awesome on cows."

She loped some circles and did a couple of stops on the mare, and it felt wonderful. She appreciated the pair of tracks the mare laid with her hind feet. Carson then rode over to the trailer that was parked nearby, and along its forty-foot length she peered as best she could into dirty windows. Seeing nothing, she moved off toward the gate.

Her mother said, "Shall we?"

Carson waited patiently to hear the gate close, and for the first time in a long while she felt herself breathe. She looked down at her hands and at the reins that rested gently on the mare's neck. She took her finger and traced the raw leather rigging that came up from the saddle and wrapped around the base of the horn—something the saddle makers did to accommodate the friction of a dallied lariat. She smiled to herself, rested her gloved palm over it and turned toward her mother as she came even with them. The earth crunched under their horses' hooves as they rode off to check on the first pasture of calves.

The cows had been divided into two groups, and Kitzie and Carson rode to the closer of the two. Carson was glad for her shearling leather coat, and noticed her mother had her chinks on—her *chinkaderos*, though she called them her "brush-poppers." A breeze blew one of the gates around as she opened it from atop her horse. The mare was very responsive to Carson's legs, and she side-passed easily to hold the gate open for Kitzie.

"Damn, she's nice, Mom," Carson said as she stroked the mare's neck.

"Glad you like her. She's a favorite of mine too. Heck, they all are. Wyker brought a couple with him that'll take some getting used to. One we had to pull out of a creek."

"No shit? Which creek?"

"This one. She got cast down over there in a heavy rain. What a mess. Cast herself good, in high water, and it took some doing to save her. After I sent the probation idiot off, it has been an interesting time for Wyker's friend I think."

Carson remembered Wyker dimly and from a child's perspective. She knew he was a good friend of the family.

"Who's the friend?" she asked absently, not really caring, more for harmless conversation than anything else.

Kitzie moved her horse up to a jog, which Carson matched for speed and tempo.

Kitzie raised her voice to say, "Seems Will has taken to helping more than just troubled horses. The guy's C.J. Not unattractive, but very guarded, stand-offish. He's Australian, and was one of the inmates in the wild horse program Will ran in Colorado."

Carson giggled and Kitzie shot her a look.

Carson said, "Is that a pun?"

Kitzie shook her head but smiled anyway.

The inmate part piqued Carson's curiosity. "A felon? Here? Really? You surprise me, Mom."

Kitzie nodded. "Yeah, Wyker surprised us both. He brought a horse for him, a big range mustang, gelded late and super tough."

They reached the lip of the creek and made their way

down. Their horses' feet clipped rocks in the muddy bed, then the horses bounded up the opposite bank. Ten minutes later, they went through another gate, this one requiring Kitzie to dismount to open. The calls of the cows were close, and Kitzie scanned the surrounding area before she got back on her horse. A short distance away, they saw a cow standing a solitary vigil over the lifeless body of her calf.

THIRTY-FIVE

Wyker led the way along a deer track that skirted the rim of a low canyon. They went along a rock face and saw pictographs, which Wyker said dotted the whole area. He also pointed out a few petroglyphs and explained to C.J. that they were carved, while pictographs were painted. C.J. wondered how the "paint" they used was made, and still visible after all this time. Wyker told him about anthropologist Luther Cressman, who had explored the country and identified numerous sites with both paintings and carvings.

C.J. was fascinated by the images of spirals and concentric circles that then developed into some kind of man/bird creature with spread wings. He saw two of these, and though faded with time, it was clear what they were.

"Isn't it odd that an Indian artist would come out to this desolate place and make these images?" he asked, but he hadn't noticed that Wyker was way ahead and didn't hear him. C.J. pressed Rio into a jog to catch up, the lead line of his packhorse stretched taut across his thigh for the first few paces until the horse moved with them.

At a good vantage point, Wyker paused and pulled out his binoculars again. Earlier they'd seen some dust and thought maybe it was the herd, but it was only a few wild mustangs and a couple of deer. Wyker dismounted and handed his horse to C.J., who asked again, "Those drawings on the rocks, why out in the middle of nowhere?"

With his binoculars up and focused, Wyker scanned the horizon. "I'm not sure. They probably followed food."

He turned and put the binoculars back in their protective covering and remounted. He moved Johnny off with his legs, packhorse in tow, his rope mecate loosely draped on his horn. Hands free, he put his gloves back on as Johnny took care not to step on Tammy.

C.J. appreciated Wyker's easy style of riding. His horses were always relaxed, willing, and ready to go if the need arose. He wanted to emulate Wyker, but he'd get ahead of himself and wind Rio up without meaning to. He watched Wyker and noted how the animals responded to his energy and consistency.

By noon, they'd found a spot to water the horses and eat. Wyker drew a map in the sandy ground of where he thought they were and where he hoped Luis and Jorge were. He decided they'd skirt closer to the Running Horse Ranch. He sent C.J. east into a short canyon that divided a half-mile up. Wyker had seen signs that cattle had been through the area, and he checked a few canyons on the opposite side. After finding only signs of past activity, the men reunited and rode on.

From afar, a man watched the riders split apart and disappear into the short canyons. The black horse behind him stood untied. Not much to look at; he was lean, shaggy, and had an old cavalry saddle on his back. The leather was worn, oiled, and tough. There was a rope rein attached to a braided noseband, which was held in place by a thread of a headstall, no bit in the horse's mouth and no metal parts on the bridle. As the rider knelt, hat in hand, the two blended perfectly with the surrounding rocks. He wasn't an old man. He wore his black hair long, and around his neck was a thin leather thong with a green stone hanging from it. His forefinger and thumb rubbed it out of habit. He had a narrow, symmetrical face and full lips, which were pursed in concentration. Below his piercing brown eyes were two horizontal black lines tattooed on his skin; tribal symbols that stretched straight across his cheekbones.

He had been following the four horses and the one dog since these two had split from the other two. He was glad the two herding dogs had gone with the other men. He watched them join back up and waited until they moved off out of sight. He knew where they were and which way they would go, and he knew they all followed the same quarry.

THIRTY-SIX

Kitzie rode to the cow and dismounted. The cows held their ground, then moved off a few feet. They were puffed-up, facing the approaching threat with calls and bellows. The calf was cold and stiff, and there were no marks on the body to indicate that it had been taken down by a predator, but its leggy body was skeletally thin. Kitzie looked it over, and then mounted her horse and they rode on. They found two more dead calves, and then came upon a live one that was very weak and sickly, eyes sunken with dehydration. Kitzie got off again and moved slowly, and scooped her arm firmly around its chest. She checked him over, then picked him up and carried him to Carson. Carson cradled him over her saddle with one arm.

"Scours," Kitzie said as she turned and led her horse toward a group of bushes. "The stress of the cold and wet weather, plus fighting muddy conditions must have weakened their immune systems. Interrupted the nursing frequency enough that they developed diarrhea."

On the other side of the bushes, another couple of cows and sick calves huddled together. Carson walked her horse forward slowly. Kitzie caught another weak calf and lifted it as gently as she could up onto her horse. She held it in place and remounted. Once in the saddle, she maneuvered the calf and cradled it in front of her in a similar position as Carson had done. They counted five more sick calves from their vantage point, then headed back to the Three Bit.

There was little conversation on the ride back. Carson concentrated on keeping the calf as comfortable in her arms as she could, and on riding her horse. It had been a long time, and she knew she'd be sore the next day.

After they arrived at the gate to the barn and had passed through it, Kitzie leaned over and reached down to latch it. "I hope Luis's cousin knows we're back, we're gonna need—"

She never finished the sentence. The calf suddenly launched up, legs flailing out of her grasp at the perfect moment. Her horse felt the commotion and moved the other way as she tried to hang on to the calf. The calf's front hoof swung wide and laid a hard scrape to her cheek, just missing her eye. She swung her head to avoid full contact, but that threw her even more off-balance. Both Kitzie and calf came off the horse and fell to the wet ground. The horse pranced to avoid stepping on anyone, Kitzie swore, the calf bellowed, and the horse shied. Then it was quiet. The calf tried to run off, but confused and alone, it stopped.

"Are you okay?" Carson asked, trying to balance her calf and calm her own anxious horse.

Kitzie tried to get up. Her right knee immediately gave way and she cried out in agony. The muddy welt on her face began to bleed in earnest. Lupe came running from the barn door as Kitzie cried out, "Oh, shit! My knee! Shit!"

The calf stood nearby on wobbly legs, bleating for a mother that wasn't there. Kitzie's horse stood trembling a few paces beyond, the rope rein hanging around his neck unevenly, one side glancing the ground. Carson hoped he wouldn't put a leg through and get fouled. She motioned for Lupe to take her calf.

"Wait here, Mom, and don't move. I'll go get the ATV," she said, then galloped her horse into the barn through the open breezeway. She hastened to unbridle the mare and put her, still saddled, in a stall. As she started the ATV and drove back to the pasture, she hoped the mare wouldn't try to roll.

After Lupe helped move Kitzie onto the flatbed part of the ATV, he lifted the calf nearby and handed it to her. Carson picked up the other one and they drove into the barn. The gelding walked there on his own. Lupe unsaddled both horses and fed them. Then he put the calves together in a stall, turned the heat lamps on, and set to feeding them.

Carson covered Kitzie with a blanket and put a saddle pad behind her mother's back to make sitting in the ATV more bearable. She called Urgent Care from the office, and it was quickly determined that she'd take Kitzie there immediately. Kitzie sat with her leg elevated and an ice pack on her knee while she waited for Carson to bring the truck. Kitzie's face was wooden. She didn't relish the idea of the bumpy ride to the hospital, but there it was.

Carson and Lupe loaded Kitzie into the truck, and she barked instructions as Lupe closed the door. Carson turned the key in the ignition, and Kitzie rolled the window down and added, "We'll have to get set up to treat and care for as many calves as we can bring here."

Lupe nodded and watched them pull away.

Carson's mother turned the flood of instructions in her direction as Carson maneuvered the truck to avoid the ruts and divots in the road. "When Wyker checks in, we need Luis and Jorge back here, and we'll call the Running Horse; ask them if they can send a couple guys to help bring calves in. We'll have to monitor the calf crop closely over the next week to ten days. We have to be aware of any other potential problems that could arise."

One line of holes was unavoidable. Kitzie tried to protect her leg and stifled a cry. "Oh shit, I've really done it this time."

The closest urgent-care facility was almost a two-hour drive away, near Burns. There wasn't anything in Martin. Once there, the medical staff stabilized the leg with a brace, did x-rays, and determined there were no breaks. They were fairly certain she'd need surgery, but that could wait a few days. Kitzie was grim at the diagnosis and expressed her frustration that the problem couldn't be fixed immediately.

Carson drove them back to the Three Bit well past midnight. She settled Kitzie on Tuff's old recliner in the living room. She gave her some pain medication, the TV remote, made her a hot chocolate, and watched her until she fell asleep.

Carson was hungry and went into the kitchen. She washed her hands and considered what to eat. Looking out the kitchen window, she saw a flashlight coming toward the house. It was Lupe, and he asked after her mom. Carson put her finger to her lips and they lowered their voices. She filled Lupe in and asked him how the calves were. He told her he was sorry but one had died. The other was holding on for the moment.

Lupe hadn't eaten either, so Carson whipped up two sandwiches, grabbed some water, some paper towels, and they headed back to the barn, eating as they went. Lupe had made a bed out of straw for the calf and it lay there, half asleep, under the heat lamps. Carson put half her sandwich on the desk in the tack room and grabbed a stethoscope. The calf's condition was marginal, and she reassured the little guy as best she could. She cleaned his raw behind with warm water, dried it gently, and applied the veterinary equivalent of Desitin ointment. She rehydrated him by injecting subcutaneous fluids. Carson made a mental note to get more lactated ringers saline from the vet, and to consult him about the use of antibiotics if signs of systemic infection developed.

She bottle fed the calf and sat in the hay with the little guy's head in her lap, her back against the makeshift fencing, and gently stroked his soft fur. He fell asleep shortly before she nodded off.

Carson was startled awake by Lupe shaking her shoulder. He told her the guys from the Running Horse were pulling in.

"What time is it?" she asked, wondering who had called them.

He said almost six, and she looked at the sleeping calf.

"He seems to be okay for now," Carson observed.

The throaty rumble of a big V8 turned Carson's attention from the calf. She left the makeshift hospital ward and walked to the barn door. The truck was quite fabulous, and obviously the creation of someone who loved mechanics. That it was dusty was a compromise to working in the environment. The exhaust tailpipe had a chrome end the size of a one-pound coffee can, and it had a manual transmission, no wimpy automatic sounds. A black-diamond metal frame rose from the back window of the extended cab, and she could just see around that to where a tricked-out quad with a matching wagon was tied down on a flatbed trailer.

The truck pulled up near the house and men in cowboy hats got out and went to the door. The one who knocked respectfully removed his hat, and when there was no answer, turned to see Carson coming from the barn.

The older of the men, a headman named Joe, made quick introductions. He directed the others to offload the gear and asked if they could use a ranch horse. "Ray there's one of our best colt starters, so you needn't be concerned for your stock, ma'am."

Carson smiled at his polite formality, and said, "I have a ride for him."

Just then another truck came into the yard. It was a man from Martin's Ranch Supply and he'd brought supplies for the nursery. Carson put them in the barn and saw that the ranch hands were all ready to go. She went to the house, Wyatt and Lulu running alongside, and checked on her mom.

"Did Lyle send what we need?" Kitzie said.

Carson nodded and rummaged in a pocket for a stretchy to hold her hair in a ponytail. She was sort of glad she hadn't had to go into town for the supplies. She still felt more than a little embarrassed about her performance the other night. "Yes, and he had some sad news. Old Hank Larsen is dead. Said his body was found outside his house and the house burned down."

Kitzie looked stricken. "Oh, no. What happened?"

"Not sure. Sheriff's out there investigating, and there may be another body, found on the road going out to his place."

Kitzie looked incredulous. "Two bodies? You're kidding."

Carson looked at the gloves in her hand, turned the soft leather over and over, and said no. She looked at Wyatt and Lulu curled up on the floor next to the recliner. "Three if you count Sonny, he was found next to Mr. Larsen."

Kitzie needed pain medication. Carson helped her to the bathroom, which unleashed a diatribe from her ferociously independent mother. While she was in the restroom, Carson got the meds, a large carafe of water, and a glass. She then helped her back to the chair. Kitzie asked Carson to set a small pillow under the damaged knee, and winced at the realignment. Once that was done, Carson suggested she eat.

"No food, not hungry," Kitzie snapped.

"Come on, Mom, you should eat something. Some broth maybe? Oh, the guys from the Running Horse are here. I didn't call them, did you?"

"Yeah, I called them last night from Urgent Care while you parked the truck. You go; I can manage."

Carson was hesitant to ride out to get more calves and leave her alone, but her mother waved her off and she started to go, but then stopped and asked about Jorge and Luis.

Kitzie told her, "I changed the message on my phone,

in case I missed their call, which I did. They left a message. They're on their way back." She picked at the coverlet absently. "The cows are probably gone. Maybe they'll all come back. I don't know."

Carson let it go. There was no answer to the speculation. She went to talk to the guys from the Running Horse.

They had off-loaded one heck of a monster ATV. It looked like it could scale walls, and it had a custom trailer it towed.

"That's amazing. We can bring back a small herd," Carson said. "My dad would've loved this. He always said V8s made this country great. Nice truck."

They told her they hunted, were proud of the rig, and her understanding of it held her higher in their regard. The conversation was brief, as Carson began to shiver in the early morning cold. She dashed back to the house to get an extra-warm coat and insulated powder pants.

Kitzie laughed when she saw her. "Don't want to be a wuss out there and get cold. That ought to do." She went on to say she'd call the vet and make arrangements for him to visit, and before Carson left, she heard her mom on the phone.

Carson rode in the ATV with an experienced wrangler named Jim, and one other guy whose name she missed. The third wrangler rode one of the Three Bit Ranch horses, which Lupe had saddled for him. They made good time going back out, surveyed the whole pasture, and got a rough count of the sick calves. There were fifteen in all, and of those, they decided two were too far gone and were put down to end their suffering.

The trailer had sides that were removable, and tall enough that the calves couldn't climb out even if they had been healthy enough to do so. A layer of straw lined the floor and the calves huddled together in it. The ride back was bumpy, and it was late afternoon when they finally came through the last gate.

The calves were unloaded and put together in a stall. The wranglers wasted little time with farewells. They loaded their rig back on its trailer, and they were gone.

Carson checked on Kitzie and found her half asleep. She asked her mother when she'd last taken anything, if she was in pain, and if she wanted anything.

Kitzie said, "I called the vet. He's on his way."

Carson went to the kitchen, dogs in tow, made some strong coffee, and fed the dogs some kibble. She carried a steaming mug back to the barn, and willed the coffee to take her fatigue away as they began to evaluate the calves.

Warm water sloshed against the sides of a metal bucket Lupe brought her. As Carson dipped a soft terry washcloth into the warm liquid, she inhaled the herb-tinged wisps of steam that came off the surface. Her hands felt a little slippery through the surgical gloves when she squeezed the excess liquid out. Carefully, she lifted the tiny tail of one of the calves and applied the towel to moisten the hardened bits of diarrhea. The warmth and moisture of the towel softened the caked-on mess, and Carson held it there until the hairs pulled apart easily and the area could be cleaned. The calf winced briefly and let out a soft mewing sound. They all needed subcutaneous hydration, they were too thin, and she was thankful that Lupe was mixing up some formula. The thought of a hot shower faded from her mind with the sound of the veterinarian's diesel truck idling outside the barn doors.

Miles away, Wyker and C.J. set up camp in a cluster of rocks on the lee side of a low hill. The rocky terrain formed a kind of stone "fort" that surrounded them, and Wyker felt comfortable making a small fire. Their dinner of stew came in foil pouches, easy to heat, and C.J. was careful not to puncture them as he set them on the fire.

At the prearranged time, Wyker walked off to find a good cell phone signal and called Luis and Jorge. When he returned, he and C.J. sat by the fire, ate, and discussed the day.

"They checked out a sheltered canyon that was freshly grazed and trampled. Could'a been where someone hid some cows. Might'a been Three Bit cattle holed up there, but it got too late to follow the trail."

Wyker stared into the fire. Nearby, the horses munched from grain bags over their muzzles, and Tammy lay dozing next to Wyker with her head on her paws.

"There's something else," he added. "They got word from Three Bit that Kitzie's been hurt and there's a situation. They've gone back."

"What happened?" C.J. asked as he swallowed the last of his dinner.

Wyker relayed the situation as he knew it, and C.J. asked a few questions about the problem with the calves.

"Are we going back too?"

Wyker stirred the fire and then threw the stick into it. It was a pleasant little fire; it would probably rain tomorrow, and he said they had better enjoy this. "No. We go on after the cows."

C.J. nodded, satisfied that the adventure would continue, and he asked who Carson was.

"She's Tuff and Kitzie's only kid, grown now, doubt I could pick her out of a crowd. Never was told what exactly happened between her and her folks, but she bailed and hasn't been back in years. Seems she's there now." He stroked Tammy's head. She shifted onto her side and stretched her legs straight. At the apex of the stretch, her feet trembled, then she relaxed with her head alongside Wyker's leg. "Luis said they called the Running Horse for some help." He stopped talking and lifted his head as coyotes howled somewhere off in the distance.

"I like the sound of those guys," C.J. said, then added, "dingoes make a kind of sound, can't say it's like that, but not so different."

The coyotes went silent and the men waited to hear more. After a few moments, it seemed they'd moved on, and Wyker added, "What's C.J. stand for?"

C.J. let it hang, and hoped if he didn't respond it would go away. "Does it matter?"

Wyker looked at him with an incredulous expression on his face. "Come on, really? It's a secret?"

"Shit, I never say." C.J. didn't look at Wyker but felt the stare. "Besides, it adds to my rep of bein' kinda mysterious."

Wyker laughed out loud. C.J. had a hard time not laughing at it too, but he held his ground.

"Just making conversation. Never mind."

"Fine. Talk about something else. What's our plan for tomorrow?"

Wyker said they'd head to that canyon, try to determine how many riders and how many cows. "Then track 'em…if it's them." He paused. "That okay by you, mate?"

Wyker said the "mate" part with as much of a bullshit Australian accent as he could muster. It sounded awful. C.J. couldn't help himself. He laughed.

In the dark canyon that Luis had described, the horse followed the man like a dog. A new moon lay on its back, and stars sparkled. Nearby, a coyote called and the man smiled. He straightened and rubbed the turquoise that hung around his neck. He reached into the leather bag slung across his chest and pulled out a piece of jerky.

The wind rustled bits of dried stuff across the ground. He adjusted an oil-sealed Outback hat. The design was such that water didn't find a path down his back, and rain was coming. He mounted, turned the horse with his legs, and retraced his way back down the canyon. He followed the tracks of the two horses and the thirty-plus head of cattle.

The air was cold, but he was warm enough in a wool coat and scarf, his long, black hair tucked into his collar. He sucked on the jerky, swallowed the juices, and drank some water from a skin that hung from the horn of the old saddle. The black horse traveled easily, head level, and to the casual eye might look like he was asleep. One might've taken the condition of the horse as underfed or weak, but he was sure-footed, and he walked straight and steady through the most uneven and unfriendly ground, barefoot, no horseshoes. The man would have no finer horse under him than this.

They walked in the dark down the slope of a canyon until it opened up to a flat, scrubby stretch of bleak, high desert with few trees. He looked up at the stars and began to hum a tune his great-uncle would sing when he'd smoke and tell stories of his ancestors. The stars twinkled and disappeared into a patch of ground fog that swallowed them.

Well ahead of the man, Stiles and Ramos covered the ground they knew well. They stopped only to let the cattle drink. Stiles pushed harder than usual and Ramos noticed it. Ramos considered asking about it but suspected Stiles had no intention of saying anything. Stiles figured the hoary old Mex felt things were different this time, and there was no point in chatting it up. Ramos shifted his big knife and became extra vigilant. Stiles rode on silently, thinking about calling Shiloh, but he knew he had to wait.

As dawn broke, Wyker and C.J. saddled up and moved

out of the rocks. It began to rain lightly. It took a couple hours to get to the general area where they thought the canyon was. Wyker no longer considered how C.J. and Rio were going—no need to. The ground was rough and it took a while to traverse back and forth down the steep scree to get to where they picked a path toward the mouth of the canyon. They spread out to scan more ground and found what they were looking for.

Wyker drank some water, wiped his mouth, and noticed something on the ground a little off to the left. Wyker nodded to C.J. and dismounted. "That's odd."

"What?" C.J. asked as Wyker remounted.

Wyker looked around. He checked for places with good vantage points. "Not sure yet. Looks like another horse was here. I dunno, but I think we have company." He looked around again and shook it off. "You up to moving out some? Time to catch up."

C.J. answered by taking the lead. Wyker caught up, and the ground opened up and the going got easier. Wyker passed Rio and set a good-paced trot, which morphed into an easy lope. The leaden gray sky stretched flat from the earth, and the horses felt heavy, as if the clouds pressed them down. The ponied horses dragged, and there was no float in the lead ropes. It took a while for them to free up.

C.J.'s face was locked in concentration and the pannier rattled with each stride. He checked his mecate, shortened it, and redallied it at the lope. Tammy ran out ahead, then circled back and took up a spot on the other side of the riders and pack horses to be sure her "herd" was together, then she'd jet out ahead again. The ground dictated the pace. They loped some and jogged some. This went on for two hours, then they walked the horses down and stopped near a creek bed. They let them catch more air before allowing them water, and then water only sparingly. They checked the gear and tightened anything that had become loose. The hair was thick on the horses' bellies and their necks were tagged with dampness. They rested long enough for them to get their wind back.

C.J. knelt and splashed some water on his face. It washed away the clinging strands of the night. He looked up at Wyker and frowned. "Kinda nerves me we're being watched."

Wyker looked at him and talked to C.J.'s back as C.J. mounted Rio. He handed C.J. the lead rope of his packhorse. "Me too."

They moved off and continued to follow the trail laid by the herd.

THIRTY-SEVEN

In a light but steady rain, Wyker and C.J. followed the trail for most of the day. C.J.'s packhorse had gotten crabby and repeatedly tried to pick an argument with Rio. C.J. adjusted what was going on and Wyker let it be. He watched C.J. read both horses, anticipate behavior, and change it up before anything happened.

The herd's trail was fresh and they crossed a broad valley area. It wasn't much in the way of cover, and they surmised that the rustlers had made a point of getting across it before dawn. A coyote gave them a brief, indifferent look before it slipped into the low brush. A crow flapped heavily past them, landed on a tall boulder, and cawed loudly as they passed.

Partway across the valley, they found an older two-track, which the rustlers had made wise use of. But then they branched off in a southerly direction when the track veered northeast. The men rode quietly without much to say, and a bitter wind came up. The rain eased to a steady drizzle, and in the distance, the skirts of a mountain range layered bare and gray-blue.

At one point in the valley, there was a rise of land, like a bump under a carpet, and a deer path wound around the side. On top of it stood a lone tree, its weathered, bare branches angled awkwardly against unseen forces. Wyker left C.J. with the packhorses and loped to its crest to take a look with the glasses. Tammy ran with him. As Wyker left, the horses moved around and bumped against each other with separation anxiety, which C.J. managed. It was fine and he relaxed, rested his elbow on the saddle horn, and waited.

Some minutes went by, and he turned when he thought he heard Wyker. And that's when it all went wrong. Hooves nervously shuffled, ears pinned, teeth were bared, and the horses went at each other's faces.

"Easy, easy there!" C.J. said as he took a tighter hold of the ropes.

Rio backed off. He wanted no part of an argument that wasn't his, and neither of these underlings wanted to take him on. They avoided him, but not each other. The two ropes slid through C.J.'s gloved hand and he barely managed to hang on to the leather tails at the ends. In doing so, C.J. stretched out at an odd angle in his saddle. One of the ropes wrapped around the front leg of Wyker's packhorse, and while he was a seasoned horse, instinct told him he was under attack. When he shied to avoid the open mouth of the other horse, it caused the rope to bite and burn. Then he stepped on it with his other foot, trapped himself, and panicked. He reared and flipped over onto his back, and the leather-tipped rope zipped from C.J.'s glove. The smell of hot leather sent up a whiff of smoke, and he was grateful it wasn't his skin. The packhorse struggled to his feet. At the same moment, Rio had had enough of the nonsense and he sent a vicious bite to the rump of the troublemaker. Rio's teeth scraped a swath of hair off the rump of the instigator, laid skin bare, and blood bubbled from a thousand yanked hair follicles. The horse let out a squeal.

"Shit! No, no! Whoa, easy, mates!" C.J. desperately tried to grab at the loose rope, and in the process, lost the other one.

Rio reared up and turned away in midair to avoid them. They bumped into him, tangled, and bounced apart. C.J. laid his reins on Rio's neck to finish the turn. He was relieved they hadn't been bowled over, and he looked over his shoulder in dismay as the two packhorses departed the scene quickly. C.J., half unseated, gathered the reins and focused on rebalancing. He slipped off Rio's back and managed to hang on to him with the twelve-foot mecate lead, which he'd had looped under his belt. As it came free, he caught it in his hand and went with his horse. He sent Rio around him from the ground and settled him. As he did, he heard the two packhorses as they continued to fight. They bumped each other and one kicked out at his adversary with a rear hoof. Helpless to do anything but watch them, an adrenaline rush swept up from somewhere below his knees. The sensation flooded his innards and he tasted bile. His hands leaned on his knees and he lowered his head until the fog cleared. He felt movement next to him and he came up a little too fast. It startled Rio, his head jerked, and he backed off a fast few steps.

C.J. saw Wyker, elbow on the horn, surveying the trail of gear on the ground, and he didn't look pleased. Tammy sat calmly by his side.

"I can't leave you alone for a minute," he said.

Rio's ears flicked between Wyker, the departed horses, and C.J. C.J. picked up his hat and brushed it off. He looked down at it, then approached Rio, ran his hand along his neck, and gathered his reins. Rio stood calmly as

C.J. remounted. C.J. said nothing as he sorted himself out and redallied his mecate loop under his belt. A good trick, he thought, as it had saved him from losing Rio too.

He felt Wyker come alongside him and was grateful Wyker spared his words. They walked together. The horses hadn't gone far, and most of the gear seemed to have stayed put. One pack sat at an odd angle, and there would be some debris to be gathered.

A hawk called out as it flew overhead. C.J. looked up and watched it fly in circles above them. It was a beautiful bird and it made C.J. think of the petroglyphs he'd seen earlier. Time had faded the images of the swirling circles of a creature with outstretched wings. He looked down at Rio's neck and patted him.

They came up to the loose horses slowly and caught them. Wyker watched C.J. as he picked stuff up off the ground and reset the load. C.J. recounted to Wyker how well Rio had handled the whole thing.

"There're days when you may not be paying the attention you should and they fill in for you. It's the nature of their relationships. Then there're days when the world is perfectly balanced between just the two of you. Unity with your horse," Wyker mused.

"*My* horse..." C.J. said it so softly that the slightest breeze would have carried the words away, but Wyker heard him and smiled.

With the packhorses calmed and ready to go, they moved on and came to a crest. A panorama opened up. The Steens Mountain Wilderness was off a ways, and they could see the Oregon Canyon Mountains. This was a remote corner of the world rarely, if ever, visited by more than the occasional hunter and free-range cattle.

Wyker looked down, frowned, and dismounted. Tammy dropped to the ground nearby and Wyker stood up. He hesitated, scanned all around them, and then walked ahead, looking at the ground.

Uneasy, C.J. asked, "What is it?"

"I see another set of tracks. One horse. At first, I thought maybe a bachelor stallion coming down from the mountains." He walked a bit farther. "It follows the herd, but then breaks off."

C.J. pulled the packhorse's head up to stop him from chewing on something, then reached to pick at a bit of Rio's mane.

"We have company," Wyker said as he got up on Johnny. "And close too."

They rode along a line of low mountains. The ground dropped away before rising to meet the base. It rose up to a long, flat tableau where the land flattened to meet the gray sky. Geologic time had eroded the steel-gray face that jutted up from the flat part of the valley, and loose stuff formed a backwash. The creek bed appeared and disappeared into winter's muted grays, beiges, and browns. Vegetation held out for spring's rejuvenation, and was thickset. It took time to find a clean way through to the water. The light was fading and they'd have to camp soon.

Suddenly, Wyker stopped so short that C.J. and Rio bumped into his horse, and C.J.'s packhorse bunched into Rio. C.J. craned his neck around to look for the reason.

A rider, sitting on a black horse, waited on the opposite bank of the creek. Wyker barely hesitated, and continued down to the water's edge. C.J. was uneasy, but he followed nonetheless. The man held up a hand in greeting and time seemed to suspend. It was a natural gesture, a stranger's greeting. C.J. thought they could be in this place at any time, now or a hundred years ago.

Wyker spoke and C.J. missed the words. He assumed it was a greeting and he noticed the rider was an Indian.

The man nodded and said, "Good horses, they didn't go far." He looked at the packhorses and toward Rio. With respect in his tone, he said, "He's a strong one."

C.J. didn't acknowledge the compliment and he watched the stranger as he would a new addition to the yard. Rio sensed the tension and moved his feet around, eager to move off. Wyker rode through the shallows and stopped alongside the black horse. He extended his right hand and he and the man shook.

"Harper Lee."

Wyker nodded, "I'm Wyker and this is C.J." Then he said, "Getting dark."

Harper Lee said, "Follow me."

Wyker pulled on the lead line to the packhorse he ponied, and fell in behind the rail-thin black horse Harper rode. They cut through a grove of eight-foot quaking aspens to a clearing surrounded by low rocks and a few large boulders. To one side, a low ring of stones had been blackened by past fires, and it was obvious someone had used this spot before.

Wyker and C.J. did a tie line for all their horses, unsaddled, and removed their packs and gear. The wind rustled the branches, but the grove provided a nice windbreak. Somehow, in all the dampness, Harper made a fire and gathered enough dry fuel to keep it going. What little he carried on the old cavalry saddle sat next to him. His bedroll was thin and the old saddle was his pillow. He sat cross-legged by the fire waiting for them. His horse was nearby, loose, no hobbles, his head down, sleeping.

C.J. brought his gear and took a spot across the fire from Harper, his back against the tallest part of a boulder. Wyker took a different approach from C.J.'s hostile silence. He sat to the left of Harper, close to the fire, with an unobstructed line of sight to the horses. He was at ease, and placed stew pouches at the edges of the fire. He'd made a few tiny holes in the tops, and the packets steamed and bubbled after a time. Wyker offered one to Harper, and he accepted. Wyker looked beyond him to the black horse and smiled.

"Nice horse." And he meant it. "He got a name?"

Harper shook his head. "No." Then he asked, "Why are you tracking the two?"

C.J. sat up a little straighter and looked at Wyker. Wyker did not look away from Harper; he had his full attention now.

"So it's just two. You saw them?"

Harper nodded and reached into his shoulder pouch on the ground beside him. It looked like a really beat-up old Pony Express mailbag. Wyker sensed C.J.'s tension as Harper pulled out a leather tube-like pouch, which contained a monocular-style expanding telescope. He removed it carefully from its bag and pulled it open to its full length. It was German made and had great optics. Harper handed it to Wyker.

"I like this better than glasses. I watched them yesterday. They were about twelve miles off, as the crow flies, but I can tell you what color their horses are and how many cows they're moving. And that they trespass across the rez like they own it."

"You're from the McDermitt?"

Harper nodded. "My uncle said they've come through before."

Wyker looked over at C.J. and willed him to dial his attitude back. What he'd thought was nervous energy was a drawn and dangerous tightness. Nerves twanged like bowstrings out of habit. Wyker made a judgment to treat Harper Lee as a potential ally, even if C.J. didn't.

C.J. caught the sign and turned his attention elsewhere. His technique was one of avoidance—avoid whatever it was until you couldn't any longer.

Wyker asked Harper if he knew the way they should go and if he was alone. Harper said yes to both. Wyker encouraged him to talk more, and as if Harper knew that words would help get C.J. to open up, he talked about himself.

He talked about his tribe and a government program, a leadership program, with a full college scholarship. His aunt had put his name in, did all the paperwork.

"She didn't tell me until I got it. I'm the first from my family to have a degree."

Out of nowhere, C.J. asked if he'd gotten a business degree. Wyker glanced at C.J., surprised he'd come out of the edges to ask.

Harper looked across the fire at him. "That was my intention, as a matter of fact, but I was distracted. Problem was, I didn't take to it like I should have. I became passionate about the sciences, specifically astronomy and geology. More a fan of looking up at the sky than down on the ground. I lost touch with my reason for being there."

Harper paused and stirred the fire. As he did, little bursts of sparks fluttered up and he watched them drift toward a patch of open sky filled with stars. The sparks mingled with the stars, then died. He put another piece of spindly wood on the fire.

Wyker asked, "What happened?"

"I became confused...at least, that's what my uncle said." He nodded toward the black horse. "Gave me the horse and told me to go. Said go until I found something."

C.J. asked, "Find what?"

"He wasn't specific. It was an awkward conversation." Harper paused. "I see these cattle and it looks wrong. I saw them and I saw the four of you."

Wyker's eyebrows went up at the last part and he shot Harper a look.

Harper nodded. "Yeah, I saw the other two and the cattle dogs."

Just then, coyotes called from nearby. They sounded to each other back and forth for a while, followed by a frenzied conversation of yipping, a greeting they made when they met up. The fire crackled and the three men listened to the music of the wilderness.

C.J.'s eyes swam as he looked into the fire. He drifted back to a time he'd long forgotten. He was twelve years old, and he'd been off on an adventure, one that got him grounded for weeks after. He went "walkabout," and he'd met an Aboriginal man, a storyteller. He sat by his fire late into the night. C.J. listened rapturously to his lilting accent as he told stories. C.J. remembered his stories of nature and the images he'd drawn with a stick in the sandy dirt. He stared into the fire and felt the memory of that encounter unfold as though it were yesterday. He thought that might be why the petroglyphs occupied his imagination. A particularly loud coyote called close and he returned to the present. Harper was staring at him.

Defensively, C.J. said, "What?"

"My grandfather said the fire visits old memories."

C.J. stared into unreadable eyes and nodded. He turned away, smoothed out his bedroll, turned his back to the fire, and said no more.

Wyker checked the horses and pulled the feedbags. Harper followed. Tammy wagged her tail as he approached, and sat at his feet for some attention. Harper stroked her upturned face and said, "Nice dog."

"She is." Wyker looped the bags over one of the panniers and asked, "Harper...that name native?"

"It's actually Harper Choco Lee. The first and last are because my dad liked the novel *To Kill a Mockingbird*, and my middle name is native and means Has No Horse."

Wyker was fascinated. "Why?"

"It's accurate." He smiled. "That's not my horse. Following the Snake War, many of the Paiute moved onto the Malheur Reservation in 1872, but white settlers took the land back when they found gold and good grazing. There was more fighting. We lost. My family ended up at Fort McDermitt. What's the story on that Rio horse?" he asked.

"Wild and doesn't trust easy."

Harper nodded toward C.J. "Like him?"

"Yeah, got to earn it. With both of them."

THIRTY-EIGHT

The personalized plates passed over the cattle guard. He was a couple hours' drive from Casa del Sol, his ten-thousand-square-foot estate and his main base of operations. He was en route for a regular meeting with his partner.

The black Escalade stopped at the gated entrance and he pressed a button in the overhead console to activate the electric gate. As it opened, he frowned at the layer of dust that flecked the shiny black paint of his vehicle. Hours earlier, Maxie had washed and waxed it, but it was always very dusty at this ranch in northeastern Nevada.

Tiny filled the leather bucket seat, seatbelt strained to its last wits, and the big rings on his fingers glinted in the light through the windshield. He used a clicker to open a succession of gates, drove over more cattle guards, and finally to the place where he'd kept the rustled cattle for the past three years. He moved them here first, and then spread them throughout his network of operations. Off to the left, he looked over a fine herd that was the product of the "business" and he observed that the batch was already sorted. He knew this because one of his better bulls was in with the cows. The market-ready ones were already off to auction; they'd be there by now.

After the final gate, Tiny parked at a big pole barn near one of those office trailers used on construction sites. Some rasty-assed work trucks were parked in a row, and off by itself was a big, shiny truck.

Tiny noted that his partner was there ahead of him, and knew he'd be in their office logged into the computer. It was their regular monthly meeting scheduled when no one else was around.

Tiny got out and looked over at the huge bales of hay in the barn. He knew, to the bale, how much was there. Inside that massive body was a keen mind, accurate as a calculator, and he had the gift of instant adjustments when price-per-pound fluctuated. He could go to the auction and know within five pounds the weights of the cows before they were scaled, and he'd calculate the total opening bid before the announcer cleared his throat. He knew by memory the account numbers and the phone numbers of everyone he needed to run everything. Tiny might have looked soft and useless, but he was a walking money-generating machine. This was why his silent partner had chosen him; he was the same way.

Tiny used his key to unlock the door. He didn't look to see if the alarm was on—he knew it wasn't—and he went through the front entry into a larger office. His partner was where he expected to find him, his hat on the rack, and his new briefcase on the expansive desk. Stains mottled its once perfect surface, like it had recently gotten wet.

The partner caught Tiny looking at it and turned away in disgust. "Don't ask. I'm still pissed off."

Tiny laughed, then he sat in a huge, overstuffed leather chair, put his feet up on the ottoman, and said, "Then we'll talk about something else."

It was his tone and his manner that caused his partner

to close the open program on the triple screen computer and rotate his chair to face him. He rolled the chair closer to the desk and they began their meeting.

THIRTY-NINE

Shiloh sat on the edge of her small bed. She felt nothing, just hollowness, as if anything could just blow through her and she wouldn't feel it. She heard the pat-pat-pat of water droplets that fell from her hair onto the bedspread behind her. She was wrapped in a bath towel, and the crests of her breasts protruded from the top. A smaller towel rested on her hands in her lap. She had intended it for her hair, but she'd looked down at herself in a self-conscious moment and had covered her chest with it instead, then let it fall to her lap. She sat there in the semi-darkness of her room, lit only by a sliver of light from the bathroom. She saw her clothes on the floor. She thought about burning them, but then she realized miserably that those were her favorite jeans. They fit her ass like no other, and it took so long to find a pair that did that.

She was sore everywhere. She could hardly move without feeling some part of her damaged body and the severe, purple-green bruises that stretched over her hip bones. She'd felt each injury as she scrubbed herself in the shower. Within minutes the hot water was gone, and shortly after even the tepid water had abandoned her. So, it was with cold water that she rinsed the conditioner out of her hair. She'd rewashed between her legs twice with the hot and then one final time with the cold water. It didn't matter what temperature, she trembled.

Shiloh tried to order her thoughts, to remember little

details, like had she left anything she really needed at the café or in the bar? What wages was she owed, and did it amount to a reason to go by and get a check?

Other than that, there was no anchor for her life in this place, and that was the truth of it. There wasn't a whole lot to pack. She had no girlfriends to call and cry to. She imagined that if anyone knew what had happened, they'd think she'd deserved it. Her mind twisted it all into a tangle. Perhaps it was payback for the debris she'd left in her wake. Then she shook it off and felt angry. She was absolutely certain of one thing; no one would have that chance to pass judgment. No one would have the opportunity to gloat at the bruise on her face. She touched where he'd slammed her head down on the hood of the car and flinched. She felt only a passing remorse at leaving Toby high and dry, but that's how it went. He'd get over it.

She reached back and squeezed the remaining moisture out of her hair. She leaned back on the bed, her bare feet dangling off the end, and placed the towel over her face like a shroud. *There,* she thought. *I'm gone, disguised, disappeared, undercover.*

She fell asleep, and awoke later with a start, disoriented. *Oh, fuck it,* she thought. *Must get moving.* She pulled out her duffle. She grabbed a worn-out suitcase from the closet and set it on the bed.

Shiloh meant to be gone before the sun came up, and she really didn't want to go to work. But she took stock of her resources and realized she didn't have enough money to go—not enough to go far, anyway. She looked at her bruised face in the mirror and thought maybe she could disguise the splotches with extra make-up. It was cloudy out, and the promise of rain was in the air. She knew she needed to talk to *him,* and his calls on the special cell would be at night. Knowing that, she tried the number anyway, but it went to a voicemail box which, according to a mechanized voice, was full. He had her money, and to go, she needed it.

Shiloh realized that going now was impractical, so she went to her tiny bathroom mirror and looked at the battered image reflected in it. Tipping her head right to left, the poorly lit vanity cast gaping shadows. She lifted her chin to see just how radically she'd need to apply make-up to hide the previous evening's assault.

Half an hour later, Shiloh emerged somewhat better for the effort and she looked at the clock. She'd be late. Her life was as packed as she felt like making it. She asked herself if she could pull it off—if she could act like nothing had happened last night. The "what if" rant went crazy in her head, but she stood up tall and reached for a sweatshirt. "I will never see these people again after today."

She grimaced and groaned as the bruising made certain movements more than uncomfortable. Even a loose-fitting pair of jeans applied too much pressure on her thighs and she never got them close to her hip bones. Reluctantly, Shiloh discarded them into the recesses of her duffle. She found sweatpants and gingerly bent over to slip them over her feet. She held the elastic well away from her hip area and settled them gently above, not caring whether she'd be warm enough. She reached up and freed her hair from the neck of the sweatshirt and grabbed her jacket. Then she thought, *Oh God, what if that asshole comes in? How do I handle that?* Then she straightened with a very empowering thought. She'd pour steaming hot coffee on the bastard and burn the shit out of him.

The morning rush would be on and Toby would be pissed—and hopefully too busy to scrutinize her appearance. She grabbed her bags, left the key on the dresser, closed the door, and went down to her truck. The damned thing started up easily for a change. Maybe it was trying to apologize for its role in her ruin.

She parked well away from the door behind the tavern, and sure enough, it was packed. *Good for Toby*, she thought as she opened the back door with her key and walked through the dark bar.

She committed herself to act normally, and it was an inner struggle to know what that was. She put her bag into her cubby, hesitated, and unzipped the hidden compartment in the bottom. She turned the cell on; it powered up and had a full charge. She left it on, grabbed her apron, and pulled her hair back with a scrunchy. She checked again for messages and sent out a silent wish that he'd call. She knew it would be breaking his pattern, but she needed to tell him she was leaving.

She approached the swinging door and the clatter of breakfast grew louder. She went through the storeroom/prep room, and past the prep counter. No one looked up to say she was late. Toby glared at her as she came in, his body a blur of motion between taking orders and the grill. The busboy looked at her with obvious relief.

Toby hissed at her under his breath, "Where the fuck have you been?"

"Does it matter? I'm here now." And she swept past

him without a backwards glance. She grabbed her chit book, stuffed it in her apron front pocket, and grabbed the half-empty coffeepot.

The first table she came to, full of wranglers, hardly noticed her when she said good morning and looked to top up cups. They usually paid a lot of attention to her, but not this morning. All she caught were incredulous "holy shits!" and "you're kiddings!" There was an odd hum about the café, and as she walked to the next table, she hoped she didn't look as uncomfortable as she felt. She'd practiced in the truck on the way to work, her lie to explain her appearance if anyone asked. She moved to the next table and Lyle Martin was the only one of the three that looked at her, nodded yes to a refill, but said nothing about how she looked.

"Thank you, Shiloh. Wondered where you were."

"Ran late this morning. What's up with everyone?"

"Everyone's talking about what happened last night," he said, and sipped his coffee.

Startled, she looked around. "What? What are you talking about?"

Before she could hear Lyle's answer, someone hollered to her in an impatient voice that he wanted to order this year, and she said she was coming.

She snatched bits of conversation and heard Del's name. She felt nauseated, and was afraid her name would come up, but oddly, it didn't. She took some orders to Toby and put them up for him to fill.

"What's up, what happened?" she asked him, but he was too busy to answer her.

Frustrated by the lack of information, Shiloh made a

257

fresh pot of coffee and saw that they needed more coffee from the supply room.

Toby didn't look up when he growled he hadn't had time to bring more in from the back. "Too fucking busy," he snarled, which was his umpteenth snipe about her being late.

She hustled through to the bar, grabbed a box cutter, and sliced open the box containing the premeasured coffee packets. She stopped and held her hand out flat, checking to see how badly it shook. The box cutter wobbled, and she was grateful to put it down. Upon her return, she rested the box on her knee and pulled the special phone out of her bag. *No message. Fuck it.* Shiloh hit redial. Voicemail picked up, and she was able to leave a brief message for him to call her, that it was urgent. Then she tossed the phone back in her handbag.

She got the fresh pot of coffee, and at the next table she served, heard the news that Hank Larsen was dead. Both he and his dog. That lonely old man and the dog? Then she heard Del's name mentioned and it was like lead in her gut. The story included him somehow and she needed to hear what the hell had happened. She brought more orders in, detoured to the back, and asked the busboy. And that was when she heard the whole story, such as anyone knew it.

FORTY

It was early and Carson sat in the straw, in a corner, her back against the wall that made one side of the pen. There were a couple of enclosures, one outside the stall, and a bigger one in the center of the main barn for the calves that were doing better. She was exhausted and the contented warmth of the sleeping calf in her lap lulled her to doze. When she woke up, she wasn't sure what had roused her. She looked through the slats and saw her coffee had tipped over. She felt something nudge her arm through the rails of the pen. It wasn't Wyatt or Lulu, but two other dogs, cattle dogs. They were interested in her, but more so in the calves. Then she heard the big barn door slide all the way open, and horses were led through by Luis and Jorge.

She stepped out of the makeshift infirmary and walked to take their packhorse's lead. "Glad to have you back."

Luis smiled through tired eyes. "Good. You look well. Welcome home." And then he added, "How's your mother?"

Lupe came in and they exchanged greetings in Spanish. Most of it Carson understood. Luis excused himself to go get cleaned up. He wanted to talk to Kitzie, but not as filthy as he was. The horses were properly put up and cared for, then Lupe got ready to leave to get back to his regular work. Carson walked with him to his car and thanked him for all his help. She came back into the barn and found Jorge in with the sicker calves. His dogs lay ob-

259

ediently just outside. Carson watched him, and it was obvious he was gifted with animals. He touched each calf and spoke to it gently in Spanglish before he left for a much-needed shower. Carson was relieved they were back and she went to tell her mom.

Spence felt beat from lack of sleep and never made it home. At around 5:00 a.m. he stretched out on the sofa in his office and caught a few minutes' rest before the phone brought him out of it. He chose to let it go to voicemail and went to the staff room to get a fresh shirt he always kept there. He walked back to his desk as he put it on, buttoning it as he went, and glanced down at the evidence bags he'd brought from Hank Larsen's place.

He stared at one in particular—one that had bugged him since he found it. He pulled open his desk drawer, pulled out a pair of powderless evidence gloves, and put them on. He opened the bag with the phone inside. He pressed the power button. His phone rang again and he set the cell phone partway into its evidence bag, removed his gloves, and answered his phone. It was the fire chief calling to discuss last night. They discussed where the blaze started and some about an arson investigation, whether it was needed, and generally what the process would be to do the reports. It was dull stuff, Spence was tired, and his attention drifted. When the conversation was finally over, he hung up and pulled out the many forms he needed to fill out, along with his notes to transcribe. He was bothered. He could see the old man's face. "I knew something was eating away at you…"

He'd barely put pen to paper when the cell phone on his desk vibrated. He stared at it, startled, and grabbed one of the gloves he'd just taken off, then cradled the phone to press the "talk" button without adding his prints to it. He didn't say anything when a voice threatened, "Listen, asshole. You mess up Shiloh and you'll never see your money."

Spence thought fast. Playing his hunch that the phone was, in fact, Del's, he coughed into the mouthpiece. He covered the distance from his desk to the half bathroom off his office and flushed the toilet. He mumbled, "Huh?" and faked a phlegm-riddled cough, then spit into the sink, hoping he sounded enough like Del to fool the caller. It was disgusting, but it was the best he could come up with.

The voice added, "We'll have the herd there late tomorrow…" Then the man said, "Hold on."

Spence looked incredulously at the phone and thought, *This guy's putting me on hold?*

Stiles did exactly that as the Shiloh cell phone vibrated in his hand. He put the Del phone on mute and answered Shiloh's call. She was in the back of the bar, behind it, crouched down, and she was relieved when "the voice" answered.

"Oh, thank God, you're there!" she gasped into the phone.

The voice sounded afraid. "What's wrong? Are you okay?"

She leaned her head against the cupboard and gathered herself. She couldn't lose it here. "Yeah, sort of. No, that's not true. I'm fucked up, but I'll live. I have to tell you, something else has happened."

Stiles was angry. "Did he hurt you? That mutherfucker hurt you? Did he?"

Shiloh was stunned. How did he know? It wasn't what she was ready for, and she hadn't planned on telling anyone about the incident. But she forged past that; she needed to tell him what had happened to Del. She wanted to focus only on the old man and Del.

"Um, I'm okay, but you have to know this, so listen. Del is dead! So's old Hank Larsen. They both died early this morning. Happened at Larsen's place. Dead bodies and the house burned down. It's all the talk here."

Stiles stared in horror at the other cell phone. *Shit, who the fuck was I just talking to?* Quickly, he replayed what he'd said in his mind. *FUCK.* He'd used Shiloh's name. He'd mentioned the herd and the money. He put the phone back to his ear.

"Shiloh, do exactly what I tell you. Got something to write on? There are things I should have told you before. It'll have to wait...no time now. You ready?" He gave her very specific instructions and told her to get out of there immediately. "Do exactly as I say. I mean it; you don't have time for anything. I think they'll be looking for you. Do this and everything will be fine, I promise. Now get gone!" And he hung up on her and refocused his attention on the other phone. He needed to buy her some time.

His mind whirled. Who had gotten a hold of Del's cell phone? He willed himself to stay calm. It was probably the police. Maybe he could stall with that and buy Shiloh time. He took a deep breath, pressed the mute button, and put the phone to his ear, "You still there?"

Spence had waited but believed the man wouldn't come back, and it startled him when he did. He mumbled his reply, "Uh-huh."

"I'll call you back in two hours with instructions."

And the line went dead.

Stiles took the SIM card out of the phone and put it in his pocket. He was about to throw the phone away when he heard Ramos riding around behind him. Stiles's horse had one hind foot cocked and he dozed. Ramos's approach woke him. Stiles hollered over his shoulder to get to the other side and pull the stragglers together. "Gotta make time today," he said, gathered up his reins, and spurred his horse.

Ramos stared after him. He'd seen him on the phone. He'd suspected he had one, just had never seen him use it. He rode off to take up the position and decided to watch his partner very carefully.

Shiloh heard Toby swear and call her name. She stood up and put the notes she'd taken into her bra. The voice on the phone sounded alarmed. He'd never sounded like that before. And there was something else, from long ago. It was something oddly familiar; it was the way he said, "I promise." She shook it off and powered the phone down to conserve the battery. The charger was in her duffle in the truck. She put her purse away and hustled back. She told Toby she had bad cramps and apologized for taking too long a break. To ease his ire, she kicked up her game, helped the busboy clear tables, and had things back the way they should be, all the while keeping her eye on the clock.

The breakfast rush tapered off, and Toby chilled out some, which made everyone dial the tension back a little. Each time she went to the register, Shiloh pulled money— twenties and tens. It was way too easy. She pretended to bag the cash from the drawer as it got too full, and slipped the envelopes containing mostly ones and fives into the floor safe. At noon Toby would take the receipts, pull the cash, and reconcile in the back office. Then he'd go to the bank and do the deposit. By then she'd be on the road. Some of the money was what Toby owed her in her check, so she justified it by telling herself she'd only be stealing a small amount. Besides, he'd just have to get over it.

At the window, Shiloh had just started to help the busboy clear a table when she caught sight of the sheriff's car as it idled by. The busboy carried the plastic tub into the back and she wiped the table down. She straightened up and checked her handiwork out of habit, and glanced up again. She saw Sheriff Spence's car pass again, though this time the driver's side was closest. He looked right at her, and their eyes locked for a moment. She turned to do another table, but the hair on the back of her neck stood on end. Her heart pounded as she collected a tip. Out of the corner of her eye, she saw the car do a three-point turn at the edge of town. He was coming back.

She found Toby drinking coffee, leaning against the prep counter in the back. "Tobe, I'm really having bad cramps. I need to run to the corner market and get…well, you know."

Toby nodded an acknowledgment at her, and she went for her things. She was certain Spence would park where he usually did, out front, but she hesitated when her hand touched the back doorknob. There was a cramped storage closet to the right of the door. It had a narrow window with a view of the parking lot out back. She slipped inside. The window was covered with welded bars to prevent a break-in. She edged up to it and craned her neck to peek through it until she could see her truck. She angled her head and saw more of the lot, quickly turned away, and slid down to the floor. Spence was in the back lot. His cruiser idled behind her truck. *What the hell?* She clutched her bag to her chest and felt her heart pounding. She waited there for what seemed an eternity. Then she heard the cruiser move off and out of the lot. She jumped up and bolted out the back door, paused, and listened. The sheriff stopped at the road, then turned right, toward his office.

Shiloh didn't need another sign to know it was definitely time to go. She got in the truck, prayed out loud for it to start on the first crank, which it did, and she drove out of the lot. She was grateful Spence had been lazy and had stayed in his car, otherwise, he'd have seen her stuff on the seat. She didn't have much, but what mattered was in there and she was ready to go. And go she did. She touched the notes with his instructions that were in her bra. Good, she hadn't lost them. She plugged in the car charger and her phone. She made sure it was on, the ringer set loud so she could hear it, and she drove away, checking the rearview mirror frequently.

The highway was a barren ribbon flanked by pale desert grasses and telephone power poles. Shiloh noticed a solar panel connected to a lone pole, lower than the taller ones, and it powered an Oregon Department of Transportation camera. She realized it would record her departure. She imagined a weary technician as he peered at a grainy, pixilated ODOT screen. She hoped that a quirk of circumstance would make her passage unremarkable for a long time. It calmed Shiloh's mind to decide she was lucky.

A scattered storm system approached from a westerly direction. Beams of sunlight spanked through breaks in the clouds, shining a bright richness among the lead of winter's last grasp.

FORTY-ONE

It was early dark, and a sliver of light sky appeared eastward. Tammy trotted up the path and settled at Wyker's feet. Wyker watched the stars fade and the sky lighten. He loved being in the wilderness with his horse and his dog. It was a perfect world after a night under a broken sky of stars mixed with low clouds. He made coffee and placed a steaming cup on the ground next to C.J., who still slept.

C.J. smelled the coffee and heard the crunch of earth under a boot. He cracked open one eye and looked up at Wyker, then at the wisps of steam that rose from the tin cup. He sorted himself out, rolled over onto his back, and realized that the ground was really hard. He sat up and reached for the coffee, then took a cautious sip. As he swallowed, he looked at the ashes of the campfire and his mind replayed his thoughts and bits of conversation from the night before. He found a sense of calm at the memory of his Aboriginal adventure. He realized how well he'd slept last night as he looked over at Rio. He felt good. He saw Harper by his horse, saddling up, and realized he never heard him get up. *Man moves like a cat. And his horse, funky-looking animal,* he thought, but it did have a really kind eye, and looks probably didn't matter.

Wyker stood by the fire, using the toe of his boot to kick dirt onto the remains of the coals. He wasn't making a serious effort of it; more like he was drinking his coffee and doing it as he thought on something. He turned and came over toward C.J. as C.J. put his bedroll in a tight coil and laced it. "I talked to Harper about the route they've been taking through the McDermitt. Seems they push them past a place called Hanging Tree. Years ago, buckaroos from the Steens Ranches tried and hung horse thieves there."

C.J. stood up and said, "Really?" He carried his gear and set to getting the packhorses' panniers on. He heard Wyker walk over to talk to Harper.

Harper spoke up, "Yes, that story is true. The tree is half fallen down and dead now. But you can still see it."

"They have a good lead on us. Is there a way to get ahead of them?" Wyker asked.

Harper didn't answer immediately. "We can go up and over, though it's a narrow and dangerous track. You should know I haven't been up there in many years."

Wyker continued, "If they get the herd loaded up, they're gone."

Harper nodded. "I've an idea where they'll do that. We'll need to really push hard to do it, but it's doable."

Wyker returned to the fire, poured the last of his coffee over it, stirred the ashes apart with a stick, and held his hand over them. There was no heat and he was convinced the fire was out. Then he tightened Johnny's cinch and slipped the bridle on. C.J. mounted up and had the lead rope to his packhorse dallied on his horn. Harper waited on word from Wyker.

"Okay, let's do this."

As the gray morning light grew, they moved off with Harper at the lead. They ascended a bluff and another ridge, and came off from the top of that at an angle that looked like there was no way through. It got colder. They covered ground with no clear trail, but the black horse moved steadily, committed to the direction. Although Harper rode him, it was clear the horse knew the way.

Wyker spoke over his shoulder to C.J. "He said the horse would know the way."

C.J. called back, "You're shittin' me."

Wyker laughed as they loped up a short rise to get momentum for a steeper climb just ahead. The hillside was covered with broken rock and shale debris. There were moments of lost traction, rebalancing done on the fly, and a lot of hustle to keep the packhorses in tow. To stop was not an option; they needed the momentum. There were many areas like that, and there was no discussion or prep, it was just "git 'er done" as Wyker put it. It was all very strenuous and after the initial "holy shit" moments, C.J. felt Rio had a good bead on the scariest parts. All he had to do was not get in his way.

Wyker's instructions had been to not dally the pack-horses; don't get hard attached in case they lost their footing and fell. "If yours does, just let him go."

C.J. noticed more petroglyphs. The images were like pages of a book and he thumbed through them in his imagination. What was the artist thinking? What did the signs mean? What animal was that drawing meant to represent? His questions piled up and he wanted to ask Harper if he knew what the symbols meant, but he held back. He was uncertain about his interest and he wasn't ready to completely accept Harper. His reticence was borne from experience and his past record of believing in the wrong people.

They made decent progress, but more than once were forced to turn back and go another way where the trail had washed out. After a few hours, they took a break at a spring that bubbled up from the ground. There was no stream, just a rocky bowl that held fresh, cool water, ice remaining in the part that was shaded. The horses all drank and C.J. rubbed the muscles on his lead rope arm, as they had begun to cramp up on the last part of the climb to the spring.

"Switch arms ponying if you can," Wyker suggested.

C.J. winced as he rubbed the knot in his arm and Wyker asked Harper how they were doing.

He responded, "We ride all night."

Wyker was quiet as he watched Tammy drink water.

"She'll be fine," Harper said. "I'll carry her if need be. For this to work, we have to keep going."

Wyker nodded and added, "That horse of yours better be as good as you think."

Harper said nonchalantly, "He is."

FORTY-TWO

Spence's hand sweated in the rubber glove and he stared at the cell phone. He willed it to ring. Eventually, he slid it back into the evidence bag and put it in his coat pocket with an extra pair of gloves. He cruised by to see if Shiloh was still at the café, and she was. Once back at his office, he looked up the number for his friend Dave, an ODA agent he knew. Years ago, he had hunted with him and had kept in touch. He hoped he wasn't somewhere without cell service and was pleased when Dave answered on the third ring. They got the pleasantries out of the way and Spence began the story with, "Dave, I have a situation, and I think you'll be interested."

Spence told him what had happened in the last twenty-four hours, what the mysterious voice on the cell phone had said, and that he'd checked on the current whereabouts of Shiloh. They discussed what her involvement might be.

Dave listened carefully, asked only a few clarifying questions, and then said, "Two DBs in twenty-four hours, a herd of cattle, and money. Yeah, you have my interest. We're working the cattle rustling case; we're at the Running Horse right now. I'm gonna get back to you."

"I'll stay in my office till I hear from you." Spence gave him the numbers and said he hoped the guy from the mysterious cell phone would call back.

Spence leaned back in his creaky office chair and

looked at the bagged evidence from the Larsen house. He rolled the chair over to the computer and began his report. He downloaded the digital pictures he'd shot and saved them in a new file, then previewed them and made a "best of" file for the ones with the cleanest frames and best angles.

Spence began to construct several sequences of events. Hank was found dead and Del had obviously killed him. Why was Del there in the first place? He studied the pictures of Del's car, and reread his notes. He'd made a note about animal tracks near Del's body. Sonny? He decided the photos of the paw prints around Del could be matched to the dog. There was a patch of soft ground and the prints were clear. What happened with the dog after Hank was murdered? What set Del off after Hank?

Spence retrieved the evidence bag containing the phone from his coat pocket. He looked at it, impatient and frustrated. He set the bag down on his desk, then picked it up again and studied it. A thought occurred to him. He recalled seeing Del pulled over alongside the road. Del had acted weird, and he'd been on a phone in his car—and Spence had seen him pulled over to the side of the road more than once. Was this Del's phone? And if so, why was it hidden in the ceramic frog at Hank Larsen's place?

Spence slid his chair over to an interoffice extension and called the tow company. They'd been at Hank's that morning and had hauled Del's car to an impound lot. He got a hold of the guy, and asked him to search Del's car thoroughly for a cell phone. The man whined about needing hazmat gear, that the car was a pigsty. Spence told him it was important and to please get to it right away.

He rolled back to the computer and scrolled through the photographs again. Spence felt certain the cell phone on his desk was Del's, and he was willing to bet that when they tested it for prints, Del's would be all over it. So how did Hank get a hold of Del's phone, and how did Del find out Hank had it? Where would Del and Hank be at the same time? Easy, only one place: the Pine Tavern & Café—or more likely, *last night* at the tavern. He picked up the phone and called Toby to find out who had worked the bar the night before. When he hung up, he saw the message light flash. The yard man didn't find a cell phone, but he did find a charger for one.

Spence mused that Hank was onto something involving Del. He recalled seeing him in the café taking notes and observing people. Somehow, for some reason, he had gotten Del's phone, Del was drunk, pissed off, and he went out to Hank's to get it back. Hank was angry and refused. Whatever the reason was, it was Del's connection to the man Spence had talked to on the cell phone. It didn't go well and it wouldn't take much to kill the frail old man. Where would the dog have been? Nearby for sure. Maybe Hank tried to protect Sonny; he would. Spence leaned back in his chair, intertwined his hands behind his head, and looked at the crime scene photos in slide show mode.

At the Running Horse, Dave hung up and plugged his cell into the car charger. Damn thing ate juice. He found his partner, Hyland Royston, in the Running Horse cattle barn office. He interrupted a conversation with the foreman.

The foreman was deep in an explanation of the microchip tracking system they'd implemented six months ago, and it was all that techie talk Hy loathed. It was Dave that the tech shit appealed to, and Hy looked relieved when Dave walked in. Dave asked for a moment and filled him in on his conversation with Spence.

"Spence is a good guy, and they don't get two dead bodies in one night in Martin very often," Dave finished, and saw he didn't have to draw his buddy a diagram.

Hy said they'd be going right away. "Get back to him, tell him we're on our way. Ask him to call out to the Three Bit and find out if they know where a Will Wyker is."

Dave called Spence back. He popped the trunk while the call rang through, and pulled his maps out. He laid the rolled and bound detail maps on the trunk. He knew Hy liked to turn the pages like a book. Dave found the map that had Martin and the Jordan Valley, all the way to Idaho and down into Nevada. Hy studied the map while Dave talked to Spence.

Dave paced as he spoke to Spence, and his boots were dust to the hemline of his jeans when their conversation was done. He joined Hy at the trunk.

Hy pointed at a large swath of land. "Hardly anyone out in that, and much of the history died with the old buckaroos who worked it." Hy ran his finger south, to Nevada, south of the Running Horse, and his finger dragged across the McDermitt Reservation. "This is an opportunity...I can feel it. The question is, are we too late?"

Dave updated Hy on his conversation. "He said he'd call the Three Bit. What's up, you have someone out there?"

Hy rolled the maps in such a way that the one he wanted would unroll first, then put them in the back seat. They got into the car and Dave guided it out of the lot.

As Dave buckled up, he said, "Actually two. Wyker has gone after some missing cattle from the Three Bit and we have an undercover agent in the field."

The Running Horse was huge, and it took twenty minutes driving on a narrow, rough, dirt back road to reach the main gate, then the highway. Dave punched the gas, hoping they would get there in time to make a difference.

FORTY-THREE

Theodoro Miranda loved technology. He loved his cell phone, his iPad, and the technology in his car. He loved all the remote-control units for the television, stereo, and disc player. He adored his laptop and his desktop, and when something got glitchy at the office, he was the go-to guy. No need to call the IT person—they had their own geek. At first, they teased him with the name "Techy Teo," but the more he worked his magic, the more respect he got. Soon the name wasn't a tease, and the abbreviated version became "Tecteo" and stuck. He liked it and was proud of it. He even got a personalized plate on his car. Computers adored Tecteo. He'd touch the keyboard, and presto! All fixed.

Before anyone knew what it was, he had the new microchip reader out of the box and calibrated. He took it home one weekend and made a point of checking every dog and cat he could find, pets that might have microchips, and he practiced on them. He prowled databases and found out who owned the animal, its history, and it was entertainment for him to stump his friends.

His supervisor was not happy when he found out, and he ordered that the microchip reader stay in the office until the training program was held, but Tecteo was quickly forgiven after two events occurred. His boss's hard drive locked up and Tecteo spent half the night, on his own time, recovering his data. And when the tech came to train the staff on the reader, Tecteo knew more than he did and taught the class. Shortly afterward, he got a job offer from the microchip company, which he turned down, and was soon out in the field putting the unit into service.

The stockyard, or the "meat rack" as the guys called it, was a regularly scheduled routine inspection. A two-man team was sent to inspect the premises, observe the general health of the animals, the records of ownership, and just about anything else the statutes required them to perform to ensure the stability and safety of the meat supply. Primarily, the big yards supplied meat products and by-products to myriad industries that the cattle were rendered to.

Semantic crap, "rendered," Tecteo thought. Many an inspector converted to vegetarian, and then quit. But he had a different perspective; he looked at his job like a detective. The attention he paid to his job affected the health and welfare of millions of people. He felt there could be no work that was more important.

His partner that day found the livestock, the alive kind, particularly distasteful. He preferred his Big Mac well done, not mooing, so he chose to be inside following the paper trail.

Tecteo enjoyed the cattle, their soft eyes and mostly mellow demeanor, and he headed to the section of the yard where trucks delivered the animals. The pens were massive, and the yard stretched as far as the eye could see. He grew up ranching with his family, and had done the cattle thing with his brothers and the extended family in New Mexico. He knew enough about the business to spot a sick or injured cow. He knew what to look for.

The chip reader was the size of an older-model cell phone and looked like a Geiger counter when the detachable handle was on it. Days before, he'd stuck his head in his supervisor's door and convinced him to let him take it. His boss had reminded him that the cost of microchipping cattle was prohibitive for most ranchers; he probably wouldn't get a thing. Tecteo was dogged in his desire to get more experience with it, and his boss relented but added that if it got damaged, it would come out of his salary.

Happy that he'd won, Tecteo now walked down the breezeway between the pens and cradled the scanner on one arm. He made his way to the farthest part of the yard. To some it may have seemed foolhardy to hop into one of the pens, what with some of the cows being fearful. Cowpied shoes were the main hazard, and he wore knee-high, heavy rubber boots. The cattle were channeled into chutes that guided them to the next step in the process. He laid a hand on a cow near its withers and slid the scanner along the crest. He used earbuds to listen for a signal. He worked the battery pack into a pouch around his waist. He passed the scanner over the back of another cow. The intensity of the sound would indicate how close he was to the chip. Once he caught a signal and found the rough location of a chip, he'd move the reader to refine the contact. A visual reading would appear on the screen and he'd press SAVE to upload the data to a PC.

The day before had been very cold, and he'd been pleased with the reader's performance. He'd read somewhere that it might get glitchy in frigid temperatures, that the screen would be hard to read. He'd jumped the first time the tone sounded, and waved the unit around until he was right over the chip, then pressed the SAVE button. Then he checked the ear tag and entered the number in his iPad database, and voilà, he knew all he needed to know about the animal that carried the chip. He was impressed when he found cattle from the Running Horse had chips; more than he would've suspected.

Today was more tedious. Tecteo wasn't getting any hits, and the thrill of the hunt began to fade the colder his toes got. It was past lunch when his partner ventured out of the heated office to find him. He was hungry. He called to Tecteo from the fence, as he had no desire to climb into the pen.

Tecteo was about to remove an earbud when he heard something. He was next to an all-black cow and he pressed the bud back in and waved the device over the cow again. Yes, there it was. He had to walk next to the cow, which politely stuck around, and he placed the device gently against its hide. It was a bit like "petting" the animal with the reader, and he was thoughtful about it. *No need to press just yet...find it first...find it, find it, there, no...no wait.* The cow was jostled from the opposite side and it pressed itself against Tecteo. He squished into a fresh cow pie. Tecteo didn't care; he was busy pressing the SAVE button and looking at the screen. Then he checked the tag in the cow's ear and made a note of the number. He called for his partner to come around to his side of the fence. He told him to stick around. Tecteo pointed his phone camera at the cow and snapped a picture.

From a window in an upstairs corner of a nearby building, a diminutive woman stood with binoculars. She focused the high-powered lenses on the activities of the young man with the scanner. She'd made a call earlier to her boss and told him about it. He'd said to watch, and that's what she'd been doing, to the point of getting a vicious headache. Her dog sat next to her as she lifted the glasses, adjusted the focus, and made her decision. She sighed as she lowered them, looked down at her dog, and told him today was the day.

The office was furnished, but hardly used, and the only thing that worked was a phone. She used her cell phone to call a certain manager at a private bank. She spoke directly to him and she instructed him to move her money to an offshore account immediately. Her second call was to a travel agent. She had prepared for this eventuality, and her false bonhomie had disguised her true nature. She had a plan—now she had to activate it and get herself and her dog well away before the real shit hit the fan. She'd carried a set of records on a thumb drive for her own insurance, and now she'd simply disappear. Her tasks completed, her hand hovered over the desk phone, knowing the last call would not be pleasant. She picked it up and dialed the number from memory. Maxie answered.

From his key fob, Tecteo clicked the trunk release as they approached the vehicle and he grabbed his laptop. There was a portable building used as a receiving point for the incoming livestock, and he set up in there. He forgot his growling stomach, but his partner couldn't ignore his any longer and he went off to find a couple of sandwiches.

Tecteo found a spot and went to work. It took him a while to access the correct program, and then he had to get to the right place to enter the numbers from that cow. It seemed to take forever until it finally loaded and he could look at the data. When the information came across his screen, he stared at it, then looked twice to make sure he had not transposed any numbers.

Another full cattle hauler pulled up by the office, and Tecteo watched it. He saw the gal with the dog walk by it, stop, and turn to speak to the driver. Then she and the dog went to a car and the truck turned around and moved off back down the road. It was leaving the site. He grabbed his cell phone and called his boss as he watched the woman start her car and leave.

He was told his boss was unavailable, and he'd have to leave a message. Tecteo considered this and just told the secretary to have his boss call him, it was urgent. He hung up and reread the screen, then accessed another screen and made an executive decision—one that would probably not please his supervisor. He knew going over his boss's head would piss him off, so he figured he'd say his boss told him to call, to make sure that his boss got the credit. His excitement was contained only by a sense of panic as to how to proceed. If there was one stolen cow here, there had to be more. He needed more authority to turn this place upside down, and the rats were leaving the sinking ship. How quickly to get help was the question.

When the voice at the other end of the line heard what

he had, the level of intensity changed. He was transferred to another extension, and this time it was a woman, and she knew her stuff. She told him a name, Agent Royston, and she said to hold while she connected him.

FORTY-FOUR

Carson washed bottles in the kitchen and cleaned up the equipment from the calves. The ones that had recovered quickly were returned to their mothers if possible. The tide of babies had ebbed to about twelve, which included those that the mothers rejected when they returned them. As she dried her hands on a towel, she heard Kitzie call to her. She told her they were going over to the Running Horse Ranch for supper.

"You sure you're up to that?" Carson asked.

"If I stay cooped up like this for much longer, they'll name an ink spot after me."

They made it to the Running Horse and their big setup that they called the "Deer Club." Everyone knew Kitzie and she was treated with a deference that Carson appreciated. Buckaroos took charge and helped her get comfortable. They found a seat for Kitzie with a chair for a leg rest. Carson frowned when they got her a tumbler of wine, but Kitzie waved her off.

The seats on both sides of the table were filled with folks Kitzie knew and needed to get caught up with, so Carson wandered the room. There were framed pictures on the walls, hundreds of them. Seems the Running Horse was the repository of the past hundred years of wild characters and tough people. The pictures were mostly worn and faded, some fresh and put up haphazardly. It was a massive collection that would have driven someone crazy to straighten and level them. Out of habit, Carson leveled a few.

A deep, melodic voice from behind distracted her, and she turned to face a man with green eyes. It startled her, the depth of them, so green they were luminescent. Forgetting to check her impulse control, she observed, "Girls must just get lost in those."

His smile was as nice as his eyes. He pointed to one of the pictures she'd straightened and told her the story behind it. He stood very close. She felt flattered, then uncomfortable; awkward, like a teenage girl. She looked over at her mother.

"She's just fine, don't worry. We heard she was coming and there were instructions to take special care of her," he said.

The Deer Club had filled and the noise level hummed with conversation. Food was served buffet style, and the long tables by the big windows gave a commanding view of the main corral and the land beyond. The late afternoon drifted to nightfall, and the soft light of dusk made it a wonderful scene. Carson wished she had her camera with her, and her mind snapped photos to add to the thousands of un-shot memories that lingered. There was lots of laughter, and one old cowboy good-naturedly cuffed a youngster for still having his hat on. The conversation was lively, and Green Eyes watched her take it all in. Carson suspected there had been instructions to see that she enjoyed herself as well.

When the buffet line shrank, he leaned in the direction of the food, extending an upturned hand, much like a butler. It was an exaggerated movement, full of self-deprecating humor, and Carson couldn't help but smile. She followed his lead and got into line. She got a plate and scanned her options. The food looked marvelous and there was plenty of it. Green Eyes followed behind her. After they had filled their plates, he led the way to two seats he'd saved. They sat down and she asked, "Were there orders to see to me, too?"

"I volunteered."

"Really?"

"I saw your performance the other night at the tavern. Enjoyed the way you clocked Shiloh. Perfect timing."

Carson was embarrassed. "Ugh. I'm not like that normally. Been through some tough times..." Her voice trailed off as she felt any explanation sounded pathetic.

"Haven't we all," Green Eyes said as he dug into his food with relish.

Out of the corner of her eye, Carson thought he reminded her of her father, especially when he didn't elaborate further. Her father never rode the same ground to dust; at least, that's how he'd say women behaved. Nearby, many jokes and good times were recalled with genuine affection. Carson found the environment reassuring, all smooth and mellow.

Her steak was amazing. It seemed she hadn't eaten a really good one in years. Across the table, an old buckaroo told her he'd known the cow personally and that he'd been as fine then as he was now. Kitzie, deep in conversation with the foreman, didn't seem to miss her daughter's company at all.

Green Eyes saw Carson's glass was empty and offered to refill it from the carafe of red wine on the table. She smiled her yes and she marveled at how good everything tasted. She looked down at the carnage on her plate and laughed.

"Usually I don't eat like a horse! It was all so good."

"One of the perks of working with this outfit. Sure, work's hard—harder than anywhere else I've ever worked—but you ride the best horses, have decent accommodations, and eat better than you'd ever expect."

She nodded as she looked around at what seemed to be a good staff.

He added, "So, beyond the appetite, how do you like the Deer Club?"

Carson looked around again and said, "I think I was here years ago as a child, with my dad. He liked to hunt and he brought me here." She took a sip of wine. "I'm pretty sure I was annoyed at being dragged along." She put the glass down, and it wobbled slightly on the bare, rough wood of the table. She felt at ease, almost happy, and it caught the edges of her mouth. She tilted her head and looked at Green Eyes with a smile of warmth she had not felt in years. "Do you know what I mean?"

And he said yes, he knew exactly what she meant.

Green Eyes lifted his glass and the immediate group joined in. He proposed a toast. "Then here's cheers to you being here again." And further toasts to her return sooner than later.

There was more laughter, more jokes, tall tales, and fun, and Carson thought there were many things about this night that she had not seen or felt in a long time. They were all good people; really nice people.

The time flew by, and in the kitchen, cleanup was underway. She saw the dessert table with pie plated near the coffee urn. Looked like apple? And people got up and conversation shifted from the tables to milling about by the coffee.

Carson stifled a yawn and realized how tired she was. She got up, excused herself from the table, and asked Green Eyes where she should take her plate. He pointed over yonder and she moved off, though she could feel his eyes on her back. There was a pass-through where folks set their dirty dishes, which were whisked away with a smile. She checked out the pie (it *was* apple) and decided that she was full. She approached her mom, who was flushed with the evening's welling of support and entertainment. The cowhands scooted over, drinks in hand, and made room for Carson. She demurred and leaned over to ask if Kitzie was tired, and when she'd like to go. As she expected, her mom inquired about when *she'd* like to go, and Carson said soon. Kitzie nodded that that was probably best.

Carson looked over to see a young woman in tight jeans in conversation with Green Eyes. *Figures*, she thought, smiled, and caught his attention. He looked brighter at her for the connection. The blond noticed his diverted attention and looked daggers over her shoulder at Carson.

Carson played it up a touch by blowing him a kiss and mouthing, "Thank you and goodnight."

He nodded and dazzled her with another smile. She was caught in the genuineness of his eyes, which sent a charge right through her, and she blushed. She shook it off, and without another thought, left for the truck.

Once inside the relative quiet of the cab, she exhaled, closed her eyes, and set her head back against the headrest. Through the glass of the windows, she heard a coyote call from somewhere close by. She brought her head up, cracked the window to get a bearing, and decided maybe the coyote wasn't that close after all. Stars sparkled in a crisp patch of sky. She closed her eyes and loved the sound of the coyote's voice. Her breathing deepened as she relaxed. She fell asleep and began to dream.

Soft lights made the surfaces of the garden plants seem surreal. And the smells of the food, beef on the grill, filled the warm fall evening. Carson walked through the gathering, smiling at her neighbors and exchanging pleasantries. It was a close group that gathered weekly. She was popular with them, missed when she wasn't there, and held the attention of each. She said the right things, hugged each with timing, and asked the right questions about family or recent events.

She pretended she didn't see him, but his presence reached out to her and he was all she thought of. Of course, he was there, and so was his wife, and she hugged her with genuine affection. There was the pleasant noise of conversation and some sort of background music. Time warped in places when Carson caught his eye, and he hers. He was as acutely aware of her as she was of him. They exchanged cleverly timed glances filled with meaning only they shared. He was so important to her...and she couldn't tell a soul. She'd never tell a soul. And no one would have believed they'd been intimate.

He acted as though she was special to him. It thrilled Carson to her core, and she fantasized about him for days after each encounter. She embellished their encounters in her mind and convinced herself it balanced her world to have him when she could. They blended smoothly, always briefly, and they never discussed what they did or what they were doing.

After they'd had a particularly delicious moment together, he said to her, "You know, if she found out, I'd be living in a trailer park. Maybe we should talk about this."

Carson straightened her jogging outfit, kissed him, and said, "Let's not."

Best not to think too deeply on it, she thought as she walked back to her house unnoticed. There was no future there, she knew it. As she walked, she couldn't find her house. There were lots of houses, ones she knew and recognized, but hers wasn't there. It was as though it had disappeared; the two houses on either side of where her house should be had slid together, and hers was erased. She panicked and began to run, first one way and then the other. She stopped in the middle of the street and looked all around her. Everything was familiar and nothing was familiar. She began to cry.

A knock on the window startled her awake. Green Eyes stood there and two cowboys helped Kitzie around to the passenger's side. Her head spun, and the dizziness was nauseating. Carson gathered herself and rolled the window the rest of the way down.

"Didn't mean to scare you. You okay?"

"Yeah, guess I was more tired than I realized."

As she drove home, Kitzie chatted about the evening and asked if Carson had had a good time. Carson said yes, she had. She was quiet and her mom asked her what was on her mind.

"I nodded off and had a bad dream."

"About losing the house?"

"No, I'm not thinking about that part of my collapse, there was something else, something aside from that...it's as if there were things..."

Her mother stared at her and waited.

Carson asked a rhetorical question. "I loved being a part of my community, Mom. I felt loved there, and I messed it up. Do things no one knows about eventually go away?"

She had promised him her silence, and she never broke it, but she wondered...did the keeping of that promise diminish her? Her mother took a while to answer. So long, in fact, that Carson checked to see if she'd heard her.

Kitzie smiled. "Some things leave a mark, like a bruise that doesn't heal. You just get used to not bumping into it. I think we each know who we were in a particular moment, good or not so good. We don't stay the same, we change. Intense feelings do fade and dull with time, and you learn to live with your mistakes."

FORTY-FIVE

usk faded fast to night and Shiloh pulled over to go pee at a rest stop, then returned to her truck. She didn't check her phone. She hadn't eaten and she drove in silence. She was numb, scared, and beyond caring what was happening back there. She had a place to go, such as it was. She followed his directions, and did it only to satisfy a certain curiosity. He'd said how to find it, how to get in, and that she'd be safe. He'd promised she'd be comfortable until he got there. He told her it was all going to be all right, he had a plan for them both and plenty of money to take care of things. That was the part that sounded the best of all, though Shiloh wondered who he was and what he wanted from her. He'd never hinted at an intimate relationship, yet he knew things about her that she couldn't explain. The thought that maybe he wanted sex had crossed her mind, but somehow she didn't feel that was a huge thing to worry on. She hadn't thought much about him until now. The long drive had given way to lots of time to dwell on things.

She'd rolled the past few days over and over in her head until she felt sick. She wanted to know what had happened to the old man and how Del got dead. She wasn't sorry he was dead; he was a shitbag. She'd wondered why "he" had included her in a plan beyond the cattle scam. She'd never met him, and so...why? She was invested. After all, he had her money. *Her* money. Why she trusted him to give it to her, she'd forgotten. Basically, that was the deal he made her and she had no choice. He ran the game and she played by his rules. Then she caught herself…had she met him? Did she know him?

Something darted fast across the deserted road ahead and Shiloh slowed. She knew where there was one deer, there would be more, and she was right. *Be careful,* she said to herself, *no need to get in a tumble on the drive to safety.* She willed herself to just get there. Vanish. She headed south into Nevada.

Shiloh got a little sleepy, found an old road where her truck could not be seen from the highway, got out, and stretched her legs. The air was clean and smelled good, and there was nothing around as far as the eye could see. Shiloh looked down and noticed that lots of grass and weeds had grown through the cracks in the old pavement. It had been a while since it had been used.

She used a penlight to read the hastily written directions once again. She leaned against the bed of the truck and wondered why the hell she was following them. She thought about the café. No telling when Toby had figured out the cash was missing, but he had to know by now. She didn't know this guy, and yet she needed a place to go. He offered her one. He made it sound so important, like it was her destiny or something. When guys talked like that—and they did a lot with Shiloh—she usually treated them like the saps they were. She'd let them spend every last dime, every cent of their savings on the hope that she'd be there, that she'd be that perfect angel, the dream lover they'd always felt would come their way like magic. She'd manipulate them into thinking they'd make her into their image of what she should be. Once or twice, she'd believed the bullshit, went along like it was working. She looked down again at the paper and smiled. *This guy's no different.*

Shiloh put the paper into her pocket and got back into the truck. More awake now, she turned around and headed back to the highway. She looked carefully to see what was coming. There was a semi that was headed the other way, toward Martin, and that was it. She accelerated down the road in the opposite direction.

FORTY-SIX

Harper was in the lead as they made their way in the dark. The horses followed each other and the men didn't talk much; in fact, they'd ridden in silence for hours. They trusted it was the right direction, though they'd had to turn and take a different route when the track became impassable again. But overall, Wyker seemed at ease in believing Harper had the correct route.

Wyker was behind Harper and C.J. brought up the rear. C.J. barely steered Rio with the reins, and when they had a tricky path to pick through, C.J. trusted Rio to take care. Animals, maybe coyotes, moved across the ground above them, and Rio checked and focused hard into the darkness. He listened and C.J. held his breath. He wondered if Rio would bolt, but he didn't. He let Rio use his senses to determine the threat, and when he decided there was none, he refocused forward.

The heavy-footed gelding packhorse was another matter. He was clumsy, stumbled a lot, and lightness on the lead rope was nonexistent. C.J. expended much of his mental and physical energy keeping him from falling off ledges, and found it to be nerve-racking. Half the time the packhorse rubbed one side of the pannier pack against rocks he edged too close to, or on a downhill he'd track unevenly and catch himself at the last second before he fell sideways. A knot developed along C.J.'s shoulders and upper back. He dallied the lead on the horn so he could rub a cramp, and the drag on the rope over his right thigh cut the circulation to his leg. He was reluctant to un-dally the rope, but finally knew he had to.

At the same moment, Rio curved his body to avoid a hard rub against an outcropping of rocks that clutched the side of the trail like a barnacle. C.J.'s hat touched the rock. He ducked just in time, and behind him the gelding bumped hard against that same bit of rock. It put him off-balance and tipped him to the left close to the edge of the trail. C.J. felt the gelding lose his footing and the horse's head jerked up. Some of the ledge of the trail had broken off and the sleepy gelding was startled by both the load shift in the pannier and gravity. Then his left front chipped loose some of the ground.

C.J. yelled, "Oh shit!"

Rio reacted to the problem and pivoted into the hill-side cliff. Rio opened his hips wide to bring them both around, and the unbearable pressure of the rope on C.J.'s thigh was exchanged by the pull of it on his saddle and back cinch as Rio dug in and held. He was sliding. The ground was broken shale, and provided little solid purchase. Gravel bits sounded like rain as they fell down the cliff.

Wyker both heard and felt the disaster unfolding behind him. He looked over his left shoulder and yelled, "Cut the rope!"

The rope was almost free of the broad horn of the saddle. C.J. smelled singed leather from where it had spun before the last loop froze on the horn. With one sweeping motion he freed his blade and swung it up so fast he thought he'd cut himself wide open in his haste. The rope cracked with the break and the release almost flipped Rio. Even in the dark, C.J. saw the white of the frightened gelding's eyes as his head pitched back and he rolled down the cliff.

FORTY-SEVEN

Spence was interrupted by the desk phone, and he wheeled away from the computer to answer. Toby's distress was clear and he asked Spence if he'd come over to the café. Toby went on to describe why he was upset and Spence's attention to the crime scene photos faded as he listened. He stood up and reached for his uniform jacket off the back of his chair, his eyes serious.

"Yes, be over in a few minutes."

He left the silent cell phone, certain it wouldn't ring again, grabbed his heavy patrol coat, and left for the café. He found Toby behind the counter. Their eyes met as he came through the door and he read the disappointment in them.

"Mornin' again, Tobe. Talk to me."

Toby explained that after the morning rush he usually did the deposit in his office in the back, only this morning he hadn't gotten to it until much later. "Everything was behind this morning 'cause Shiloh was late getting in, and then she's all banged up and not right. Then she left early and we had another wave come in. So by the time I go back there and do the money...well, right away I can see something's not right. The totals are wrong, and there's about three hundred dollars missing."

Spence noted the time he'd seen her through the window when he drove by earlier to check up on her. He knew she'd seen him. He asked Toby, "You said she was late? And all banged up? Like, what do you mean?"

Toby described what he'd seen and recounted when she came in, how long she worked, and when she left.

Spence raised his eyebrows as he looked over his pad. "What was going on in here this morning? Anything out of the ordinary?"

Toby said the place buzzed with rumors about old Hank Larsen and Del. People were shocked and it did kinda dampen the mood. He said she worked a little over an hour, then said she had "female" troubles. Toby scratched his head, "I dunno. She was in and out of the back. I didn't keep track of her, you know? What the hell happened last night?"

Spence relied on his public relations training and recited the usual law enforcement line, said he couldn't comment, and that the investigation was incomplete. But he asked more questions about Shiloh; what had Toby meant by she was "not right"? How long had she been doing that? And he kept after the description of "banged up."

Toby said she'd been off her game for a few days really, and she'd gotten her face hurt a week earlier at the bar. He recounted the story as it had been told to him, though he did go on to say, "Today's bruises were different, they were all up the side of her face, and she walked sore. Ya know? Like when it just hurts to move at all sore?" He grabbed a towel and wiped the counter off, reset the napkin holder, and fussed like it was easier to be busy while he spoke. "I didn't want to embarrass her by looking too closely. Ya know, women, they just get temperamental when you ask what happened and such, then they start to telling you and maybe crying and then you can't get any work out of them. Most times just send 'em home or they get on the phone to their girlfriends or the boyfriend who did it...and then they go on about all the boring details...over and over."

Spence hid his impatience until he interrupted Toby to ask if he wanted to file charges. Toby hemmed and hawed, but Spence encouraged him to do so. He didn't tell him why. Toby agreed and Spence inquired about any records he might have on Shiloh, or her employment application.

Toby looked dolefully in the direction of his office and the pitiful excuse he had for a desk. "Some. You know, I'm lucky to get anyone to work here. Always surprised me that a looker like that stayed as long as she did. Men came from miles just to watch her pour their coffee. You know what I mean? I'm gonna have some very disappointed customers...and some happy ranch wives."

Spence smiled at that and followed Toby into the back. "Did she have a locker or something here?"

Toby pointed to the cubbyhole Shiloh used. An apron was shoved in it, and Spence pulled it out. A slip of paper fell to the floor. He started to go for it, checked himself, and looked around. In the kitchen, near the prep area, he saw what he needed. He pulled out a pair of plastic gloves used for food handling. He returned to pick up the paper on the floor, unfolded it, and angled it toward the door where the light was better. It was a diner's receipt, but what she'd written didn't make sense. He went back into the kitchen, found a small plastic baggie, slid the note inside, and sealed it. He found Toby sitting on a hard folding chair at his desk. In the center was an old-style calculator with a solid roll of paper protruding out the top. Piles of papers covered the rest of the surface completely. On the wall hung a black phone, its bunched and twisted cord strangling its length to a fraction.

"Toby, please look at this. What does the shorthand on that mean?"

Toby reached for his "cheater" glasses and peered at it.

Spence continued, "I know that restaurants have their own code, abbreviations that tell the cook how someone likes this or that. It's just that I've never known anyone to order thirty eggs over easy."

FORTY-EIGHT

C.J. thought he was gonna eat shit. He was sure of it, and then it was over and he hadn't. He was speechless as he stood next to Wyker, looking down into the dark. Tammy paced. Their eyes adjusted somewhat to the darkness, and as the initial adrenaline rush backed off, their senses returned. The packhorse seemed to be about thirty feet down in some rock and low brush.

Harper hadn't said much. He held all the horses farther up the trail, then his voice came out of the darkness. "That horse is lucky. He's not hurt that badly, he landed on the ledge-like section. There's a way to lead him perpendicular to the trail, and we won't have to double back."

C.J. couldn't believe it. "You can see that? What the hell?"

Harper laughed. "Yeah, this trail continues a ways and then drops down, and when you get him up, it shouldn't be a big deal."

Wyker said, "That's a fine, positive attitude."

Wyker attached his coiled rope to his belt and put his heavy leather gloves back on. He commanded Tammy to stay. It was obvious she didn't like that, nor did she want to. Wyker set his hat on a boulder and adjusted a headlamp to his head.

He handed C.J. a flashlight. "Careful with the light, not right in his eyes if you can help it, or mine."

They edged back along the trail, picked a spot, and began a descent. When they got near the gelding, he was still and appeared to be dead. C.J. watched for the rise and fall of his side, and was relieved to see he was breathing. Aside from nasty, raw scrapes that had taken hair clean off, the horse looked better than he expected. Granted, they could see only one side of the horse. Miraculously, he'd finished the fall on his side with legs flat on the ledge and pointed downhill. There was enough ground around where he'd landed that he could get up. The horse's left ear flicked toward the sounds of the men climbing over the rocks to get to him.

Wyker came up to the horse gently, his voice soothing. "Easy, easy there, easy." The last few inches, he crouched and placed his palms firmly on the horse's neck, which prevented him from moving. He instructed C.J. to stay clear of the legs and to come around to a position near the horse's withers and back.

The horse had come down in an area where there were no major boulders and C.J. sensed a measure of relief from Wyker. Pieces of equipment and gear were scattered behind and above him in the scree of the mountain. C.J. found parts; the harness was broken up, though most of it was still attached to the gelding.

"That may have helped break his fall," Wyker observed.

The sharpest part of the fall was where he'd slipped off the trail, and they had been very lucky. Leather straps were tangled and scarred, and C.J. worked to get them off.

"Easy, mate, easy," he said.

It took a few minutes and some effort, and the gelding

didn't thrash, which helped. The back cinch was a bugger, but C.J. finally got it free and dragged the mess out of the way. The downed animal tried to lift its head and scramble its legs when he heard the sounds of the equipment move over the rocks. It was the first reaction from him, and Wyker steadied him. They weren't set yet for him to try to get up.

"Good…that's good…he has something left, he has to get himself up or he won't at all."

C.J. took the lead rope on the halter and got ahead of him.

"There's a lot of loose stuff there, you need to clear some space in case he comes forward on you."

C.J. began to clear the ground with his boot.

"Yeah, that's good," Wyker said as he followed C.J.'s movements.

C.J. pulled on the rope and Wyker coaxed the horse to get up. The horse flailed a bit, legs swung in the air, and he grunted. Then he stopped and acted as if he had given in. C.J. pulled on the rope, which lifted his head and stretched his neck, but he didn't help. C.J. was surprised when Wyker began yelling at the gelding, using his coiled rope to smack him hard on his back and rump. It looked awful, and sounded worse.

The horse struggled. Sweat dappled his neck, but after a couple of failed starts and stops, he was finally on his feet. Besides the places where the hair was scraped off in the fall, the horse had a couple of deep scrapes and shallow cuts. He stood calmly as Wyker checked him over, though he shook from the cold and shock of his ordeal.

"As a good friend of mine would say he's banged up

some, but it's far from his heart and he'll heal."

"Would that have been Tuff?" C.J. asked.

"Sure was. I hear him to this day."

They decided to proceed and give the gelding a better going over later, when it was light. C.J. started the climb back up. He went through the wrecked gear as he went, and took what was worth carrying to where Harper had the horses. He stowed what he could in the pack on the other horse. He was startled to hear Harper off his horse. He'd taken his bridle and tied it to his saddle. He climbed down the slope toward Wyker and the horse.

Over his shoulder, he said, "He'll follow you. I'll lead that one and meet up with you."

Harper took the rope from Wyker and moved the gelding off before more stiffness and pain set in. Wyker climbed back up to the trail, much to Tammy's obvious relief and joy.

Harper's horse did more than follow; he led the way. Wyker laughed at the naturalness of it. The horse seemed to know what was expected of him, and did it. It took an hour and a half, almost two, before Rio's ears flicked to his left and the sound of pebbles and displaced rock gave way to the shadow of Harper leading the packhorse to the trail. He bridled his horse and ponied the wounded pack-horse, and the group continued down to the crevasse floor.

"It breaks off that way and drops down into a valley over there. If we've made the time, we'll be ahead or even with them. There used to be a spring tucked back in a canyon close by, I think it's behind and between those walls. We'll water there."

The temperature dropped a predawn chill. Wyker took the injured packhorse and suggested Harper move out on ahead to take a look around. Both Harper and C.J. laughed in that way people do when they've had a long night, then Harper vanished into the dark, and in moments the sounds of him faded.

Wyker used his light to check the injured horse as they rode, knew to keep him moving was best, and followed the trail as the sun rose. The banged-up gelding walked stiffly with a noticeable front-end limp. The steepness of the descent made it harder for him, but soon the going became better as the trail became a series of switchbacks. C.J. hoped the worst was behind them.

Two hours later a hazy light, diffused by bands of clouds, cast bare shadows among the rocks and sparse bushes. The bottom of one long switchback was in the cleft of blended ridges and Harper was there waiting.

"They're in the valley off to the west, we're about even with them. They're on the move."

Harper started to lead the way, but he turned and spoke to Wyker over his shoulder. "There's a protected area down close to the valley floor, a short canyon with a spring. We should take the pack off that one and leave the two of them there. Just carry what we need, then we catch them for sure."

Wyker thought on it and said to Harper's back, "They'd probably stay together."

Harper answered, "They'll stay."

C.J. overheard and asked, "What? Come back later and get them?"

Wyker nodded over his shoulder.

They rode in silence for a while until Harper made a couple of stops and starts as he looked for the entrance. It was flanked high with boulders and a stone slope higher on the mountainside. If Harper hadn't turned, C.J. wouldn't have seen it at all. It didn't look like you could ride "into" anywhere. It was a narrow crack, deep in shadow and a tight squeeze, but they wiggled through.

Rio didn't like the confined spaces and jigged a bit while C.J. steadied him. C.J. was impressed with what felt like a hideout. It appealed to the sneaky part of anyone— the perfect place to be invisible.

"Shit, this is great," he said to himself, but his whisper carried and Wyker laughed.

Sound carried loud until the crack opened up to a tiny "box" in the mountain. Not really a canyon, but unless you were a goat, it was not climbable.

Wyker said to Harper, "You weren't kidding when you said 'protected.'"

It was a very short area, about a half-acre floor at the most, and it had some forage for the horses. There was an actual rock promontory that formed a kind of cave. C.J. saw drawings on an innermost curved wall, and he smiled. They were barely discernable and he rode closer to lean over for a better look.

A spring oozed out of the high-sided rock face and dribbled into an erosion indentation in the rock before it overflowed the bucket-sized pool onto the rocky ground. It wasn't a creek per se, it didn't flow, but rather made a dark stain for many feet around it before it vanished. Where it crept and spread, it fed the grasses to a greener hue; a splash of color in a gray and brown palette.

Wyker dismounted and handed Johnny's mecate up to Harper, and he tended to the horses they'd leave behind.

C.J. asked Wyker if they'd hobble the horses. Wyker shook his head, then looked at Harper and smiled. "I thought I saw a clever bramble gate tucked away near where we came in here."

Harper smiled. "You did."

Wyker put the gear in the cave and got the grain bag. Rio's ears locked on that and he stretched his neck long toward Wyker. Wyker went to him and gave him a couple handfuls. He did the same to Johnny, Harper's horse, and then found a couple of good spots to leave the rest. He fed Tammy, too. With the packhorses settled as much as they could be, the men rode to close the "door" to the canyon with the bramble gate.

Harper's horse stood quietly next to Wyker and Johnny as Harper disappeared into the crevice to secure the gate. There was a nicker of separation anxiety. Rio nickered back and again jigged a tight circle.

When they were all mounted, they moved off down the trail quickly. Rio's anxiety eased the farther away they got, and Wyker asked Harper what the story was on that canyon.

Harper said his uncle told him several different stories, that it had been used for lots of things. "Over the millennia it has been a meeting place, a spiritual sanctuary, and a hideout."

FORTY-NINE

itzie couldn't sleep. She felt unsettled and thought about the guys out there. She thought about the cows, the pile of bills downstairs, then she didn't want to think at all. She rehashed the evening in her mind and the conversations at the Running Horse. Eventually, she gave up on sleep and worked to stand up. The sensation of the cold floor on her bare feet seemed to clear her mind and she looked out the window. She was surprised to see the barn slider open slightly, with a faint light coming out through the opening. She put the brace on her leg and struggled into some warm clothes. She hobbled her way through to the kitchen, got an extra coat from the mudroom, and worked her way out the door. Wyatt and Lulu slipped out ahead of her as the cool air splashed her face. She opened her mouth to call them, but then thought better of it. It was probably Jorge or Luis out there. She managed to position the top of the crutches into armpits layered with clothing, which were bruised and tender from the pressure of the crutches.

Carson was in her dad's chair in the tack room and had her feet up on the desk, the only light cast by a solitary brass lamp. Its green glass focused the light onto the blotter. She pulled at the edge of an old, faded picture tucked into the leather corner. She held it in her hand, then turned it over. Written on the back were her name and the date. It was a picture of Tuff holding his little girl.

She wore his heavy shearling coat and a throw over her legs. A box of Kleenex and an open bottle of California merlot sat nearby. She put the picture back where she found it and cradled a glass in both hands. The dogs found her and Wyatt stood on hind legs, his paws on the armrest. Carson spoke softly to him as her mother came in. She got up, but Kitzie raised a hand.

"Don't. I'm fine."

Kitzie looked around and found a four-legged stool to use as a leg rest, and a folded saddle blanket for cushioning. Carson settled her mom into the big leather swivel chair and put a throw over her lap. Kitzie flinched and lifted her bum knee into the best spot.

"Don't fuss," she said. "Pour me one."

Carson found a clean Mason jar for a glass and filled it. Kitzie took it and laid a hand on Wyatt's upturned head, then sent the dogs to the big dog bed in the corner, where they nestled together. Carson's tears had ceased, but the raw pain of them was etched on her face and in her eyes. Carson dragged another chair over and sat down.

"You're wearing your dad's coat," Kitzie said.

Her father's coat was too long in the arms, just as it had been when she was a child. "Coats like this last forever and are so warm. I love the permanent creases from age and the dark stains on the cuffs."

Kitzie said, "I do too."

A gust whistled the window and bits of hay skittered down the concrete breezeway past the door. It fluttered the pages of a calendar that hung by the door. Carson's eyes wandered around the room's old pictures, articles, and awards. They were stuck to the wall with whatever seemed handy at the time—a thumbtack, a farrier's nail, yellowed tape—and each image or ribbon stirred a memory. It was quiet except for the wind.

Carson blew her nose, took a sip from her glass, and asked what would happen if they didn't find the cows.

"I'll have to manage," Kitzie answered.

Then Carson noticed the calendar on the wall was old, from the year her father had died. "I've been taking stock of my situation. Apparently, my timing hasn't improved. Didn't mean to become another barnacle on your hull."

Kitzie smiled. She missed the funny metaphors Carson used. "That's crap. You're here because it was time for you to be here. Did you forget it's a working ranch? It's always something. Something's always happening."

"Oh Mom, I've made such a mess." Carson took a hit off the glass. "I'm sitting here in Dad's chair, and can't remember the sound of his voice. I desperately want to say I'm sorry, and I can't." Tears rolled, unabsorbed, down the coat. She emptied what was left in her glass and poured some more.

Kitzie waited for the right words. "Funny. I come out here, sit in this chair to get his strength and find my own courage."

Carson wiped her face. "You know when the money dried up my, 'friends' did too? I fit in when I had it, and was jettisoned when I didn't." There was a solid layer of rage in her that went beyond frustration.

Carson gave it all up. She talked and cried and talked some more. She told her mother everything. And when she grew silent, they sat together for a while. Kitzie reached out her hand and Carson took it in hers. In the eaves of the barn, the owl returned and made sounds of settling down. Kitzie wondered what time it was and glanced over at the window, surprised that it was getting light outside. Kitzie handed her daughter a Kleenex box, and Carson smiled and took some.

Kitzie said, "If some of the mess does manage to find you, you'll figure it out; we'll figure it out together. The forgiveness part is all yours, that's an inside job, and the most difficult."

FIFTY

As he approached the shabby apartment block, Spence saw that her truck was gone. When he tried the door to her apartment, he was grateful she hadn't locked it. He put on a pair of latex gloves and entered with the customary law enforcement announcement of his presence on the premises. He found food in the refrigerator, unwashed dishes in the small sink, and dried goods like stale cereal and crackers. It seemed she'd grabbed just what she needed and abandoned the rest.

There were some bits of paper on the dresser, and with a gloved forefinger, Spence moved them around to get a better look. He noted that she'd even left some clothes in the closet. He checked the pockets and found a receipt from the diner. It was old and she'd made changes to the numbers. Each amount that was scratched out kept growing. Oddly, she had written first ten, then fourteen, and up to thirty-five. In all caps after that was scribbled "fifteen fat ones" underlined with a large exclamation point after. The paper had been balled up, maybe thrown away. He decided it had been tossed, reconsidered, and retrieved to be disposed of elsewhere. She must have forgotten all about it. He bagged it and slid it into the breast pocket of his uniform.

He left everything else as he found it and retreated to his patrol car. Before he left, he stuck his card in the door of what looked like the landlord's apartment, and headed back to the office.

The first thing he did was compare the receipt he'd just found to the one he'd gotten at Toby's. He rolled his chair to the computer and punched up enough informa- tion from the Oregon Motor Vehicle database to get the registration on Shiloh's pick-up. He was surprised it wasn't currently registered, and wondered how he'd missed that. Then he thought about it, realized she'd never parked where he could see the tags, and she didn't cruise around much. He rolled his chair to the computer and inflated the urgency on this suspect. He made a detailed log of his ac- tions and the suspect's physical description on an attached sheet.

With evidence gloves, Spence removed the cell phone from the evidence bag and turned it on. After it had up- loaded its features, he noted there were no messages and no missed calls. He surmised the man he talked to knew that Del was dead and he'd warned Shiloh off.

He sat back and tried to put himself in the picture. There was the conversation he'd had with Hy Royston, the question of who had roughed up Shiloh, why Sonny and Hank were killed, and what Del's part was in it all. It was intertwined—a conspiracy with several moving parts—and he was certain it was the cattle rustling operation coming undone. The missing piece was where the cattle had gone. That was a lot of animals that had to go somewhere. He figured Hy knew this too and that was why he was on his way. He knew one thing; he wouldn't want the job of un- tangling the knot in terms of who to charge and with what, and who to make a case against when all the players were revealed.

He called Hy's number and got Dave, as Hy was driving. "Dave? That you? Hey, it's Spence, where are you right now? Oh, that close? I was gonna ask to meet. Breakfast tomorrow at the tavern? But maybe lunch today? Okay, breakfast it is. See you then."

FIFTY-ONE

Although Stiles and Ramos pushed the herd, they still had another day's ride at their present pace. Stiles knew they could push through; they'd done it before. They came to a shallow ravine with water and some grass growing at the water's edge.

Stiles said, "Water them and take a half-hour break. Let 'em graze."

The cattle waded across the shallow bit of stream and a couple of the heavier cows lay down. Ramos rode to a small mound of boulders with a lone skinny tree growing at the base. He dismounted, tied his horse to the tree, and settled at the base to doze.

Stiles found a good spot well away from him. He dismounted and loosened the girth, and glanced over to be sure Ramos was sleeping. He pulled out the Shiloh phone and saw there were no messages. He turned it off to save the battery. All he could do at this point was hope she had done what she was told and had gotten out. It bothered him that Del had gotten himself killed and that the old man was dead too.

His fatigue messed with him when he stopped moving. *Must keep moving,* he thought, and guided his gelding to another bit of stuff to eat. He put the phone in his pocket and pulled out some beef jerky. His breath made clouds and ground fog developed in pockets. That would make finding the way a little more interesting, but no big deal.

Nothing like jumping off that cliff that one time in the snow, he thought, and smiled.

The weather changed about halfway down the switch-backs. Wyker and Harper were silent and C.J. wanted to ask how far out they thought the storm was. Tammy trotted along behind Wyker. Rio seemed to like following her. She was the silent fourth "man" and never wavered in pace or posture. Wyker had full chaps on and an older-style duster, and C.J. was similarly clothed. The men moved out at a good trot or lope, and were able to go much faster without the packhorses.

The band of rain that moved through was cold, almost slushy, and stung as it hit their faces. Rio shook off the accumulated drops from his forelock, which added to the cold spray into C.J.'s face. C.J. was grim; this was a reality dose of weather. It sucked. Well, at least it hadn't begun to snow.

C.J. found fresh manure, and they followed the trail to a shallow creek area where it was clear the herd had stopped for a short rest. Harper trotted back to Wyker after making a wide circle. Tammy sat down to rest while they were stopped. She looked tired. Wyker studied her, then looked up as Harper returned. "You act like you know what you're doing."

Harper smiled through what looked to be a very cold face. His lips weren't exactly blue, but they had a tinge. His breath, and that of his horse, clouded with each exhale.

"We're on the rez. They use our land like their own free-way, and we either didn't know it or didn't care."

Through clenched jaws, C.J. asked Harper how long ago he figured the rustlers were there.

"Couple hours ago, like this morning. They're not going to stop, they'll ride all night."

They pushed it at an extended trot, and Harper rode alongside Wyker. Tammy kept up, but C.J. noticed that Wyker continued to watch her closely.

And then a gust of wind blew, catching the manes of the horses and blowing them to the left. And it brought with it snow. They rode for about thirty minutes before Wyker stopped. He dismounted, and from his saddlebag he pulled out a coat for the dog. He checked her paws. Tammy waited patiently.

"She's okay, but I'll carry her on Johnny when it gets dark," Wyker said.

He remounted and they picked up the trot again. The dusting of snow would make the trail of the herd easy to follow after dark. They were in high-desert terrain with little brush and few trees; rocky, open country and soft hills. The steeper hillsides rose off to the side of them. In the gullies, the wind blew over them rather than on them, and it was a relief. At the higher points of ground, the wind-driven snow/sleet/rain combination was no longer on their faces, and now pelted the backs of their necks. Thankfully, that was as bad as it got. Harper proved he was tough, and that horse of his never swished his tail or shook its head in protest. Overall, he was an amazing animal.

With daylight waning, Wyker used his binoculars and

scanned ahead. He saw the broken, snow-covered ground appearing and disappearing in a broken trajectory. He didn't actually see them, but he knew they were closing in. They'd made up time and ground. They needed a short rest and then some luck.

There was a short break in the weather and they picked out a cluster of rocks and low trees. C.J. grained the horses. Tammy ate some dry kibble and rested. The saddles they left on, but loosened the girths, and covered the seats so they wouldn't become soaked. They'd break for an hour or so, then continue after them.

FIFTY-TWO

Shiloh's truck defroster fan had so little power that it defrosted only two small circles, each the diameter of a teacup saucer, at the base of the windshield. She hunched low to see through them. The truck was a rolling wreck and she knew it. The bald tires barely held the slick pavement as she looked for the unmarked dirt road off a frontage road that ran parallel to the highway. She ran a verbal dialogue of bargaining with the truck to not run out of gas.

The adrenaline of being a fugitive had worn off. The flush of a successful escape had faded. Alone in the dark, Shiloh's bravado evaporated. She crept along, seeking an old piece of board with five numbers on it. He said the numbers would have slash marks between them, and they would be hand-painted and on a board fastened to a post at windshield level.

Shiloh thought she saw it through the little defrosted portholes in her windshield. She stopped and backed up so that her one high beam illuminated the sign on the post. Shiloh opened the driver's side door and got out to look over the roof of her truck. The wind-driven sleet smacked the side of her face, and she gasped. Her hair whipped across her cheeks and she pulled it away from her eyes to stare at the sign. It was the one she was looking for, but something else made her eyes widen in surprise. The numbers were a date—the date she was born. Those numbers were her birthday and it creeped her out. And if she'd had a full tank of gas and money to go on, she'd have made the choice to not go down that road at all.

How weird... Shiloh thought as she got back into the truck. She navigated down the badly kept road for about a mile. The gas gauge was at empty and when it dipped below that for a few miles, she knew she'd be dead in the water. Then her lights found a slight bend in the road, and the road widened into an area of open ground in front of a good-sized, rectangular wooden barn. There was a small side door and two large swinging doors that must have locked from the inside because there were no handles on the outside. Shiloh parked in front of the small door to the barn so that her headlights illuminated it. Her heart sank as she saw that it was padlocked. He had not given her the combination. *Shit!* But she got out of her truck and went to the door to look anyway. It was different from any tumbler lock she'd seen in that it needed five numbers to open. She tried her birthday, which didn't work. *Crap!*

Shiloh was cold, she was tired, and now she was pissed off. She had both hands pressed flat against the metal door, and her forehead pressed against its icy coldness, when she had a bizarre thought. Could it be that simple? She tried the numbers again, but in reverse order. The lock opened.

Yes!

Shiloh opened the door inward to see the hulking shape of a huge, forty-foot motor home. It was covered loosely with some kind of net-like tarp. Her truck headlights illuminated it just enough that she could see as she walked forward and pulled on the closest edge of the tarp.

She stepped toward the back, pulling the tarp away enough to see the front end of the coach. It had a passenger's door and she reached up and tried it. It was unlocked, so she opened it, and a forward interior light went on.

Okay...

Shiloh climbed up and inside. It was cold in there, freezing cold, and it smelled new—that wonderful new-car smell, only bigger. She didn't know much about motor homes, but this was super nice. She guessed that she'd need to light a pilot light somewhere in order for the heat to work. Shiloh went into the sitting area/kitchen and found an overhead light. The light cast a welcoming glow and she began to feel better.

She saw that the unit was long, with a hall to the left past the kitchen, and she found another light in the ceiling, which illuminated the area. To the right was a small pocket door. Shiloh opened it and found a pretty decent bathroom. She tried the tap and heard a pump somewhere, and water trickled out in fits and starts, then to a steady stream. *Cool...*she smiled.

There was a short hall that led to a master bedroom with a nice, queen-sized bed. The décor was fancy, but not extreme. Shiloh's hand felt the handsome bedspread, and she gave the bed a test. It felt like it had one of those foam-topped mattresses. Then she noticed two control units, one on each of the small side tables next to the bed. She pressed a button and the dial lit up and digitally read "Hi." She spun a little side dial and the Hi went to nine, then eight, then seven. She looked at the matching unit and investigated. It took her a minute to realize it was a heated mattress. She turned both controllers to Hi.

She looked in the dresser drawers and they were clean. She slid open the mirrored closet door, expecting to see clothes hanging there, and found nothing but a large cardboard box on the floor tucked back against the wall. Curious, Shiloh saw that the box had been opened. She peered inside at an odd-looking machine. It was heavy as she slid the box over to get a look at the side of it. It read "Super Canner" along with a model number. *A canner?* she thought. *How odd,* and moved on.

Shiloh smiled and turned around to see a flat-screen TV in the upper section of a wooden, built-in dresser/storage wall. She saw a remote and tried it. It turned on and the screen was blue. She figured there'd be a manual somewhere. *This is getting nicer all the time,* she thought. There was a thermostat on the wall in the bedroom. Shiloh adjusted the dial and to her surprise, she heard it click on and a fan somewhere started to whir. *Huh? Really?* She found a register in the carpeted floor and cool air gently blew into her hand. *When it's light out tomorrow I'll have to take a better look around the outside of this thing,* she thought. It was connected to power and he had thought this out, so there was probably propane there too; had to be. Shiloh dialed the thermostat to the original setting and it shut down. She went back to the kitchen/salon area, and found another thermostat that also worked.

She saw a big, flat-screen TV just above the driver's area and saw the remote that operated it. She turned it on and it warmed to a lovely glow, then the news popped up on it. Shiloh adjusted the volume and a surround-sound speaker system perfectly balanced what she heard. *Sweet!* Below it was an electric fireplace, one of those new ones that looked like a real fireplace. She fingered the top panel until it plopped open on a hinge, revealing the controls to turn it on and adjust a fan that blew hot air into the room. It warmed up very quickly, and Shiloh held her cold hands to it. The warmth was delicious.

She felt much happier. The kitchen was galley style and had more room than the one in her apartment. She tried the side door, which opened, but was blocked by the tarp. She went forward to the driver's side door and exited. Shiloh felt her way all around and tried to pull the tarp off in the semi-dark of the barn. It hung up on some stuff on the roof, and she decided she'd better not force it. Her truck headlights still cast long shadows, and she just missed tripping over an electrical cord and a thick hose that ran to the side of the building. She walked around the exterior of the unit and located the intake grates of each heater.

Shiloh went back to her truck. She would have preferred to park it inside, out of sight, but for now, she backed it up and tucked it next to the barn. As she moved it, her headlights illuminated a large propane tank about thirty-five feet away from the barn. There was a fitting of some kind on the side of the barn, and maybe an electrical connection. A satellite dish was nearby with another connection to the outside of the building.

Shiloh didn't care about the particulars, it all worked for her at that moment. She turned off her truck, silently grateful it had run on fumes, and grabbed her things. She saw the letters GMC emblazoned on the front grille of the motor home, and noticed it had four wheels in the back, like two axles back there.

Shiloh put her stuff on the bed and settled in on the sofa with the remote control for the TV. She figured out how to change the channels, then realized she was hungry. The refrigerator was not on, and the side-by-side doors and the freezer doors had been left propped slightly open. She searched the cupboards, found some unopened crackers, and that fake cheese that one can pack in school lunches. *That stuff probably lasts a lifetime,* she thought. There were a few small, sealed packages of nuts, the airline kind, and she opened those. Then she found a bottle of Chardonnay whose name she'd never heard of before. *Excellent,* Shiloh thought, and she rummaged through one of the drawers and found a corkscrew.

She ate her gourmet meal and drank the wine, and felt better for it. Oh yes, things were way better now. The little fireplace thing worked like magic in the front salon area, and it became very cozy. Shiloh brought the wine and settled into the warm bed, and soon fell into a dreamless sleep.

FIFTY-THREE

Spence arrived at the Pine Tavern & Café about the same time Hy and Dave did. They greeted each other, shook hands, chatted lightly, and went inside. A light snow dusted the street and sidewalk, and the windows of the café were clouded with condensation. The warmth was welcome, and the men shed their winter gear and found a table.

The café was crowded and there was a definite void in service. Toby hardly looked up. The busboy helped with orders, serving, and clearing. An imperfect arrangement, but everyone understood and they were patient.

Toby gave Spence an inquisitive look. Spence shook his head and spoke quietly, "There was no sign of her, and it looks like she won't be back."

Toby didn't answer, but swore under his breath.

Hy was grumpy in the morning without his coffee, and Dave ignored him until he was civil. Spence said they were like two old ladies, which got him a glare from Hy. Spence raised his hands, palms up, in surrender. Dave was more amiable and they ordered breakfast. Dave pulled a melon baller out and set it next to his plate. Spence was curious but said nothing. Hy woke up more and they talked about their time at the Running Horse, what they'd learned about their microchip program, and the cameras they'd installed. They'd heard Kitzie Collins was on crutches and Spence asked what had happened. Hy said she'd gotten hurt on a horse.

Breakfast arrived. Toby's breakfasts were legendary and they never disappointed, even though he was short-handed. The hearty meals that Hy and Spence enjoyed were fantastic, and they said so. Dave had English muffins and fruit—a half a cantaloupe to be precise—and he used his baller instrument to make perfectly shaped balls of melon, which he then lightly salted and ate with a fork. They spoke in hushed tones as they ate.

Spence commented, "So, the better payoff is the calves and reproduction. There's that much better a return on the rustled cows."

Dave answered, "They've been very successful. They've figured out a system to locate the best cows from some major ranching outfits."

Hy added, "There's a lot of speculation about how they do that part."

Spence shared his theory that it was a team—a tight team—and they had a system.

"So, they had a system..." Spence mused.

Dave suspended his fork with its perfect combination of flavors in midair, and said, *'Had?* Why did you say had?"

Spence took his notebook out and set it on the table. He outlined the theory that the deaths, the disappearance of the waitress, the cell phone caller, and the rustlers were all connected. The conspiracy, he felt, led to the very place where they were eating breakfast. He told them about Hank's behavior, that maybe he was onto something, that he had seen something.

"There was an anger keeping him going these past

weeks. And I think he broke it wide open. I think he stole Del's phone and I think I talked to the main cattle thief yesterday."

They finished breakfast without going into it further inside the crowded café. Spence suggested they leave and examine the evidence in his office.

FIFTY-FOUR

It was damn cold and uncomfortable. Tucked into the lee side of a rock formation, they'd found protection from the wind. Tammy slept peacefully by Wyker, but for the men, sleep was impossible. They talked about the rustlers and their ability to handle the cattle and the elements. They had to admit how hardened they had to be. They talked around what they had to do to get the cattle away from them. Finally, it was Harper who put it out there—they would have to *take* the cattle from them.

They were all quiet for a few moments, until Wyker said they should discuss a strategy; a plan. He asked Harper if he'd seen weapons. Harper said he hadn't looked specifically for them, nor had he been close enough to.

C.J. toyed with some rocks on the ground, moved them around into patterns like the petroglyphs he'd seen, then said, "I won't risk Rio. Me, I risk, but not him." C.J. went on to say he didn't feel smart enough to know what to do on his own, but that he was impressed with their combined abilities. "You tell me what to do, and I'll do it."

Their rest over, they rode off in the direction they'd been following, and when cracks of light split the sky, it was clear the storm had brushed past them. The clouds had swung to the east and streamed the unstable air north of them. Visibility would be good, and with a bit of luck, they'd soon catch up to the rustlers. There was an uneasy quiet between them. They knew that whatever was going to happen, it would happen soon.

As Wyker reached the crest of a long slope, he stopped suddenly and reached for his binoculars. Harper, beside him, extended his scope to its full length and saw them too. C.J. and Rio held back, C.J.'s paranoid nature feeding his caution.

Tammy stood at Johnny's feet and Johnny dropped his nose to her. C.J. watched his steaming breath blow down and wisp up around her. She turned her head toward him in what C.J. thought looked like silent gratitude.

Harper nodded when Wyker said, "I make out two riders." Wyker lowered the binoculars and said, "Only two..." But the way he said it, it was almost a question.

Harper said that was all he'd observed before meeting up with Wyker and C.J.

C.J. said, "Amazing that it's just two guys."

Wyker started downhill. Johnny's back end slid, legs braced wide for balance, and his front legs managed the speed. Tammy made her way to the bottom and turned around to wait. Rio handled the hill the same way, and they did it with workmanlike efficiency. They galloped a flat area, about a half-mile, and then gentler ups and downs altered the pace. They had their goal in sight. The sun was to their left, and it would stab a beam and then vanish as they swept down the hill. The ground in the shadows was frosty slick, and softened where the sun hit.

They rode fast across uneven ground that required a certain level of expertise and focus. Wyker rode lead. He let them know about any hole or rock that could trip up a horse and rider. Bits of mud and debris flew and the horses' chests were splattered, as well as the men's legs. All three horses were sure-footed, yet still there was the inevitable stumble, the brief loss of balance, then finding it again in the following strides. It wasn't a pretty ride.

Rio caught a foot and slid down a slope on his knees. He started to tilt sideways and C.J. stepped off him onto the hill. Rio recovered his balance and came up on his feet. C.J., in stride next to him, jogged a step or two and popped back up into the saddle without missing a beat.

Harper had been slightly behind them, and saw the whole thing. He came alongside the surprised but pleased C.J., and they both laughed. On the fly, Rio maintained his pace and C.J. reorganized himself and his rein. He looped the muddy mecate under his belt again, where it had been before the slide.

They trotted along a draw, parallel to the broken ground and the tracks from the cattle. To ride in the churned-up earth would suck the shoes off their horses' feet. C.J. patted Rio's damp, muddy neck. There were bits of broken twigs and debris in his mane from plowing through dense shrubbery in order to stay out of the line of sight of the rustlers. They were so focused on their pursuit that the adverse conditions were a minor consideration, almost forgotten. The cattle—Kitzie's cattle—pulled on them like a powerful magnet. The momentum was on their side. They could feel it. Even Tammy felt it. They were close and she could smell the herd.

FIFTY-FIVE

The cattle were tired and it now required more effort to move them. The night had been miserable. Bands of bad weather had broken off of a front and swept over them. It had snowed, it had rained, it had sleeted, and it had blown. Stiles and Ramos were finally out of the steeper hills into the high desert, close to the rendezvous spot. The sky cleared as the storm moved north of them. A kindness, but Stiles was concerned about timing. The truck would be there that afternoon, and by his reckoning, they were still on the rez. They needed to be at least two hours ahead of where they were. They had to move faster. He rode behind the herd, and hollered and slapped his leg with his rope. The cattle moved at different speeds, some a little faster than others. Ramos muttered something that was hard to hear, as he had a scarf wrapped over his face.

Stiles didn't respond, so Ramos lowered the scarf and said it again. It sounded like *"Siguendo."* Then he spat on the ground.

Stiles couldn't believe what he thought he'd heard Ramos say in Spanish. "Somebody's back there?"

Ramos only nodded and Stiles turned and looked, but saw nothing. His first concern was to meet the truck. That some rez Indian was out hunting rabbits for his supper didn't matter to him. Stiles pushed the herd to move faster. He signaled to Ramos to keep going, then rode up onto a promontory to take a look around. At first, he saw nothing, and he was convinced the Mex was nuts, until movement caught his eye. He stood up in his stirrups and stared. There was a rider out there, and he was close.

He loped back to the herd. His speed startled them, which sped them up. He yelled to Ramos,- who nodded and angled his horse toward the side of the herd. Stiles upped his pressure and focused his energy on the lead cows. The others followed them.

Wyker had Tammy heel with him. She'd seen the cows, but he kept her from tipping their hand. Harper was close, and led them on a parallel course that had kept them out of sight of the rustlers. Wyker was surprised. There were only two of them and no dogs.

Harper raised his hand in a silent "whoa" and they fell into single file. All three horses sensed something, a heightened energy. Harper stopped. Wyker moved Johnny up next to him and leaned over toward Harper to hear him say, "They've seen us."

C.J. asked, "You sure?"

Harper shot C.J. a look that would have been funny in another time and place.

Wyker said, "Well, if they know, let's go get a better look. Quit fooling around."

The three rode to the top of a rise and Wyker used his glasses.

Harper said, "They have to go straight through that

valley." Then he added, "There's a road that sweeps close to the rez boundary. They've come through there before."

Wyker put the binoculars away. "They're in a hurry. Could be they've seen us and are moving out. Or maybe they're late."

Harper said, "That's where they're headed."

Wyker nodded. "We're taking the cattle. Let's all be sure we have the same story when it's over."

C.J. quipped, "I suck at stories, mate. I'm better at lying."

Wyker nodded again but was cautious. "We'll figure it out later. Let's go get some cows."

Harper left them to get ahead of the herd. Rio paced when Harper's horse left them. Wyker asked C.J. if he was ready, and C.J. nodded as they picked up a trot, then broke into a lope in direct pursuit.

If they could have ridden as the crow flies, they would have been on top of them in no time, rather than taking the better part of an hour. When they did catch them, they were very close to the edge of the rez and Wyker signaled to C.J. to take Rio down along a dry creek bed off to the right. He made a circular hand motion, a signal to go around and flank them.

Rio threw his head. He was covered with sweat. He loped sideways, settled, and changed his attitude. C.J. took him down into a wash and around a curve in the dry streambed. Part of the bank had eroded and crumbled, so it was good footing, not too rocky. They moved well until Rio slid to a hard stop. C.J. couldn't figure what had stalled him. He had his head down and was blowing and sniffing at a spot just ahead of them in the creek bed. The area was sandy, soft, and it looked fine to C.J., but Rio wouldn't go there. He held firm that he would not move forward. Frustrated and impatient, C.J. pushed him. Rio resisted, took one step in, and his front leg sank to the knee. He scrambled backwards, leaped hard to the right, and spun a one-eighty to face the threat. It happened in a flash and scared the shit out of C.J. He realized he'd almost foundered his horse into an unrecoverable situation, and his horse had tried, against his better judgment and experience, to believe him. It was a bad moment where Rio's faith in C.J. had been tested.

C.J. stared at the benign ground that was really a sinkhole, stroked Rio's neck, and murmured a sincere apology. He looked for an option. He saw a small, narrow wildlife trail, and wound a circuitous bypass around it. Apparently, the wild animals knew to avoid the sinkhole too. He followed the trail, even though to go straight through would have been the obvious, faster way to go.

On the other side, C.J. turned Rio up the slope and they moved carefully to the rim. Rio froze, stock still in the lee of the slope. They were out of sight and perfectly positioned to get a look. Without being seen, C.J. stood tall in the stirrups, looked, sat back down immediately, and bent low over the horn. They were within a few yards of the bigger man.

He came up again slowly, standing in his stirrups to look again, and took measure of a classic confrontation. He crouched a bit, not believing what he was seeing. Harper sat on his horse, blocking the rustlers and their horses, and words were being exchanged. The skinnier of the two rustlers faced him from the front of the herd, and Harper was within yards of him, the sun at his back.

C.J. saw that the man who spoke to Harper was armed with a rifle. He ducked back down and sat in the saddle, flattening himself on Rio's neck, and shook his head. C.J. was scary close to the big guy, and he realized the guy didn't know he was there. He edged up again and saw a scabbard-like sheath attached to the man's saddle. C.J. watched him reach down, quietly undo the leather strings that held the flap over the knife, pull the flap up, and fold it over. This cleared the knife's massive handle.

The wind had come up and C.J. felt the sweat on his face go cold. He sat back down again, out of sight, and thought that was about the biggest blade he'd ever seen. *Must be a bad-ass throwing knife,* he thought. Thankfully, he hadn't seen a gun. Sweat beaded on his upper lip and he wiped it with his sleeve. Then he considered something and looked back down the path he and Rio had just come up.

He stood up in the stirrups again and took another look. The big guy hadn't moved and Harper was in a bad position. The skinny guy had had enough, and began to raise the rifle barrel toward Harper. The wind brought his words crystal clear to C.J. "...then they'll never find you..."

But before he cocked the rifle, there came a shot. The retort bounced off the hills and spooked the cattle. The skinny guy's horse shied. Harper ran his horse toward a group of boulders, and the horse really moved. The guy raised the barrel of the gun skyward as he tracked the departing Harper.

C.J. chose that moment and did it. He moved Rio up

to the top of the rise and yelled, "Hey asshole!" which scared the shit out of the big man.

Ramos had turned his horse slightly, ready to help his partner, but the voice from behind him caused him to inadvertently spur his horse. The startled horse leaped forward, spooked, and almost unseated him. Pissed off, Ramos turned and spurred his horse up the slope after C.J., his knife in hand.

Rio wheeled, slid ass-low down the slope, took a broad leap halfway down, completed a running landing, and picked up a full gallop down the draw. It was tight, the big man was quick, and they were close. C.J. and Rio retraced their steps and took the arching path around the treacherous sinkhole.

The big guy saw an opportunity. He chose the clear open ground of the creek bed to cut C.J. off and take him down. C.J. glanced over his shoulder to see him flip the blade. He was getting ready to throw it.

C.J. doubted his plan for that millisecond between success and failure. Rio responded to C.J.'s cues and ran the crooked trail up around the wash. They were now only a few feet apart, C.J. and Rio slightly above the big man, both horses running at full speed. The brush along the wash prevented their pursuer from getting a clean shot at them. The big man held the blade poised over his shoulder, waiting for the right moment to release it.

C.J.'s devotion to Rio had never been greater. His horse, possessed with an ineffable trait of courage and faith, covered the ground without a missed step. A stumble meant the knife would find its mark. C.J. didn't look over his shoulder again. At that point, it wasn't up to him.

He held on to Rio, and let him take care of them.

Separated by less than twenty feet, when Rio and C.J. were coming down the track almost level with the creek bed, the big man threw the blade. In an instant, C.J. felt something hit him in the back. Then he heard a horrible wreck behind them.

Success happened so fast that it took Rio many yards to slow up and turn around. There was no sign of the big man or his horse. C.J. felt cold up his back and reached around to touch it, expecting his hand to come back bloody. Instead, he fingered a huge slice in the back of his coat. It was split wide open.

C.J. looked back down the creek bed and saw the Mex's horse flailing in the sinkhole. He didn't see the Mex. C.J. hoped the wreck had snapped his neck, and that his broken body was in the sinkhole under his horse. But when the horse managed to get up and out, he saw the big man was not there. C.J. thought, *He must've moved like a demon up the steep draw.* C.J. didn't stick around to find out where he'd gone.

Harper moved fast and Stiles watched the Indian run. Could've had him, but decided not to waste the shot. He slid the rifle back into the scabbard and looked to the cattle. They had run off a short distance, some had split off, and some had stayed together. It was a much smaller group now and steam rose from their overheated bodies. He looked around, aware of his vulnerability out in the open, and he braced for more trouble.

Ramos was nowhere in sight and it was silent. As Stiles rode his horse toward the herd, he took stock of his situation. He wondered where the hell Ramos had gone. Not like him to run. He considered it was a hunter's shot, and not connected to the Indian. He decided to move what part of the herd he could on his own. He figured he was close, about an hour, maybe an hour and a half to the truck from there. He wanted to salvage this group if he could. He didn't want to cut and run...not yet. They'd used this way enough to have a couple of emergency escape routes, and he knew the country. He had an idea; one never used before, but he had marked it to memory just in case. He pushed the cows, alone, down the valley as quickly as he could.

C.J. and Rio made their way to a spot where he had a view of where things had happened. It was quiet now, and he saw no one. Paranoid, C.J. stayed low and out of sight, and made a wide circle around to another place where he might get a better view. The silence unnerved him, as did the memory of that rifle the rustler had.

He rode in the crevice of two hills, which gave them cover and a way to get closer to where Harper had confronted the rustlers. He almost had a heart attack when two lost and confused cows trundled out of the brush. They ambled toward him like they were happy to see him. C.J. let them follow as he and Rio found another sheltered, secure vantage point. He saw nothing but another couple of stranded cattle, and no sign of riders. C.J. wished he knew where the hell everybody was.

In the shadow of the rocks, the two cows, C.J., and Rio stood together. It was an odd little group, and the sight would have been funny in another context. They'd been after a whole herd, and C.J. had gotten two.

After what seemed like an eternity, he thought he heard someone coming, and he cursed the fact that he had no way to defend himself. C.J. backed Rio into the least-exposed position available and rotated Rio's body to face the enemy. The cattle seemed unconcerned.

C.J. let out a sigh of relief as Harper walked his horse out from between the boulders and brush, the horse's footfalls quiet without shoes.

"Oh mate, you scared the hell out of me!" C.J. said loudly.

Harper put his finger to his mouth, remounted, and rode over to Rio. They positioned their horses nose to tail so the two men could speak to each other in hushed tones.

C.J., still pumped, said, "Holy shit! What the hell was that?"

Harper answered, "Got a little crazy. You hurt?"

"No. What now?" C.J. asked.

C.J. filled him in on the big guy. Harper looked at him and said he'd wondered where he'd gone. They decided to go the way Harper had just come, and the cattle followed. The men picked another vantage point to check things out and spotted Tammy down in the flat area herding some cows. Harper scanned around with his scope. There was no sign of the rustlers or Wyker.

He lowered his scope and asked C.J., "That dog listen to you?"

C.J. said, "Hell, I don't know, maybe a little."

Harper nodded, put the scope away, and they moved cautiously forward out into the open. When Tammy saw them, she wagged her tail. She looked around, agitated, anxiously circled, and then crouched down, hooked on the cows. C.J. and Harper approached, split apart, and took positions to move the cattle. The two cows with them trotted to join the small group and let out relieved sounds as Tammy circled them in. C.J. didn't bother Tammy; she knew the job and set about doing it.

Harper said his uncle's place was very close and it would be nothing to move the cattle there.

C.J. said, "What about Wyker?"

"He followed the rest of the herd," Harper answered.

"We should go help him," C.J. said.

Wyker had followed the scattered cattle. A loose horse galloped out from somewhere and Wyker recognized it as the big Mexican's horse. It had a broken rein, snapped ten inches below the bit, and the saddle was askew. He saw no sign of the man, and Johnny pinned his ears when the horse ran toward them. He didn't like this new horse so close, but he focused on what had to be done.

In the confusion, the main group of cattle had split off into smaller groups, and Wyker was surprised to see the one rustler still trying to gather and push a few cattle ahead of him. Wyker didn't know the geography, and it looked like the rustler had angled to go up a sharp turn in the valley. A broader track went straight and there were sloped canyons off either side.

Wyker closed the gap from behind at a long trot. He figured the rustler was aware of him, even though he didn't turn to look.

The rustler split off suddenly and made for cover. He galloped around a bend and was lost from sight. The cattle slowed and settled to nibble at what forage could be found. Wyker hoped the rustler had abandoned the herd and made a run for it. He could see the brands clearly now, and he smiled. They were Three Bit cattle. He held back some distance and waited.

Wyker and Johnny slowly swung wide, far enough to be out of range, but there was still no sign of the rustler. He waited a few more minutes, then moved cautiously to get around and gather the cattle back together. Suddenly, Wyker checked Johnny hard and did a rollback to his left. The ground exploded in the place he would have been had he not done so. Wyker had realized the trap just in time, and the gunfire spit rock and dirt into the air. Johnny was a big Quarter Horse but he had speed. Wyker opened him up back the way they'd come, as fast as he could. He heard another report echo against the landscape but did not feel it or hear it hit.

He stole a look back. The loose horse had disappeared, and Wyker saw he hadn't been followed. He should have expected an instant response to confrontation, and kicked himself for miscalculating. He was glad that Tammy wasn't with him.

FIFTY-SIX

Spence unlocked the door to his office and the three men went inside. They kicked off the ice and dirt on the mat and shed their warm coats and gloves. Dave grabbed a chair and Spence showed them the evidence and pictures from the crime scene. They discussed what might have been the sequence of events. Spence described where he'd found the phone. All three were silent as the images of Sonny's body resting with Hank flashed on the screen.

Dave got on the phone to secure phone records and cell tower traces. He also accessed a link to the highway cameras. Over his shoulder, he said, "They'll need a little time to sort out the phone. They have a guy working on it now."

Hy nodded and moved on to Spence's theory. Spence handed them the evidence bags with the diner receipts and consulted his notes from his interview with Toby. He described the theft of the money from the till, and surmised it was traveling money, some owed to her, the rest stolen.

Dave queried how she could have taken advantage of so many. Spence described her as any man would, and said it was hard not to fall for her wiles.

Hy simply stated, "Can't say I recall the girl, but I get it."

Spence added his thoughts. "She was good and in a position to overhear conversations. The receipts don't make any sense to Toby, and he was very puzzled by them." He filled them in on what Toby said about the bruising on her face and how she'd been odd the past week or so. He stopped in mid-sentence and Hy asked what he was thinking. "Now that I think of it, she must have been watching...I'll bet my cruise through...I was just checking to see that she was still there and hoped that the guy would call again." He hesitated. "I'm almost certain something happened that night between Del and Shiloh, and the voice on the phone was, well...was upset about it."

Dave turned away from perusing the highway camera footage and said, "What if Del was the one who gave Shiloh those bruises? Hank had this phone and he hid it...in that butt-ugly frog thing...and Del was out there to scare it out of him...only it got physical. It wouldn't take much to kill an old man."

Spence said Hank was very frail. Hy asked Spence about what he thought had happened to Del. Spence admitted that he didn't know.

"That part didn't make sense. He must've been fleeing the scene, his car was outbound, and then he wrecks for some reason. He reeked, his hair was wet, and it stank...and not of water. That may get explained with a thorough autopsy. There were tracks from an animal, well you see, I took extensive photographs before the scene was disturbed by the firefighters."

Dave went back to fast-forwarding through the highway camera video records.

Hy sat back and said, "It's possible specific cattle were targeted and this Shiloh manipulated men to get the information. She was in a perfect position to capitalize on that. I'd be curious to know the connection between her and the man on the phone. Who is he and how did he set her up?"

Spence added, "So, you're confident she was part of the rustling operation? They stole millions...but where was her share? She had to steal money to get out of here? She had nothing? That part has me wondering where the money went."

Hy simply said, "And dead guy Del's money...you say he was hard up too? So where's the money?"

Spence's desk phone rang and he excused himself to answer it. It was a call for Agent Hyland Royston. Spence covered the mouthpiece and mocked, "Is there an Agent Hyland Royston here?"

Dave laughed.

Hy took the phone, listened intently to the other end of the line, and quickly relayed the information to his partner. He covered the mouthpiece with his hand and told the news to both men as fast as it came. He was excited—or as excited as Hy ever got.

"An inspector at a yard in southern Idaho messed around with this new scanner. He went to a yard to practice with it and he found some of the Running Horse cattle. He's quarantined all the cattle about to be slaughtered. It's a major slaughter yard, manager's screaming to the department. Kid's out there alone holding things till we get there."

FIFTY-SEVEN

C.J. and Harper moved the cattle down the valley cautiously. Both were aware that they were dangerously exposed. Rio stopped suddenly and locked on to something. Harper's horse saw it too. Tammy was preoccupied with the three cows that had stopped on a patch of green. She was set to move them when she suddenly took off. C.J. looked up and saw Wyker, the sun at his back, making his way toward them on Johnny. Tammy reached him first and was ecstatic. He dismounted and loved on his dog, remounted, and trotted over to C.J. and Harper. Tammy leaped and ran alongside them.

C.J.'s relief was all over his face. "About time you showed up."

Wyker had a tired smile. "Good to see you too. Everyone okay?" When he saw C.J.'s back, he asked what had happened.

Wyker fell in at the walk next to them as they moved the cattle. They talked about the big Mexican and how C.J. had gotten the back of his thick coat ventilated.

Wyker leaned over to speak to Harper across C.J. "When I said a distraction, I'm not sure that's what I meant. I thought you were a goner back there."

Harper replied, "Speaking of distractions, you ever shot that thing before? Or was that your first time?"

Wyker laughed. "When he lowered the barrel...well, I thought my timing was rather excellent." He paused. "You ever run that horse before?"

That set the three of them off into uncontrollable laughter, which broke the tension and dissipated the adrenaline. Minutes later, Wyker wiped his eyes as they all recovered themselves and got to the business of solidifying the herd.

Harper asked where the other rustler had gone.

Wyker's expression hardened. "Damned if I know. This country is deceptive. He melted away fast."

They made for Harper's uncle's place on the rez. Harper scanned the area for both rustlers, and the herd moved along easily with three riders and a dog. Harper said they'd be at his uncle's around dark.

They approached the area where Wyker'd had his last encounter. There was no sign of the rustlers, and the cattle were still there. C.J., Wyker, and Tammy held the herd while Harper went on a quick reconnaissance ride. He vanished like the rustler had, and C.J. commented on his gift of stealth.

Harper returned and said it was clear. They couldn't believe their luck. They had recovered almost Kitzie's entire herd, healthy, and no one had been hurt. Wyker was very pleased. In passing, he said he looked forward to telling his friend Hy all about it.

Harper's head turned sharply at the comment and asked who that was. Wyker told him. Harper listened with an amused look on his face, but said nothing.

Shiloh woke up often during the night. It was hard to get comfortable. She got up the next morning still very sore and in more pain. She distracted herself from it by taking stock. It hurt to dress, but it was cold out. She pulled all her things out of her truck, brought them in, and set them neatly on the table in front of the sofa.

Eventually, pangs of hunger sent her to search the kitchen. She found a microwavable bowl and looked in the pantry. She appreciated how neatly everything was stacked and stored; so well organized, she thought. Shiloh picked out a can of chicken noodle soup and explored a few drawers until she found the can opener. As she held the can on the counter and lined up the opener over it, she thought the can didn't feel quite right. She picked it up and shook it and no liquid sloshed inside. *Oh great,* she thought. Probably spoiled and a solidified "science project" would be all she'd find. She almost didn't open the can, as the smell from something like that would be really gaggy, but her hunger and her curiosity got the better of her.

There was no soup inside. *What the heck?* Instead, she found a dense, very tight paper spiral. It was packed so tightly that she couldn't get it out. Frustrated, Shiloh opened the other end and pushed the mass through. It rolled across the counter, bumped against the marble backsplash, and ricocheted onto the floor. She looked at the backsplash and thought, *What a nice detail... marble.* But then she bent down to pick up the runaway and was stunned. The tight paper spiral was all money. Lots of it. She tore off the paper binding ring and unfurled the currency. A new one-hundred-dollar bill, and another, and another. Shiloh could barely breathe as she unrolled it and it became clear that they were all hundreds.

She sat at the table, unrolled the wad of cash, and tried to count it. The new bills were difficult to unroll, uncooperative to flatten, and impossible to stack. Stunned, she gave up counting at six thousand dollars. Then she opened the cupboard and saw lots of soup. She randomly picked out a few cans and shook them. They each felt the same and she stepped back, realizing how much trouble she might be in.

Shiloh took all the canned goods out and found some slender boxes of packaged pasta and rice side dishes. She chose Rice-a-Roni Pasta Parmagiano, her favorite, and she pried the cardboard open at the top. She looked inside to see the tops of tightly compressed bills and a flavor packet. *Cute.* She pried one stack out and fanned the crisp edges. She whistled through her teeth. These were also hundred-dollar bills, also tightly rolled, three across and three deep in the box. Shiloh stared at them and put them all back as they were. She closed the cupboard and began to feel paranoid. What if the man who'd sent her there walked in right now, and found all his money stacked on the table and his pantry bank open?

And she was hungry. Was there nothing to eat?

FIFTY-EIGHT

Uncle was a man of few words, a flashlight, and the gift of taking charge. He met the herd well before they were within sight of the house. He said nothing. He simply turned and walked ahead of them down the dirt road toward a structure with a single light on the outside. As they got closer, C.J. saw that it wasn't on the building, but rather on an old lamppost between the building and a corral. Uncle swung open the panel gate to a large corral and waited for them.

Harper took point. C.J., Tammy, and Wyker followed up the herd, and they moved the Three Bit cattle into the pen. Wyker and C.J. stopped just outside, and Uncle closed the gate after Harper rode out. The cattle went over to a long metal trough and set to eating the hay that was in the feeder.

Out of the dark came a woman and a teenage boy of about seventeen. Silently, they approached the horses and held them. C.J., too tired to argue, dismounted and let the boy take Rio. To his surprise, the boy swung up into the saddle and the woman handed Johnny's lead to him after Wyker dismounted. Harper and the boy took the horses and disappeared around the corner of the barn.

C.J. muttered to his horse, "Traitor."

Uncle and the woman led them down the dirt road, which turned left to reveal a small ranch house. Tammy had it figured and she made a beeline for it. There was a

349

feeble light by the door on the front porch, and the weather-beaten wood rang hollow under their boots.

The door creaked in protest as it revealed a small living room. Inside was a tired easy chair that was obviously loved, a cluttered table by a three-seat sofa, and an old television set tuned to a news program. A fire welcomed them from the fireplace in the corner of the room. The warm smells of cooking came from a well-lit kitchen. Tammy sniffed a greeting to an old dog lying by the sofa. The old dog thumped his tail but didn't get up. Tammy followed the woman and sprawled out under the kitchen table.

C.J. removed his hat when he entered the home, and sat down at the table. The chair was tight in a corner, and it was easy to relax against the wall and close his eyes. He woke a little while later to see Harper speaking their language softly to the woman as she stirred something in a pot. He saw him reach up to the cupboard and take down two large mugs. The woman ladled something hot into each and got two spoons. He turned and placed a mug in front of C.J., and handed the other to Wyker. The woman retrieved two bottles of beer from somewhere outside, chilled by the elements, and handed one to C.J. and one to Wyker.

C.J. looked at the beer and then to Wyker, who nodded. "Go on, you deserve it."

C.J. smiled, thanked them, and ate the soup, which was hearty and filling. The beer tasted divine. Wyker was grateful for their kindness and Harper pointed Wyker to his uncle's chair. Wyker shook his head, but they insisted, and it felt like a feather bed. Wyker smiled as he recalled that his father once had something much like it…much to his mother's dismay. He put the cup on the windowsill and got his cell phone out. He turned it on and found that he had no signal. He gave up and thought he heard Harper say, "If you fall asleep, I'll wake you both shortly."

Stiles rode straight to the truck. He made it just in time. They'd almost given up and were set to leave. Stiles saw they had a horse trailer hooked up to a pick-up with them and it suited his needs perfectly. They asked him where the cattle were, and Stiles said Ramos was right behind him with the herd, and told them to wait for him. He also told them his horse looked to be colicking and he needed to use the rig and get him to a vet. Stiles hustled his horse into the two-horse stock trailer, saddle on, jumped into the truck, and headed down the dirt road as fast as he could reasonably go. *Let them figure it out,* he thought.

Stiles hoped she was there by now. He put his cell phone on the seat next to him and listened to its startup tones and clicks. There were some nasty ruts and an old creek bed that had some snow in it, and he focused on not getting stuck. The rig bucked and sputtered. He needed enough momentum to get beyond the creek, and it almost caught him. He realized how frightened he was. To get caught now would screw everything up for sure.

The light turned to dark and he turned on the truck's headlights. It would take him a couple of hours to get there. This dirt road took him in the wrong direction from where he needed to go, but he needed gas and found a convenience store with one pump. The engine was a bit worse for wear from neglect, probably a typical ranch truck. He checked the tires and fluids and that was a smart move. It needed topping up on just about everything. He checked the registration and saw fresh tags on both the truck and the trailer. *Good.*

He bought some groceries and some ice. Back on the road, headed in the right direction, he tore open a package of bear claw breakfast pastries and devoured them. He washed it down with orange juice of the "fresh-squeezed" plastic kind. He'd also grabbed some coffee, which the woman at the counter assured him was freshly made. He picked up the cell phone and saw there had been no calls. He dialed Shiloh's phone. It rang and rang and then went to voicemail. Stiles convinced himself the phone was not turned on at her end and he left a message. Basically, he said to sit tight, and in a moment of warmth, he got a little chatty, said he hoped she liked the motor home. He added his plan for a trip across country, someplace warm and sunny, well away from this cold. He finished with some words about being by the ocean. He hung up and felt his horse shift in the trailer. He'd need food and water soon.

FIFTY-NINE

The storm had passed and a layer of fog now blanketed the Three Bit Ranch. The light filtered through a haze of gray amber and it was quiet. Carson had gotten up early, like she had as a child. She had always been a morning person. She felt like an early ride in the arena. There were none of the sounds she remembered from childhood, just the early birds chirping in the steel rafters of the barn. A breeze jostled a long strand of old cobweb and she watched it sway with the current. Dust and debris colored it to a mousey brown and the string of dust pearls hung long like moss from the trees.

She warmed her mare up slowly, felt the even smoothness of her gaits, and rode alone for the better part of an hour. After her ride, near the tack room she slipped a rope halter around the mare's neck and loosely tied her, hung the bridle on a nearby hook, and heard her mother in the office. The coffeemaker gurgled and Carson poured a Styrofoam cupful and added sugar.

She asked Kitzie, "What are you out here for? You should be in the house resting that leg. Have you heard any news?"

Kitzie shook her head. "Oh, bother that, I was watching you ride and enjoying the barn. And in answer, I've heard nothing…yet."

Carson looked at her mom and smiled. "Ah, ever the optimist. I really enjoyed my ride, though this place is like a ghost town. I miss the activity. It was too quiet."

Kitzie sat back in the swivel chair, her leg up, and nodded that she knew what Carson meant. "I never expected Wyker to show up and actually help. He surprised me, you know? I hope they're okay."

Carson smiled and said, "It's kinda nice when something about people surprises you."

The phone rang. It was an old-style dial phone, heavy and black. Carson caught bits of the conversation. It was a man, someone Wyker knew, an official of some kind. Her mother grabbed a piece of paper and a pencil from the desk and took down information. Carson waited and saw relief on her mom's face.

Kitzie looked up at her daughter with a smile and mouthed, "They got our cows. They got our cows!"

Carson mouthed the word, "Where?"

"On the reservation."

Carson mouthed back, "Reservation?"

Kitzie said into the mouthpiece, "Yeah, I'll hold," and said to Carson, "they're somewhere on the McDermitt."

Carson thought about it, and looked to the map on the wall. "Really? That's a ways."

"One horse is pretty banged up, one of the packhorses. They have to go get that one, had to leave it. Long story I guess. They are at some guy's house on the rez. But they are okay and the cows seem to be fine. They need Wyker's rig. We need Jorge to go with you and his dogs. Would you go get some gear together? Gonna be cold." Then whoever was on the other end came back and she continued with that conversation.

Carson started off to find Jorge.

They loaded Wyker's rig with supplies, vet stuff, food,

and whatever else they could think of. Kitzie returned to the house and Google mapped the location on her laptop. It didn't really have an address. Carson looked over her shoulder at the computer. She considered looking at her e-mail, then decided she probably didn't have an account anymore. She had a Facebook page, but did she really want to look? As though reading her thoughts, Kitzie asked if she wanted to check her mail.

"It was a bundle connected to the house…cable, computer, and some other stuff in a package deal. I'm sure it's disconnected by now. It was way overdue before I left," Carson said with an edge in her voice. She felt embarrassed. "Sorry, I guess I feel guilty. I made such a mess of things."

Kitzie tidied the desk and shut down the computer. "I recall a quote from Alexander Hamilton in the *Buffalo News:* 'A well-adjusted person is one who makes the same mistake twice without getting nervous.'" Then she slipped in something that startled Carson to her core. "Did you love him?"

Carson was stunned. Her mother moved on without a beat and hobbled into the kitchen. They gathered their gear and were out the door to the truck in no time. Jorge's dogs were in the bed of the truck, crated. He had his horse ready to load, saddle on, and the bridle hanging on the horn.

Kitzie watched Carson get into the driver's seat. Carson asked her mom to hop in for the short ride. Her mother laughed that natural, easy way and said, "That's all I'm doing!"

Carson drove the truck to the hay barn, where Luis

waited to help Jorge load bales of hay onto the roof of the trailer and secure them with tarps. They loaded hay into the bed of the truck and put as many as would fit in a single layer in the rack on top of the trailer.

Kitzie and Carson sat in the truck together and Carson looked down at her hands, emotion in her throat, and she struggled to find a voice. Her mother waited and Carson took a deep breath. She looked at her and answered the earlier question. "No, he wasn't mine to love."

Kitzie said, "I see."

Carson plunged on, "I thought maybe I'd go back. But, if it's okay with you, I want to stay." Then, scared, she quickly added, "You don't have to answer now."

Kitzie looked at her daughter. "You know the answer." She reached over and touched her daughter's hand and squeezed it. "This has always been your home. It is yours to make of it what you will."

Jorge opened the crew cab door. His dad said a few things in Spanish, to be careful and take care. Wyatt tried to get in the truck and Luis stepped forward and gently pulled him back. Carson took her mom back to the house and Kitzie reluctantly got out. She crutched her way around to lean on the sill of the driver's side door, smiled, managed her way to the front door, and waved goodbye.

Maxie had just served Tiny his dinner when the phone rang; the *house* phone. Tiny heard him ask the caller to please wait a moment. Tiny had a thing for "real" phones in the house; he didn't like remotes. Maxie carried in the gold-plated phone and long cord. He plugged the cord into the closest outlet (there were dozens of them strategically placed all over the sprawling home) and placed the phone next to Tiny, lifted the receiver, and spoke into it. It was almost ritualized the way he did it.

"Mr. Bellamy will speak with you now. Hello? Yes…Mr. Bellamy is now available."

It annoyed Tiny to be disturbed during dinner. Maxie had prepared one of his favorites too. He looked with distaste at the offending phone Maxie handed him, and Maxie retreated to hang up the other one.

Tiny listened carefully and he slowly pushed his plate away. Maxie silently appeared at his elbow, took the plate, and disappeared into the kitchen. He would keep the food warm.

But Tiny lost his appetite and the dish went uneaten. The call was a long one; it was one of his foremen, Mark, at the site waiting with the trucks. They'd brought two cattle trucks, and it was late and the cattle weren't there. The foreman told him that Stiles had arrived alone, that he'd left and he hadn't seen or heard from him since. They were nervous about sitting near reservation land with trucks and men, and felt exposed. They wanted instructions. More specifically, they wanted to leave. The conversation was interrupted by one of his men and Tiny could hear him say that he heard someone.

Tiny said, "Don't hang up on me…I want to know what the hell is happening."

At first, there were just some garbled sounds, then a raised voice. Then more words and the tone was both defensive and conciliatory. Tiny tried to get a bead on what he was hearing.

"Sir, the Mexican is here, he's alone, and there are no cattle with him. He's pissed that Stiles isn't here and he says he doesn't know where the cows are. He says they were ambushed and he thinks it was Indians. He says he wants his money. I need instructions."

"Get the fuck out of there are your instructions! Leave that son-of-a-bitch; tell him he's on his own."

Tiny hung up the phone and left the dining room. He went to his study and pulled out a cigar and sat in his favorite chair. The room was octagonal, finely paneled, and unread books lined shelves that circled above his head. It was a beautiful space, perfect for work and reflection. Maxie came in, went to the bar, and poured Mr. Bellamy a snifter of expensive brandy. He lit an antique warmer, heated the liquid to a perfect temperature, and placed the snifter on a coaster on the table. He knew not to say anything when Tiny was in such a mood, and he retreated as silently as he had arrived. Tiny smoked and drank for almost forty minutes before the house phone rang again.

Maxie, posted just outside the door, entered and set the phone on a mahogany table by the chair. Tiny raised his hand, answered it himself, and waved Maxie out with his cigar.

This time it was another fellow, not Mark, and this guy was freaked out. He was out of breath, like he'd been running, and he said something about blood everywhere and then yelled something about a big-assed fucking knife.

Tiny was confused, "Where's Mark?"

The hysterical voice said, "I don't know! Behind me a

ways. He went down. That Mex went crazy and we all scattered! Mark was cut bad, his arm, his neck, and I tried to get him outta there. Everyone ran…we all took off into the dark! Shit! Shit! I'm bleeding bad!"

Tiny's heart pounded, but he stayed calm. "How did you get this phone?"

"Oh…fuck…I need stitches! Help!"

He repeated again, "How did you get this phone?"

"When Mark fell, I couldn't carry him, so I grabbed it out of his hand and kept running. Oh man, oh, I'm gonna be sick…"

And Tiny heard a cough and gagging. *Disgusting,* he thought. "Where are the trucks?" he asked. He raised his voice and said it again. "Where…are…the…trucks?"

"I don't know where they are. Mark said to get in the trucks and go, and that made the Mex mad! Mark wasn't telling him anything, just that we were leaving. When the Mex saw that we were leaving him, he pulled out a big fucking knife, the yelling started and I ran. Mark…he got cut first…the Mex ran up behind him and cut him….I think Mark bled out…I don't think he…"

The guy sobbed. He was scared and his teeth chattered. Tiny considered the possibility he was going into shock, and then there was his blood loss. Tiny bit his lower lip and hung up without another word. He knew the trucks were untraceable. The phone, however, was a huge problem. This number—how stupid! And there were severely injured people out there. He had to think what to do to clean this up. He needed to call his partner and he would have to go do salvage. He'd know how to clean up this mess. He'd need the helicopter and a trusted pilot to fly out there and back by dawn.

Tiny paced furiously, mentally preparing for the call he had to make. His silent partner wouldn't like any of this, but he had a way of monitoring law enforcement and he had the head for wet work. He dialed his private number.

His partner answered and was pissed. Pissed off because he was asleep, pissed because he had to get up, and really pissed because all hell had broken loose and he had to fix it, and fix it fast. He hung up on Tiny and got out his radios and monitoring gear. Then he dressed all in black. He called a number and asked, "Where's the pilot? Wake him! Prep for immediate departure. Get my team—you know who."

Thirty minutes later, he waited at the airport for his crew. He calculated flight time and made sure the body bags were loaded. He wasted no time with pleasantries when they arrived. They got in and the helicopter took off.

They came in low, below radar, and he used his night vision goggles to see the area as they approached. He knew the pilot was combat trained and had his own night vision gear. He saw that one of the cattle trucks was still there. He saw several bodies and someone leaned against one of the tires. The wounded man waved weakly and tracked the chopper as it landed.

Anonymous in his black garb, and sans his trademark fancy boots and hat, Dale and his two guys got out with their gear. Dale told the pilot to use night vision and make a sweep of the area to look for anyone else, and the pilot took off immediately. The injured man was exhausted and cold, but able to describe what he'd personally seen. Yeah, the Mexican took the other truck. Stiles had taken the pick-up and stock trailer and that just left the two cattle trucks. Dale told the guys to grab the dead bodies and put them in the back of the remaining cattle truck. Dale lifted the wounded man, walked him to the cab of a cattle truck, and helped him inside. The man started bleeding again and Dale found a dirty towel behind the seat and told the guy to keep pressure on his wound. The helicopter pilot radioed Dale and said he'd found another body, and there was a bloody guy waving like crazy at him.

Dale barked instructions to put down and get the body and the wounded guy. The pilot said they'd make a mess of his bird, and Dale told him to shut up and just do it.

As he released the talk button on the radio, he relaxed it to his side. He looked to the west, saw the stars vanish behind clouds, and silently hoped for a good rain to wash this mess away. One of his guys found a good-sized buck knife on the ground near where the other truck was parked. Dale figured the Mex had taken the better of the two trucks and was now armed with the guns that were in the cab. He didn't need his knife.

"Bag it and stow it in the chopper. We'll dispose of it over a lake or something on the way outta here."

Minutes later, the chopper landed. The bloody, freaked-out guy leaped out and ran to Dale. He was a mess and he still had Mark's cell phone, though the battery was dead. Dale took the phone with his gloved hand.

Dale convincingly reassured him as he led the guy toward the cattle truck. Dale was thinking this one was too freaked out and might be a problem. He put the man in the cab. Dale went to the back of the cattle truck and saw that they'd covered the bodies securely, and he told the bigger of his guys to drive the cattle truck to one of Tiny's special yards. He'd be waiting for them. The big guy asked about the guy in the truck. Dale gave him a look and the guy nodded, and Dale knew the freaked-out guy wouldn't be a problem after all.

Dale and the other "muscle" walked to the idling chopper and got in. The pilot's mouth was a hard line and Dale saw the stains in his beloved bird.

"Let's go, make a pass over so I can see we got it all, and then let's get out of here."

They'd been there less than an hour.

Hy and Dave met agent Tecteo Miranda at the yard. There was a lot of tension from the yard managers. They'd been reluctant to hold out a huge section of cattle from the production line. This inconveniently forced them to alter schedules, which they didn't seem to do very easily. Tecteo had to call his manager, and he had to call his boss, who had to page his superior, who then had to call another agency, which had closed for the day. This caused an emergency page to an underling of a department head at the state level who called his friend in the State Capitol, who then barked an order back down the chain to another agency, which finally made a late-night call to someone who could make a decision and was fortunately married to a district court judge, who rolled over in bed and said to her husband that a warrant would be sworn. The warrant arrived and several pens of cattle were sealed. None were removed. Tecteo had stayed up all night with his partner and a local sheriff (who happened to have family ranchers in the Malheur County region). All were motivated to track down as many rustled cattle as possible.

Tecteo had found a can of bright-orange spray paint, and to keep himself awake all night, he had set to scanning about sixty-five head. It wasn't a waste of time; he came up with eight more microchipped cattle, which he marked with the spray paint.

Tecteo limped to the agents' car as they parked, and everyone introduced themselves. Hy asked Tecteo why he was limping.

"Got me a nasty bruise from getting kicked last night."

Dave asked him what happened as he unloaded a laptop from the trunk of the car.

"I'd found a chip in a cow and had taken a reading. So I used a can of spray paint to mark the hide. Cow didn't mind the scanning, probably felt a bit like a massage, but the nozzle on the can had become clogged or something and it made this sound that sort of spit and crackled and the cow bolted and let fly."

Hy asked if he should get it checked out.

Tecteo laughed. "Heck no, it'll heal." Then he added, "The guy in charge here has managed to find tracking info on most of the cows in the two large pens we quarantined. He seems genuine enough, kind of simple. He's got a good reputation, from a good cattle family. Maybe got this gig through nepotism. I checked him out while I was waiting." He continued, "The secretary is a contradiction. A Little Miss Sunshine with a shit of a dog that has nipped two people. I'd tell you to watch out for it, but I think she left and I don't think she's coming back…just my gut feeling."

Tecteo's assessment of the secretary didn't miss the mark.

Hy didn't care. "Do we know where the cattle came from?"

"I've narrowed it down to three operations that regularly ship cattle in. All of them are LLCs and a tangle of ownership…corporations, limited partnerships and so on. Layers of shit to sift through. It'll be an accounting forensics job, and a legal maze, like usual. When this kind of profit is involved, I figure they can afford good lawyers. It'll be a hard wall to penetrate."

Then Hy said, "But not impossible, and we have a few good lawyers too. Good job, Agent Miranda."

Tecteo looked at both men and smiled. "Pleased you boys could make it to the party!"

Stiles dropped his horse off at a nearby ranch. He walked him back to their gate in the dark and turned him out in their big pasture with their cows. He'd seen the place enough times to know that they took good care of their animals. Besides, he thought, they're getting a fine working cow horse.

He climbed back into the truck and drove until he picked up the dirt track. His anticipation was building. He was about to meet his long-lost daughter. The adventure he'd planned, a journey to get to know each other, was about to begin. Sure, he thought, it might be awkward at first, but he felt confident that they'd have a proper relationship once he showed her all the trouble he'd gone to for her.

He parked the rig on the other side of the large structure, opposite the propane tank and satellite dish. He rubbed his hands together to warm them and went to a side door, which he opened with his key. He stepped inside, fumbled for the switch, and flipped on the overheads to illuminate the inside. They bathed the structure in brilliant white light, and he stared at an empty space in numbed silence. The tarp that had covered the motor home lay crumpled, torn, and strewn across the floor of the building. Next to it was an abandoned truck.

Tammy walked up the dirt road. She paid little attention to Uncle's dog, which walked obediently beside them. Wyker and Harper talked casually. Wyker's cell phone buzzed and he answered it. It was Hy Royston, and Wyker was surprised he already knew all about the Three Bit cows. Said there was more to the story, but it could wait. Then Hy asked him if he could speak to Harper Lee. Puzzled, Wyker shot a look at Harper and said, "Well, funny you should ask, we're here at his uncle's place waiting for Carson Collins. What the…"

Hy said, "Yes, I know all about it. He works for me. He's one of my agents. May I speak to him, please?"

Always formal, thought Wyker, and he handed the phone to Harper.

The first thing out of Harper's mouth was, "Yes, sir."

Harper walked a short distance away from Wyker and the conversation lasted a good ten minutes.

Wyker went in search of C.J., who was out walking with Rio. Harper had a dozen cousins who had come out of the woodwork to feed and clean early. They thoroughly fussed over and enjoyed looking after the new arrivals. They'd taken to the cows too; they seemed to love all animals. They kept asking C.J. if they could ride, that maybe they could go to get the packhorses for them. They wouldn't mind, they said, like it was up to him.

Their enthusiasm was a breath of fresh air and C.J.'s mood was uncharacteristically light around the kids. He laughed at the antics, the roughhousing, their stupid jokes, and marveled at how far Rio had come. The boys climbed all over, around, and even under him, showering him with affection. Johnny did not escape their favors, and they asked if they could brush him too. C.J. saw no harm in it and said yes. And that was the scene when Wyker walked over to him.

"What's up? Where's Harper?"

Wyker was smiling. "On the phone."

"Who's he talking to?"

Wyker answered, "His boss."

Harper walked up and handed the phone back to Wyker, and then it was Wyker's turn again with Hy. C.J. looked from one to the other and Harper just smiled.

"No shit?"

Harper reached forward with his right hand and introduced himself as Undercover Agent Harper Lee.

C.J. shook his head and smiled. "No shit?"

Harper replied, "No shit," then turned toward the house.

C.J. stopped him. "Please know I am grateful...for everything."

"You're welcome."

Harper collected an armful of wood cut to fit in the barrel stove and went inside.

The kids bombarded C.J. with questions about the horses. How old were they? How long had Wyker had Johnny? One of the boys started petting Tammy and brushing her with the horse body brush he'd used on Johnny. Wyker came back after hanging up, listened to the rapid-fire questions, and smiled at the sorrel hair from the body brush that had transferred onto Tammy's black fur. Tammy sat patiently and Wyker answered questions about Johnny before the children ran off to feed the cows.

C.J. asked what was next, and said that whatever it was, to count him in.

Wyker said he'd keep that in mind and added, "Sounds like you don't want this to be over."

C.J. searched for the words he wanted. He hoped he'd found a place he could be for a while—a place where familiar old patterns of trouble would not find him, nor he them.

He let the moment pass and asked, "So really, what happens next?"

"We'll go get those packhorses. Hopefully, they haven't strayed from that little canyon.

"Those kids want to go too."

Wyker watched them and said, "Yeah, that'll be fun if they let them. We'll talk about it. We'll wait for Carson and

Jorge. They're on their way. They have a couple of ranch horses, his cattle dogs, and they are bringing feed too. The weather looks like it'll hold."

C.J. leaned over the rail, brush in his hand. "Funny, when we were getting the cattle, all thoughts of the future went away. Now, all I want to know is if we have a future."

Wyker looked at him. "We'll just take it one step at a time. Not much of an answer...sorry. The best I have right now."

The group returned to the house, which was crowded but cozy. Four squeezed around the linoleum table in the kitchen and whoever got the corner seat was a prisoner. They were drinking black coffee and a couple of kids were parked in front of the color TV that got a signal from an antenna on the roof. They liked sports and cartoons. Harper's aunt washed dishes and they spent most of the day right there telling stories and tall tales. They talked about the rez, learned more about Harper, and Harper learned more about them. C.J. was relaxed and talked openly about prison. Wyker joshed C.J. and retold the story—rather, several stories—about the now-infamous partnership of C.J. and Rio.

When the stories of Wyker's time spent with the inmates and the wild mustangs came up, the kids abandoned a half-played checkers game on the floor and leaned on the jam of the door or on the backs of chairs and listened. Wyker really got into it about the mustangs; how they were to work with, and how the inmates were. What it was like when they first met each other. How the wildness in both brought out the best in each other. It was a day well spent, and when Harper's aunt said it was time for the younger kids to get home, of course, they didn't want to go. Wyker, Harper, and C.J. grabbed heavy coats and gloves and went with them. It was good to get up and stretch their legs.

Tammy alternated between trotting close to Wyker and going faster into a run to be with the boys. It was a roundtrip of a couple of miles to their homes.

Carson called and said she had missed the turn-off. Harper got on the phone and talked her back in the right direction. It was dark when she finally found them. Harper borrowed a big Maglite and the three men walked down the road to flag her down as she drove up it. As they walked, they listened to coyotes yipping and barking to each other up in the low hills to the right of the road.

C.J. asked Harper what his aunt's and uncle's names really were.

Harper replied, "Aunt. Uncle. That's all I've ever called them and they've never corrected me."

Wyker's fifth wheel, big as it was, was easy to turn around. Carson managed not to wake Jorge when she did it, though he was awake when she slowed to make the turn onto the road she'd missed. She spotted the light that waved them in.

Wyker walked to the window and smiled at her. "Well, haven't you grown up since I last saw you," he said.

"Just a little. Good to see you, Uncle Wilbur." And she laughed.

Wyker had forgotten that she always called him that—his silly name, she called it when she was little—and it pleased him that she still took to it. The sparkle in her eye, the curve of her mouth, and the shape of her teeth spurred vivid memories. He was struck dumb by the instantaneous, crystalline recollection of his good friend and mentor; by how the child resembled the woman Tuff loved. There was solidness to the deep, enduring beauty of this family. They were a huge part of him.

It was a pivotal moment for him and one where he knew he'd done the right thing, been in the right place, and surrounded himself with the right people. The air around him felt lighter and brighter. And while he just wanted to drink that reality in, time wasn't there, and he pivoted to some quick introductions in the dark, then she slid over and let him take the wheel.

Tammy leaped up and sat on Carson, who laughed at the dog's enthusiasm. The guys hopped into the back of the truck on top of the hay bales.

Once at Harper's uncle's place, Wyker found level ground. Carson opened her door and Tammy jumped out. Jorge's dogs were released from the carriers in back and they were off to smell everything. C.J. and Jorge set to unloading the horses and Harper was in the shed, working out where all the horses would go.

Carson was glad she had remembered to bring sleeping bags. She found the interior lights in the fifth wheel's front compartment. The exterior lights cast ghostly glows on faces, and when Wyker came over, she hugged him around the waist.

"If Dad were here..." she started, and then she looked up at him with her father's eyes.

Wyker saw them moisten with tears.

"...he'd thank you for helping us," she finished.

"Tuff would've had my hand swallowed in that big paw of his and then chewed me out for leaving those two horses out there."

Carson shook it off, pretended to be Tuff, and thrust out her right hand, which Wyker shook good-naturedly.

"You don't have his grip. When he shook your hand, you either needed a drink or a doctor afterward!"

They both laughed.

C.J. came around the edge of the trailer to tell Wyker the horses were all set. He checked himself for a stride as he took a good look at Carson. In the pale lights, hair askew, no make-up, she smiled with affection up at Wyker, and C.J. saw her mother in her for sure. C.J. walked over to them and saw how happy she was to see Wyker. That energy turned toward him when Wyker introduced him. Carson extended her hand, shook C.J.'s firmly, and thanked him.

She said her mother had asked after him and "some big Rio horse."

C.J. mumbled something short and escaped back to the barn. He'd been awkward about it and that surprised him. He'd always found it easy to charm the ladies, but this moment was an uncomfortable one for him.

Jorge and Harper pulled hay down and carried a couple of fifty-pound sacks of grain from the bed of the truck. The teenaged kids approached, wanted to help, and grabbed hay hooks. Many hands made light work. The fit was tight in the barn for five horses when they were all in there at once. The overhang helped, and they stood together for warmth and everyone got along. They each found a pile of hay and were quiet as they fed. Jorge said he'd grain in the morning.

Wyker asked Carson if they'd eaten, and she said they'd brought sandwiches. They were good to go in and meet their hosts.

The next morning the tiny kitchen was more than cramped, and they ate in waves at the table. Aunt made ham and eggs, toast and coffee. A chill hung in the air and they discussed the plan and worked out whether they would take the kids with them.

Harper was quiet. Whatever was decided, he'd leave it to the others. He knew the kids would play a game of "Indian tracker" and follow them anyway. He said as much to Wyker.

Carson, in the corner chair against the wall, enjoyed the banter. It felt like family. Even Harper's dour uncle enjoyed the activity in his tiny house, though he grumbled that the plumbing couldn't take it.

They prepared to ride and bundled up in layers. Harper and C.J. went to see to the horses. Wyker, Carson, Jorge, and the three dogs checked on the cows. The herd had moved off to the far side of a pasture and bunched together about a half-mile away. They'd rested and grazed most of the day before.

The kids loped up on borrowed horses. Harper said something and Wyker agreed they weren't about to miss an opportunity for adventure. Jorge said he felt he and the dogs should stay there with the herd. He didn't think they needed so many riders to go retrieve two horses. Wyker agreed with him.

Carson found herself in the space between conversations and noticed C.J. working with his red horse. The connection between them was clear; there was something special there. She'd heard what a tough horse Rio was, and how well they'd done together. They made an iconic Western silhouette against the gray weathered barn, and C.J. was the image of a true cowboy.

C.J. adjusted his mecate, lifted his gaze to the group, and found her eyes. She resisted the urge to look behind her, as though maybe his stare was meant for someone else. She froze, held there by an energy. They stared at each other.

C.J. touched the brim of his hat and smiled. He was captivating, and the most striking human she'd ever seen. There was gold sparkling in those intense brown eyes, and she couldn't help the smile that found the edges of her mouth. Her hair caught up in the wind and danced.

GLOSSARY

Banamine: Available by prescription from a veterinarian, Banamine is a potent analgesic (relieves pain) with anti-inflammatory and fever-reducing capacity.

Boot Jack: Sometimes known as a boot pull, it aids in the removal of boots. A u-shaped mouth grips the heel of the boot, you stand on the back of the device with the other foot and pull the foot free.

Bridle: Headgear used to control a horse, consisting of buckled straps to which a bit and reins are attached.

Bridle Horse or Finished Bridle Horse: A horse developed far enough that he can be ridden and worked one-handed in a leverage curb or spade bit. The original vaqueros developed their methods and took lots of time to build true leadership, partnership, and refinement.

Bute: Phenylbutazone is an analgesic (relieves pain) and anti-inflammatory medication commonly used for the treatment of lameness and pain in horses.

Chaps: Sturdy coverings for the legs of the rider, consisting of leather leggings and a belt. They are buckled over jeans with the belt and they have no seat.

Chinks: Chinkaderos, Chingaderos, also called armitas, chivarras, or brush-poppers, are short, lightweight leggings that provide protection to the rider's legs.

Cinch: A strap that keeps the saddle in place on a horse, runs under the horse's belly and is attached to the saddle on both sides.

Dallied: Tied without a knot.

Easy Boot: A quick alternative to shoeing when a horse loses a shoe. A lightweight rubber boot that fits on the horse's foot with a semi-aggressive tread, and can be used over various terrains. Cable buckles and ice studs can be installed to provide extra traction.

Fender: The adjustable part of a saddle that serves as a barrier between your leg and the horse, keeping your leg from contacting the horse's sweat or creating friction. Attached to a stirrup leather.

Flag: Desensitizing tool to train a horse.

Headstall: The central piece of the bridle that goes behind the ears and has cheek pieces that attach to the bit on either side.

Heritage Roughstock boot: Square-toed boot built for working cowboys, durable enough for the range, and steeped in solid tradition. This is one of the best-loved boot styles that the Ariat Company manufactures.

Horn: The knob at the front of a Western saddle positioned on the pommel; rider can hold on to it to balance;

also allows vaqueros to control cattle by wrapping a rope around it.

Gooseneck: A truck trailer for transporting livestock with a projecting front end designed to attach to the bed of a pick-up truck.

Lace-up Ropers: A boot with a rounded toe and flexible fit. Many are lace-up boots, which provide a great fit and ankle support. If thrown from a saddle and dragged, this type of boot poses an issue because the rider's foot will not slip out of the boot.

Mecate: A long rope, traditionally of horsehair, approximately 20-25 feet long and up to about ¾ inch in diameter. In this story, I use the variation sometimes called mecate reins or McCarty, which is used as a rein system for a bridle with a bit. This design, usually of nylon rope, has a single looped rein attached to either side of a snaffle bit with a lead rein coming off the bit ring in a manner similar to the lead rein of a traditional mecate. This set-up is most often seen today among some practitioners of the natural horsemanship movement.

Pannier: Rectangular boxes typically made of canvas, leather, or wicker. For horse packing, they are supported by a pack saddle to distribute weight more evenly across the back of an animal.

Previcox: Chewable tablets used for the control of pain and inflammation associated with osteoarthritis and for the control of post-operative pain and inflammation associated with soft tissue and orthopedic surgery for dogs. In recent years, owners of aging horses and horses with lameness issues have used this product when long-term consistent use of bute is undesirable. It is an off-label usage and against regulations, but many horse owners use it successfully.

Reata: A long, noosed rope used to catch animals.

Rope Halter: A device made of rope that fits around the head of an animal and is used to lead or secure the animal. The ones described in this book have no metal components and the placement of the tied knots on the halter affect pressure points for refined training.

Stirrup: Holds the foot of the rider and is attached to most saddles by adjustable stirrup leathers to fit both the size of the rider. They are used to remain in correct position over the horse's center of balance.

Tie Line: Also called a high line or a picket line, this is a line stretched between two trees to which you tie your horse.

Vaquero: A horse-mounted livestock herder of a tradition that originated on the Iberian Peninsula. A cowboy, or more common in the West, a buckaroo. A cattle driver.

Worlds: Final scores from shows for the year are calculated in various show divisions, and the total qualifies a horse and rider to go. There are Open, Non-Pro, and Amateur divisions, and riders have to qualify for a limited number of slots to join the World Competition, which is referred to as "the Worlds."

Coming Soon...

THREE CORNER FIRE

ALSO AVAILABLE...

Three Corner Rustlers Audio Book

Available for download at iTunes and Amazon

and

Three Corner Rustlers CD Box Set

Includes bonus music CD
"Three Corner Blues" by Lorin Rowan

Available only at www.kimvogee.com

Made in USA - Kendallville, IN
1180705_9781657836280
10.14.2020 1336